FOUR NIGHT STAND

GEORGIA MOORE

Serendipity, 51 Gower Street, London, WC1E 6HJ
info@serendipityfiction.com | www.serendipityfiction.com

© Georgia Moore, 2024

The right of the above author to be identified as the author of this work has been asserted in accordance with the Copyright, Designs and Patents Act 1988. British Library Cataloguing in Publication Data available.

First Published in Australia by Escape Publishing

Print ISBN 9781917163729
Ebook ISBN 9781917163736

Set in Times.
Cover design by Ditte Løkkegaard

All characters, other than those clearly in the public domain, and place names, other than those well-established such as towns and cities, are fictitious and any resemblance is purely coincidental.

All rights reserved. No part of this publication may be reproduced, stored in or introduced into a retrieval system, or transmitted, in any form, or by any means electronic, mechanical, photocopying, recording or otherwise, without the prior permission of the publisher. Any person who commits any unauthorised act in relation to this publication may be liable to criminal prosecution and civil claims for damages.

Georgia Moore is an Australian author of steamy contemporary romance. Her stories feature competent heroines who are still figuring out what they want from life, and heroes who've got emotional baggage to unpack.

When not consuming copious amounts of pop culture (mostly romance novels), Georgia can be found singing in a choir, eating an endless amount of carbs, or being overly competitive at board games and trivia.

To keep in touch with Georgia, sign up to her infrequent, but exciting newsletter:

georgiamoorewriter.com/newsletter

You can also follow Georgia on social media:

Website:
georgiamoorewriter.com

Instagram:
www.instagram.com/georgiamoorewriter

Facebook:
www.facebook.com/GeorgiaMooreWriter

Tumblr:
georgiamoorewriter.tumblr.com

This first one's for me. Deep breaths. You did it.

CHAPTER 1

Jules: Think I'm getting busted for reading a novel at my desk.
Cat: Reading what?
Jules:...
Jules: That erotica Tori was raving about.
Tori: HahahahAHHhhahah!
Cat: What makes you think you've been busted?
Jules: I've been summoned to Patricia's office.
Jules: Do you think I'll have to do a course about work appropriate activities? I probably should. Bet she's with HR.
Cat: Deep breath. I just saw her on level 4 with Jonathan. She's probably running late.
Tori: Or they're preparing your termination notice?
Jules: Don't joke about that!
Tori: It'd save you having to make the choice...?
Jules: :(
Tori: Jokes. They'd never fire you. The IT team would fall apart without you.
Jules: Thanks.
Jules: Oh! Think that's her. I'll catch you up later.

Jules pops her phone down and folds her sweating hands on her lap, looking around Patricia's office. Just because she was caught reading a workplace erotica at work, doesn't mean she has to feel embarrassed. Which she's not. She's aware work isn't the best place for it, but lately, her job hasn't been holding her attention, even with the extra responsibility of covering her boss's role while she's on maternity leave. And the numerous daily phone calls from people in this company with an 'urgent' tech issue that has to be fixed 'ASAP' because they have 'deadlines' only add more stress to her doubled workload. They don't provide enough of a challenge to alleviate her boredom, hence the ill-advised stress relief reading material.

Patricia's cloying perfume signals her arrival a second before she enters. Jules straightens and watches the door as her boss's boss slides into the room, still graceful in heels in her seventh decade.

'Julianne. Sorry to keep you waiting,' she says with her Irish lilt, dropping a stack of books on her desk before sorting them onto the shelving behind her. 'I was in a meeting with Jonathan and getting anything succinct out of him is like asking my grandkids about their day. I do not need to hear what time you woke up and what you had for breakfast. Bless them.'

Patricia sits behind her desk and readjusts her cat-eye frames on her face. 'No doubt you're wondering why you're here.'

Jules swallows. 'I have some idea.'

'Samantha spoke to you, did she?' Patricia asks.

'Uh...'

'You're all good to cover her, I assume. I would have expected to hear from Samantha before now if that weren't the case.'

'Yes?' Jules's shoulders creep towards her ears. She hasn't spoken to Samantha since she left for maternity leave a few months ago, but it seems like the right answer.

'Perfect. It's a week-long conference. Everything has been booked already.' Patricia rifles through her filing cabinet as she talks.

Jules blinks. 'Conference?'

'The Australasian Publishers Conference. Down in Sydney. You'll be going to represent Infinity Press.' Patricia pulls out a lime green folder and passes it over. Jules stares at it for a second before taking it. 'That's a full itinerary for you. Have a look through and if you've got questions, email Lindsay and she'll help you out.'

Jules opens the folder. There are dozens of printouts. She skims the top sheet, trying to absorb the information, then flips the page and reads the next header. 'Hang on.' She lifts her gaze to Patricia. 'This is next week?'

'Yes. Samantha did mention that, didn't she?'

'Uh... yes. Of course,' Jules says, not wanting to be caught in a lie. Besides, this is all much better than what she thought she was summoned for.

She flips through pages until she finds the conference program, running her gaze down the list of presentations. This might be the exact thing she needs to reinspire her sagging motivation.

'Perfect. Lindsay will update everything with your details,' Patricia says, assuming Jules is onboard though she's said nothing to confirm that. Jules has always admired Patricia's full steam-ahead attitude but this is the first time she's the one getting steamrolled by it. 'You'll be going with our new marketing expert. Joined us about a year ago from Cable and is finally making some decent digital progression with the company.'

A knock sounds from behind Jules.

'Ah. Just in time.' Patricia readjusts her glasses. 'Come in.'

Jules swivels to watch a man enter the room. She can't help her appreciative once-over. He's got the look of someone in marketing, that put-together beauty which belongs in magazines. Not that his navy slacks and loose white polo shirt are especially magazine-worthy. He's got the light brown eyes and dark brown hair combo, that Jules loves, and a strong jaw graced with stubble that would feel amazing between her legs.

Jules's eyes widen and she lifts her gaze over his shoulder, feeling her palms tingle. Wow. Where did that come from?

She stands and tries to keep her smile polite and not sleazy when his focus shifts to her.

He extends his hand and Jules does *not* think any inappropriate thoughts about how thick his fingers are. 'Hi. I'm Cameron. Nice to meet you.'

Jules's legs tremble and her smile slips. Oh dear lord. She knows that voice. She's *fantasised* about that voice.

At least once a week, often more, she's been getting a call from someone in the marketing department wanting help with their image archiving system. Someone with a beautiful voice and a rare patience and politeness that had her eager to keep him on the line instead of hanging up to get back to her own work.

Apparently, that call has been coming from Mr Stubble and Caramel Eyes.

Holy shit. Tori and Cat are going to flip when she tells them she's finally seen Cameron in the flesh. His company profile doesn't have an ID picture, so they've been trying to convince her to find his desk for months, but Jules has held firm in avoiding where marketing sits. They tease her about having a crush on a disembodied voice, but by god it's a voice. Deep, but not smooth, it's got some grit to it. Their phone calls have become the best parts in her monotonous weeks.

His hand still hovers in front of her and Jules is a little eager when she grips it. 'Nice to meet you too. I'm Julianne.'

There's only one guest chair in Patricia's office so Cameron stays upright and gestures Jules back into the seat.

Jules shifts in place, fixing her gaze determinedly on Patricia's face as she talks. A little bit of harmless fantasy about a co-worker who was just a voice on the phone is one thing. Now, she has a visual and is going to be spending a week in Cameron's company.

Jules's fingers twitch around the folder in her lap, her thoughts skittering to the possibilities of next week, until something Patricia says brings her back.

'I have to make a speech?' Jules checks she heard correctly.

'Yes,' Patricia says. 'Samantha was going to be presenting about the e-commerce system the company developed. You'll be fine to cover.'

It's not a question. Jules swallows roughly. 'I can handle it,' she assures Patricia. 'I co-developed the site with her.'

After that second bombshell – or was it the third? – there's not much more to discuss. Patricia dismisses them from her office and suddenly, Jules is standing by the lifts with Cameron.

'Julianne.' The way Cameron spaces her name out makes Jules's stomach wobble. Plus he's looking at her with questioning eyes, which only adds to her wobbling stomach situation. 'You're the one who keeps helping me out with the image archive, aren't you?'

'That's me.' She lets out a relieved sigh. 'I normally go by Jules.'

'Jules, of course,' Cameron nods, smiling now he's placed her. 'Can't believe I didn't pick it from your voice. I think I speak to you more than some of my team members.'

Jules lets out a breathy laugh that barely resembles her normal laugh. In her defence, Cameron's eyes are really beautiful up close and he's staring right at her from less than a metre away. Cameron. In the flesh. Close enough to touch.

'I hope that's a good thing?' She bites her lip. That came out far too sincere.

Thankfully, Cameron's still smiling when he answers, pressing the button to call the lift as he does. 'I don't mind. I do feel bad for taking up so much of your time, though.'

'Don't be. I enjoy our calls.'

She wants to take the words back as soon as they're out, especially when Cameron turns his head and his caramel eyes fix steadily on her flushed face.

He holds her gaze for an electric three seconds before simply saying, 'Me too.'

Jules breathes out slowly, hearing something else in his tone besides polite congeniality. *Imagining* something else in his tone. She's gotten so good at conjuring it in her mind these last few months that her fantasy is bleeding into reality. That's what she gets for fantasising regularly about his voice.

Her phone vibrates in her hand, and she glances at the screen to see new messages from Tori in the group chat.

'So,' Cameron says. 'I'll pick you up from here on Monday, or is your place better?'

Jules nearly drops her phone, then fumbles so badly to catch it she does drop it, along with the folder of conference documents. The excursion to pick them up brings her face where it ought not to be at work – crotch level. Then Cameron drops down to help her and it's even worse because his *face* is *right there*.

She shoves the papers back into the folder, accepting some from Cameron, and quickly rights herself.

'Your place or here?' he repeats.

Jules's cheeks heat. She's imagined Cameron asking that in any number of scenarios. The real thing has her sweating in a less fun way. 'For?'

'The conference. The company hired a car for the two of us to drive to Sydney.'

Jules nods slowly. 'Right. The two of us.' Alone. In a small space together. For hours.

Jules's insides goop all over the place. It's tempting to say her house for no other reason than he'd be at her house. But also, then he'd see her place and she's not sure that's wise considering Tori and Cat also live there and would turn the simple event into an *Event* complete with spying at the windows and maybe wolf-whistling.

Away from Patricia's office, she can smell him for the first time, which sounds strange, but when you've been fantasising about a voice and suddenly the other senses get to come out and play, they go overboard. He smells like coffee and something floral. Jasmine? Rose? She's never been good with plant stuff. The house plants in her share house aren't alive because of her. Maybe if she shuffles closer, she can pick what it is.

'Jules?'

Her body trembles hearing her name in his mouth unfiltered through a phone line. 'Here would be great.'

'I'll meet you in the foyer at 7 am Monday then.'

'Okay,' Jules says faintly, so busy gaping like a codfish at the early departure time she misses the chance to check out his ass when he steps into the lift ahead of her.

CHAPTER 2

Jules is barely through the front door when Tori marches up and blocks her way. Her long curly brown hair is in two buns on her head. She's been cooking.

Holding her phone aloft, Tori dramatically recites, '..."False alarm. Actually potentially good news. I'll explain at home. Need your help please." What kind of bullshit message is that?' Tori throws her hands skyward.

Jules doesn't believe in stereotyping, but Tori sure does have the Italian proclivity for exaggerated hand gestures down pat.

'My apologies for being so inconsiderate,' Jules says with a faux-British accent.

Tori snorts. 'Accepted. But can I at least get a hint before Cat gets home? I was stuck in boring planning meetings all day and I'm dying for a distraction.'

'Nope.'

'Urgh. Fine. Cat threatened to change the Netflix password if we start without her anyway.' Tori saunters off down the corridor, curvy hips swinging back and forth in her short skirt. 'But I've made homemade pizza so you better have a story to match that effort!'

'It matches. Trust me,' Jules tells Tori's back before following her down the foyer into the living room. Tori branches off for the kitchen and Jules heads down the back corridor and into her bedroom.

She dumps her bag on her messy desk and unearths the conference folder. Now she's not being distracted by Cameron and his caramel eyes, she can actually take in what the pages say. She's only been to the Australasian Publishers Conference once, after her promotion to senior IT officer years ago. She was like a kid let loose in a lolly store. She'd crammed in so many talks, filled dozens of pages with notes and came back to the office with several ideas for improving the company's image archive and metadata systems. Inspiration had fuelled her and she worked long hours because she'd wanted to, not because she was doing two people's jobs at once, like now. Could attending the conference again reinspire her?

Though part of her is ready to move on from Infinity Press. A small part. The bigger part makes her shoulders hunch whenever she thinks about it. A risk-taker she is not, and Infinity is a comfortable and secure job, the place she met her two best friends – though only Cat still works with her – and close to where she lives. A patch of boredom isn't enough to push her out, as lengthy as it's becoming.

She sits in her desk chair and flicks through the disordered pages. Four nights in a hotel near Sydney Harbour. Arrival on Monday, with a welcome speech followed by drinks. Then three days of talks and a trade-stall day on Friday, which she's not involved in.

Jules grabs a pen from her desk and scans the list of talks, circling ones of interest to her. She finds the session bearing Samantha's name. 'From Computer to Consumer: E-Commerce Technology from the Readers' Perspective'.

Jules taps a finger on the paper. Sounds straightforward, and thankfully her talk is on Wednesday, so she has time to cobble something together. She knows from experience the IT talks are less popular than publisher or editor talks, or even marketing, but she's fine with public speaking. Plus, considering she worked alongside Samantha on revamping their website she could wing it and be fine. Not that she will, but it's an option.

Speaking of Samantha, she did say to call in case of an emergency. Jules has been reluctant to interrupt her new-mother life and nothing at work has been an emergency anyway. Unless you count the staff kitchen running out of coffee pods that one time.

Samantha answers quickly. 'Jules. Hey.'

'Hey. Are you whispering?'

'Yeah. Angelica's finally napping. Way too late in the day for it but that's a future-me problem. Hang on, I'll just—' There's the sound of a door opening and closing, then Samantha asks at a regular volume, 'How's it going at the office?'

'Fine. Busy, but that's usual.'

'Urgh. Sorry you got stuck filling in for me on top of your other work. The company wasn't keen on me having a newbie trained up to temp my role. I did bug Patricia to get a temp in at entry level instead, but she was sure you could handle everything.'

Jules takes the compliment with a grain of salt. She's confident that before she had stepped in for Samantha, Patricia wouldn't have been able to pick her out of the IT department. And there's only four of them, two of whom are men. More likely it was a budgeting thing, because god knows that's the way the company has been heading since the new CEO came on-board last year.

'Speaking of Patricia... she spoke to me today about a conference next week?'

'Oh, fuck. I mean, duck,' Samantha corrects. 'Jules. I am so sorry. I was meant to talk to you about that ages ago and it completely slipped my mind! You know how it is, baby-brain and all that. Well, I guess you don't know, but it's real. I'm getting interrupted sleep every night and I can't remember the last time I had a proper sit-down meal. Don't get me wrong, little Angelica is my greatest love, but my head feels like one of those lotto ball things; lots going on inside but it's a bit random what comes out as action.'

Jules has fatigue merely listening to Samantha talk. 'It's okay. I said I'd go.'

'Thank the IT overlords,' Samantha says. 'You'll be great, I know it.'

'Any insider tips? I've only attended once and it was years ago.'

'It probably hasn't changed much. You'll have more free time than you think, so bring stuff to do. What else... Of course, it's fantastic for networking if you're into that, plus they have an open bar at the welcome night which is a hoot. Beware of the marketing people though, they can get a little handsy.'

Jules knows one marketing person she wouldn't mind getting handsy with. Maybe Cameron can be her 'stuff to do' in her spare time. The thought makes her insides melt, like thoughts of him usually do, but her fantasies have never had the possibility of becoming reality before. She doesn't appreciate the new sensation of ants crawling over her shoulders because of it.

'Okay, thanks,' Jules says. 'Had you started prepping the presentation? It'd be good to get a sense of what you were going to say.'

'Yes. Yes, I have. I started a list and put it... somewhere. Can I send it to you later? It's a thirty-minute talking time then audience questions. I was going to go into UXD and navigability of the e-commerce site, but focus more on our research and the focus groups we did. You know, bridging the gap between product and consumer.'

'Sounds great. I'll flesh out whatever you've got.'

'You're a lifesaver. Some people's presentations are shockers, so don't stress too much. You're gonna kill it. Don't kill it too much though,' Samantha jokes, 'I want my job to be there for me in another few months!'

Jules's gut spasms. 'I don't think that's going to be an issue.'

The sound of a baby crying carries through the phone.

'Oh, duck. That's Angelica. Better go. Text me if you need help!'

Jules throws her phone to the foot of her bed, feeling better about the conference part of next week at least.

She searches her desk for a blank sheet of paper to start listing talking points which will hopefully supplement whatever Samantha's going to send through. It should be easy to fill her allotted time. Start with the high-level concept of e-commerce driven by individual consumers, then go through the research process, covering how they selected for focus groups, the methodology behind the questions, before ending with development of the actual site.

Forty minutes later, she's filled two sheets with notes. If only she had notes on how to approach three hours alone in a car with Cameron.

* * *

The pizza, like anything Tori cooks, is fantastic. As is the wine Cat brings home to accompany it. In true Friday-night fashion, they sit in front of the TV with the music channel playing in the background. Jules and Tori share the couch while Cat sits on a cushion on the floor at one end of the coffee table, eating her pizza with a knife and fork, the blonde pixie-cut she's growing out held back with a cheap plastic hairband.

'So you're going to be away all next week attending this conference. With Cameron. Who is the marketing man you're interested in. That's what's happening?' Cat lays out after Jules's recount.

'Correct,' Jules says through a mouthful of mushroom pizza.

'Lady, this is your chance!' Tori exclaims, leaning forward to whack Jules's leg. 'Make your move. Throw your hat into the ring. Show him what you've got.'

'Yes, because that sounds like me.' Jules rolls her eyes and reaches for another slice of pizza from the trays on the coffee table.

'Please tell me you've at least thought about it?' Tori says.

'I've thought about it.'

Tori laughs and salutes her with a slice of pizza. 'Atta woman.'

Jules flushes, but the overly enthusiastic support is exactly what she needs. It's been ages since she's done anything about her lack of romantic relationship. Not since her last grand romantic gesture ended with a break-up and a wounded heart and zero dates for three years.

'How did you react when you realised who he was?' Cat asks.

'My knees legitimately went weak, and I had about a dozen inappropriate thoughts at once.'

Tori laughs.

Cat gasps. 'Do you think he could tell?'

Jules chokes down a bite of pizza. 'I hope not. I tried not to act sleazy, but he's super attractive, and I'd been reading that rival CEOs office erotica, so my thoughts kept sliding into the gutter.'

'Are you sure it was the erotica and not, I don't know, the massive sexual crush you've had on this dude's voice for months?' Tori teases.

'That may have played into it,' Jules concedes, body heating. 'The voice is even better in person.'

'I wish I'd been a fly on the wall during that meeting,' Cat sighs.

'You don't think it's a little weird though?' Jules asks. 'Going after someone I work with?'

'So?' Tori shrugs. 'How do you think people meet these days?'

'Uh, Tinder. Hinge. Bumble,' Jules lists the dating apps off on her fingers. 'I think speed dating is back in fashion, too.'

'Felicity and Bianca met at work and they've been married almost three years,' Cat points out. 'Besides, you're in completely different divisions and have different bosses and *you've been crushing on him for months.*'

'Urgh. I know. I do not need the reminder.' There's only so many times you can fantasise about a disembodied voice before it becomes weird. Though oddly, no less sexy, even though it's started to feel a little... lacking. Empty.

'What's there to lose by trying?'

Cat doesn't ask it like a challenge so Jules answers honestly. 'My comfort. And our chats on the phone. He'll call me up for IT help and it'll be super awkward because he knows I want him and he shut me down.'

'Lady, that's assuming he shuts you down,' Tori says. 'But look at you! You're gorgeous and intelligent and single. And even if you weren't that last one, what happens on conference stays on conference.' Tori winks exaggeratedly.

Ignoring Tori apparently condoning infidelity because she knows it's only in jest, Jules asks, 'What if I don't want it to stay on conference, though?'

'Wait. Seriously?' Tori spins to lean against the couch arm and face Jules. 'I've been assuming this was just a sexual fantasy crush.'

'It is! It is, but it's also...' Jules plays with her pizza crusts. It's different now they've met in person. There's a little ache in her chest that wants to *know* him. 'I mean, we connect so well over the phone – half our conversation aren't even about IT – and you know I care about having that connection before having sex.'

'View it as a trial run,' Cat suggests, topping up everyone's wine glasses. 'You know, like that bit where you're going out before you make it official.'

Jules cocks her head. 'Like when we soft-launched the e-commerce site at work?'

'Exactly,' Cat says. 'I mean, I know you get on well on the phone, but what if in person it's awkward, or there's no physical chemistry?'

'The chemistry is there. On my side, at least.' Jules sips some wine to try and cool the sudden heat in her body.

'In which case,' Tori says, 'a conference fling is definitely still an option. Climb that man and get him to whisper sexy things into your ear with his beautiful voice. Then you can cherish the hot, sweaty memory for years to come.'

An appealing idea, at least on a physical level, if it weren't for three hurdles. One, the foreboding ants-on-her-skin feeling when she thinks about putting herself out there with Cameron for real. Two, that ache inside her that craves more than sex. And three.

She levels Tori with a look. 'And how would I initiate that kind of relationship at a *work conference*, huh? That's textbook inappropriate behaviour.'

'Though not against the company code of conduct, if you were concerned about that,' Cat says, 'since you're not in the same chain of command.'

'Great. Thank you. I'll be asking why you know that later,' Tori says while Cat blushes, before angling back to Jules. 'Samantha said the welcome night gets boozy, right?' Tori wiggles her eyebrows. 'That seems like a perfect time.'

'When we're both inebriated and unable to consent? How's that better?'

Tori rolls her eyes. 'I'm not saying have sex with him that night. Hell, don't have a fling at all if you're not up for it. But maybe... use the liquid courage to lay some groundwork. Flirt a little. Wear something revealing and see how he reacts.'

'Cat?' Jules asks her more reasonable friend.

'I was going to say 'ask him out', but with the Todd stuff —' Jules shudders.

'Yeah, you probably don't want to do that,' Cat finishes. 'So, Tori's isn't a bad idea. See how he responds to some flirting before you make any big moves.'

'See!' Tori gestures broadly to Cat, a piece of pepperoni flying off her pizza in her enthusiasm, narrowly missing Cat's sewing machine set up in the corner of the living room. 'Thank you. And it's perfect for you because you're a flirty drunk.'

Jules rubs a hand over her face as Cat retrieves the flyaway meat. 'If I'm going to try and get closer to Cameron — and I haven't said I am yet – can we have a plan that's more realistic than 'get flirty-drunk'?'

'I think that's plenty realistic,' Tori says into her wine glass. 'In fact, I've seen you pull with that tactic before.'

Jules narrows her eyes. 'If you're talking about at Felicity and Bianca's wedding—'

'You know I am,' Tori winks.

'That doesn't count. You know I'm not big on spontaneity.'

'Emotional-security is your middle name, yes,' Tori nods. 'But when orgasms are on the table, you might be convinced to step outside your comfort zone.'

'But what if I don't want it to be about orgasms? What if I want it to be about, you know, a relationship.'

'Without orgasms?' Tori's jaw drops.

'Connecting on an emotional level.'

'*Without orgasms?*'

'Okay, okay,' Cat interrupts. 'Moving on.' She grabs a clean napkin and a pen from the stack that lives on the coffee table, ready to be used for her crosswords.

'"Sober plan to win over Cameron",' Cat narrates, writing on the napkin. 'This'll be your game plan. Step one is—Hang on.' Her head snaps up, gaze locking on Jules. 'Do we know for certain he's single?'

'Yes.' Jules takes another sip of wine as her body heats. 'He, uh, told me on the phone the other week.'

'He told you, huh?' Tori smirks, extending her leg to dig her toes into Jules's thigh. 'Did you tell him you were also single?'

'Maybe.' Jules tickles Tori's foot when she starts winking exaggeratedly. 'Stop that.'

'Moving on *again*,' Cat brigs their focus back with a snap of her fingers. 'Here's your plan. Step one is flirt, while sober, and see how he responds. Step two is—'

'Sex,' Tori says.

'Tori! You can't jump straight to sex from flirting!' Jules argues.

'Why not?' Tori shrugs. 'I do it all the time. Works out brilliantly.'

'Because I want to use this week to test if we have longevity, not sexual chemistry. Or not *only* sexual chemistry.'

'Step two,' Cat continues, ignoring their arguing, 'is having a face-to-face conversation. Actually, maybe that's step one.' Cat readjusts the numbers on her list. 'Step three is a trial date.'

'Hang on.' Jules moves to kneel beside Cat on the floor. 'That feels like a jump too. Talk, flirt, date? Shouldn't step two have, like, sub-steps?'

'You want specific tips on how to flirt?' Cat asks, turning her pale blue eyes on Jules.

'I know how to flirt.'

'The past few years say otherwise,' Tori jokes.

'Hey.' Jules throws her used napkin at Tori's head. 'I may not have dated in a few years because of... Todd. And work has been sucking all my time and energy—'

'Sorry,' Tori apologises. 'I know it has.'

'—but I still know how to flirt,' Jules finishes her point. 'Though step three may be an issue. I don't know any date places in Sydney.'

'Google it later,' Cat says, though she adds a sub-entry between step two and three for it.

'Okay. This is looking achievable.' Jules scans the napkin like a sitemap to her dating life. 'Step one, we talk face-to-face.'

'So you can make sure he's not boring in person,' Tori says.

'Step two, I flirt a little. Step two-point-two, find a date place. Step three, trial date. Perfect.'

'I'll help you pack some flirty outfits,' Tori offers. 'And I'll see if my Sydney siblings have thoughts about a date place.'

'Thanks, Tor.' Jules spins on her knees to face her. 'That'd be awesome. But nothing too flirty, since it is a work conference.'

'Got it. I'm excited,' Tori grins. 'I see sexy things in your future.'

'Agree,' Cat says. 'See, it says it on the plan. Step four is hanky-panky.' Cat barely gets through the sentence before dissolving into giggles, laughing so hard water leaks from her eyes.

Jules snatches the napkin but the damage has been done.

'Are you seri—Cat! You actually wrote 'hanky-panky' on my planning map!'

Cat gasps and doubles over, pressing her hand to her stomach. Tori joins in with her snorting laugh and Jules can't fight against their mirth. She's got a plan for her presentation and a plan to make things happen with Cameron, vague as it may be. Now if only the ants would quit marching across her skin when she thinks of acting on it.

CHAPTER 3

Cameron checks the tags on his polo shirts as he lays them on the bed, making sure not to pack any of the smaller size that show off his biceps and torso. He doesn't want to invite that kind of attention in a work setting. His presentation speech is printed out as well as downloaded onto his phone and iPad, same with the itinerary. No chance for his technological bad luck to kick his ass this year. Everything in order for a productive work conference.

Except him and his racing heart.

Walking into Patricia's office yesterday – less than 24 hours ago – was like stepping through the looking glass, but instead of a white rabbit, he'd come face to face with a goddamn beautiful woman. Light-brown hair that fell straight over her shoulders, deep blue eyes, a smile that was like a cool breeze on a hot day. The second he'd heard her voice, he should've picked who she was, but he'd been too entranced by her smile. Jules. The woman in IT he's been talking to for months.

Their conversations had been one of the few bright spots since leaving Sydney. Then he fucked that up by wondering what it would be like if they were more than friends. If this woman who made him laugh and made his tech problems seem momentary delays instead of endless hurdles would want to talk to him face-to-face. If her smile was as stunning as it sounded over the phone.

He can't have that happen.

It's why he's been avoiding her in the office. Going on coffee runs when he knows she's coming up or racing into the bathroom. He knows his patterns. He knows how quickly he falls. He knows that falling can lead to a downfall. It's what landed him in Canberra working at Infinity Press with Jules in the first place.

He needs to focus on his conference presentation anyway. It'll be the first time seeing his old Cable co-workers after the unprofessional exit he made, abandoning his team right on the cusp of a massive marketing campaign he'd spearheaded. He wants – *needs* – to redeem himself, to them and the wider publishing industry. It's a small sector and reputations travel. It's why his whole damn speech is about targeting Gen Z, even though Infinity has a tiny YA list. He may as well have called his session 'To my old Cable colleagues: I'm sorry.'

His phone ringing jars him so much he swears.

Pulse racing, he accepts the call from his older sister. 'Hey, Carrie.'

'It's Chloe,' his younger sister answers.

He double-checks the caller ID. 'Chloe? Why're you on Carrie's phone?'

'We're brunching. You're on speaker.'

'Hey, Cam,' his older sister speaks finally.

'So how's it going?' Chloe leaves him no time for a hello. 'All ready for your trip back to the hometown?'

'Packing as we speak,' Cameron manages to insert, putting his phone on speaker and setting it on his bedside table so he can continue packing.

'Brilliant. I'm so excited to see you. I've barely seen you since...'

The three seconds of silence is long by Chloe's standards. It's enough for Cameron's stomach to start eating away at itself.

'Well,' Chloe ends lamely, avoiding mentioning anything specific.

'Since you broke up with Braden,' Carrie finishes for her,

having no compunctions about exacerbating Cameron's self-flagellating stomach.

'*Anyway*,' Chloe says loudly, but not loudly enough to cover the sound of someone being slapped on the arm. 'Lunch for us on Monday is all booked.'

'Don't you have uni?' Cameron folds his polo shirts and stacks them into a pile on the bed, then starts on the pants.

'I can't miss the family reunion! And everything's online anyway.'

'You're still arriving late-morning?' Carrie asks.

'That's the plan,' Cameron says.

'Okay. I'll come grab you from the hotel and we can walk over together. Chloe's coming straight from uni.'

'See?' Chloe says. 'I'm not completely unstudious.'

Cameron laughs as he grabs his suitcase from his wardrobe, contentment a warmth in his chest, a rare feeling since he left Sydney.

'And we know you have the welcome drinks Monday night,' Chloe keeps talking, 'so Carrie reserved tickets for you to see the symphony on Tuesday.'

'I'll meet you at stage door after. We can grab a drink,' Carrie says.

Cameron shakes his head, placing his suitcase on the bed. 'Am I going to have any nights to myself?'

'You get Wednesday night off so you can prepare for your presentation on Thursday,' Carrie says.

'Gracious of you.' He says it with sarcasm but his shoulders loosen knowing he has the night to run through his speech a few times.

'Everything good with you?' Chloe asks of his silence. 'You don't sound thrilled to be spending time with your family.'

'I am.' Cameron starts arranging his folded clothes in his suitcase.

'Really selling it there,' Carrie says.

Cameron sighs, hands stilling. 'Braden's going to be there.'

'Ah,' Carries says. 'That explains it.'

'Yeah.' Cameron drops onto his bed, the pile of polo shirts listing towards him.

'You know, maybe that's a good thing,' Chloe says.

'Seeing the woman who made me leave Cable, who has since taken my old job, will be a good thing?'

'Maybe you can get closure.'

Cameron grabs the tilting polos and drops them into his suitcase. 'I was the one who broke things off with her. I don't need closure.'

Carrie hums.

'Spit it out,' he says, shoving a pair of socks into his suitcase.

'You've become a social recluse since you two broke up, I'm just saying.'

He rubs his knuckles in a circle over his chest. The barb stings because it's true. 'How would you know? We don't live in the same city anymore.'

'I have a network.'

Cameron rolls his eyes. 'Does the network start with 'S' and end with 'teven'.'

'It's sad you have so few friends over there you immediately know who's ratting you out. But yes. I pay him well. He gets free Sydney Symphony Orchestra tickets whenever he and Friedrich are in Sydney.'

'And Clo? You're in on this too?'

'Well, yeah. Sorry. But it's true! You can't have walls up against proper intimate social connection forever. You need a support network. And not a, like, *these people will grab drinks with me after work* network, you need, like, a *these people will pick up the phone at three in the morning and drive me to the emergency ward*. Do you have anyone like that over there?'

Cameron wants to have a positive answer but aside from Steven and Friedrich, there's no-one. Not even Jules, and she's—

He shakes his head. He's not thinking about what she is or

isn't or could be. He's not dating anyone from work again. It's not worth it. His career has been battered enough.

'I've only been here a few months,' Cameron says, though it's been almost a year. 'Relationships take time.'

'Who's attending the conference with you?' Carrie asks. 'You can start there.'

Cameron hesitates for a second. 'A woman from IT is coming as well.'

'Oh my god.' Chloe's voice increases in pitch and volume. 'Is that the woman you told us you liked?'

'There is more than one woman in our IT department.'

'You're hedging.' He can hear the evil smile in Carrie's voice. 'Shit. It is her, isn't it?'

Cameron takes a second to figure out how to lie convincingly. There isn't a way. Carrie has an abnormal ability to detect dishonesty, even over the phone.

'Yes,' he says. 'But don't get any ideas. I didn't tell you willingly. It was pestered out of me after too much wine and tequila shots. And I didn't say I liked her,' he clarifies, 'I said she was likeable.'

'Details,' Chloe dismisses with a hand-wavey air to her words. 'But she's going to be in Sydney with you the whole week, so this is the perfect opportunity for you to let your walls drop. Oh! Carrie can get her a ticket for the symphony so you can go together. Like a date.'

Carrie laughs. 'Consider it done.'

Cameron grabs his phone, taking it off speaker and pressing it to his ear. 'You're getting ahead of yourselves. And aren't you forgetting something?'

'What?'

'I don't date people I work with.'

There's silence while his words are processed.

'Fucking Braden,' Carrie groans. 'I wish you'd stop letting her affect you. You know you've got trust issues, right?'

This time the barb hits like a shard of glass in his spine. 'It's smarter not to get involved.'

'No matter how caring and funny you said this IT lady was?' Chloe reminds him unnecessarily.

'Yes.' He's well aware, every day, of all those things. It's why avoiding her is his main tactic. 'So will you drop it?'

'We'll table it until you're here in person,' Carrie says.

Cameron sighs. It's as good as he'll get. 'I've got to finish packing. I'll see you Monday.'

He ends the call and pockets his phone.

His distraction has resulted in a messily packed suitcase so he pulls half the clothes out to start again. He could have happily carried on holding an uncomplicated, phone-based friendship with a co-worker forever, regardless of Chloe's thoughts on his 'wall against social connection' or whatever she described it as.

He doesn't have a wall. Sure, there was a certain safety in Jules never having seen him, so he knew she liked him not because of how he looked, but because of who he was. And his technique of physical avoidance isn't stopping them having a connection. Friday proved it, because when he saw Jules in Patricia's office there was a definite connection, like a pull in his chest, a pull that only got stronger when he realised she was the woman from the phone. Clearly, he doesn't have a wall. Though it would make sticking to his 'don't date colleagues' thing easier if he did.

But considering he does have a connection with Jules, he's banking on the conference and daily family commitments to help him keep his emotions on lockdown. And his hands to himself, because shit, the way he felt on Friday? He hadn't felt desire – hell, *any* emotion – that strong in over a year.

He zips his suitcase closed with force. He's focusing on the wrong things. Jules is making him *feel* and he needs to be shutting his emotions down if he's going to get through coming face-to-face with his old colleagues. And his ex.

CHAPTER 4

When Jules's alarm goes off at 6 am on Monday, she wakes regretting having told Cameron to pick her up from work. She could have slept more and she was having such a nice dream where Cameron was feeding her chocolate mousse.

She groans and rolls out of bed with the coordination of whatever the opposite of a ballerina is. It doesn't help that it took her ages to fall asleep because she kept worrying about the three-hour car trip and what on earth she and Cameron were going to talk about. What if they *can't* talk face to face? What if they end up talking about the weather? Or what if Cameron turns out to have no interests, or it's something odd, like collecting tiny decorative spoons?

Jules arrives at the office three minutes early – a miracle considering the hour – but Cameron is there before her.

'Good morning.' He looks entirely awake and perfectly assembled and not even in need of a coffee, though he's holding two. He's clean-shaven today and the square cut of his jaw is somehow more distinguished without the stubble.

'Morning.' Urgh. Her voice sounds like she's gotten too familiar with the bottom of a bottle of wine.

'Not a morning person?' Cameron asks.

Jules would reply with something witty if a) she had the brain power to think of something, b) she had the energy to say it, and c) she wasn't distracted by noticing Cameron's hair is still damp from a shower he would have been naked for.

She pinches herself. Despite what happened in Patricia's office the other day, she's not normally prone to sporadic indecent thoughts. Must be the poor sleep.

'For me?' She points to one of the coffees.

'Yeah. It's a cappuccino. Hope that's alright. I remembered you mentioning it on the phone once.'

Her stomach goes momentarily weightless. 'It's my usual, yeah. Though any caffeine in the morning is great. Thanks.'

She takes it and guzzles a few mouthfuls.

'I'm sorry,' Cameron says. 'I requested an early check-in for my own benefit. We could have met later.'

Jules groans. 'You tell me this now?'

'Sorry.' Cameron grimaces and Jules has the urge to comfort him by placing her hand on one of his well-muscled arms, on display in another polo shirt.

'No, it's cool,' she says, gripping her coffee tighter instead. 'I could've paid more attention to the times on the schedule. But I'm here now and I've got caffeine.' Jules inhales the precious scent of it to drive home her point, fluttering her eyes in ecstasy.

She stops that quickly. She doesn't want to go thinking the word 'ecstasy' when she's about to trap herself in a car with Cameron for hours.

Cameron leads her to a shiny silver hatchback in the company carpark and pops the boot. A black suitcase and a satchel bag already sit inside.

'Here.' He lifts her suitcase into the boot and she watches his biceps flex. It's going to be a long week if even the routine lifting of a heavy object has her thoughts sliding into the gutter. Could he lift her? Press her against the car and—

Cameron slams the boot shut. Jules startles, biting her lip. A few minutes in and she's having erotic thoughts, even though she purposefully avoided reading any more of her office erotica. She made a point of cramming the weekend with packing and planning and trying on outfits for Tori instead.

Her previous relationships have provided no precedent for handling this level of randy daydreaming. Even with Todd it was never like this.

'Ready?' Cameron heads for the driver's side, sliding easily into the vehicle like he might slide—

Woah. Nope. Jules takes an overlarge sip of coffee. She's not thinking those thoughts.

'Hope so.'

* * *

Cameron is quiet as they drive out of Canberra. Jules slowly relaxes into her seat, drinking coffee and biting her lip every time she has an inappropriate thought about him. Her lip gets tender quickly. Adjusting the rear-view mirror makes the muscles in his arms stand out, and every time he changes gears, her gaze drops to his thick fingers. Even the fact he's navigating without using a GPS system is a turn-on. Something about the confidence, probably, and the pre-planning that would have contributed to it.

'You can put the radio on, if you like,' Cameron says as they hit the freeway.

'Oh. Thanks.' Jules puts her coffee in the cup holder between them while silently freaking out. Music preferences are like an insight into someone's soul and Cameron is casually asking her to bare hers. That's got to be, like, a step six on the dating plan at least.

Jules turns the radio on and Duran Duran blasts from the speakers.

'Shit, shit.' Jules fumbles for the volume control, shoulders bunched up around her ears. 'Sorry—Got it.'

She flops against her chair and presses a hand to her chest. 'Well. I'm awake now.'

Cameron laughs and Jules's entire body goes taut before a shiver slides down her spine like ice-cream melting down the side of a cone. She's heard the husky sound through the phone before but in person it's as luscious as his voice and his smell.

Jules reangles the air-vent on her flushed cheeks.

'Could you imagine having that as your alarm?' Cameron asks on the tail end of his laughter.

'Yes. And it's a horrifying thought. I'll stick with the generic annoying buzz, I think.'

'Generic? That doesn't seem like you.' He turns his head to smile at her, revealing literal dimples in his cheeks. *Dimples*.

Jules's insides melt. 'Oh. Uh, thanks. I did have it as a Bangles song at one point, but then whenever I heard the song I thought about sleeping.'

"Manic Monday'?'

Jules twists to face him and narrows her eyes. 'I thought you didn't think I was generic?'

Cameron laughs, glancing over at her. 'I don't. You're not.'

Jules presses her lips together to keep her smile from growing overlarge. 'Neither are you.'

Cameron clears his throat, attention back on the road. He shuffles his hands along the steering wheel and the conversation peters out, leaving only the sounds of George Michael on the radio.

Jules taps her fingers on her thighs, stealing glances at Cameron out the corner of her eye. It's been a while since Jules engaged in flirting, but handing out compliments and dimpled smiles seems very flirty. Are they at step two already? She hasn't established yet if he's boring in person or has weird hobbies.

'So. Uh. Have you been to the conference before?' She winces at her own question. It's only marginally better than asking about the weather, but she wasn't ready for silence to announce the death of conversation and she's not sure how to get the flirty banter back. She should have taken up Tori's offer of practising flirting with her over the weekend.

'Most years I've been in publishing,' he says. 'My first was in Melbourne, about four years ago?'

'No way. I think I was at that one! I wonder if we saw each other?'

'I don't think so. I would have remembered you.'

He doesn't say it like a line but with his voice, anything he says sounds like he's whispering it directly into her ear. She presses her legs together and grabs for her coffee to do something with her itching hands.

'Hang on. I think that's—' is all Cameron gets out before she takes a sip.

Her eyes widen and she nearly spits the liquid out before swallowing it.

'Mine,' he finishes.

Jules coughs, looking between the cup and Cameron. 'Is there coffee in this or is it just sugar?'

'There's coffee.' Cameron takes the cup from Jules and brings it to his own lips.

Jules gulps as he drinks. Far out, how can drinking a hot beverage be sexy? First, lifting her luggage into the car, then drinking a coffee. What's next? He'll blow his nose and she'll go weak at the knees? Ridiculous.

He returns the cup to the holder and shoots her a quick, one-dimpled smile. 'There's also caramel and hazelnut syrup.'

'Do you—' She pulls her gaze from his mouth and bumps the air-con temperature down a notch. 'Do you have a sweet tooth?'

'Massively. I go through about two blocks of chocolate every week.'

'Two blocks!' Jules files the fact away with glee.

'You sound scandalised. I bet you've got your own guilty food pleasure.'

'Meringue. And marshmallows. Oh, speaking of.' Jules pulls her handbag onto her lap and digs through it for the brown paper bag Tori thrust at her last night. 'Chocolate shortbread?'

'You brought snacks?'

'It's a three-hour car ride. Of course I did. Want some?'

He laughs. 'Sure. Can you—' He drops his jaw and holds his mouth open.

Oh. He wants her to feed it to him.

She breaks off a section of biscuit and slowly lifts it to his waiting mouth, holding her breath. Her fingers graze his lips and tingles shoot up her arm to her heart, which somersaults in her chest.

'Thanks,' he says.

Jules swallows, shocked by the intensity of her body's reaction. Her arm is still tingling. If they ever do anything physical like she's fantasised, she may combust.

'It's good,' he says after swallowing. 'You make it?'

'No way. I can't bake. One of my housemates, Tori, did. The kitchen is like her Zen space, so there's always food around.'

'Sounds like a good arrangement.'

'Yeah, it is.'

Cameron leans in his seat and opens his mouth for Jules to slip some more shortbread into. No contact this time. Jules doesn't need to give herself a heart attack by sparking any more cardio gymnastics.

'So we're both sweet tooths,' Cameron says, 'hated by dentists all over the world.'

'Gosh, I hope not. Dad's a dentist.'

'Did he let you eat sugary stuff when you were young?'

'I see where you're going with this,' she says, returning the shortbread to her handbag. 'And yes, he did. It's mum that was always wary of sugary foods.'

'She also a dentist?'

'No way. She hates going to the dentist, which dad is always teasing her about. She just didn't think kids should consume heaps of sugar.' Jules gestures to the stereo. 'She works in radio, actually.'

'Ah.' Cameron nods slowly and his now-dry hair fans over his forehead. He brushes it back and Jules's insides goop like a lava lamp. 'Makes sense.'

'What do you mean?'

'Your encyclopaedic knowledge of 80s music. Had to

come from somewhere. You're too young to have actually been around in the 80s.'

'Yeah. I'm a 90s kid.' Jules shoves her handbag back at her feet. 'Encyclopaedic is taking it a bit far, though.'

'Is it? You always manage to name the songs I'm playing at work when we're on the phone.'

Jules's cheeks heat. She readjusts her skirt, which got rucked up by her bag. There are goosebumps over her legs. 'Well what about you? Who did you catch the synth-pop bug from?' Thanks to Cat's HR position and some unasked-for meddling, she knows he was also born in the 90s.

'My piano tutor, oddly. She was obsessed and used to squeeze 80s pop into every lesson alongside the scales and arpeggios.'

'You play piano? I'm learning so much about you.'

Jules double-takes as they drive past a 'Welcome to Sydney' sign. Has the time really passed so quickly? It's like that one time they spent a half-hour on the phone at work after an IT solve that took three minutes.

Her phone buzzes. Seeing it's a text from Samantha, she grins and unlocks her phone, hoping for the presentation notes so she can knock it over this afternoon and spend the rest of her free time during the conference focusing on steps one through three of her plan, and having more conversations like this with Cameron.

Jules opens the picture attachment and sighs.

'Bad news?' Cameron asks.

'Not bad, just a bit of a letdown. Samantha – the woman I'm filling in for – said she'd started prepping the conference presentation, so I asked her to send me her notes.'

Since they're stopped at a red light, Jules holds her phone up for Cameron. 'Look.'

'That's a post-it note.'

'Yeah. And not even one of the big ones.'

Jules pulls her phone back as the light turns green. 'Oh, hang on. She's typing something. Maybe there's—Nope. She says sorry, she thought she had more and—Oh. Now there's a picture of her newborn.'

'Maybe you can put that in the presentation,' Cameron suggests. 'People love babies.'

'I can picture it now. A whole audience cooing at once.'

Cameron laughs. Jules shivers. It's getting to be a pattern.

'You haven't started your presentation yet?' Cameron asks.

'I only found out I was going to the conference on Friday.'

'What?'

The car swerves for a second before Cameron gets it back under control. 'Sorry. Sorry. I just... That's the stuff of my nightmares. I mean, I've printed off multiple hardcopies of the timetable and my presentation already.'

'Really?' Jules says, a smile slowly blooming across her face. 'But you always come across so calm on the phone. Like you can handle anything.'

'Thanks for the vote of confidence. Very off base, but I appreciate it. I think all technology hates me. The radio being at full volume earlier was probably my fault. But I figure if I act calm when I have a tech emergency, maybe I'll feel calm.'

'Has that ever worked?'

'Not really. But if you answer the phone when I call IT, it always helps.'

Jules doesn't think her insides are ever going to return to a solid state at this rate.

Her phone buzzes again. 'And... another picture of her baby. Well, there goes my chance for a conference fling. I'm going to be using all my free time to work on this presentation.'

Cameron clears his throat. 'Conference fling?'

Shit. Jules's eyes widen and she grips her phone tight to her chest. She'd gotten so comfortable during their conversation she stopped running every word through in her head first. Big mistake.

'No. I didn't—I was joking. My friends and I were chatting about the trip and they brought it up.'

The silence that follows is that awkward silence that calls

attention to how awkward it is. Jules's mouth opens to fill it, and the essence of Tori takes over her hands as she gesticulates to bat away the silence.

'I mean, I wouldn't say a flat-out no – it has been a while for me – but only if the right person offered. And I have no idea why I gestured so strongly at you then. Please ignore that.' Jules buries her face in her hands. 'This is awkward. I'm much less awkward when we talk on the phone.'

'You are.'

Jules emits a strangled laugh. 'Thanks.'

'Sorry. That wasn't meant as a critique. It's... interesting seeing this different side of you.'

'Interesting like actually interesting, or interesting like you're dreading the next week of my company?' Jules looks at the car door and wonders how achievable jumping out of a moving vehicle to escape this conversation is.

'The first. Definitely.'

It's something, at least.

'You know what? I'm just going to—'

Jules cranks the volume up on the radio. The floor of the car vibrates so much she feels it travelling up her legs. If it gets loud enough, maybe it'll vibrate her right into another timeline where she didn't embarrass herself in front of Cameron.

She grips the sides of her seat and stares ahead. She's going to be silent for the rest of the trip. No speaking. No more embarrassing herself. She'll try for step one another time.

Cameron kindly keeps the music at that volume for half a minute before he turns it down. 'Seriously, Jules. Don't worry about it.'

'I think I should stop talking for the rest of the drive.'

'Don't stop on my account.'

'Oh no. This would be for me. So I stop embarrassing myself and giving you the impression I'm some terrible employee who doesn't do the work and has sex on the brain constantly.'

Cameron makes a noise that's some combination of

a cough, laugh and groan. 'I don't think you're a terrible employee. You've helped me out so many times in the office, and you only found out about the conference on Friday. I'm impressed you agreed to fill in.'

It's sweet of him to defend her on that count. She doesn't want to hear what he has to say about the second part of her statement.

How can she fail so badly before they've even made it to the hotel? She almost spat coffee over herself, confessed to thinking about a conference fling, and told him she's basically going to be winging her presentation. She's probably pushed herself back to negative steps and now she only has a week to get back on track.

'Do you collect tiny spoons?' she asks after a few minutes of silence.

'No.'

At least there's that.

CHAPTER 5

Jules speeds through check-in like a category five hurricane. Or she tries to. She and Cameron have been placed in rooms beside each other, so she has to ride the lift up with him, their luggage, and all her embarrassment taking up the rest of the space like an invisible monster.

She grips the handle of her suitcase and jiggles her leg up and down. Cameron doesn't mention anything from the car ride but Jules keeps replaying over and over when she gestured to him and said she wouldn't turn down a conference fling if the right person offered. Fuck. Tori kept teasing that Jules had been single too long, while Jules was certain it would be like riding a bike to get back into the whole flirting and banter thing. She supposes it is, if that bike has misshapen wheels and no handlebars and brakes that don't work.

She steps into her room, Cameron continuing to the next one along the carpeted corridor with a polite smile. Jules shuts the door before leaning back against it and exhaling. She tries to keep the embarrassment out, but it creeps in and wraps around her until she starts overheating. She fumbles in her handbag for her phone and messages her group chat with Cat and Tori.

Jules: Tori, you were right. I've forgotten how to flirt! Car ride was so awkward! Not sure the plan will work now.

She shakes her body out and takes in the room, hoping to distract herself. It's a big, open space decorated in shades of blue, with a bathroom immediately to the right, and a kitchenette stocked with teas, coffee, a kettle and a mini-fridge to the left. She wheels her suitcase through and rests it in front of the wardrobe, which runs along the wall behind where the bathroom is. There's a small lounge chair and a queen bed with way too many pillows against the right wall, and a table with two chairs on the left side, along with a wall-mounted TV. The only character in the room comes from two pop-art style photo series either side of the doors leading out to the balcony, one of the Sydney Harbour Bridge and one of the iconic Luna Park entry.

Trying not to look too closely at the creepy Luna Park clown face, she heads for the glass doors and out onto the small balcony, body relaxing when the cool breeze hits her skin. She stares out at Sydney city and takes a deep breath. Traffic noises float up to her but if she looks out between buildings, she can see the sparkling blue water of Sydney Harbour.

She takes another slow breath in, trying to reset her emotions, but is interrupted by her phone pinging with incoming messages.

> *Cat: Oh no! I'm sure it's not as bad as you think.*
> *Tori: Do not back out of this! You deserve it.*
> *Tori: Think of the endgame.*
> *Cat: Exactly. You can't give up after a single set-back. It's like the soft launch, remember? So there's time to fix things.*
> *Tori: You are an intelligent, sexy, single woman!*

Jules shuts her eyes and imagines the endgame. Her and Cameron. Dating. Hanging out outside of work. The ache in her chest stretches, ready for fulfillment.

So the car ride over was a failure, it's not the end of the

world. She's still here, and Cameron's still here, and she's got her plan and a whole week to make things happen. He did say not to worry about the things she said in the car. If she wants to move forward, she'll have to trust he meant it.

She releases her breath and texts her friends back.

Jules: You're right. Going to try again.
Tori: Hell yeah!
Tori: Be proactive! Not reactive!
Cat: Good luck. You're an amazing person and Cameron's going to see that.
Jules: :) :) :)

Jules puts her phone away and stares out at the water again. She takes another deep breath, then turns on her heel and heads to the bathroom to freshen up.

* * *

After splashing water on her face and running a brush through her hair, Jules paces her room for a reserved six minutes before finding the courage to say screw you to the incessant prickling like ants across her shoulders. Considering the last time she'd been brave with a man she ended up abruptly dumped by her partner of four years, she's pretty proud of it only taking six minutes.

She marches down the corridor to Cameron's room and knocks on the door which is propped open by a doorstop.

'Come in!'

She pushes through into a room that's a mirrored copy of her own. And a good thing too, because it means she has all her brain power to focus on the fact that Cameron isn't wearing a shirt.

Jules's insides fizz as her gaze travels unbidden over Cameron's body. Beneath the loose polos he favours for work, this man has been hiding abs. Like, proper, defined abs.

Holy shit. She wants to run her hands over those ridges,

then use her tongue to lick along that trail of hair down to where his jeans are riding low on his hips.

And the jeans! She's been so distracted with the abs she hadn't noticed the tight fit of the dark blue denim. Damn, this man has thighs too.

Cameron shifts, arm wrapping over his torso like he's trying to cover up his glorious muscles.

'Oh gosh. Sorry. Sorry.' Jules spins to face the door that is still slowly coming to rest back against the doorstop. With the sultry voice, then the face, and now the body, her dream man keeps getting dreamier. But ogling him in his hotel room without his permission? Her hormones are making her misbehave.

'I thought you were my sister,' Cameron tells her, sounding flustered.

Good. That makes two of them.

'You have a sister?' Jules asks, honestly curious and also because she's desperate for a distraction from her unresolved horniness.

'Two. One older, and one younger. You can turn around now.'

Cameron is still buttoning up his light green shirt so Jules gets to say a slow goodbye to the abs she's hoping she can somehow see again under more honourable – well, not honourable, but with full consent and awareness – circumstances.

'So, uh.' Cameron finishes buttoning his shirt. 'Did you need something?'

Jules peels her gaze from his fingers to his expectant face. There's a faint pink on his cheeks.

'Oh. Right.' The pricking sensation of tiny ant feet spreads out from her shoulders down her back. She focuses on maintaining a normal breathing pattern as her hands go clammy. 'I was wondering if you wanted to grab lunch together,' she asks, trying for step one, take two. 'I thought that might be nicer than eating alone.'

'Ah.' Cameron shuffles on his feet, thrusting his hands into the back pockets of his jeans. 'I have plans already.'

'Oh. Okay. That's totally cool,' Jules says in what she hopes is a breezy voice, even though she's failed step one. Again.

'Maybe another day?' Cameron offers. For the sake of the ache in her chest, Jules hopes it's legitimate and not merely a soft let-down thing.

'Nonsense. She's very welcome.' A woman's voice sounds from behind her.

Jules spins once more to the doorway to see a tall woman walking through. Jealousy licks at Jules's heels as the woman strides with confidence into the room, toned arms on display in a thick singlet-strapped top over high-waisted slacks. Then Jules realises her hair is the exact shade and thickness of Cameron's, her eyes that same caramel colour. This must be one of the sisters, though she can't pick if she's older or younger.

'Hi.' The woman shoots her a smile as she heads for Cameron to wrap him in a big hug and ruffle his hair.

Jules smothers a laugh. Must be the older sister. Her brother has done the same with her countless times.

'Cam.' The woman pushes back and looks him over. 'Nice to see you back in the home city.'

'Thanks, Carrie.'

Cameron extricates himself and pats down his hair. A good move for Jules's sanity since the ruffling had turned his hair from styled, to I-just-had-really-great-sex-and-I'm-not-afraid-to-show-it. Her insides are still bubbling away, like a pot of water on simmer. One good flame could spur it back to boiling and then who knows what she'll do. Possibly blurt something inappropriate – again – or stare at Cameron's crotch for too long. The jeans are tight enough there's a potential she might see something.

'This is my sister, Carrie,' Cameron gestures between them. 'Carrie, this is Jules.'

Carrie rounds back to look at Jules. 'Hello, Jules.'

'Hi. Nice to meet you, Carrie.' Jules holds her hands behind her back and smiles politely. It's never too early to make a good impression on the family.

Carrie's gaze goes between Cameron and Jules, a strange look on her face like she's thinking hard. 'You're more than welcome to join us,' Carrie says eventually. 'Any friend of Cam's is welcome.'

Jules looks to Cameron to gauge whether he's amenable to Carrie's suggestion. He doesn't look like he's projecting a 'no' vibe, but he also has a little crease between his eyebrows that makes Jules shift on her feet. She wants to get to know him more, but she doesn't want to intrude on his family time.

Carrie looks between them again. 'Can I tempt you with some intel into the working of Cameron's brain and the first round of drinks on me?'

'Carrie,' Cameron says, shooting his sister a look.

'Come on, Cam.'

There's some non-verbal sibling communication that goes on for a few seconds, before Cameron steps past his sister and stands in front of Jules. 'You're welcome to join.'

Jules stares into his caramel eyes but the little smile on his face makes it seem he's not saying it only out of politeness.

Cameron's invitation combined with the promise of more personal stories about the man is too tempting to turn down. Plus, with his sisters there as chaperones, she's far less likely to go blurting out inappropriate sexual fantasies. Who knows, maybe she'll finally adequately manage an entire conversation with him.

'Alright. I'd love to.'

Carrie grins as she strides past the pair. 'Fantastic.'

* * *

They end up in a restaurant on the twelfth floor of a building overlooking the water at Darling Harbour. It looks schmick and makes Jules re-tuck the t-shirt she's wearing into the band of her knee-length skater skirt, the same outfit she's been in since this morning. Thank goodness she took the time to freshen up a little before striding into Cameron's room. She still feels underdressed beside Cameron in his button-up shirt and with Carrie now sporting a blazer over her singlet.

'Are you alright?' Cameron asks softly, leaning down closer to Jules, his voice sending shivers along her arm.

Her nod is shaky. 'This just feels a lot like meeting the family.'

'You are meeting my family,' Cameron points out as they follow Carrie and the maître de through the restaurant.

'I know that. But like, I feel like I'm psyching up for an interrogation.'

'You'll be fine. You're great at talking to people.'

'How do you know?' Jules asks, watching Carrie take a seat at a table where a woman is already seated, sketching something in a notepad. She hugs Carrie when she sits, and the two lean their heads close together, Carrie whispering something to the other woman.

They both turn to look at Jules and Cameron, and Jules's heart rockets up into her throat.

Cameron's family is clearly genetically blessed because his other sister is stunning too. She's wearing a multi-coloured flapper-style dress with wedge heels and several bracelets, and her hair is a bright blonde with pink and purple highlights. She and Carrie are smiling at Jules in exactly the same way. It makes her gulp.

'You take my calls a lot at work, remember.' Cameron answers her question.

'Oh. Yeah.' Jules watches Carrie say something else to the other sister, so she's not really focusing on what she's saying when she keeps speaking. 'But you're the exception to the rule. Most of them leave me wanting to resign or escape to the breakroom to read some erotic romance.'

Cameron stills beside her. 'Erotic romance?' he asks politely.

Jules freezes. Time stops while she stares into Cameron's inquisitive eyes, déjà vu an unpleasant weight on her chest. She has a very detailed vision in which a tear in the fabric of reality appears before her and she can step into it and be taken away from Cameron and the mounting embarrassment of her mentioning erotica in front of him. Again? Seriously? Telling him she's creepily and inappropriately read erotic romance at work is not an approved method for starting something between them.

'Let's both ignore I said that last part,' Jules begs, since the tear in reality has not appeared.

Cameron clears his throat and pauses for almost as long as before. 'If you want.'

She crosses her arms over her chest as her nipples peak. God damn Cameron and his sexy voice.

Jules strides across to his sisters at the table, nerves about meeting them totally annihilated by her recent embarrassment. If she can survive accidentally mentioning her reading habits to Cameron, she can survive making chit-chat with his siblings over lunch.

CHAPTER 6

Jules sits at the table like she's about to be interviewed for a job. Tension in the lines of her neck and shoulders. Cameron has the urge to rub her back and tell her to relax but no way is he doing that in front of his sisters. And Jules probably wouldn't appreciate the uninvited physical contact anyway.

He takes a fortifying breath then drops into the seat between Jules and Chloe.

'Hey, Cam.' Chloe wraps him in a hug. Her hair tickles his nose but something loosens in his chest. He's missed her. Carrie too.

'Hey, Clo. Good to see you again.'

'And you.' Her eyes flick between him and Jules like she's watching one of her reality dating shows.

A waiter comes by the table to fill their water glasses and hand out menus. Cameron guzzles half his water at once, watching his sisters look between him and Jules with glinting eyes.

'So, Jules...' Carrie begins what's sure to be an interrogation. 'It's nice finally meeting you in person. We've heard a lot about you.'

Cameron's chest tightens.

'You have?' Jules turns her wide blue eyes toward Cameron.

'Why'd you sound surprised?' Chloe asks her.

'Well, uh...' Her gaze flicks over his face before turning

to Chloe. 'I guess I didn't, um, think I made much of an impression on Cameron.'

She could not be more off-base. Though thank fuck she hasn't picked up any interest from him. Of course, by the time this lunch is over, his sisters may have dropped enough hints that she'll be digging into why he mentioned her to them. He can imagine the conversation now. 'Why'd you tell your sisters about me?' — 'Because you're the only person in Canberra I've felt a connection with'. Yeah. That needs to be avoided.

Carrie laughs. 'You underestimate our brother's lack of social life in Canberra.'

'Carrie. Seriously?' Cameron curls his fists on his thighs.

'I'm only saying what's true.'

And giving Jules a shocking impression of him.

Cameron turns to Jules. 'They know you help me with IT stuff a lot. That's all.'

He directs the last bit at his sisters. Chloe goes for the I'm-so-innocent Bambi eyes but Carrie's quirked lips promise she's not done needling. He needs something stronger than water.

'Right.' Jules tucks a strand of hair behind her ear. 'That makes sense.'

'Tell us more about that,' Chloe chimes in. 'What does an IT person do at your company? Aside from help my Luddite brother over here.'

'I'm not a Luddite. I have bad luck with technology.'

'He put together a photo slide-show for my engagement party,' Carrie tells Jules. 'It got stuck on a picture of me and Jesse glaring at each other for half the night.'

Cameron leans across the table. 'Hey. I warned you to give that task to someone else.'

'Enough.' Chloe interrupts, waving her bangle-clad arm. 'I wanna hear about Jules.'

Jules's gaze flicks between him and his siblings, eyes wide. 'Uh, about my job?'

Chloe nods.

'Well, I'm the senior IT officer at Infinity, which means lots of trouble-shooting when our systems don't work as they should, basically.'

Cameron frowns. 'Why're you always answering my phone calls then?'

'Our department got shrunk when the new CEO came in, so everyone's had to pick up some odds and ends.'

'But aren't you also covering for Samantha right now?'

'Yeah.' Jules smiles in that exhausted way Cameron's seen on Carrie's face when she's in the middle of a weeks-long program with the orchestra.

Cameron, driven by an unexplainable instinct, bumps his knee against hers beneath the table.

Jules startles and turns a wide-eyed gaze to him.

Shit. That was forward of him.

Then Jules bumps her knee back softly against his thigh, sending him a quick smile. Cameron smiles back, feeling a heat in his chest he hasn't experienced in years, his sisters momentarily forgotten until one of them taps their foot to his beneath the table.

He tears his gaze from Jules. Fuck. What is he doing? This is exactly why he avoided meeting her in person at the office. He's... leaning in. Conversationally and physically.

Saved by the approach of a waiter to take their orders, he clears his throat and straightens up in his chair, pointing randomly at the menu since he was too enthralled by Jules to have looked over it.

'Excuse me,' Jules says after ordering, 'I'm just going to the bathroom.'

Cameron watches her walk away, skirt swishing around her knees. His sisters are staring at him when he turns back.

'What? *What*?'

They don't say a word, merely stare at him. If he were to label their expressions, they'd be something like 'told you so', and 'you're in trouble, mister'. Cameron starts overheating and they haven't even said anything yet.

'So.' Carrie folds her arms atop the table. 'Jules.'

Chloe sighs. 'Cameron, she's wonderful.'

'You've only spoken to her for a minute.' He fiddles with the top button of his shirt, working it loose.

Chloe shrugs. 'I got a good vibe from her. And from you, when you're with her.'

'Agreed,' Carrie says.

'I don't — Can we — ' He stands abruptly from his chair. 'I'm going to the bathroom too.'

'You can't run from this conversation!'

But he can sure as hell delay it.

Yes, Jules is wonderful and he likes how he feels around her, but that's it. He won't give history a chance to repeat by dating someone else he works with.

He rounds the corner to the bathrooms and slams into someone. His hands wrap around their arms and only when they're steady and he's staring into their summer-sky blue eyes does he register he's clutching Jules.

His breath catches. 'Oh, hey. Jules. Sorry.'

Her skin feels soft and warm beneath his hands.

'That's alright. Thanks for catching me. Falling on my ass would have been one too many embarrassments in front of you today.'

'Embarrassments?'

'You know the... the... the car ride stuff.' Her gaze darts around, avoiding his face, catching on the hollow of his throat. She gulps, then mumbles, 'And mentioning my, uh, reading proclivities.'

Oh yeah, that. His hands heat. Jules. Erotic romance. It's quite a combo. 'Seriously, don't worry. I'm not going to judge how you fill your spare time. I go through several paint-by-numbers every month.'

'You do?'

Shit. He didn't mean to bring that nerdy hobby up, but Jules looks less embarrassed now that he has, so it's a win. 'Really.'

Jules laughs softly. 'Thanks.'

Her gaze settles on his face and her pupils expand across the blue of her eyes. The lighting in this alcove is dim. It's kind of... intimate, hidden away from the restaurant's patrons.

He hears her breathe in and feels her shift in his arms.

Crap. He's still touching her.

'Sorry. Sorry.' He pulls his hands away and runs one through his hair, trying to forget the feel of her skin. 'Um. How are you coping with lunch? I know you were nervous before.'

'I was, yeah, but... I'm enjoying myself.' Her hand comes up to cover her arm where his had been a moment ago. 'It's nice seeing you around your sisters. You obviously have a good relationship.'

'Yeah, I'm lucky in that way. I know a lot of people who don't get along with their families. But I've missed them. Didn't realise how much.'

She nods. 'I can hear it.'

'Don't you mean see it?'

'No. I can hear it in your voice. You sound relaxed.'

Cameron isn't sure what to make of the fact she can hear his emotions in his voice. 'Probably because whenever we've talked on the phone before I've been in the middle of a tech crisis.'

'That's true.' She laughs, then sighs. 'Well now I feel bad about intruding on your family lunch. I know Carrie kind of sprung the invite on you.'

'You're not intruding. I wanted you here, too.'

Her eyes narrow. 'Really?'

'I've... It's nice chatting with you outside work. Being able to see your face when you talk.'

Christ, he's leaning in again. At least his sisters aren't around to hear it.

Might be worth it though, because Jules smiles at him and says, 'I think so too.'

The clenching in his chest happens again.

* * *

Their food has been delivered by the time they make it back to the table. Carrie and Chloe wait until they're seated before digging in, which Cameron knows is only because Jules is around.

He lets his sisters take over the conversation as they eat. He doesn't want to give them any more ammunition for their two-woman mission to tear down his supposed emotional intimacy wall.

For all her embarrassment at the start, Jules handles lunch with his sisters with ease. She asks all the right questions, makes them laugh, gushes over the food with Carrie and talks about costume design with Chloe. She fits into his family like marshmallows in hot chocolate.

Cameron has a less pleasant lunch. Oh there are some great moments, like whenever Jules absentmindedly touches his arm or his shoulder when she speaks to him, or hearing her get nerdy explaining her job and the various IT systems she helped streamline. Cameron keeps catching himself staring softly at her, feeling light as a feather. That's the bad part, because any time he makes eye-contact with Chloe or Carrie they give him *a look* and he has to work hard to get his expression back under control.

The way Jules makes him feel is hard to fight against though. She's so open; everything on the surface. Her joy and passion and intelligence and friendliness. No hidden agenda like with Braden.

Thinking of his ex sours his mood, but it's the reminder he needs to reign in any wayward feelings.

Jules leaves eventually, claiming she needs to work on her presentation before she gets distracted by the conference officially starting. Cameron half-stands up when she pushes back from the table, then awkwardly reclaims his seat. He's hoping his sisters missed the action but knows by the way one of them kicks his shin he's shit out of luck.

He settles for not watching Jules as she walks out.

Imagining the sway of her hips is a poor substitute for the real thing.

'Oh. My. Gosh,' Chloe says. 'This was totally worth skipping class today. You *like* her.'

'No, I don't,' Cameron says automatically, used to it now from all the times he's tried to convince his own internal voice of that exact thought.

'Uh-uh-uh,' Chloe wags her finger. 'You already fessed up that you did, but I thought it was more like, chill. But this is *serious* liking. Your eyes were all over her.'

'I was looking at you guys, too.' Cameron defends himself.

'Sure, Cam,' Carrie says, 'but you weren't looking at us like we were the pot of gold beneath a rainbow.'

'So what? Was I meant to not look at her when she was talking? That's rude.' It comes out defensive and has Carrie and Chloe sharing a look that makes Cameron sit up straight. 'Stop that,' he tells them.

They turn to him in unison, Chloe with big innocent eyes and Carrie like she's keeping a secret.

'No. Whatever you're about to say or suggest or tell me. The answer is no.'

'We think you should go for it with Jules,' Chloe says. 'Ask her out.'

Cameron tilts his head back to stare at the ceiling. 'No.'

'Come on. Why not?' Chloe asks with the whine of a hopeful romantic. Or a woman who watches too many reality dating shows.

'You know why. I can't go through another Braden.'

'Okay,' Carrie says, 'but you're ignoring the part where *Jules isn't Braden*. You have to get back in the game at some point.'

'Do I? Why can't I just focus on work. Nail my presentation and be single?'

'Because that's not you.' Chloe reaches across the table to place her hand over his. 'You're a relationship guy. Honestly, you're a bit of a romantic. You like people and company and caring for others.'

'And the only person you've got to care for down in Canberra is Steven, so there's certainly room in your social calendar.'

Cameron shuffles in his chair. His sisters aren't incorrect about his personality. That's why avoiding seeing Jules at work was the cornerstone of his tactic to not date anyone at work. Being in her presence makes him want to reach out. He'd flirted with her in the car, for fuck's sake. Absolutely no chill, and no commitment to the one dating rule he has.

Chloe pinches his wrist. 'Would it help convince you if I said you were so busy fawning over her, you didn't notice she was doing the same with you?'

Cameron's heart squeezes. 'She was?'

He answered too quickly. It earns a smirk from Carrie.

'Totally!' Chloe says. 'She was looking at you with these bright eyes, totally engaged and endeared by you.'

'Not to mention all the arm touching.' Carrie adds. 'Felt like I was watching a Hallmark film in real life.'

Cameron's chest inflates like a balloon, but a balloon is hot air inside a thin skin, easily burst.

'You've only just met her. How can you tell?' He questions Chloe.

'Because she looked into your eyes like she cared what you were saying, not at your mouth like she was picturing it on her.'

Jules may not have been picturing it, but now he is. Picturing kissing Jules. And it's hot like fire and also, in his daydream, happening in the hire car like they're horny teens who've snuck out for a night. He'd thought about it at the time, too. When she mentioned a conference fling and that traitorous part of him, half-emotion half-desire and zero logic, perked up in interest.

Cameron reaches for his water to cool the heat travelling down his spine. Far out, imagining one single kiss isn't meant to make him feel like this.

'Even if that's true,' and fuck, the horny-teenage-esque part of him longs for it to be, 'it makes no difference.'

'*Cameron*,' Carrie snaps his name. 'You've got to stop letting Braden ruin your life from beyond the relationship.' She leans over the table and her gaze traps his. 'You moved out of Sydney, you've shut out old friends, you haven't dated, you've lost your joy. We've been letting you grieve and wallow because that shit Braden did earned you some recovery time. But now it's time to pick up the bow and get playing again. Or whatever is more applicable to you.'

Carrie's always been a pro at rousing speeches – probably from her time as captain of every netball team she's ever played in – and Cameron feels something stirring inside him, like little eddies of wind picking up discarded dreams. He recalls Jules's smile, and the warmth that bloomed when she touched him.

Is he really going to keep literally running away from Jules as long as he works at Infinity?

As the eddies pick up, he forces himself to recall everything that went down after he found out about Braden. The sickening feelings and the anxiety. Quitting his job in the middle of a campaign he spearheaded. It helps put a stop to the hopeful stirring.

'Hey,' Carrie draws his attention back to her. 'We're only saying it because we love you.'

Cameron sighs. 'I know.'

He toys with the edge of his napkin, gut twisting now that Carrie's played the love card. It doesn't change anything though. He and Jules still work together, and his highest priority for this conference needs to be making things right with his ex-colleagues, not getting to know Jules more. Pursuing a relationship with Jules would be a distraction from his presentation that will help redeem his professional reputation. It's a risk he can't take.

CHAPTER 7

Cameron waits for Jules outside her room that evening, having agreed earlier to go with her to the welcome night. He paces to expel the restlessness from his limbs which has been there since lunch. His sisters are insistent he make a move with Jules tonight, despite him repeatedly reminding them a relationship was off the cards. Even if what they say is true and Jules is interested in him. They've texted him constantly all afternoon, giving him advice about complimenting her and asking about her interests outside of work, like the issue is he doesn't know how to have an adult conversation, and not that he's choosing not to pursue a relationship with Jules for legitimate reasons. He loves them, but they are terrible at taking no for an answer.

He's not sure he buys Jules's interest, anyway. There were a few... *moments* in the car and at lunch but they could all be attributed to friendliness.

But then again, here he is, having only met her in person three days ago, and already he's been leaning into those moments.

So maybe there *is* a possibility she's interested in him. As more than colleagues and maybe more than friends. Maybe following his sisters' advice won't lead to the disruption of his career like it has in the past.

And *that* is why he can't ditch the jitters. Part of him is actually thinking about doing something. Goddamn.

He leans against the wall opposite Jules's room, circling his fist over his chest. Why's he even thinking about this?

Jules steps out of her room. Attraction moves through him like wildfire, desire roaring in his ears, and Cameron feels that tug again. It's migrated lower than it had been in Patricia's office. Jules is wearing a deep blue wrap dress with silver heels and a matching purse hanging off one shoulder. Her hair is out and it falls over her shoulders in a way that makes Cameron want to fist his hands into it.

He balls his hands into his pockets like he can trap all the fervour in his fingers. No touching. That's a one-way highway to flirting and feelings, and he's avoiding all the toll roads with Jules.

'You look great. Beautiful,' he tells her. Friends can compliment friends, right?

'Thanks.'

Her smile fills him with warmth and he pushes his hands further down in his pockets.

She swishes side to side and Cameron gets a flash of her upper thigh when the dress parts along her right leg. His heart thuds an extra beat against his chest and he knows he's in trouble.

They head for the lifts, the strength of attraction enough that his blood still rushes loud in his ears.

'Do you think the welcome thing is going to take a while?' Jules asks, pressing the button to call the lift. There's a slim silver bracelet around her wrist he hadn't noticed before.

'I think the speech will be short and the drinking and mingling will be longer. Why?'

'No reason.' The doors open and they step inside, their shoulders brushing. 'I haven't networked in a while, is all. Is that expected after the speech?'

'No. Unless you want to?' Cameron hits the button for the second floor and stays by the lift panel. More space between them is good.

'Maybe.' Jules shrugs and leans into the back corner of

the lift. 'But what if I introduce myself to someone and they ignore me or shut me out of the conversation or something?'

She fiddles with the strap of her handbag, projecting unexpected nervousness.

He steps in and covers her fidgeting hand with his own, giving in to a swift and undeniable urge.

She sucks in a sharp breath as their hands touch, her eyes widening.

So much for keeping his distance. It'd be rude to pull away now though and he doesn't want to anyway. 'Think of it this way. If someone came up to you and said hello, would you say hello back or ignore them?'

'I'd say hello, of course. Wouldn't anyone?'

'Exactly.'

'Oh.' She laughs softly, chin dropping for a moment. 'I see your point.'

That's his cue to move his hand. It goes back into his pocket, though that was a shit deterrent earlier. 'But if you're not interested, we can always grab a drink, listen to the speech, then bail.'

'We? You wouldn't want to hang around?'

He turns to face the numbers above the door as they count down. Every decreasing number brings increasing tension to his arms as his hands curl into fists. 'There are some people here who... I'd rather not see tonight.'

There's a slight pause. 'People from Cable?'

His tongue grows heavy. 'Yeah.'

The lift doors open and Cameron takes long strides away from the conversation.

Jules doesn't ask anything further as they join the check-in queue outside the function room where the welcome event is being held. It's not too busy when they step through, only a few people mingling in small groups around the space. The bar at the back of the room has a queue though, and a handful of the tabled booths around the walls are already taken.

'I'll grab you a drink?' Cameron offers. A quick scan of the room hasn't revealed any Cable staff yet, but it's inevitable they'll be here. He could do with the liquid fortification.

'I'll come with you. I don't know anyone here.'

They join the bar queue, Cameron still with hands in pockets. Jules cranes her neck to look at the ceiling. Cameron glances up to where two massive chandeliers are sparkling. It's a bit gothic, with the velvet curtain-draped walls, but Jules seems enthused, and her fascination gives him a chance to appreciate the length of her neck and the smooth expanse of her skin. He could lean in and kiss her right below her ear, or under her jaw.

Wow. He lasted an entire two minutes without noticing how attracted he is to Jules. He pinches himself through his pockets to nix the desire and eagerly steps up to the bar to give his order. Maybe alcohol can dull that too.

'I've heard this welcome night can get a little boozy,' Jules comments.

'It's true. Get any group together and put a cap on the bar tab, and people tend to go in hard and fast.' He presses his lips together at the poor word choice.

'Is that your technique?' Jules braces her hands on the edge of the bar. 'Hard and fast?'

Fucking hell. Is she trying to make an innuendo? He'll take it over her digging into his history at Cable.

'Depends.' His body leans against the edge of the bar while his brain reprimands it for getting so comfortable.

'On what?'

Cameron's pulse speeds up but there's something in Jules's eyes, ocean-blue under the lights, that feeds his recently re-awakened desire when he replies. 'My drinking partner.'

Eyes on her face, Cameron catches the minute widening of her eyes. The biting of her lower lip is more obvious and damn is it sexy. Ignoring the need to touch her bare skin is getting bloody hard with the way his body is leaning into hers.

He keeps his attention on Jules, ready to back off, rein himself in at the slightest hint of discomfort. She holds her ground. In fact, he's certain her eyes drop down to his lips for a split second.

His heart beats wildly against his ribcage.

There's no harm in a little flirting, right? As long as he doesn't cross any lines he can't come back from. They can be the kind of friends who flirt but never take it further.

The bartender sets their drinks down and the moment breaks.

Cameron shakes his head and grabs his wine, following Jules toward one of the booths. The swish of her hair across her back looks like temptation and the alcohol isn't going to help his brain win the war against his body tonight. Which he wants it to. Doesn't he? It's hard to be sure when they edge around a group of people and Cameron's hand is suddenly resting on Jules's lower back. It's like he's magnetised to her skin. His awareness narrows down to that point of contact, feeling her body warm beneath her dress.

Before they've made it to the booth, someone calls out his name.

'Cam? Oi, Cameron!'

Cameron turns slowly, hand dropping off Jules.

'Should we ignore them?' Jules leans close to him, her body pressing against his arm.

Cameron's chest heats – Jules is trying to protect him – but as soon as he spots the olive-skinned fridge of a man clearing the floor toward him, he smiles down at her. 'We're good.'

'Cameron!'

'Matteo.' Cameron accepts the extended hand and bone-shuddering back slap, careful to keep his drink out of harm's way. 'It's been too long.'

'Mate, I was just about to say that.' Matteo pulls back, grinning with shining white teeth. 'How long have you been in Canberra. One year? And the past few months, you've become a ghost. No phone call, text, DM, hand-written letter expressing how much you miss your best friend in the world.'

'Okay, let's not get carried away.'

Matteo laughs, dropping his hands from Cameron and turning to Jules.

'My apologies, *bella*. The rush of reconnection was too strong. Worked with this one for years at Cable before he jumped ship.' He holds his hand out and Jules takes it. 'I'm Matteo. Buongionro.'

'Ciao, Matteo. Mi chiamo Julianne.'

'Parli la mia lingua nattiva?'

'Sì. La mia coinquilina è italiana, del Nord Italia.'

'Perdonerò la tua associazione con un nordico a causa della tua bellezza.'

Cameron loses the conversation quickly, not speaking Italian, which leaves him free to notice how Jules's hand is still in Matteo's grip. She's not making any move to free it.

Whatever Matteo says next makes Jules blink rapidly and a flush spreads over her cheeks. His stomach lurches. Shit. She told him she was looking for a conference fling. Is he watching the start of it right before his eyes?

So what if he is? Jules is a no-go for him. They work together. And he can't fault her choice. Matteo's striking and a decent man – even if the idea of them together turns his stomach.

It just rubs him wrong. He's here fighting off feelings, ignoring matchmaking texts from his sisters, holding back from connecting with Jules the way he wants, and meanwhile, Matteo is swooping in with his affable, put-you-at-ease-so-you-don't-notice-I'm-coming-onto-you way he has.

Something hot rises like a geyser and Cameron moves to press his arm against Jules's. Matteo's gaze drops to the point of contact and he raises an eyebrow at Cameron.

'Okay then,' Matteo says, finally dropping Jules's hand. 'It's been a pleasure meeting you, Julianne. I'm sure we'll see each other around. And you.' He spins to Cameron and claps him on the shoulder. 'We need to catch up, okay?'

Cameron would put money on Jules being a conversation

topic. He'd damn his baser instincts for making him react so strongly, but it made Matteo back off.

'My number is still the same,' Matteo says. 'Text me. Or I will send you pictures of ugly cats every hour until you do.'

'I'll text,' Cameron agrees, accepting another hard slap on the arm. He's missed the guy and his affable charm and his obsession with British television. His stomach turns because the months with no communication is all on him. He left Sydney and let his connections fall to the wayside. It'll be nice to connect with Matteo again – just not when Jules is next to him pulling his focus like a flower bending toward the sun.

'Bye, bellissima. Bello.' Matteo disappears into the crowd as much as a 6-foot-3 man can.

Cameron watches him rejoin a group of people on the other side of the bar. He recognises them all. The Cable staff are here. Apinya, Fen, Wade, Munir, Rose. And Braden.

He turns his back before any of them look his way.

'I thought you didn't want to see anyone from Cable tonight?' Jules asks as they continue toward one of the few empty booths.

'Matteo's the exception. We used to be close before I left for Canberra.'

'Did something happen between you?'

'Between us? Nothing.'

'So with someone else?'

Cameron's neck prickles but he resists turning around.

'I think it's the distance thing,' he bluffs, pressing his hand to Jules's back to get them moving again. 'Me in Canberra, him in Sydney.'

'I get it. My parents live overseas now and my brother is in Hobart.'

They make it to the booth, Jules sitting on one side while Cameron slides into the seat so they're perpendicular. Cameron angles his body away from the crowd but the sensation of being stared at remains.

He needs a distraction.

'Where're you parents now?' he asks Jules.

'Ireland. Mum and Dad have still got lots of family up there. They always spoke about moving back when they retired, so it was a bit of a shock to me and Finn – that's my brother – when her and Dad went three years ago.'

'Have you been to visit them?'

'Twice. Feels like home, being around them, even if it's a different country.'

'I get that. Sydney feels like that to me.'

He might not have realised it if Jules hadn't made that comment about hearing it in his voice at lunch. It's true though. Driving past the Harbour Bridge was comforting in its familiarity.

Feedback squeaks through the speakers as the MC steps onto a raised platform across the room and introduces the keynote speaker, a publisher from New Zealand. As she speaks about the changing landscape of the publishing industry, Cameron keeps his eyes on the crowd – specifically, Braden.

The last time they saw each other, he'd been boxing up his desk at Cable and she stopped by to offer empty platitudes along the lines of 'I'll miss you' and 'let's catch up when you're back in Sydney'.

He's glowering. Fuck, he hopes she wasn't serious. There's an itchy, dry feeling in his chest that the wine has no effect on.

The speech ends to hearty applause and chatter starts up quickly. Queues form at the bar and Cameron keeps his eyes on the Cable group like they're a spider in his bedroom he doesn't want to lose sight of.

Jules bumps her knee against his and he shifts his attention to her.

'You good?' she asks, her eyebrows drawn down in concern.

'Sorry. Yeah.' He takes another sip of wine. 'I'm good.'

Jules's gaze is too shrewd, so he looks out at the room again.

Matteo catches his attention. He gestures between Cameron

and Jules, then grins and gives him a thumbs up, which is when the geyser inside him flares again and Cameron is hit with inspiration.

Holy shit. The answer has been staring him in the face this whole time. He feels ridiculous for not seeing it sooner. His libido has been distracting him, but maybe he can make it work in his favour instead.

There's a way he can uphold his no-dating colleagues rule but offer Jules something else. Something he knows she wants, that will give them both satisfaction without endangering his career.

'Matteo seems...' Jules stirs her drink with the straw. She must have caught Matteo's unsubtle gesturing. 'Friendly.'

'He is. And probably open to a conference fling.' It's completely unsubtle but he's not about to bring up his idea without at least a sign he won't be shot down.

Jules's skin flushes and she covers her forehead with her palm. 'You had to bring that up? I thought we were forgetting everything I said in the car.'

Cameron wraps his fingers lightly around Jules's wrist over her bracelet and moves her hand off her face. 'I don't want to forget the car ride. I learned a lot about you.'

Jules sighs. 'Yes, that I ramble when there's awkward silences.'

She downs a large gulp of her drink, then looks across to where Matteo is chatting up the MC. 'I'm sure he would be down for a fling, but he's not really my type.'

'What is your type?' He jumps on the opening, keeping his attention on Jules to read her reaction. Is the flush on her skin from the alcohol or something else?

'Um...' Her gaze skitters over his face before bouncing off. 'I plead the fifth,' she says into her G&T before taking another large sip.

'Fair enough.'

'Oh, hey.' Jules pushes her loose hair behind her ears. 'I was thinking. You grew up here, right?'

It's a clear conversational shift, but Cameron goes along with it, waiting for his sign. 'Eastern Suburbs, yeah.'

'Maybe you can be my tour guide this week? The last time I was here was with my Grandma. Lots of cafes and art exhibitions, so it'd be cool to see the adult side of Sydney.'

Cameron can't pass up the opportunity, craving another of Jules's blushes. 'Adult?'

'Not like that!' Jules play-shoves at Cameron, who fake tumbles down onto the booth.

Jules laughs and grabs his arm to pull him upright. 'You're a bit of a goof, you know.'

He doesn't feel goofy, but he does feel looser around her, even as he keeps looking for that sign. 'I like hearing your laugh.'

Jules's hands tighten a fraction around his arm. Her eyes are suddenly very focused on his, with a smouldering intent that has him thinking of strewn pillows and messed up sheets. He shifts so his knee presses against hers beneath the table, and she sucks her lower lip into her mouth. It's the sign he was searching for.

'I've had an idea,' he says.

'What about?'

He drops his voice so she has to lean in to hear him. 'About your conference fling.'

She pulls away slightly, taking a sip of her drink. 'You think I should go for it with Matteo anyway?'

He shakes his head slowly, pulse jumping when her gaze drops to his lips for a second. Time to play to his strengths. 'I want to be your conference fling.'

'What?' Her eyes widen. 'I... what?'

He doesn't mind her confusion. He has been keeping his feelings in check, so to her, his offer must seem to come from nowhere.

'Jules.' Her shiver is an aphrodisiac to him. He slides around the booth so they're sitting side-by-side. Not close enough to touch, but close enough he can smell her shampoo and feel the heat of her body. 'You want a conference fling. I want to have a conference fling with you.'

They've not broken eye contact, so he can see a hesitancy creep onto her face even before she speaks. 'Where is this coming from?'

Cameron takes a beat to think. He doesn't want to force it, so the truth is perfect for this situation. Some of it, at least. 'I've been thinking about it ever since you mentioned it in the car.'

Jules licks her lips. 'You have?'

''Course I have. It's you. I feel good around you. I think it could be… good for the both of us.' *And I can appease my desires without giving them the chance to damage my career again.* 'So, what do you say?'

She takes ages thinking it over, spinning her bracelet around her wrist as she does. He wants to take her hand and run his thumb over her knuckles, but he wants to hear her confirmation first. He settles for drinking her in, catching up on all those months of never seeing her in person, even though that was a purposeful decision. The warmth of her eyes, the glossy shine on her lips, the way her hair sits against her neck where he wants his hand to be sitting, right against her flushed skin where her pulse is found. The first place he's going to kiss her. One of them, at least.

If she says yes to his proposal.

He hears her breath fluctuate, sees the minute nod of her head before she says, 'Yes'.

Cameron's chest expands with heat. He pulls gently on her hand until they're both standing, then drops it as they make their way through the crowd, into the lobby and across to a waiting lift. As the doors slide shut, Cameron exhales, then gives in to the desire that hasn't abated since she stepped out of her room.

He spins to press Jules against the mirrored wall, hands on her hips. She moves smoothly with him. If this is a precursor to what it'll be like in the bedroom, Cameron can't wait. He's already getting hard and they've barely done a thing. The illicitness, the reprieve from having to deny this physical connection with Jules, it's heady like the scent of hot chocolate on a winter's day.

He breathes deeply, smelling Jules's fruity shampoo. She stares up at him, eyes bright and clear, a smile soft on her lips and her fingers curled into the bottom of his shirt. She looks like everything he's ever wanted. Every opportunity, every long weekend, every dessert. He wants to taste. He's only got a few days with Jules and he doesn't want to waste a second.

He leans in but Jules throws a hand against his chest.

'Wait,' she says.

'Yes?' He pulls back.

'Shouldn't there be more, I don't know, flirting? Gaging of interest? Aren't there steps to these things?' Her fingers twist beneath his shirt to his skin, even as she asks. Seems she's also having the brain-against-body fight tonight.

'Flings?' he asks.

'Yeah.'

'Not really. They're normally pretty truncated.' He pushes her hair behind her ear so he can run his fingers over the curve of it and down the side of her neck. Her pulse trips beneath his fingers. He's definitely kissing her here.

She licks her lips. 'So you've done this – had a fling – before.'

'Yeah. You?' He runs his thumb under her jaw from ear to chin, then up to rest it below her kissable lips.

'No. Actually, yes. Once.' Her skin flushes pink. 'At a wedding. It was... not something I thought I'd be interested in doing again.'

Cameron lifts his thumb off. 'But you're interested now?'

Her eyes burn as they look into his. 'Very.'

Cameron's lips curve into a smile and he traces her parted lips with his thumb. He leans in, ready to pull her plush lower lip into his mouth and finally know what she tastes like when Jules covers his mouth with her hand.

He freezes. 'I get the strong sense you're having second thoughts.' It comes out muffled behind Jules's palm.

'No. No. I am so on board.'

He lifts his eyebrows.

'I am! I am. If you slipped your hand into my undies you'd feel how wet I am already.'

Cameron groans and drops his forehead to press against hers. 'Christ.'

Jules's hand slips off his mouth. 'Crap. Didn't mean to say that last part out loud.'

'Hey, I do not mind.' He grips her face between his hands, probably too tight but he's desperate to kiss her yet knows in his gut he needs to let her make that final step. 'It's fucking hot.'

'I'm not having second thoughts, I'm just nervous and overthinking. And how am I the one overthinking this? You're the person who printed off multiple copies of the schedule, yet you're cool as a cucumber.' Jules groans, but not in the sexy way. 'And I'm saying things like 'cool as a cucumber'.'

Cameron laughs. 'Stop thinking so much.'

'Ha ha.' Her eyeroll makes Cameron smile. 'You know it doesn't work like that.'

'Maybe if you actually let me kiss you it will put you at ease.'

Jules's eyes narrow. 'I'm not sure 'at ease' is going to be the effect.'

He hopes not. He was hoping for something more electric. He's half-hard already, eager for this to start properly. The fling is something Jules wanted, but he's not going to rush it if she needs a moment to come on board with his impromptu offer.

'We have been flirting, by the way. I'm offended you didn't notice.' He says it lightly, making sure she knows it's a tease.

'We have?' Jules winces. 'Sorry. I'm rustier than I thought I'd be. It's—'

'Been a while. You told me in the car.' Cameron moves

his hands to rest at her waist and encourages her body to bend into his. She does. 'And I told you how beautiful you looked tonight. When you asked if my drinking technique is hard and fast and I said it depended on the drinking partner.' He moves his head to whisper into her ear. 'I wasn't talking about drinking.'

Jules's breath catches then releases on a shaky exhale. Her hand slides up his back to curl over a shoulder. 'And in the car, when I said I didn't know why I gestured to you when I said I'd say yes if the right person offered? I was lying.'

If the small space in the lift was hot before, hearing Jules's confession has the temperature skyrocketing. Cameron cants his hips into hers and she pushes right back. He needs to strip his shirt off, peel off Jules's dress to press their skin together.

First things first though. They haven't even kissed.

'If there's any area of life that deserves less thought, it's sex,' he whispers into her ear before slowly dragging his lips across her cheekbone. 'Especially a one-night stand.'

'One night? Is that all this is?'

Feeling his body react to her, the strength of his desire... maybe one night would be smarter. It was hard kicking back feelings for her when she was a voice on the phone and now, with her trapped beneath his body, her warmth lighting him up, her smell and her voice driving him slowly desperate to taste her, it's a slippery slope ahead of him. He's not sure if more exposure will build his resistance or erode it so feelings come tumbling in.

All he knows is that the longer he stares at Jules, the more he wants.

'You said conference fling. That's four nights.'

CHAPTER 8

Jules is sweating so much she's sure rings of it are obvious on her dress. Totally unsexy, and yet, she still feels wildly turned on. Like Cameron has flicked a switch and her body has lit up. Like he's switched a dozen switches and she's buzzing with excess energy. And only part comes from her freaking out because nowhere on the napkin currently safe in her suitcase was this eventuality covered.

She'd almost turned down his offer because of it. Her friends suggested a fling but it's not her number one priority. She wants to know Cameron in the non-carnal way. Yet when she'd considered voicing that to him at the welcome drinks, ants had started marching all over her skin. Down her back, and along her arms, even the bridge of her feet and around in her throat.

Because she wasn't ready to lose her access to Cameron by blurting out her intentions the second he showed interest in her beyond friendship. He probably wouldn't have reacted poorly, but probably isn't good enough. She chickened out.

Then while she was hesitating, her libido grew louder and louder until that ache in her chest to *know* Cameron was teeny-tiny, subsumed by pure, unadulterated want. And so she'd said yes.

Yes to four nights. Four nights of Cameron. Four whole, entire, sexy nights.

Is it possible for a brain to short-circuit?

The lift opens on their floor and Cameron pushes off from the wall and wraps his hand around hers, tangling their fingers together like they're a couple on a first date and not two adults about to go and make hanky-panky.

She laughs aloud at the thought. Cameron turns his head to her. 'You good?'

'Totally.'

'Because we don't have to have sex because you said yes downstairs.'

She shivers as his husky voice caresses her, then laughs at herself.

'Do you want to call it?' Cameron slows their approach.

'Sorry. Yes. No. I just...' She shakes her head roughly. 'I have a thing for your voice? And hearing you say 'sex' was like foreplay for me.'

Cameron stills. 'My... *voice*?'

'Yeah.' Jules bites her lip. Why hasn't she let this man kiss her yet? Where's Tori's voice in her head when she truly needs it.

'I can work with that.' Cameron shoots her a grin that's one hundred per cent devious promise, before he speeds up again, pulling them towards his room.

Even walking, her thighs rubbing together, the feel of her own dress fluttering against her skin, is sensual. She's not going to last a minute once Cameron touches her properly. 'Should I be worried?'

'That depends.' Cameron's voice drops low, the rasp coming out like actual friction against her skin. 'Is me stripping that dress off you, kissing down your body, tasting you, feeling your quiver against my tongue... is any of that worrying?'

Jules's breath catches, heart trying to beat right out of her chest. Her voice sounds strangled when she says, 'Not worrying.'

Cameron makes quick work of opening his door and rushing them inside.

They're both breathing heavily when they resume their previous arrangement from the lift. Cameron's body presses Jules back against the door, heat up and down her front and the obvious hardness of Cameron against her hipbone.

She exhales shakily. She's doing this. *They're* doing this. She's about to have sex with the man she's been lusting after for months and it's not happening in her head this time.

Little ant-feet pinpricks play across her neck as Cameron's hands frame her face and he leans in slowly, eye contact unbreaking, giving her the time to freak out again like she did a half-dozen times in the lift for silly, nervous reasons.

She's not going to give herself the chance this time.

She fists her hands into his shirt and closes the distance between them, finally fitting her lips to his.

Fire. That's the word that rises like smoke signals from flame when their lips meet. Holy hell. Cameron kisses her like he needs it, slow but deep. Jules whimpers into his mouth and curves her body closer, tasting wine on his tongue when it darts into her mouth. She's burning up, clenching her legs together.

Cameron's hands skim down her sides then pull their hips together, his hardness pressing where she needs it. Jules's head drops back and Cameron's lips are on her neck, kissing and sucking on her pulse point. She lifts a hand to hold his head in place so he'll continue paying attention to this newly discovered erogenous zone.

Her other hand slips under his shirt so she can feel that deliciously heated skin, the abs she got a sneak-peek of earlier today. She thinks she swears but the fog of lust is quickly crowding out sense. She's panting like she's run up ten flights of stairs.

Cameron leans back to tug his shirt off before moving back in to kiss her. Hard. His hands move around to her back, spinning her around and walking them further into the room.

Jules stumbles over Cameron's discarded shirt and can't

make her limbs respond quickly enough to save her from falling onto her ass. It knocks aside some of the lust-fog.

'Wait, wait. Can we—holy shit.' She swallows roughly, crab walking backwards away from the discarded shirt while staring up at Cameron. His abs are a work of art. What will they feel like beneath her tongue? God, she might combust. She's already aflame, molten lava in her belly, down lower, at her fingertips. 'Can we clarify what's going to happen?'

'I'm going to get you naked,' he says, low and steady like the sexiest documentary narrator of all time. 'And then I'm going to make you come. And then I'm going to push inside you so slowly that you'll feel every inch.'

Jules's gaze drops down to the bulge in Cameron's pants. Every inch?

She clears her dry throat. 'I meant, how are we defining fling? What are the parameters?' *Why are you asking these meaningless questions?* Ah. There's Tori's voice.

'Well,' Cameron steps towards her, muscles moving in hypnotic action. 'What if—'

'Stop.' Jules throws her hands out and Cameron freezes. 'Sorry. I can't think straight when you're shirtless and stalking toward me.'

Cameron laughs, gravelly and low, with a smile like he knows hearing it makes Jules quiver. 'I told you to not think so much.'

'If we get this sorted, I promise to stop thinking so much.' Jules places a hand over her speeding heart.

'Alright.'

'Thank you.' She breathes deeply, trying to be polite and focus on his face and not his torso. 'So. Fling. Only while we're at the conference?'

'Agreed. This ends before we get back to the office.'

'And, um...' Her focus drops to his abs. Lower.

Cameron's lips quirk. 'Anything else?'

'Uh.' Shit. Her brain is melting. 'Are you—have you gotten tested recently?'

'Yes. I'm all good. You?'

She bobs her head up and down. 'And, um... what about...?' Questions spring to mind like 'why?' and 'how?' and 'really?', but Tori's voice reappears, telling her not to make this into a big deal.

Cameron props his hands on his hips. 'Are you stalling?'

'Maybe?'

It's been three years since she had sex, not counting the fling. What if she's as rusty at it as she is at flirting?

'Jules.' He says it soft. No judgement, but with a suggestion of, what, understanding?

Jules stares at him, totally at ease in only his pants, none of that embarrassment from when she accidentally walked in on him earlier. She counts all six sections of his abs, stares again at the bulge in his pants, feels her insides clench, ready and waiting.

'Can I come over there and kiss you?' Cameron asks.

'Please.'

His voice drops low and the pulsing ache at her core pushes the worries away.

'Please.' Jules grabs Cameron's outstretched hand and he hauls her upright.

They meet in the middle, lips on lips and hands grabbing. It's nothing like a first kiss anymore. No hesitation or testing the waters. It goes off like a firework, a big boom in Jules's chest and then sparks cascading down her spine to her core. Cameron tastes like wine and spearmint and heaven. Jules grabs onto his shoulders and pushes her body against his bare, solid chest.

'Fuck,' Cameron swears. 'This is a really—' is all he gets out before his lips are on hers again like he's hungry for it. He kisses her like she can take whatever he feels like giving her and he knows she'll enjoy it.

And she does. She enjoys when his tongue licks the roof of her mouth, and when his fingers undo the tie of her dress. She enjoys it when he pulls back to push the dress off her shoulders and proceeds to stare at her with unbridled desire. She enjoys it when his mouth ghosts across the mounds of her breasts in featherlight kisses before he thumbs her nipples to taut peaks then unclips her bra and gets his mouth on them.

'Cameron,' she sighs. He's not even gone close to her clit and she feels that wave approaching. 'Bed,' she gasps, as he grazes a nipple with his teeth. 'There's a bed right there.'

Cameron herds her toward it and Jules lays down quickly, dragging Cameron's body on top of hers.

Her insides are on fire in the most delicious way. It's like being high but also totally cognisant at the same time.

Cameron drops his hips onto her and moves his hardness in circles on her mound. Jules may whimper. She certainly spreads her legs wider to give him more room to work with.

'I've been thinking about this since you stepped out of your room in that dress,' Cameron says.

'You have? I had no idea.'

'Let me give you some idea, then.'

He kisses down her body, laving attention on her collarbones, her aching breasts, down over her hip bone, right to where she's hot and wet. He presses a kiss over her underwear and Jules shudders, hands fisting into the sheet by her sides.

Worries come to her about how she looks, and what's going to happen tomorrow and when they get back to the office, but then Cameron looks up at her, waits for her to whisper 'yes', and drags the fabric down her legs. When he licks up her folds to the tight bundle of nerves all she can think of is bliss and pleasure.

'Cameron.' She shudders as his tongue works over her clit, little flicks then big circles all around until she's shaking, hovering. 'I need...'

Words fail, but Cameron's already there, sliding a finger inside her, rubbing at her entrance and with one more lick she's gone, shuddering through an orgasm that leaves her flushed all over and breathing heavily.

Cameron grins at her from between her legs, lips wet with her slick. Jules's insides clench.

'You need to be naked,' she says.

Cameron unbuttons his pants and starts dragging the zipper down. Jules is transfixed. Holy shit. She can't get a deep breath in.

'I... fuck.' Cameron stops, sitting back on his calves. 'I didn't pack any condoms.'

'I did! I did. They're in my—' Jules jumps out of bed, any notion of self-consciousness gone with the promise of another orgasm and finally feeling Cameron inside her. 'My friend insisted on packing one into every bag and pocket I have. Ah-ha!'

Jules spins, triumphant, and almost drops the condom when she realises Cameron is now naked on the bed.

Cameron. Naked. On the bed.

Her mouth pops open. He's leaning against the headboard, arms extended across the back of it, making no move to hurry Jules as she stares like he's a masterpiece in a gallery. Tanned skin, muscles everywhere, abs and arms and *thighs*. Jules gulps. His erection stands proud and thick enough she's glad he said he was going to push in slow.

'Wow,' she breathes.

'I could say the same.' He extends a hand to her and Jules follows it right back to the bed and manoeuvres until she's beneath his body. It feels like she never left. How could she have gotten used to this so quickly? It's like her fantasies have been studies for the real thing.

He slides the condom on with practised ease and then he's right there at her entrance and things between them are about to change.

'Ready?' Cameron checks.

'Yes.'

He kisses her as he pushes in, as slow as he threatened.

'*Fuuuuck*,' he groans, echoing Jules's thoughts.

Jules feels every inch of his hardness filling her, stretching her until she's breathless. He's so hot inside her. But he needs to— 'Move.'

Cameron nips at her jaw then does as she asks.

It builds quickly, Cameron setting a steady pace that Jules is happy to match. Her mouth finds his again and the messy kiss is hot in a new way. This is what her books tell her a fling should be. Uncontrolled. Passionate.

Jules drags her hands up Cameron's sweat-slick back, sliding them into his thick hair while her legs lock around his waist. Cameron finds that sweet spot on her neck again and then his thumb is skating over her collarbone, her peaked nipple, dragging down her chest then rubbing over her sensitised clit and she's bowing her body, needing to be closer to his heat and his everything.

It's a blur and it's amazing, hurtling toward the cliff's edge with him again. His thumb is relentless and her second orgasm of the night comes without warning. She shudders, clenching around him while he swears above her, stimulating her through it until her body goes loose. His pace picks up and seconds later he's coming inside her, face screwed up in the beautiful mix of painful pleasure, telling her how good she feels around him.

Jules focuses on breathing while Cameron comes down from the high before carefully pulling out of her. Her body tingles. Her heart is a bass thump in her chest. Holy shit. *Holy shit*. The sex alone might be worth it, even if she never gets to have her relationship with him.

CHAPTER 9

Jules wakes up the next morning in her own bed in her own room. She rolls over to silence her alarm and *bam*, the knowledge she had sex mere hours ago with Cameron crashes into her like a bird into a glass door. Better than coffee for getting the blood flowing in the morning. She touches her lips, which feel tender in ways they haven't felt in years. Along with other parts of her body. It's a good sore though, because it's a reminder she had sex with Cameron last night.

Oh my god.

Twenty-four hours ago, she was meeting him in the lobby at work, worrying about what they were going to talk about in the car and hoping to cross step one off her dating plan. Now, she's turning into a molten goo-ball remembering precisely the shape of Cameron's shoulders and hips and thighs and the exact feel of him inside her.

Her body tingles and she swears, grabbing a pillow and shoving her face into it. Last night was incredible but *far out*, it was not how this week was meant to play out. What was the point of writing those steps down because she didn't want to get drunk and fall into bed with him on night one, if she was going to then proceed to fall into bed with him on night one? At least neither of them was drunk.

And what happens now? There's no step five on the napkin. Nothing that was meant to come *after* sex, or 'hanky-panky' as Cat so beautifully wrote it. There's no alternate pathway to seeing if they could date once they've hooked up. She wanted to be closer to Cameron before getting to the sex part. Hence steps one, two and three. Is it even possible to slide back to step one now that step four has happened? You can't hit undo on a real-life decision like that.

Having sex with Cameron was... her body flushes and her toes tingle. Mind-blowing. But what if she's accidentally made it so that's all it is? And, oh god, what if it ruins their entire dynamic. What if they can't talk to each other anymore? What if the carnal knowledge they now possess of each other means it's going to be all blushing and stammering and politeness. Or what if it's just all sexual innuendo and foreplay, all the time.

Her nipples perk up at that and she slaps her arm across her chest. Her body is clearly on board, but she'd like her brain to get there too.

She's burning up and it's much less pleasant than the kind of burning she was doing in Cameron's bed last night. She kicks the sheets off her body and starfishes out. She doesn't regret it and she wouldn't take last night back, but she has no idea how to turn a fling into an emotional connection. They were only beginning to learn more about each other. She wants more of *that*, not the bedroom stuff.

Well. She wants more of that too.

Why did her past self have to get so caught up on having structure and guidelines in place? She's probably shot herself in the foot with all that 'what is this', 'define a fling' stuff.

Urgh. This is why she avoids spontaneity and taking relationship risks. She grabs her phone from the bedside table. She needs advice.

'What,' Tori answers the group call bluntly, her 'I've not had my tea' voice firmly in place.

'Morning ladies.' Cat's probably been awake for at least an hour already.

'Ugh,' Tori groans. 'It's not even daylight yet.'

Jules checks the clock. 'It's after seven.'

'My blackout curtains are awesome, then.'

'I'm coming in,' Cat announces.

A video request comes through from Cat and Jules accepts it in time to watch Cat march into Tori's room and pull open the heavy curtains so a strip of light falls exactly onto Tori's gigantic, rumpled bed and the rumpled woman within it.

'No, Cat. Do not interrupt my—Cat!' Tori throws a pillow at Cat and her phone clatters to the ground. Jules gets a wonderful view of Cat's slippered feet before the phone is retrieved.

'See. Daylight.' Cat's voice echoes in Jules's ear as it's picked up by Cat and Tori's phones.

'I hate you.' Tori pulls her doona back and shuffles over so Cat can climb onto the bed and sit beside her.

'Hate you too. Can you hang up your phone? The feedback is getting ridiculous.'

Jules clears her throat. She loves her friends and ordinarily she finds amusement in their bickering, but her stress levels need attending to.

'I had sex with Cameron.'

There's total silence, aside from her own voice echoing back to her before Tori hangs up her phone.

'Can you—Sorry.' Cat moves her head closer to her phone. 'I think we misheard.'

'I had sex with Cameron.'

Cat breaks into a grin. 'What! You what!'

Cat's steady-hand phone holding technique becomes more like a shaky-cam as Tori bounces on the bed beside her, cheering. Apparently, hearing about Jules's sexploits is as good as caffeine to wake a person up.

'Good on you,' Tori says, literally applauding her.

'Is it? Is it good?' Jules scrambles up into a sitting position. 'We wrote that list out so I could build a proper relationship in proper increments with Cameron and I skipped straight to step four somehow and I'm starting to freak out. The whole point of writing the steps out in that order is because I didn't want this to just be a conference fling – no offense,

Tor – and now it's clearly a conference fling with no long-term potential.'

'Not necessarily,' Cat says. 'You can get to an emotional relationship through a sexual one.'

'No I meant, like, we literally verbally agreed it was a conference fling with a very definite end date.'

Tori throws her hands up. 'Why the hell would you agree to that?'

'I don't know! I was flustered. He was half-naked at the time and I was horny and stressing that we had no clear structure to our engagement and also, I may have, accidentally,' Jules starts slipping back down into a recline, dragging the sheet over her head, 'told him in the car ride over that I was interested in one,' she finishes in a whisper.

Tori's head drops to her chest. 'Woman.'

'You know how I get with silence and the filling in of it when I'm nervous.'

'You couldn't have filled it in with talk about the conference?' Tori's face is all pinched up, visibly pained. 'Or the weather?'

'Again. I'll refer you to me and silences and nervous rambling without proper forethought.'

Cat drums her fingers on her collarbone. 'You know,' she says slowly, staring off beyond the screen, 'this doesn't seem like as much of a problem as it could be.'

'How?'

Cat's focus shifts back to the camera. 'Have you considered he agreed to a fling expressly *because* that's what you told him you wanted? Maybe he's doing it to please you.'

'That's ridiculous. How did you reach that conclusion?'

'Well, because if it isn't that, then it's quite lecherous of him to proposition a co-worker, or take advantage of your desire for sex.'

Tori shudders. 'Yikes. That's so true.'

'He wouldn't do that,' Jules says firmly.

'So if it's not that...' Cat starts the sentence for Jules.

Jules emerges from her sheet cocoon. 'You're saying he knows I want a fling, and he likes me so he wants to give me what I want?'

'Your banter is good enough over the phone that you've been crushing on him for months,' Tori says. 'Who's to say he's not feeling the same way?'

'And see, now we're back to 'I should have stuck to the pre-planned steps' which literally included me trying to figure out if we had emotional chemistry. Now I'm not going to be able to tell if it's just sexual.'

'What if you tell him you want more than sex?' Cat suggests. 'If he says yes, you'll have your answer.'

Jules shudders, pinpricks digging all over her back. 'After we've hooked up? No way. I'll seem like some desperate person who's fallen in love with him because of his powerful sexual energy and massive penis.'

'Woah. Have you?' Tori's eyes widen and she grins gleefully. 'Is it?'

'His penis isn't magical, so no. And I'm not commenting on its size.'

Tori leans back against the pillows, nodding. 'It's huge. Knew it. With a voice like that.'

'There's no correlation between depth of voice and penis size, which doesn't matter anyway,' Cat directs to Tori, before pointing to the screen and saying. 'And you read too much workplace erotica.'

'I do not. Just because you prefer fantasy settings, doesn't—wait. I'm getting derailed.'

She pushes herself to sitting again, glancing in the direction of Cameron's room as she does, then lowering her voice and leaning close to her phone so her face takes up the entire screen. 'I can't tell him I want more. You remember what happened with Todd? What if that happens again? I'd prefer just sex with Cameron than no Cameron at all.'

Her friends fall silent, possibly remembering, as she is, the wreck she was after Todd broke up with her. She'd bought him a ring and planned a speech and while she didn't get down on one knee there *was* a romantic dinner. She opened her heart to him and instead of a 'yes, I'll marry you' she got 'we should break up'.

Then the ants came marching in and settled somewhere inside her, ready to stomp their scratchy little feet whenever she thinks about jumping into the dating pool again. Or taking an emotional risk. Like telling Cameron how she feels.

Cat clears her throat. 'That situation is a little different.'

The ants disagree.

Jules shakes her shoulders but the feeling lingers, so she pushes past the topic instead. 'Ignoring the huge actually-impossible-to-ignore issue that I'm apparently having a fling with a man I want to see if I want a proper relationship with, what am I meant to do this morning? Look him in the eye and ignore what happened last night? Do I bring it up? Say thank you?'

'Woah. Slow down,' Tori says with a lifted palm, thankfully going along with the abrupt topic change. 'You're way overthinking this.'

Jules fists her hand into her tangled hair. Now Cameron, **and** Tori have told her that. Probably because it's true. 'I know. But you know I don't have experience to draw on in this situation.'

'Just act normal,' Tori says.

Jules rolls her eyes. 'Proper advice only, please.'

'Fine. Take your cues from him,' Tori says. 'Say good morning, see how he reacts, then continue from there.'

'Okay. Okay.' Jules bobs her head up and down. 'I can do that. But what if I start getting awkward. What if I look at him and, like, picture his O-face or something.'

'Then he'll read it on your face and whisk you away to a closet somewhere.'

'Tori!'

'Hey. You'll be fine,' Cat says. 'You're great at conversation. You do it all the time at work with people I know you'd rather ignore or yell at or stick pins into a voodoo doll of. Yet you get through all of those with aplomb. It's one of the reasons you're covering Samantha's maternity leave.'

Jules nods, taking a deep breath.

'So you can handle interacting with Cameron in a calm, regular way. The conference starts properly today, anyway,' Cat says. 'It may not be such a big issue. You'll be seeing him far less than you would have yesterday.'

'Cat's right,' Tori agrees. 'And bringing it back to seriousness for a second, this isn't the end of any romantic prospects for you. If you think it's too soon to ask him for more, fine, but I think it's definitely still on the table. In the meantime, think of your situation as serendipity.'

'How?'

'You were saying it's been a while for you, and now the guy you're crushing on, who you've been having sexual fantasies about, has offered to have sex with you, not just once, but for an entire week. Why're you trying to find a downside to this?' Tori grabs the phone off Cat so she can stab her finger to the screen. 'Lady, grab this opportunity. Get some. Get filthy. Have fun. Be spontaneous in a safe, structured way and use those post-orgasm pillow talk moments to get a little closer to him.'

'That's... that's actually a fantastic point,' Jules says. Much better than straight-up telling him how she feels.

'I agree,' Cat says, reclaiming her phone. 'Nice pillow talk idea, Tor.'

'Thank you.' Tori dips her head, arms extended out in a seated bow.

'So for now,' Cat says, 'the new plan is sex and pillow talk. Got it?'

Jules nods, pinpricks fading from her skin.

'Great. We'll help you write a new list when you get back. "How to turn a conference fling into a real relationship in five easy steps."'

Jules laughs, dropping her shoulders, tension unspooled. 'I love you guys.'

'We love you too.'

Jules hangs up feeling less like an overworked car battery. In amongst the teasing and the overtly sexual comments, her friends provided some solid advice. She and Cameron did agree to a fling, and if last night is any indication, it's going to mean a week of incredible sex. She's not going to shy away from that. She can't be the only person in the world who's tried to work out if a fling can turn into something more, and her friends will help her figure it out. After the conference.

Jules nods and climbs out of bed, heading to her wardrobe. For now, she's going to be like the protagonist in one of her erotica novels – or like Tori – and get some. She'll commit to the fling, focus on enjoying herself and catching up on all the sex she wasn't having these past few years. And when pillow talk opportunities arise, she'll grab onto those with both hands too.

CHAPTER 10

Cameron gulps down a glass of water as he waits for Jules in the hotel restaurant. He hasn't been to this hotel before, but it looks like every other he's been in for these conferences, with a continental buffet in the middle of the space and various sized tables spaced around it across the room. The host had tried to lead him to a table to the left of the buffet when he arrived, but he spotted Braden's blonde head with some other Cable people and asked to be seated elsewhere. He hasn't braved the buffet yet in case he ends up trapped in the loop with Braden.

Thankfully, his phone provides plenty of distraction. His sisters and Matteo have been texting him all morning. Questions about Jules from the former, and the promised ugly cat pictures from the latter. He ignores his sisters for the moment. He doesn't want to trip Carrie's lie-detector ability with some half-cocked text about Jules.

Matteo must have found a way to auto-generate the texts because there'd been half a dozen on his phone already when he'd woken up. Now, Cameron finds a picture of a python online, knowing Matteo's deep fear of snakes, and sends a message.

Matteo: Finally! Thought you were abandoning me again. (A snake though? Really?)
Cameron: You deserve the snake for all those ugly cat pics.

Matteo: Haha. I've got a work call in a few minutes, but catch up later today?
Cameron: Sure. Is that Italian bakery in The Rocks still open?
Matteo: Hell yeah, it is. Meet you there. We'll figure out a time later.

Smiling – and salivating already for a slice of apple cake – he closes out of the chat, then scrolls through his text chains. It's not a pretty picture. In the past few months, he's texted his parents and his sisters, a few colleagues, Steven, and someone from his bank.

Chloe can never see this. It's damning evidence that he's been doing exactly as he's been accused – shutting himself off.

A tingle down his spine makes him look up. Jules walks toward him through the tables, a shy smile on her face. His gut clenches and heat shoots straight down to his crotch.

After last night, he wasn't sure how he'd feel around her this morning.

Randy, as it turns out.

Is it any surprise, when last night was some of the best sex of his life? So raw, but fun too. It was like he was a kid let loose at a theme-park. So much to do and see and experience. Earlier this morning, after his run around Sydney Harbour, he'd knocked on Jules's door to invite her down to breakfast. She'd opened it looking like a fantasy of the morning after. Dishevelled hair and sleep-flushed skin. He couldn't help the once over he'd given her, and when he saw her nipples taut beneath her oversized Duran Duran shirt, it had been hard to keep from pushing her back into her room and down onto her mattress for more.

He's having the exact same reaction now, his blood rushing loudly in his ears as his gut clenches again. He runs his hands through his hair. He's got to get his body under control or he won't last through today's conference events before dragging her back to his room.

But work has to come first. That's the whole point of this arrangement, that it won't get in the way of his professional life at Infinity, or his goal to reclaim some dignity with his old Cable colleagues. Running away to Canberra gave him the benefit of 'out of sight, out of mind', but now that he keeps seeing people from his past, all the feelings of guilt and shame about his no-warning resignation are sitting on his skin again. He needed space from Braden, but his team bore the brunt of the fallout from his decision. His professional reputation must have taken a hit as well. Publishing isn't a big sector, in the scheme of things. Word of mouth matters, and his abrupt exit would have earned him a mark against his name. It's why it's so important he nails his presentation. He's got to wipe that mark clean.

His worries woke him this morning and it took reading through his marketing presentation twice for the emotions to settle. Now, seeing Jules pushes those feelings deep down inside him again, until they're barely a whisper in the back of his mind. He could get addicted to that reaction. But a few days of being with Jules is the only way he'll let himself be with her. A few days where he can help her tick 'conference fling' off her to-do list, then back to the office and the way it was before, where any pining happens from a distance.

Assuming this week doesn't make that impossible. Even now, as Jules reaches the table, a little whirlwind starts in Cameron's chest that speaks of emotions to come. He stops the sensation with a hard pinch to his upper thigh.

'Sleep well?' he asks as Jules sits across from him, hair brushed and tied back, dressed in a knee-length blue skirt and a simple black top. Stunning. And sexy. He can have *those* kinds of thoughts all he wants.

'Yes. I normally don't on the first night in a new place, but I think I was, uh...' A flush spreads over her cheeks. Cameron knows it's probably extending down her chest too.

'Worn out?'

'Let's go with that.'

Cameron preens at the secret smile she gives him.

They grab food from the breakfast buffet, Cameron checking first to make sure Braden isn't there, then retake their seats.

'So, what session are you—' Cameron is interrupted by his phone ringing. Seeing it's Chloe, he dismisses the call. 'Sorry. What talks are you going to today?'

'There's a half-day series on subscription models that I want to check out,' Jules says, putting salt and pepper on her scrambled eggs. 'And Samantha texted me last night. She wants me to watch James McCarthy's talk on UXD research methodology, which isn't really my specialty, but she's my boss, so.' Jules shrugs and picks up her knife and fork. 'What about you?'

He's got it memorised, but he pulls the paper program from his pocket and moves his bowl of yoghurt and muesli to the side so he can unfold it flat on the table.

Jules covers her mouth with her wrist, but the laugh gets through.

'What?' Cameron asks.

'Nothing. Nothing. It's just...' She scrunches up her nose. It's both adorable and hot. 'It's kind of cute that you have a hard copy of the schedule that you've literally highlighted and annotated.'

'Cute?'

Jules shrugs, still holding in laughter.

'Just wait until you've only got five minutes between sessions and can't remember where the next one is and your internet connection lags,' he warns her.

'Has that happened to you?'

'Yes. Because technology hates me, remember? That's why I have this.' Cameron taps the program.

Jules finally laughs properly, making Cameron's inner whirlwind pick up. 'I'll take my chances. Me and technology have a good rapport.'

He's halfway through telling Jules his plans when his phone buzzes on the table. He flips it over to see Chloe's face, *again*, and dismisses the call.

'Do you need to get that?' Jules nods at his phone.

'Nah. She'll probably end up texting anyway.'

Of course, as soon as he says that, the phone rings again.

'I don't think she's going to text,' Jules says.

'Sorry.' He accepts the call and half-turns away from Jules, who's demolished half her plate already. 'Chloe. It's not a great time.'

'Oh. Have the presentations started already?'

'No. I'm with Jules having breakfast.'

Jules taps him on the shoulder. 'Say hi from me.'

'Jules says hi,' he tells Chloe.

'Hi Jules!' Chloe screams through the phone.

Cameron winces. 'Hear that?' he checks with Jules.

'Loud and clear,' she laughs.

'I'm actually super glad I caught you together!' Chloe continues, back to normal volume. 'You need to invite her to the symphony tonight.'

Cameron glances at Jules, who's started scrolling through her phone, chewing on her bottom lip. 'No, I don't.'

'Come on. You promised you'd give it a go with Jules, and you've been ignoring all the texts from me and Carrie, so we know you backed out.'

He cops the reprimand on the chin and crosses his fingers they never find out the real reason he's ignored the texts.

'The symphony is perfect for you two. It's totally romantic.'

Which is why it's a bad idea to invite her. He can keep his emotions in check when things are confined to the bedroom, and he has to keep them in check if he's going to get to the end of this week without hurt feelings. Put him and Jules in a 'totally romantic' set up and things could get sticky. Jules made it clear last night. This is a fling. He wants, no, *needs* it to be that too.

'I didn't promise. I said I'd think about it.' He'd had to

concede that far so his sisters would let him escape the lunch table yesterday.

'You can think about it while you're listening to the performance.'

'That's not a convincing argument.' Cameron shovels some muesli into his mouth.

He turns to watch Jules, who glances up at him and smiles, quick and cheerful, before dropping her attention to her phone.

'Hang on,' he tells Chloe, remembering something Jules had asked him last night, about wanting a guide to show her the 'adult' side of Sydney. Seeing the symphony must count as an adult activity. Classical music and champagne. And he knows from their phone calls and her choice of sleep shirt that she's as into music as he is, so she'll actually enjoy it, not like the one time he brought Braden along.

The chest whirlwind stirs hopefully, but this is him being friendly, not romantic. Jules wants a guide and he has access to tickets. It makes sense.

'Okay,' he tells Chloe. 'Do it.'

Chloe lets out a gleeful screech that pulls Jules's attention to him again. Her eyebrows raise in a question.

He presses his phone to his chest so Chloe can't eavesdrop. 'Do you have any plans tonight?' he asks Jules.

'No.'

'Do you want to come see a concert at the Opera House with me? The Sydney Symphony Orchestra is playing.'

Jules's mouth pops open. 'The Opera House? Tonight?'

'Yeah.'

A smile spreads out over her face. It's like watching the sun appear. 'Yes. I want to do that. Oh my gosh, that would be incredible.'

'Great.' The whirlwind picks up speed in Cameron's chest, spreading warmth through his torso. He pinches himself hard enough to bruise.

Returning Jules's smile, he picks up the phone again. 'Jules is in,' he tells Chloe. 'I'll get Carrie to text me the details.'

'It's a date!' Chloe proclaims. Cameron doesn't bother correcting her before hanging up. He's got better things to concentrate on, like Jules staring at him like he's a knight in shining armour. It makes him want to grab her round the waist and kiss her. If she's this excited by the idea, what's she going to be like when they're actually at the Opera House?

'I can't believe you got me a ticket to the symphony,' she says.

'Technically, Carrie did,' he says. 'She's played cello with the orchestra for years.'

'I had no idea Carrie played. That's incredible.' She folds her arms on the table and leans over them.

Cameron echoes her position, bringing their faces closer together. Her eyes are bright and sparkling and he can't take his focus off them. They look different in the morning light than they had in his bed last night.

'Have you seen the SSO perform before?' he asks.

'No, never. But I used to listen to a lot of classical music with my Grandma, and she'd try to listen to any of their recorded concerts when they ended up on the radio.'

'Sounds nice,' he says, hearing fondness clear in her voice.

'Yeah. It was nice. She's where I got my love of classical music from.' She reaches for the salt shaker, shaking even more onto her half-eaten eggs. 'Do you remember those Bugs Bunny, Looney Tunes symphony things they did? With, like, Ride of the Valkyries, William Tell.'

Cameron squints, a hazy memory coming to mind. 'Was there one set in a barber's shop?'

Jules leans back in her seat to laugh. Cameron watches her joy like she's the New Year's Eve fireworks, echoing bursts of pleasure going off in his own chest. She's as hot and bright and as *dangerous* up close.

'Yes. Yes!' she says, still laughing. 'Barber of Seville.'

'Huh. I should've known.'

He eats a mouthful of his abandoned muesli. The conversation is easy. Fun. Like talking with her on the phone at work always is, except now his eyes keep dropping to her lips, and he's fighting the instinct to lean in and smell her skin.

'Grandma owned them on VHS,' Jules continues. 'Every time I went over when I was younger, she'd pop them on. I was totally transfixed.'

He can see it. A younger version of Jules sitting cross-legged in front of a boxy TV with those same twinkling eyes. 'And then your mum came along and lured you from symphonies to synthesisers.'

Jules laughs. 'I wouldn't say lured, we listened to all kinds of music at home. If anyone was luring anyone, it was my older brother trying to get me into country.'

'What's wrong with country?'

'Musically, nothing. But, I'm a lyrics person, and I get too fussy finding faults in some of the messaging of certain kinds of country music. Not saying there isn't stuff I like, especially more recent stuff, but, you know.' She shrugs.

'I'm not a lyrics person, but I get it. There are songs I used to enjoy that I don't listen to any more for that reason.'

'Really?'

'Mm-hm.'

Jules's eyes twinkle at him, and when her focus drops to his lips, his gut jerks. It'd be easy to lean across and kiss her, taste the salt on her tongue. But they're surrounded by colleagues. The thought quells some of the heat in his limbs.

'But symphonies and synthesisers are my main musical loves,' she concedes.

'Feels like that should be on a t-shirt.'

'Oooh, yes!' She points her fork at him and twirls it as she speaks. 'With some kind of fun illustration. You design it, I'll figure out printing. We can wear them on casual Fridays in the office.'

'I didn't realise we were at the matching outfits stage of our relationship.' It's meant to be a tease, but Jules's face floods with colour. Crap. He's embarrassed her. 'Poor joke. Sorry.'

Jules grabs for her water. 'It's fine.'

He knows that's an 'it's fine' that really means, 'it's *not* fine' because she's avoiding his gaze. What set her off? Was it the implication this is more than sex?

Jules straightens up and slaps her glass down on the table. 'Oh, shit.'

Cameron's heart flips. 'What?' He sits up straight and extends a hand across to her side of the table.

'I just realised... I don't have anything to wear tonight.'

'Oh.' He draws his hand back. 'What about that dress from last night?' he suggests, only partly driven by the ulterior motive of seeing her in it again. It made her legs look phenomenal, and her eyes an even deeper blue.

Jules frowns. 'That's too casual. This is the symphony.'

'It'll be fine,' he tries to reassure and get the frown off her face. 'There'll be tourists there in shorts and t-shirts.'

'I know but... it's the Sydney Opera House. I want to wear something fancier.' She chews on her lip which puts useless – at this moment anyway – sexual thoughts in his head. 'Do you think I'd have time to shop for something?'

Jules pulls Cameron's printed program toward her on the table and runs a finger along the day's session times. Cameron wishes he could offer some helpful advice, get Jules to look at him with that stunned smile again that makes his insides glow, but he's struck out already with last night's dress suggestion. Fashion emergencies are more Chloe's forte than his.

'Hang on.' Cameron grabs his phone as an idea comes to him. 'I'll do you one better.'

Chloe picks up on the first ring. 'Cameron? Everything good?'

'Chloe. Hey. Jules needs an outfit for the symphony.'

Chloe gasps. Across the table, Jules looks up at him, mouth open. Cameron smiles, seeing Jules put the pieces together until the frown clears from her face and she's back to awe. The whirlwind gains momentum, spreading warmth until he feels ten feet tall. He could get addicted to seeing that look on her face.

CHAPTER 11

Jules was hoping to grab lunch with Cameron after the morning session on subscription models, but she makes the responsible choice and heads to her hotel room to tidy up her presentation for tomorrow and do a practise run. It means she won't see him until the show tonight and she's pre-emptively missing him. A tad pathetic? Maybe. But she'd had so much fun at breakfast with him, talking about music and making a start on appeasing that ache inside her that's eager for all things Cameron. The more they chat and the more she gets to experience the full Cameron – the little eyebrow twitches and dimpled smiles and huffed laughs and his floral scent – the fonder she gets. She's not ready to definitively say they have longevity, but so far, no red flags.

She knows the symphony invite wasn't him *asking her out* asking her out, but it's got to be a good sign that he's making plans to spend more time with her away from a bed. Cat and Tori had thought so when she'd texted them the news.

Experiencing the full Cameron, after having *experienced* the full Cameron last night, has also built a need in her core. All morning, her thoughts have been scrambled from the great sex of last night. The seminar she attended was fascinating, but she kept daydreaming about Cameron's hair and his thick fingers and his wicked smile instead of soaking up any knowledge. She even pulled out her phone at one point to text him before realising she doesn't have his number. How is she meant to organise spontaneous fling-related sexual rendezvous without it? Though that would make them less spontaneous.

The point being, she intends to have many rendezvous with this man, however they may come about. After this morning's confab with Cat and Tori she's all aboard the conference fling train, stopping frequently for orgasms.

She pauses her run-through as her thoughts get the better of her, necessitating a trip to the bathroom to splash water on her face. Her lips tingle. They feel flush with blood and tender despite not having been kissed at all today. Her eyes sparkle at her in the mirror, her pupils blown wide from the sensual daydream of a minute ago featuring Cameron, limited clothing, and the desk in her room.

Drying off her face, she takes a few deep breaths, trying to refocus so she can finish her run through.

* * *

Her lips are still tingling when she heads off to the James McCarthy talk which Samantha has been texting her non-stop about like she's some stalker-fan. She gets lost in the rabbit-warren of level six and ends up racing down corridors to get to the talk on time. She's puffing as she enters the packed room, and heads immediately swivel to her. Wow. Samantha isn't alone in her appreciation of this James person.

She's already hot from the racing around, but the attention sends a new flush over her skin. Jules's chest is on fire but she attempts normal breathing and heads to an easy to get to seat on the edge of the front row. She cranes her neck to see if she can spot Cameron, but no luck. She didn't expect him to be here. His printed schedule had a circled session on brand fluidity or something like that at this same time, but her kiss-desperate lips inspired some wishful thinking.

She does catch his friend Matteo's gaze though, and he waves at her. There's no little fizzle in her gut today like there was last night when he'd introduced himself. He's pleasing on the eye and if Cameron hadn't offered himself to Jules for her conference fling, there's a chance she would have followed Matteo down an empty corridor and into a secluded stairwell for some beneath the clothes fumbling in the name of a conference fling.

Who is she kidding? She wouldn't have been brave enough for that. And after last night it doesn't matter, because Cameron made a move and he's the only man Jules wants to follow into a secluded stairwell for a heavy make-out session anyway. Her skin buzzes as she thinks about it, imagining his large hands pressing her against a wall, his lips on hers. If she shuts her eyes and concentrates, she can actually taste him on her tongue.

The noise in the auditorium drops away and her eyes snap open as an older man looking like the dictionary definition of 'scholar' strolls onto the stage. Tan chinos, a checked shirt, glasses perched on his nose and a jacket with actual elbow pads.

It makes her daydreams seem indecent and she smooths her skirt down over her knees. It's probably a good thing Cameron isn't in the room to break her concentration.

'Welcome everyone,' the man greets them, spreading his arms wide. Jules pulls her laptop from its case and hovers her hands over the keyboard.

'My name is James McCarthy. I'm the founder of McCarthy Media. I'll keep the intro short because it's all online and I know you're not really here to listen to my bio.'

He speaks with confidence and a self-aware manner that has half the audience laughing, even at the dry stuff about how he founded his company that runs marketing and research methodology workshops and critique services. She gets sucked in despite herself. It's the energy he has, that enthusiasm and utter belief in what he's talking about. Like she used to have when she first started at Infinity.

The session flies by. Jules takes plentiful notes for Samantha's benefit, but also because she's drawn to James's charismatic way of talking. For a man who looks like a stereotype, his presentation is anything but stereotypical. Filled with funny anecdotes, colourful animated graphs and musical excerpts,

Jules appreciates the presentation on more levels than she was expecting. Not only is it well presented, but the information is new to her. It's lateral thinking problem-solving techniques that make sense and she can see herself applying them at Infinity to make further improvements on the archiving system, and even the intranet. Her notes for Samantha are peppered with asides to herself she'll need to delete later. 'Can we use this for image tagging?' 'Improve search function – eBook site?'.

The applause when James finishes speaking is thunderous, and Jules claps as hard as anyone. James might have found himself a new fangirl.

People hover outside the auditorium afterwards, but Jules heads for her bedroom where she left her portable charger in her haste to make it to this session.

A man steps out of a plain door ahead of her and she almost crashes into him, pulling back at the last moment.

'Sorry, Mr McCarthy,' she apologises, recognising the patched jacket immediately.

'That's quite alright.' James turns to her, pushing his glasses up the slope of his nose. 'Hang on.' He assesses her quickly. 'You're the lady from the front row! You were certainly taking plenty of notes during my presentation. I think you must have gotten a full transcript!'

His cheerful laugh reminds Jules of her dad and she finds herself laughing along with him. 'Yeah. I probably did. It was a fantastic talk.'

'Thank you, thank you. I hope you learned something while you were busy typing away?'

'Oh for sure. So much. I actually loved it more than I was expecting, to be honest.'

James purses his lips. Jules's skin heats at her slipped confession, and she rushes to say, 'Not in a bad way, I promise. I meant, I've never considered how strongly contextual and social factors can influence how people interact with technology, even in the publishing sphere, and how that can influence their responses to surveys and in focus groups and the like.'

'Ah.' His lips lift into a smile. 'Most people don't. It's why I run a whole company to teach people that exact thing.'

'Yeah. I'll have to look into it.'

'Here. Let me give you this.' He flicks open his briefcase and passes her a business card. 'Website, email, phone number are all on there. Enjoy the rest of your day,' James says, starting to leave.

Jules looks at the card. She should send a picture of it to Samantha.

Thinking of Samantha has her calling out. 'Excuse me again. Sorry.'

James turns to her and her tongue gets heavy in her mouth. She takes a deep breath and asks anyway before she loses the spark of confidence that made her stop him. 'This is probably a big ask, but are there copies of the conference slides available? I'm filling in here last minute for my boss and yours is the one talk she was sad to miss.'

James rubs the underside of his chin with his knuckles. 'Hmm. Who's your boss?'

Jules goes to tuck her hair behind her ear but it's already pulled back in a ponytail. 'Samantha Liu? We work at Infinity Press.'

'Ah, Ms Liu.' He smiles, nodding his head. 'I know the woman. I remember hearing her talk at the last Sydney conference. Spoke a mile a minute but great stuff, great stuff.'

'So you'll send me the slides?'

'Why not.' He pulls his phone from his pocket and passes it over after unlocking it. 'Give me your email and I'll sort it out.'

'Thank you so much.' Jules enters her details.

'Will you be giving her presentation then?' James asks as she types in her work address. 'I noticed she was on the timetable.'

'Yes. Tomorrow afternoon. I just finished polishing it up at lunch.'

'Working on it right up until the deadline. That's always

been my technique too.' James smiles at her, taking his phone back, then glancing at the screen. 'Julianne, is it?'

'Yes. Julianne Doherty.'

'I'm looking forward to your talk, Julianne.' James walks away with a nod of his head.

Jules watches him leave, tapping her finger on the corner of the business card still in her hand. There's an energy sparking in her chest that lingers from her talk, the energy she felt when she first started working at Infinity. She reads the business card again before slipping it into her phone case.

* * *

After the last of the day's talks, Jules showers at the hotel then catches a bus to Chloe's university where they've arranged to meet. She steps off the bus with her make-up bag, some hair stuff and two pairs of shoes that Chloe asked her to bring, with a promise she'd drop them back at the hotel so Jules could go straight to the concert. She spots Chloe's pink-and-purple streaked hair immediately. A good thing too, because the hug comes in swiftly, and suddenly Jules is surrounded by slender arms and she's got curls up her nose.

'Jules! I'm so excited you're letting me dress you.' Chloe pulls back with a bright dimpled smile so similar to Cameron's it makes Jules's stomach swoop.

'Thanks for agreeing to it,' Jules says, falling in beside Chloe as she sets a fast pace into the campus. 'I probably could have gotten away with something I have in my suitcase, but I wanted it to be special.'

'First time going to the Opera House?' Chloe stops at a bay of lifts and presses the up button. The doors open and they step in.

'No, I've been before, but not for years.'

'I've gone so many times since Carrie got into the orchestra. Which sounds like I'm bragging, which I'm totally not. It never loses it's cool and I always dress up.'

They exit on level four and Chloe takes them around

enough corners that Jules loses all sense of orientation, before Chloe pushes open a wide door.

Jules steps into an explosion of fabrics. 'Woah.'

She swings her head a full 180 degrees to take in the racks upon racks of clothes of all kinds and styles. In the middle of the room are a few bays with sewing machines sitting on them, and dress forms adorned in outfits at various stages of completion.

'This would be my friend Cat's wet dream,' she tells Chloe.

Chloe laughs and grabs Jules's wrist to pull her into the back left corner of the room, taking her bags off and dumping them onto one of the sewing tables. 'It's a chaotic mess, but I love it.'

Chloe's like a firecracker, sparking around Jules and making her try on outfit after outfit while she keeps up a steady conversation about the musical she's helping out with and the collection she's creating using all scavenged fabrics. Eventually, after Jules has tried on so many outfits she's lost all sense of modesty, Chloe settles on a midnight blue dress.

Chloe pushes Jules over to the full-length mirror with surprising strength. The top half of the dress clings to Jules's body from the wide, off-the shoulder bands to her waist. The bottom half is made with thick panels of fabric in varying dark shades of blue. Jules swishes side to side and they reveal flashes of skin up to mid-thigh, though there's a tan slip underneath for security.

Jules twirls, feeling like Cinderella after her Fairy Godmother waves that magic wand. The dress does amazing things to her breasts and brings out the colour of her eyes. She'd love to slowly descend a curving staircase wearing this and have Cameron waiting at the bottom with barely-banked fire in his eyes. The need that's lingered since this morning flares hot inside her.

'It's not too scandalous for the Opera House?' Jules paces in front of the mirror to see if there's any underwear on show.

'Not at all.' Chloe dismisses the worry, pulling out a set

of electric hair curlers from a storage container and plugging them into a wall socket. 'Just think of all the scandalous operas that house has seen.'

'That's a fair point.' Jules spins to peek over her shoulder at the back of the dress where there's a V that comes down low enough it would have shown her bra had she not taken it off. The dress is supportive enough and the fabric thick enough to temper the worst of any nipple visibility, which around Cameron, is as inevitable as Cat and Tori buying her flowers for her birthday.

'Plus, I know Cameron will be wearing a nice suit, so you need to match his level.'

Jules wobbles on her stilettos. Cameron in a suit. Now *that's* an image. Would he let her peel it off his toned frame slowly? She'd love to unbutton his shirt and just push it to the side to reveal those abs that make her mouth water. Kiss slowly down that exposed skin, sinking to her knees so she could undo his belt and then—

Chloe pushes Jules down into a chair, jarring the image from her head. Probably a good thing.

Jules rearranges the panels on her dress so they show slightly less thigh while Chloe grabs a smock from a storage chest.

'Cameron's going to see you and lose his breath,' Chloe says as she ties the smock around Jules like she's at the hairdressers.

'What makes you say that?'

'You're a ten out of ten and Cameron's predisposed to smart women who make him laugh, anyway.'

Jules bites her lip, watching in the mirror as Chloe rolls sections of her hair into the heated curlers. He's probably predisposed to women he's had sex with as well, but Jules still gets melty inside hearing someone close to him confirm she's his type. There's hope for 'how to turn a conference fling into a real relationship in five easy steps'. That really needs a better name.

'Thanks again for helping me,' Jules tells her.

Chloe waves a hand in front of her face, pulling out items from Jules's make-up bag. She locates the foundation and starts smoothing it over Jules's skin. 'It's totally my pleasure. I love dressing people up and making them feel confident. Besides, Cameron asked me to and I love my brother, and you and him are obviously close, so you and I are friends by default.'

The assumption catches Jules by surprise and her stomach does a hopeful lift upwards. 'How do you know we're close?'

Chloe moves onto her eyeshadow. 'He told us about you months ago.'

Jules almost gets an eye-full of eyeshadow as her eyes fly open before she snaps them shut again. 'He did?' Her heart beats a samba in her chest. At lunch, Chloe and Carrie said they'd heard about her, but she didn't realise he'd been describing her like they were *close*.

'Sure. You were the woman he geeked out with about music. The only other person he talks about regularly is Steven, who's a family friend, so it doesn't really count. Done.'

Jules opens her eyes, watching Chloe reach for the blush and highlighter. 'But we only met face-to-face on Friday.'

'Woah.' Chloe's eyes widen. 'Seriously?'

'Yeah. We've been talking on the phone a while, but, I mean, that doesn't really make us friends.' Plus there's all the very not-friend-appropriate things they did to and with each other last night. But she's not sharing that with Chloe.

'I think it does. Who cares if you hadn't met in person?' Chloe resumes applying Jules's make-up. 'You were so comfortable around each other at lunch the other day, and you don't get chemistry like that with someone you're not close to.'

Jules's heart does a little flutter at 'chemistry' being applied to her and Cameron.

'It's why me and Carrie were so keen to meet you,' Chloe continues. 'Sorry if we came across overbearing, by the way.'

'You didn't.'

'Good. We were just so happy you were real and a good person. Doesn't hurt that you two are super into each other, either.'

'What? No we're not.' Is she that obvious? Does Cameron know she's been crushing on him for months? She bites her lip, worry dancing up her spine.

'Sorry. Gah! Ignore me.' Chloe snaps the blush and highlighter cases closed. 'I'm a little too open off the bat, I've been told. I didn't mean to make you uncomfortable.'

'It's fine. It's just...' Jules's heart lurches from a samba to a two-step. It's just what? What *are* her and Cameron right now? Hooking up? Friends with benefits? Should she deny her crush to Chloe?

'Hey. No need to respond.' Chloe grips Jules's chin to steady her while she starts applying mascara. 'Like I said, Carrie and I were just happy to meet you. Cameron's been a little knocked about after breaking up with Braden.'

Jules doesn't have a claim on Cameron – yet – but her fingers still curl into her palm hearing about him with another person.

'I personally don't think moving to Canberra was a great choice for him,' Chloe continues while Jules's stomach grows heavy. 'It seems like he's isolated himself, which isn't great for him. Or anyone, for that matter. But he seems his old self with you.'

Chloe gives her an unguarded smile but Jules is still stuck a step behind. 'Braden?'

'Oh, yeah. He was dating this woman at his old work and things did *not* end well,' Chloe says with a dark look on her face. 'Not to get into the specifics, but it really shook his confidence. She's actually attending the conference with you guys.'

'Really?' Jules asks, stomach stirring uncomfortably.

'Uh-huh. Honestly, me and Carrie have been worried about him seeing her again.' Chloe recaps the mascara, returning it to Jules's make-up bag, and taking the time to pack the rest of her stuff away, except for a tube of lipstick. 'That's why we're glad you're with him. Otherwise, he'd be getting all trapped in his own head, turning into a doom and gloom guy. He needs some sunshine around.'

Chloe steps behind Jules to start undoing the hair curlers. With each perfect curl that unravels over her shoulders, the ache grows inside Jules, the one that can only be filled by learning more about Cameron than just his body.

She was riding that post-orgasm high after last night if she thought the sex alone would be satisfying. No way will she be satisfied with just a fling. She wants to know him in all the ways partners know each other. Like what he's like early in the morning and when he's tired, what he wears to bed and how he sleeps, what makes him laugh so much he cries, if he's ticklish anywhere.

Knowing his sisters approve of her – which they must if Chloe felt able to drop so much info about Cameron on her today – helps her stomach settle, though her legs feel shaky as she stands in front of the mirror. Chloe's made her look classy but still sensual, and in less than an hour, she'll be seeing Cameron. Her insides clench and she watches in the mirror as her pupils dilate. She hopes Chloe's right, that he loses his breath when he sees her, because she could use the confidence boost to follow through making this week about sex and pillow talk.

They can ride the conference fling-train together, destination potential long-term dating. Even if it includes a baggage compartment filled with bad break ups and an ex who's going to be around for the rest of the week.

CHAPTER 12

Cameron takes the long route from the hotel down to The Rocks, walking through Circular Quay and following the wide path around Sydney Harbour. People crowd onto ferries bound for beaches, the zoo or nature reserves, tourists stop to take photos with the bridge or the Opera House in the background. Kids in school uniforms mill around eating hot chips or ice-creams or both.

It's... there's a looseness to his limbs and something light in his chest.

He didn't expect being in Sydney to feel like coming home.

He's lived in Canberra for almost a year. Shouldn't he have settled in there? He unpacked all his boxes. He bought new kitchen utensils. He changed his address for every service he could think of. But stepping through his front door never brings that immediate release like stepping onto these sun-soaked pavements has.

Walking through The Rocks, he passes the sole office of Lin & Luther, one of the biggest publishing companies in Australia, and the one he's dreamed about working for since he graduated from university. They publish some of the most progressive stuff, especially in the young adult space, and he'd been planning on using his YA-centric work at Cable as a portfolio to apply for a job there. And then the shit with Braden happened and he couldn't stay and see his largest project through, not to any standard he'd be happy with. Not without costing his mental health.

He doesn't let himself pause outside the building, but it prompts an inconvenient thought anyway.

Was leaving Sydney a mistake?

Carrie and Chloe would say yes. In fact they have, many times, right from when he first mentioned the idea to when they helped him unload moving boxes from the rented van. His parents didn't express a view either way, which means they also thought it was a mistake but didn't want to influence his decision.

He'd been so stuck on the idea of putting distance between himself and Braden, but leaving the state may have been overkill. His CV and professional reputation took a hit, but it's bigger than that, because the distance has done more than get him away from Braden. His relationship with his family is different, and he and Matteo haven't spoken in months. He can slip back in with his sisters like no time has passed, but will it be the same with Matteo?

Out of all his old friends at Cable, Matteo is the only one he'd bothered to keep in contact with. Communication fizzling out between them is on his shoulders. Yeah, there was the distance, like he told Jules last night, plus Matteo had the misfortune of being there at Cameron's lowest. He knows Matteo isn't on Braden's side though, and hell, it's not Matteo's fault Cameron felt echoes of the gut-churning discomfort and sweaty palms whenever a text came through. He shouldn't be punished for being a reminder of what Cameron lost due to a relationship with the wrong woman at work.

Hopefully, today can start them back to the friendship they used to have.

He feels at home and out of place at the same time as he takes a seat at the tiny cafe in The Rocks, waiting for Matteo to appear. At least this place hasn't changed. The sandstone building and hand-painted 'Giorgio's Bakery' on the glass window are as he remembers. The tables still wobble on the cobblestones. The servers are still quick to welcome patrons and bring out menus and a water jug and glasses.

He pours himself a water and holds it between his palms, squinting across to the sun-drenched sails of the Opera House peeking between buildings. He'll be seeing Jules there tonight. A spiral of warmth twists up his spine. She's probably with Chloe right now, choosing some fancy outfit that's going to turn her already stunning looks into bombshell levels of devastating. His blood rushes thinking about it. He hasn't seen Jules since this morning and there's a part of him that misses her, and it's not his dick. Or not *just* his dick.

Which isn't a part he wants to look at too closely. Missing is a little close to emotions, which he shouldn't be having this week. No-strings. A fling. Emotions out of the picture. He nods to himself.

'Cameron.' Matteo's looming presence cuts across his vision as he plops in the seat across the table. 'Stickler for being on time, as always.'

'If you're on time, you're late,' Cameron echoes the favourite phrase of an old music tutor he had, setting thoughts of Jules aside to enjoy later.

'I'm worth the wait though,' Matteo jokes, running a hand over his shaved head and catching the attention of a passing group of women. He smiles at them and at least two of the women blush. None of them look as cute as Jules with colour over her cheeks though.

'You? Not so sure about.' Matteo turns back and reclines in his chair.

'That I'm worth the wait?'

'You've been ghosting me for months. I thought what we had was special.' Matteo pouts, stretching an arm across the table.

Cameron knocks their knuckles together. 'I'm sorry for icing you out.'

'You should be. My friendship is a gift.'

'Sorry for not cherishing it.' He says it with an eyeroll but the meaning is sincere.

In all the hubbub of his sisters trying to convince him to ask Jules out the other day, they'd made some points he didn't disagree with. There are times when he's so sick of doubting himself and his relationships, and not only the romantic ones. So sick of faltering in situations he used to not think twice about. It's like a cold he can't shake, that cough that lingers weeks past when it should have gone away.

'I'm being serious,' he tells Matteo. 'I shouldn't have gone radio silent on you.'

'Look, mate,' Matteo says, bracing his forearms on the table and staring at Cameron. 'I'm a bit hurt, not gonna lie, but I know you've had stuff going on. You moved to a new town, new digs, new people, new work and all that.'

Listed like that, they sound like weak excuses. Cameron sighs. 'But I shouldn't have stopped texting.'

'Damn straight.' Matteo straightens in the chair and grabs a menu. 'Okay. Dragging you portion of the catch-up is over. Let's pick up where we left off, alright? No awkward finding our feet again. We're not lovers reunited after a war.'

'Sure.' Cameron smiles, stomach settling as he relaxes into his chair at Matteo's easy acceptance of his apology.

Joking around with Matteo, it loosens something in his gut he didn't realise had been wound so tight since moving out of Sydney. Same way being with Jules does.

'Great. So as your best friend, it befalls me to ask...' Matteo's eyes scan over the menu. It's a shock when he asks, 'What's going on with you and the brunette?'

Cameron's eyes widen. 'You weren't kidding about jumping in, huh?'

'You know I don't lie.'

It's true. He never does, which means offending people, including Cameron, more than a few times, but at the end of the day, Cameron appreciates the bluntness. Knowing where he stands with Matteo, and knowing he'll never play pretend or run rings around him with petty games. And he's never mean about it. Always very clear that he's speaking from his own experiences.

'So. Julianne?' Matteo prompts again after they've ordered coffees.

'Jules. We're...' He has a moment of wanting to keep Jules to himself, but Matteo with relationships is like Carrie with lies. He *knows*.

'We're hooking up.' It doesn't feel adequate to assign Jules to a 'hook up', but it's what they agreed to and what he needs to keep her as to stop her from distracting him from work.

'Urgh. That is my least favourite relationship phrase. It's so vague. What does that mean in this situation? Expand.'

'Sex.'

'Mate. *Mate*.' Matteo shakes his head. 'I said expand and you gave me even less words.'

Cameron fiddles with the cutlery a server dropped off. 'You want the full story?'

'Look at my face.' Matteo leans across the table and frames his face with his hands. His dark brown eyes are wide. 'I want the full story.'

The full story starts months ago, when Cameron called up the IT line at work and a woman answered and their conversation slipped beyond work, despite Cameron's rule not to get close to anyone at Infinity. But they were in different departments and had never met so the slip didn't seem crucial. Then it kept happening and he found himself calling for even the simplest IT problems. The number of 'have you tried turning it off and on again' conversations was, frankly, embarrassing, but worth it to get to the part of the calls that happened after, where she'd guess the music he was listening to at his desk and they'd talk for ten, fifteen, once even thirty minutes about music. One time, he caught himself smiling and humming to himself in the bathroom after a call. That was when he knew he was heading into the danger zone. The danger in this case being falling for a co-worker.

He doesn't tell Matteo any of that, but it's not like he has anyone else to talk to about this. His sisters want him to actually date Jules, and he doesn't want to be talking to them about his sex life anyway. It's weird enough when Chloe drops hints about hers, and the time he discovered Carrie's vibrator collection was scarring.

Matteo's energy is so open and he's looking at Cameron with a ridiculous wide-eyed gaze and a little pout on his lips. If this is what it will take to atone for his months of silence, so be it.

Cameron inhales deeply then lets it out. 'Right. Well, we drove up together and she let slip she was interested in a conference fling.'

'Damn, that woman is forward.'

Cameron shakes his head, remembering the rambling and facepalming that happened after. 'I don't think she meant to say it at all. She wasn't propositioning me. She actually made it pretty clear she wasn't.'

Matteo sucks a breath in through his teeth. 'Ouch.'

'At the time, sure.' Because even though Cameron was busy ignoring any mushy feelings for Jules, it still hurt to hear he wasn't even being considered. 'But then we had sex last night.'

'Wait. Damn.' Matteo slaps his hands onto the table. 'Are you telling me I was this close to being Jules's conference fling if I'd played a little harder at the welcome drinks?'

'Don't be gross, man.'

Matteo laughs him off. 'Kidding. So this a one night thing?'

'No. Throughout the conference.'

Matteo slaps his knee repeatedly. 'You've picked up some game this past year.'

Cameron has a sip of his water. It's not game, it's playing to his strengths and minimising risk. If Matteo wants to think he's some sex-god, that's fine with him. Jules certainly made him feel that way last night. All those noises she was making, the way her hands were all over him.

Thankfully, their food is delivered before Cameron's blood travels too far south from the memories.

'So.' Matteo dunks a potato chip into some aioli with the energy of a villain stroking a cat. 'What happens after conference?'

'Nothing happens,' Cameron says, spearing off a chunk of apple cake and shoving it into his mouth for further conversational protection.

'Come on. You've got a woman like that interested in you and you're not considering keeping things up – a fling, or maybe more – beyond the conference?'

'No, because we'll be back working together in the office and that's a bad mix.'

'Sometimes the combos that sound terrible work the best. Like corn chips and melted chocolate.'

Cameron shudders. He knows Matteo's going for some kind of meaningful analogy but of anyone in the world, Matteo knows what's in his past. He should get where he's coming from.

'Well, I've tried it before,' he gives Matteo a loaded look, 'and it's ruined me for corn chips forever.'

Matteo narrows his eyes. 'I know I introduced the metaphor, but now I'm lost. Is not eating corn chips the equivalent of not dating women? Because that's—' he blows out a huff of air, shaking his head.

'It's not dating women *I work with*.'

'Right. Okay. Thank goodness. So where do your feelings come into play?'

'Nowhere. I have no feelings for Jules.' Sure, he's imagined taking her to see that Duran Duran cover band next time they're in town, but that was a subconscious daydream at best and doesn't count. It's not like he's set an alert for concert announcements.

'No feelings?' Matteo shakes his head. 'Man, that's cold.'

'Not *no feelings*. I like her, obviously, but...' How can he say he's worried about developing deeper feelings so he's going to deny himself until his dying breath? That he's worried they're already there inside him and this new arrangement is going to bring them out into the open.

'So the way you were staring at her last night was merely a lustful gaze,' Matteo says when Cameron falls into silence.

'And I imagined the envy-monster eyes you got when I held her hand?'

Cameron can tell he's fishing so he keeps his reply short. 'Yep.'

Matteo narrows his eyes. 'You're full of shit.'

'I don't have feelings for Jules, and if I did, it wouldn't matter anyway, because I don't want to date someone I work with and she wants a fling. She told me she wants a fling.'

Matteo stills during Cameron's tirade with a chip halfway to his mouth. His expression still conveys, 'you're full of shit'.

Cameron deflates as quickly as the outburst appears. 'Sorry. Sorry.'

'No need to apologise. You know bottling emotions up isn't good for anyone. Got any more you want to let out?'

There he goes using the 'emotions' word again. There's clearly some merit to it since Cameron just raised his voice at his one friend when all Matteo was doing was trying to knock sense into him. Totally wrong sense, but the intentions were honourable.

'Nope. Nothing.'

'Okay, well I've got something.' Matteo pops the chip into his mouth and swallows. 'This new attitude is about Braden, isn't it? Because you didn't used to have a no-dating-colleagues rule. In fact, I remember you heavy-handedly trying to set me up with Fen.'

'What's your point?'

'My point is.' Matteo stops to look at him like he's looking *into* him. It's disconcerting and he crosses his arms over his chest. Cameron doesn't want anyone pointing a magnifying glass at his insides. There's stuff he's not proud of in there, and feelings he doesn't want to be aware of.

Matteo shakes his head. 'I'm sorry I didn't realise the Braden stuff got to you so much.'

'It didn't.'

'You sure? Because last time I was at one of these conferences with you, you were Mr Networking at the welcome drinks. Out there saying hello to everyone from every publishing house, chatting with so many people it was like you were running for Prime Minister. This time? Nada.'

'People change.'

'I see that clearly.' He gestures to Cameron, who stiffens at the look in Matteo's eyes. Man, he'd forgotten how sincere Matteo can get when he wants. Disappointing him is like disappointing both parents at once.

Cameron sighs. 'If I say it is, will you drop it?'

Matteo holds Cameron's gaze for a moment before he relaxes back into his chair. 'Yeah. I'll drop it.'

'Thank you. I've gotten enough of that from my sisters.'

'The Parker sisters!' Matteo smoothly pivots the conversation, serious face departing on the wave of his grin. 'You've met up with them, then?'

'Of course.' Cameron eagerly grabs the new conversation topic. 'Had lunch together yesterday, and I'm seeing Carrie again tonight.'

'How is Carrie?'

'Married,' Cameron replies, seeing the panty-dropping look in Matteo's eyes.

'Shame.'

'She's quite happy, actually.'

'Found herself a nice country boy, like she was always joking about?'

Cameron hesitates over saying the next bit, knowing what he's setting himself up for. 'A conductor.'

Matteo catches the implication immediately. 'No shit. So someone she works with?'

'Worked. Past tense.' Though it started when he was conducting the orchestra she plays in. Cameron keeps that part to himself.

Matteo stays true to his word, and his no lying thing, and doesn't bring up Jules again. They carry on their conversation, catching each other up on the last few months of lives lived separately. It's easy, like rewatching a favourite movie. He laughs, Matteo tells anecdotes, Cameron shows him pictures of his new place and Matteo invites himself down for the next long weekend.

After what feels like no time, Cameron needs to head off to get ready for the symphony. And seeing Jules, who he is having a conference fling with, which he is completely satisfied by.

'Enjoy,' Matteo tells Cameron as he stands. 'Let Carrie know if the marriage goes south, I'm available. And tell Jules if she wants more than a fling, I'm open.'

The sudden jealousy-geyser that erupts inside Cameron makes him knock into his chair as he walks away. He tries to cover it with a laugh but it's not convincing even to his own ears. 'Not happening.'

CHAPTER 13

Jules walks around to the Opera House from Circular Quay, shoulders back and hips swinging. She draws looks from passers-by and they inject her spine with confidence. The sun has started to set, painting the sky with oranges and pinks, and the city lights dance on the water of the harbour.

Cursing herself again for not having Cameron's phone number, and not thinking to ask Chloe for it, Jules walks slowly along the railing by the Opera House, on the lookout for Cameron and his luscious hair.

She almost walks past him until he lifts a hand in greeting and she does a double-take at the man she'd dismissed a second earlier.

Her lips part as she drinks in Cameron as he leans back against the railing. Gone are the chinos and loose polo shirts. In their place is a well-fitted navy suit that doesn't hide his well-muscled thighs or the breadth of his shoulders. He looks like he's stepped out of one of her fantasies, the one in the office where he sits across from her and tells her what to do in that alluring voice of his and watches while she gets herself off to his instructions.

Jules gulps and floats over to him, caught in a sexual haze, thoughts of skipping the symphony to make music of a different kind with Cameron at the forefront of her mind.

'I've never seen you in a suit,' is her dull greeting.

Cameron's lips quirk. 'What's the verdict?'

He stands tall and holds his arms to the side.

'It—you—' Jules licks her lips, gaze sliding down the buttons of his shirt, the crisp seam in his pant legs, the shined leather shoes, then back up to Cameron's face to see him doing the same with her.

His eyes glide over her bare shoulders, her heavy breasts, down to her feet and up again, setting off a heat in her belly.

He finds his words first. 'I wish we'd met at the hotel.'

'Why?'

'So I could have turned you back around and we could have gone straight to my room.'

Jules quivers. The heat in Cameron's eyes promises fun and endless pleasure.

'We could always skip the symphony?' It's not like she wasn't thinking about it already herself.

She's constantly taken aback by her body's visceral reaction to him, which hasn't diminished at all after having sex with him. She can barely feel that ache in her chest right now over the heat between her legs. Can that ache go another night unfulfilled? Would it matter in the long run if she chooses fanning the flames of her desire instead?

Cameron laughs, low and husky. He closes the distance between them until they're close enough she can smell his aftershave. 'No way. You were so excited to go this morning. I'm not letting you skip it.'

Jules's heart flutters in her chest. She appreciates the sentiment, but damn, parts of her are disappointed to not immediately come into contact with parts of Cameron. She may combust spontaneously from unresolved arousal trying to make it through the next few hours of the pre-show drinks with Cameron, the concert, then meeting Carrie for a tour of the green room. Staring into Cameron's eyes and seeing the not entirely hidden desire makes her certain the delay will be worth it.

A breeze moves along Jules's exposed skin and she shivers. Cameron wraps an arm around her shoulders, tugging her close to his side. Is this normally part of a fling? She needs a Tori hotline to ask these pressing questions. For now, Jules gladly snuggles in close to the furnace that is Cameron as they descend to the Opera Bar and grab a table with a view of the Harbour Bridge.

* * *

They share food and drink while fending off the overeager seagulls, during which they talk about the conference so far and Jules fantasises about peeling Cameron out of his suit and having her way with him. She means to pepper in some personal questions to help take the edge of that ache inside her – persistent despite her arousal – but then Cameron looks at her like he's undressing her with his eyes, and her clit starts pulsing and she loses all her good intentions.

Afterwards, they join the masses moving into the Opera House for the concert. Cameron keeps his hand on Jules's back as they ascend the wide stairs into one of the giant arching sails. Heat spreads across her skin from the point of contact, like a drip of ink on paper, until it's curling around her front and making her breasts ache.

It's like this man has some kind of cheat code that gets him to bypass all the usual steps to arousal. One light touch over her clothed skin and bam, her internal muscles are clenching, ready for him.

Cameron leads them confidently through a door to a quiet section outside, nestled between two of the Opera House sails, where the cool air helps take the edge off Jules's lust.

'Wow.' Jules walks to the railing and looks across to the Harbour Bridge. Darkness has fully set and the lights around the arch stand out. She's seen it before, of course, but it feels different tonight. It's probably the fancy dress, which sits a little tighter than she's used to, or the curled hair she'd never bother to do herself. Or Cameron.

'Quite a view, isn't it?' he says, walking over to join her, his presence managing to compete with the famous bridge.

'Yeah.'

She pulls her phone from her clutch to take a picture so she can send it to Tori and Cat.

'Do you want me to grab one of you?' Cameron offers.

'That'd be great. Thanks.'

She passes the phone over, fingers tingling when Cameron's graze hers. She rearranges the fabric of her dress then smiles toward Cameron.

Cameron's slow to lift the phone, gaze roaming over her body in a way that leaves no doubt what he's thinking about. Sitting beside him for the next two hours may be torture. Or incredibly drawn-out foreplay. The line is thin.

'Are you ever going to take the photo?' she says as Cameron dawdles with particular focus on her legs.

'I'm taking a mental one first.'

Jules rolls her eyes but her insides go goopy as he finally lifts the phone and takes a few pictures.

'Can I put my number in your contacts?' he asks, joining her at the railing.

Jules's stomach continues its happy squirming. 'Please.'

He enters his details and sends a text to himself before handing the phone back to her.

'Beautiful,' he says, brushing the back of his knuckles across her cheekbone and down her neck, leaving a trail of fire across her skin.

Jules's gut lurches like it's trying to sway her into Cameron for a kiss. His lips look so delectable, all pink and perfectly shaped. She's not sure if kissing for the sake of it is an acceptable part of a fling. Does it always have to be driven by uncontrollable need? Or to lead to orgasms? She really needs another napkin to lay it all out for her. Or a tiny Tori on her shoulder.

She pulls back from Cameron before her gut wins the fight to connect their lips, and wraps her hands around the banister, looking out at the harbour.

'You know, when Grandma lived with us for a while, she'd put classical music on every evening while we ate dinner,' she tells him, trying to distract herself from the part of her screaming *kiss him kiss him*.

'Sounds special.' Cameron braces his left arm along the railing and turns his body toward hers. The wind ruffles his hair and she grips the railing tighter. 'Was this the same Grandma with the Looney Tunes video?'

'Same one. She had this collection of old records that I loved play-conducting as a kid. They're with me now back home. I like putting them on over the weekend.' Jules slides her fingers closer to Cameron's on the railing.

'What about you?' she asks, the cool air on her skin having cleared some of the sexual haze. 'Are you into classical music, or just here to see Carrie? I know it's a far cry from 80s synth pop.'

'I do listen to other genres, you know.' He moves his hand so their pinkies overlap. Jules's body tightens.

'I know. That's what we first bonded over though, so I associate it with you. You remember when you called me up at work that first time?'

'Yeah.' He shakes his head and his hair displaces itself. Jules reaches over unthinkingly to fix it up. Her fingers bury in the thick strands for several seconds before she recalls herself and slowly removes them.

Cameron's eyelids are heavy, his pupils large black drops on a bed of caramel. Jules sucks in a deep breath, recalling the same expression on his face last night after he'd made her come with his mouth.

'Sorry,' she says breathily. 'Keep going.'

Cameron's gaze settles on her lips for a drawn-out moment. Jules wouldn't say no if he leaned up to her, but he follows her wishes and she's left licking her own lips instead.

'You got halfway through explaining how to navigate the image database when you stopped talking. I thought the connection had cut out. Then you asked if I was listening to Spandau Ballet.'

'And you were. I thought it was cute.'

Cameron pushes out of his lean to stare at her with a furrowed brow. 'That's the second time you've called me that.'

'What. Cute?'

'Yeah.'

'You are cute. In, like, a daggy kind of way.'

'Cute and daggy.' Cameron nods roughly and looks out over the harbour. 'Thank you. They're words I aspire to be called. That many men aspire to be called.'

'Sorry.'

'I don't accept your apology.' He moves quickly, turning to face her and snapping his arms around her lower back so he can pull their bodies tight against each other.

Jules's hands get trapped between their chests. She tilts her head back to look into Cameron's eyes. The caramel is molten heat.

Cameron's hands slip down her back, until the tips of his fingers reach the top of her ass. 'What're you doing?' she whispers.

'Touching you.'

'I can feel that.'

Cameron smiles and his hands dip down further.

Jules tries to arch away but all that does is push her front harder into Cameron, where she can feel he's half-hard inside his slacks.

'We're in public.' It's a weak refute. There's barely anyone in this tiny wedge between the sails, only an older couple drinking champagne and two young women engrossed in their phones.

Cameron's smile grows even wider and Jules feels her insides heating as Cameron unlocks some previously hidden kink.

'I know.' Cameron moves his hips oh so slightly, knowing exactly where to put the pressure to tease Jules. 'I'm trying to get you to call me something other than 'cute and daggy'.'

'Indecent? An exhibitionist?'

Cameron drops his face alongside hers, and whispers. 'Warmer.'

His breath ghosts over her ear and she shudders. Her

nipples bead under her dress and she wiggles her hands free to grip Cameron's biceps.

'I was thinking,' Cameron says slowly, lips against her temple, 'something more like "sexy", "desirable".'

Jules is aflame. Hot from where their bodies connect, chest to chest, hands to ass, lips to temple. She's in public and she's wet and Cameron's only been touching her for a minute.

And she doesn't want him to stop.

Dear lord, Jules is like a beast unleashed around him. Her protests are insincere because right now all she can think about is lifting her leg up onto Cameron's hip and thrusting herself against his thigh until she shatters apart, getting to know more about his musical interests be damned.

The pre-show warning bell starts to ring.

Cameron's lips press to her ear. 'Say it, and I'll let you go.'

Jules bites her lip. No-one ever told her flings made you drunk on horniness.

His arms flex and crush their bodies somehow tighter together. '*Jules*.'

When was the last time she got a decent breath in? She feels lightheaded. Does she want his hands to move off her? If she doesn't say it, what will he do next? Thrust a thigh in between her legs? Kiss that spot on her neck that makes her shudder?

The warning bell is still ringing but they're alone on the balcony now. No-one would see.

'I'm waiting.' Cameron's warm breath tickles her ear and she shivers against him.

She can't deny that voice anything. 'Sexy. You're incredibly sexy.'

Cameron draws away from her and all the cool air that moves to take his place pebbles her skin.

'See. That wasn't so hard.'

Jules narrows her eyes at him. She feels bereft without his arms around her, and in need of release. Her only consolation is knowing he is, too. That they'll both be sitting listening to that symphony with their libidos through the roof.

'I'm going to get you back for that,' she warns, walking past him and grazing her hand across the front of his slacks.

Cameron hisses, but he's all grins as he shoves his hands into his pockets and follows her inside. 'I can't wait.'

CHAPTER 14

Cameron readjusts in his seat for the one-thousandth time. He only has himself to blame for being so turned on that focusing on the music is near impossible. He was the one to taunt Jules before the show. But can he be blamed when she looks like she does? In that fucking incredible dress that exposes her shoulders and chest up to the top of her breasts, and that clinging blue fabric showing off every curve. When he had first seen how low it dipped down at the back and realised she couldn't be wearing a bra, he almost lost control of his sanity right there on the boardwalk in front of the Opera House. How does she do this to him?

Now he's sitting here, thinking of all the things he wants to do to her. Meanwhile, Jules seems entirely wrapped up in the symphony, moving minutely with the flow of the music, her fingers lifting off her knee every now and then to conduct through a section of the piece.

It feels wanton to be imagining sliding his hands between her legs when she's caught in innocent enjoyment of the music, but, as he's been made aware of since meeting her in person last Friday, put him in a room with Jules and his thoughts turn devilish. Not that she seems to mind. He didn't plan on a conference fling, but it's good for his sanity that it's happening. He wouldn't be able to handle the sexual hunger his body insists on having for Jules otherwise.

The end of the program finally arrives and Cameron releases a shaky exhale as the lights come on, decreasing the temptation to get his hands between Jules's thighs only slightly.

'That was incredible,' Jules gushes as they exit the concert hall.

'I'm glad you enjoyed it.'

'So much.' Her cheeks are flushed pink and her eyes sparkle. The hours of blue balls suddenly don't seem so bad seeing the joy in her face, and warm, glowing pride spreads across his chest because she's giving him that look again. Like he's the knight in shining armour.

He's still counting the minutes until he can get her back to the hotel.

As the bodies of people converge at the exit doors, Cameron reaches for her hand. Even that innocent touch is erotic after so long with no contact. Jules grins at him and lifts their joined hands to press a kiss to his knuckles. Cameron's skin tingles where her lips pressed and while the pride blooms stronger across his torso, it also sends blood rushing down to his stirring dick. Shit. Is he really going to have to wait another hour to get her alone and naked?

Once outside, Cameron pulls her in the opposite direction to the crowd, taking her around to the stage door where Carrie, still in her concert blacks, is already waiting for the pair.

Carrie's gaze goes to their joined hands and she raises an eyebrow at Cameron. He reflexively separates from Jules and shoves his hands into his pockets, not wanting to give Carrie the wrong idea.

'Hey, Jules.' Carrie goes for a hug and a kiss on the cheek. 'Lovely seeing you again.'

'You too. Thank you so much for getting the ticket for me. It was really special.'

'You're welcome.' Carrie turns her attention to Cameron and though her voice remains light, he can see the question in her eyes. 'Cameron told me you're a music buff, so it seemed appropriate.'

Jules laughs. 'I really am. And I haven't heard live classical music in ages. I forget how it sweeps you up in it.'

Cameron feels the same about Jules herself.

He follows both women through security – Carrie signing them in – and up into the green room. Jules's dress parts tantalisingly as she moves, showing off her long legs and making Cameron's pulse sluggish and heavy inside him. He's caught up in Hurricane Jules.

Carrie pushes through the doors to the green room and Jules's head starts swivelling to take it in. Cameron's seen it all before but he smiles watching Jules pointing to the pool table in one corner, and the multiple screens broadcasting live footage from the various stages.

Carrie drops back beside him while Jules walks slowly through the tables and chairs, past the lounges and to the big windows at the back of the space that look out over Sydney Harbour.

'Hand-holding?' Carrie asks him, with a single-eyebrow raise perfectly emulating their mother.

Cameron shrugs. 'I didn't want to lose her to the crowds.'

'Sure.'

Cameron heads for Jules and away from Carrie, but it's not easy to shake off either of his sisters when they have something to say.

'It's your life,' Carrie says, following him, 'but you know what the parents would say.'

'Don't use your phone at the dinner table?' Cameron says, curling his hands into fists in his pockets.

'Don't deny yourself the chance because you're scared it may not work out.'

'That was meant to be encouragement in our professional lives.'

'I think it applies here too.' Carrie grabs Cameron's arm to stop them before they get too close to Jules. 'Look. The way you look at her, the way you are around her… maybe you can't see it, but she lights you up. Anyone who makes you feel like Sydney on New Year's Eve is worth taking the chance on, don't you think?'

Cameron's gaze falls on Jules. His chest expands seeing

her, the warm brown curls falling down her back and the smile on her face as she types something on her phone.

'It's a big risk.'

He doesn't need to specify. Carrie knows what went down with Braden. Rehashing it tonight when Jules is standing metres away from him looking like a goddess is the last thing he wants to do.

Carrie steps in front of him, blocking his view. 'With a big reward.'

He'd brush it off as meaningless nonsense, but Carrie's talking from experience.

Carrie's gaze flicks over his shoulder. 'Susannah! One sec.' Her attention comes back to him. 'I've been trying to catch her all evening. Meet you both in the dressing room? You remember the way, yes?'

'Yes, of course,' Cameron happily takes the reprieve. 'We'll see you there.'

'And this conversation is not over, by the way.'

Cameron pulls his hands from his pockets and looks over at Jules.

Is she worth the risk? Parts of his anatomy say yes, but their instant connection on the phone, and then physically in person, is so similar to how things started with Braden, and look how that ended up. Battered confidence and leaving the state abruptly to move to Canberra. He still gets guilt flushes about his unfriendly, unprofessional exit from his old job. He thought it was worth it because he was protecting himself, but being back in Sydney has made his decision feel like all he's done is hit pause on his life for a year.

He can't put himself in a position where he'd need to make that choice again.

What he can do is cave to the sexual connection he and Jules share and embrace the arrangement they have in place. One week for a conference fling, like Jules wanted. Whenever, wherever, whatever. With Jules he's down for it all. Then it ends and they'll both have gotten what they want. He'll have been with Jules but there'll be no risk to his career, and she'll have had her conference fling and broken her sex drought, or sated whatever urge it was that made her want the fling in the first place.

There should be zero doubts when he's got one week of companionship with an incredible, sexy woman who lights him up when she smiles at him.

Like now.

He's metres away but her smile hits like lightning between his ribs. Pure need threads through his veins like ichor, evaporating Carrie's words from his mind.

He stalks towards Jules, watching her eyelids grow heavy and her grip on her phone go limp.

The green room isn't busy. He knows from hearing Carrie talk about it that after mid-week shows the performers tend to rush home. It's why he feels no compunction whatsoever as he takes Jules's hand again, feeling a sizzle through his body, and leads her on a detour instead of heading straight for the dressing room.

'Where're we going?' she asks, but doesn't pull from his hold. 'The sign said the dressing room was that way.'

'It is. But first I need to do something.'

He pulls her into a hidden alcove behind a stack of room-dividers that always seem to be there, and finally, *finally*, gets his mouth on her.

There's no hesitation before she's kissing him back, giving as good as him, kissing him with so much force that he knows, despite appearances, he wasn't the only one who's been thinking about this for the past two hours.

He presses a hand to the bare skin between her shoulder blades and the other grips her hip and pulls her in closer. Her tongue licks at the seam of his lips and he opens up, stroking her tongue with his and tasting salt and wine and Jules.

She pulls back, breathing heavily, gripping onto his shoulders like she needs it to keep her upright. 'Your sister is just around the corner. I had no idea you'd be such an exhibitionist.'

He buries his face in her neck. 'I'm not usually, but you drive me wild.'

'Same.'

He runs his nose along her skin, kisses where her pulse races beneath his lips, scrapes his teeth over the same spot. She shudders.

Jules wiggles a hand between their bodies to his shirt, slipping the top button free and pressing her palm to his skin. 'You have a way of making me throw all my rules out the window.' Her voice is breathy. 'When you were touching me before the show... I seriously considered it.'

'Considered what?' Cameron's lost the train of conversation, busy kissing the exposed skin between her collarbones and her breasts.

Jules moves her hands to his neck and angles his head to hers. Cameron's heart bangs so hard against his ribcage, it's probably a medical disorder.

She looks at him through hooded lashes. 'Exhibitionism. Letting you keep holding me against your body while I rubbed off on you until I came, right out there on the balcony before the show.'

'Holy fucking hell, Jules.' Cameron's dick twitches. He presses his forehead to hers and steals a kiss from her.

'I know. I've never been this adventurous with sex,' she says while they kiss, her fingers sliding into his hair and scratching his scalp, sending goosebumps down his neck. 'You're bringing out sides of me I didn't even know I had.'

'You too,' Cameron confesses, slipping his thigh between her legs and pressing. Jules arches against him and rubs, like she'd apparently been imagining doing on the balcony. And fuck if that doesn't make the blood rush faster to his dick, thinking of how wanton he can make Jules.

And how she makes him feel the same. 'This dress hugging your curves has had me horny all night,' he confesses. 'Sitting next to you in the dark was torture. The things I wanted to do to you. I could barely focus on the music.'

'What things?' she demands breathlessly. 'I shared mine. It's only fair.'

Cameron leans into the rough edges of his voice, knowing Jules likes it. He grips her ass, grinding her against his thigh, staring into her eyes as he talks. 'Things like placing my hand on your thigh. Like hooking my foot in between your legs and holding your legs apart. Like slipping my hand between the layers of your dress and cupping you, so I could feel that burning heat and know you were as wild with desire as I was.'

Jules's pupils expand until he can barely see the blue. 'Cameron.'

His name on her lips is heaven. He can't wait to make her say it again and again. Whimper it and whisper it and moan it low and long as he fucks her into bliss.

'Something to think about between now and getting back to the hotel.'

Jules locks her arms behind his shoulders. 'No.'

'No?'

'No. Haven't you been listening to me? You've had me *dripping* for you since that little stunt on the balcony.' She leans up quickly to nip at his lower lip and pleasure races right down his front to where he's already hard and aching. 'You *do not* get to rile me up, again, and leave me aching for you while we go make nice with your sister.'

The words sucker punch desire deeper into his bones. 'I don't, huh?'

'No,' she growls.

'What do you want me to do about it?'

Jules backs herself against the wall and drags his body by his jacket lapels onto her. She kisses him like an attack but Cameron doesn't hate it. Not one bit. Her leg lifts up over his hip and she grinds hard, her core against the steely heat of him. Cameron grips her thigh with one hand and gets the other up at the nape of her neck. Her skin is fevered beneath his hand. If he couldn't hear the unsteady thrum of his own pulse in his ears, he would swear this was a dream.

She stares into his eyes and he's at her mercy. Her gaze gives off enough heat he's glad there's no-one else around to be drawn in by her. She's so different from last night. There's no hesitancy, no second-guessing. Something must've changed between then and now and whatever it is, Cameron's all for it. Confident Jules, shy Jules, impatient Jules, desperate Jules. He'll take any and all and be a happy man. For a week. For *longer*.

It's a split-second's thought that has his gut lurching, before Jules smashes through it and it disappears from his consciousness.

Her hand circles his wrist with a strong grip and she maintains the eye-contact as she says, 'I want you to get me off right here and now.'

Cameron's heart slams against his chest as she guides his hand up her thigh to her underwear. 'Hard and fast. No more teasing.'

She pulls her underwear aside and Cameron can't help dragging a finger slowly between her slick folds. 'Fucking hell, Jules. You weren't lying about being wet.'

His dick twitches. She's been sitting beside him all night like this. Ready for him.

'I'm too on edge to lie. I wasn't lying about you making me throw out the rule book either. Now hurry up, or I'll —'

Cameron plunges two fingers inside her. Jules's head snaps back and she groans loud before biting down on her lip. Cameron sets a brutal pace but Jules matches him from the off. She moves against his hands with the desperate energy that only a truly horny person can achieve. Her eyes are shut tight and her head is thrown back, exposing that gorgeous neck and all that skin to his lips. She's fucking beautiful, chasing her bliss. Her skin flushes pink and that spot on her neck that makes her quiver calls to him. He licks at it before nipping the skin lightly. Jules's fingers dig into his biceps. She rides his fingers like a pro, but he can tell by the whimpers she needs more.

Cameron brings his thumb into play on that bundle of nerves, rubbing tight circles. His other hand fixes onto her breast and kneads. The top of her dress is too goddamn tight for him to take the time to wriggle his fingers beneath the hem and directly onto her skin, but he can feel her nipple peak beneath the fabric and he flicks a finger over it, while he bends the fingers inside her, trying to find that spot that makes her—

Jules clenches around him in a silent orgasm, shaking through it while he keeps moving his fingers until she whimpers, her whole body loosening as she slumps back against the wall.

Her eyes flutter open and she fixes her attention on him, breathing heavily. 'I needed that.'

He can see in her eyes that all he's done is take the edge off. Her gaze travels down his torso, dick twitching in his pants as her pupils blow out again.

He can feel the ghost of her hands on him when his sister's voice calls out. 'Cameron?'

'Shit. That's Carrie.' He adjusts himself in his briefs, rebuttoning his shirt and smoothing it out. Jules's lipstick has smudged off and she's flushed, but hopefully Carrie only assumes they've been kissing. Still bad, and no doubt she'll be texting Chloe as soon as his back is turned, but it's more palatable than her knowing Cameron got Jules off with his fingers in a semi-public place.

Jules makes a noise of annoyance. 'But I didn't even get—'

'Later.' He presses a fierce kiss to her mouth.

It's probably for the best. He's so riled up she'll barely get her hand around him and he'll go off like a teen being touched for the first time. Better to save his dignity.

CHAPTER 15

Cameron's fingers, the ones inside her a half-hour ago, squeeze her hand as they hurry down the corridor to his hotel room, Jules vibrating with need. The green room was cool to explore and Carrie is someone Jules could easily be friends with, but Cameron wearing a suit with his hair mussed from her fingers running through it was too great a temptation. She rushed through a farewell as soon as was polite. Now, her flushed skin and damp panties are a reminder of what they've just done.

They had semi-public sex. And she was the one who initiated it.

What's gotten into her? This confidence and ability to ask for what she wants without first spending hours convincing herself is so unlike her. It took her months to find that comfort with all her exes, yet something about Cameron alleviates all worries and doubts about voicing her desires. The need inside her may be explained by her three years of abstinence, but that confidence can't be.

It's Cameron. His heat and his presence and the sure way he touches her. The way he looks at her with those caramel eyes, like he's touching her even when he isn't, like he's seeing right into her thoughts and he likes them. How he's not shy in telling her how she makes him feel so she knows she isn't drowning in desire alone. She needs him to touch her properly again.

He does the second they're in his room, pinning her against the wall and kissing her, wasting no time in licking his way into her mouth. Jules melts into him, sweeping her hands up his back, feeling the strength of him. She'd fantasised about undressing him slowly but abandons the idea as his fingers dive between the panelled layers of the skirt, zinging tracks of heat over her skin.

'Careful with the dress,' she warns. 'Chloe needs it returned undamaged.'

'Let's get it off you then.' Cameron's fingers search the dress for a zipper. 'I've been hard for hours and I need to be inside you.'

'I've got it.' Jules pushes his hands off her, sure he won't read it as dismissal, and reaches for the invisible zip at her side. 'You do you and I'll do me.'

'I thought we were doing each other,' he jokes, jacket already off and thrown away, shoes and socks tugged off.

'Strip, Cameron. I want you in me fast, too.'

Her dress hits the floor and she wastes a few seconds laying it on the back of a chair before sitting on a corner of the bed to watch Cameron complete the world's fastest strip tease. It still manages to send Jules's blood to her needy clit as his shirt gets yanked over his head, and his pants and briefs are shucked quickly, leaving him naked and proudly erect in front of her.

'You're beautiful,' she says, gaze travelling up his body as he walks to her.

'We've been over this. You mean "sexy", or "irresistible", or—*Fuck*.'

Jules wraps her hand around his cock and puts her mouth on him. He's right there and she needs to taste. Salt and musk and Cameron coat her tongue as she moves up and down his length, learning the feel and taste of him. She swirls her tongue around the head before dropping back down, settling into a rhythm with mouth and hand.

'*Jules*.' Cameron's hands stroke over her hair before fisting in the strands.

She grabs the back of his muscled thigh to pull him closer, sucking his pleasure out, feeling herself become wetter with every noise he makes above her. Throaty grunts and rough exhales and aborted curses. Compliments in that rough voice that let her know they're finding pleasure together. 'You feel so good' and 'Your mouth, Jules, fuck'.

'Stop, stop,' he pants, hands dropping onto her shoulders. 'I want to come inside you.'

Jules pulls back, staring at his wet cock, so stiff and red in front of her. She tilts her hips and grinds herself against the mattress, seeking to relieve her clit's pulsing need.

'Fuck, you're—' Cameron's gaze drops to her rotating hips. His chest rises and falls unsteadily, and a lickable sheen covers his torso. 'I need to be inside you. Now. I want you doing that while you're riding me.'

'Hurry up, then.'

Despite his words, he drops to his knees in front of her, bracketing her flushed face with his hands and kissing her hungrily. 'You're so demanding tonight.'

'Yeah, well.' Jules rotates her hips into the mattress again, unable to look away from Cameron's eyes, the ones that wrap her in a caramel cocoon and make her beautifully brave, even as a wedge of vulnerability slices through her desire. 'I feel confident around you. Like I can be honest about what I want.'

Cameron's hands tighten on her face and he sucks in a harsh breath. 'You can be. Always.'

'Will you do the same?' Her heart's on fire as she asks. It's about sex, but it goes deeper than that. For her, at least.

'Yes. *Yes*.'

His thumb rubs along her cheekbone a moment before his hands drop to her waist, thumbs skimming the sides of her breasts on the way down. Her skin pulls tight, nipples hardening. She watches Cameron stare at them as they do, need bare on his face.

She grabs his arm and pulls him up to lean over her body. He kisses her as they scramble up the bed, skin sliding and hands reaching, until Jules goes to roll him onto his back and realises.

'Oh, shit. I don't have any condoms on me this time.'

'Hang on a sec.' Cameron reaches across to the bedside table. His pec hovers tantalisingly over her mouth for a second before he pulls his arm back, clutching a box of condoms. 'I grabbed some on the way back from my run this morning.'

Jules digs into the box for one. 'Clever. Smart. Genius.'

'It wasn't done altruistically.'

Cameron throws the box onto the floor and presses his chest into her body, laying her flat on the bed.

Jules shivers. 'I find it very sexy that you used the word "altruistically" while we're having sex.'

Cameron kisses down her neck and she cranes her head to give him better access.

'Jules,' he says directly into her ear. 'I don't think it's the word you find sexy. I think it's the voice.'

Goosebumps erupt over her skin.

'I could recite the alphabet to you and by the end, you'd be a quivering mess.'

'Please don't test that,' she breathes.

'Ay, bee, cee, dee, ee, ef —'

Jules turns her head and kisses Cameron, swallowing the sound of his laugh. Goddamn he's right. His voice is so rough that the alphabet makes her insides melt, weighing her limbs down with delicious heat.

He glides a finger between her folds then brings the digit between them. It glistens.

'See?'

'I was already wet, Cameron.'

'What a prissy tone,' he teases.

'Prissy?'

'Don't worry. I liked it.'

'Oh, I know.' Jules lifts her hips up, gliding her wetness over his hard cock.

Cameron grins and drives his hips down, pinning her harder to the mattress. He glides through her folds until Jules is squirming and desperate to feel him inside her.

'Wasn't I promised a ride?' she asks.

Cameron rolls them with efficient speed until Jules is straddling his muscled thighs. She gets the condom on quickly, and then she's sinking down onto him, watching his face tense in pleasure, pleasure that remains as she works herself on him, bracing her hands on his chest. She goes slow a few times to find the right angle, then she moves.

Loud breaths and the dull thump of the bed against the wall fill the air. Cameron watches where their bodies are connected and Jules whimpers when his hands find her breasts, kneading and tugging at her nipples. Her rhythm slips but then he pulls her down against his chest, kisses her with fire on his tongue.

'Like you were before.' He grabs her hips and grinds her against his pelvis. 'Make yourself feel good.'

They kiss as her hips circle, seeking the friction she needs, feeling her orgasm build slowly and surely, until she's right there, *right there,* but she needs—

'I need your fingers on my clit,' the new-found confidence has her asking aloud instead of hoping he'll intuit it.

Cameron's hand slips immediately between their bodies and his thumb presses hard to her clit and rubs. Pleasure rushes through her. Magma spiralling out from her core, into her lungs and breasts and fingertips. Her mouth gapes at the intensity of the orgasm, especially after having come already tonight.

Cameron's hands grip her hips and he bucks up into her. 'You look phenomenal when you come, Jules.'

She has to kiss him.

Then she keeps kissing him, messily, wanting to taste him as he plants his feet on the bed, gets his hands on her hips, and drives in and out of her until he tenses and comes on a low groan that's as much music to Jules's ears as the symphony was.

'You need to ride me again,' Cameron says after several soporific moments filled with nothing but the sound of their breathing.

'Gladly.' Jules manoeuvres off him and flops onto the mattress. 'But let me catch my breath first.'

'Wore you out, did I?' Cameron grins, sitting up to deal with the condom.

'Someone sounds smug.'

'A little.'

'Well, it's well deserved.' Jules looks at the clock on the bedside table and sighs, pushing sweaty hair off her face. 'I should probably get back to my room, though. I've got my presentation tomorrow.'

'Ah. Of course. What time do you speak?'

Cameron heads for the desk in his room, where his conference documents are organised in neat piles. Jules shamelessly watches his bare ass, thinking about running over and biting it.

'Jules?' Cameron lifts his gaze to her and Jules doesn't even care she was caught ogling him. She can tell by his half-smile he doesn't mind.

'One pm.'

He checks the documents again. 'I can come watch you,' Cameron says.

'Oh. Really?' Jules sits up in the middle of the bed, not bothering to bring the sheet with her. Cameron's attention drops to her bare breasts and as thoroughly debauched as she's been already tonight, her core clenches. 'You don't have to. I know IT's not really your area.'

'True.' His attention returns to her face. 'But when you were telling my sisters about it the other day it was pretty interesting. You're face actually lit up with excitement. Might be a nice change from all the marketing-focused ones anyway.'

Jules's stomach wobbles happily. This definitely falls into the 'supportive boyfriend' side of the score sheet. Not that she's keeping score.

Cameron returns to the bed, sitting against the headboard with his long legs stretched out atop the sheets. 'Do you want to run through it with me tomorrow morning?'

'That'd be awesome, actually. I haven't had a chance to do it with an audience.'

Cameron grimaces and Jules laughs at the expression.

'I know, I know,' Jules says. 'Your total nightmare. I've been a little distracted these past few days.'

'Oh?'

'Yeah. Some really hot guy said he wanted to have a conference fling with me and he's got the sexual appetite of a teen with a porn addiction.'

'Oh, he does, does he?' Cameron shifts to his knees, using his body to encourage Jules down onto her back while pressing kisses all over her skin.

Jules squirms beneath him, laughing until his mouth gets to her breasts and then sighing instead. She should actually go to her room, but Cameron's naked and pressed against her. She can feel his dick hardening against her thigh and her insides set to tingling again. Her sexual voracity continues to surprise, and she spreads her legs for him to fit better.

The sex that follows is hot, of course, but it's also fun. Has she ever had this much fun during sex? The answer comes quickly. No, she has not. Maybe some of that was on her, assuming that sex should always be sexy or sensual. Being spontaneous with Cameron is opening her mind to entirely new ways to enjoy herself and it's only been two days.

CHAPTER 16

Cameron forgoes the gym again to do his morning run around Sydney Harbour and The Rocks. It's quiet this early, the sun only beginning to rise, and the energy is different from last night when he was here with Jules. He sucks in lungfuls of air, tasting the salt of the ocean, and keeps his gaze focused up on the buildings and street signs he passes. Places he hasn't been in a year that are as much a part of his past as the two-storey brick home he grew up in.

Passing the Lin & Luther offices, he jogs on the spot in front of the sandstone building, wondering if it's worth setting an alert for any job listings from them, because it's like night and day, comparing this to his morning jogs in Canberra. He's actually got a smile on his face. He can feel it.

At the end of his loop he slows down, stopping at the end of Circular Quay to look out at the water as he stretches.

He nominated himself to attend the conference because he wanted the chance to prove to his old Cable colleagues he wasn't the unprofessional asshole he appeared at the end of his time there. It wasn't meant to be a homecoming, but as he stares at the water, feeling how steady his heartbeat is, that's what it resembles.

He doesn't want it to feel like this. He's started a new life in Canberra. He's got a good job, a good place, a good cafe around the corner. Sure, he never pictured himself there, but when he was looking for an escape, Steven had that connection at Infinity and a spare couch to crash on. It seemed fated.

Yet that pesky question shines through in the morning air,

as clear as the sun reflecting off the water. Was leaving Sydney a mistake?

* * *

He ducks into a cafe on the way back to the hotel when he notices they're selling meringues as big as his fist. Jules will probably appreciate one after her presentation. He grabs coffees and breakfast for them both so they can skip the buffet and he can enjoy her company without checking over his shoulder for people from Cable.

At the hotel, Cameron knocks on Jules's door. His hair drips water down his back, but he needed to shower after his run. No way was he greeting Jules in his sweaty gym clothes. He may have rushed through the drying part, not wanting the coffees to get too cold. Keen to see Jules, too. It's been, what, seven hours? And he had the urge to see her smile.

He shakes his head, sending droplets onto the carpeted corridor. These are dangerous urges he's having.

The door opens, and there she is, still in pyjamas with her messy hair in waves over her shoulders, looking like a fantasy.

'Cameron. What're you doing here?'

Her gaze skates over his damp hair and down his body, heat flaring in her eyes. She's clearly braless because he can see her nipples poking at the fabric like they were the other morning too. Taunting him.

Ignoring his heated blood, he says, 'I'm here to help with your presentation, remember.'

'I remember.' She smiles and his gut does a happy tremor. 'I meant, like, here at my room. I thought we'd meet at the breakfast buffet again.'

'Breakfast.' He lifts the bags with the croissants and banana bread. The meringue is sitting in his room for after her presentation. 'And coffee, of course. The more important part.'

Jules laughs, eyes locking onto the coffees. 'You better come in then.'

'Thanks.'

Cameron slides past her, getting a whiff of her fruity shampoo.

'I grabbed the coffees on the way back from my run,' Cameron says, dropping them in the kitchenette. 'So you may want to top them up with hot water.'

Jules takes the kettle into the bathroom to fill it with water, and Cameron takes a second to look around her room. The bed is a mess, and there's more pillows on the floor than on furniture. There's an e-reader sitting on the side table next to a glass of water and her phone is plugged in and charging. He smiles. She's managed to make the lifeless room feel like her space.

Not that Cameron knows what her actual space looks like. Not that he will.

Ignoring the pang in his chest, he turns around as he hears Jules opening the takeaway bags.

'Croissants and banana bread,' he says. 'I figured a little sweetness wouldn't go amiss.'

'Good choices.' Jules grins at him, pulling a croissant out and tearing an edge off before popping the pastry into her mouth.

Cameron sits on the chair closest to the kitchenette, pulling his phone from his pocket and placing it on the table before pushing aside conference papers and Jules's laptop to make room. He opens the bag with the banana bread and cuts it neatly in half since he only bought the one slice, then transfers half of it onto a napkin and slides it across to Jules.

She smiles at him and he smiles back and it all feels normal. Which is odd. He rarely eats pastries for breakfast, his hair is still damp and his shirt is sticking to his back, and she's in pyjamas and hasn't brushed her hair. They're in a hotel he's never been to before, in a city that used to be home and still feels like it. Yet he's certain he could sit across from Jules at this table for hours and be content.

'Should we get started while we eat?' he suggests, not wanting to get too comfortable in the moment.

Jules shakes her head, gesturing at her croissant. 'Breakfast first. I'm still waking up.'

The kettle boils and Jules goes to top up the coffees. Cameron watches her walk past. He's a fan of her sleep shorts. They end just below her butt, leaving her long legs on display, which he runs his gaze over, recalling them wrapped around his hips the other night. Why hasn't he taken his time kissing up them yet? He needs to fit that in before the conference is done.

'I can't believe you've already been out,' Jules says as she returns to the table with the coffees. 'It's barely past seven.'

'It was a nice morning.'

'I had a nice morning, too. Sleeping. In bed.'

Cameron glances over at the unmade bed. It's easy to picture Jules spread out across the covers. To picture kissing up those bare legs, sliding her shirt up over her stomach, kissing the valley between her breasts, licking—

'Which is the one that won't rot my teeth?'

He tears his gaze from the bed to see Jules smiling teasingly at him. He wants to bite those lips, then nibble some other places, too.

'Haha,' he rolls his eyes. 'The one on your left.'

She grabs her coffee, takes a sip, then sighs happily. 'Coffee.'

Cameron shakes his head at her but his chest is warm.

He looks away, taking in the rest of the room. 'Holy shit.'

'Huh?'

'Sorry. I just noticed the artwork in your room. I thought I had it bad.'

Jules looks over her shoulder. 'Oh. The Luna Park face? Creepy, isn't it.' She shudders and turns back to him. 'I don't remember it being so scary when I was a kid, but I was probably too caught up in the excitement of visiting a theme park.'

Cameron tries to ignore the lifeless artwork, focusing on Jules. 'Did you live here when you were younger?'

'No. I'm a bit boring. I've always lived in Canberra, didn't even leave for uni. But Grandma lived here, so we came up and visited a bit.'

'Do you want to fit in a visit?' He gestures to the tacky artwork. 'They're open late some nights, I think.'

Jules pulls a face. 'No thanks. Last time I went, I ate too much fairy floss and then went on that spinning one that sticks you to the walls.' Her face pales and she presses a hand to her throat. 'It was not fun. I'm emotionally scarred.'

'We've all been there.'

Jules makes a little choking noise in her throat. Cameron lifts his eyebrows at her, then she bursts into laughter. *Loud* laughter, like he hasn't heard from her before. They can probably hear her in the room below.

'What? What'd I say?' he asks over her gasping.

'You—you said—' Jules can barely get the words out. It's an infectious laugh, and his lips twitch to join in, but Cameron's also worried she's not breathing. Her face is turning red and her eyes are leaking.

'Jules? You're scaring me a little, here.'

'Sorry, sorry.' She wipes below her eyes, blinking up at the ceiling. 'I didn't mean to laugh so hard. It wasn't even funny. It was just, the way you said it, like, with such empathy. "We've all been there".' She shakes her head, wiping at her eyes as another burst of laughter breaks from her chest. 'You were so serious!'

He snorts. 'Yeah. I was empathising.'

'About vomiting at a theme park.'

Trying to mimic his tone from earlier, he nods sagely, holding her gaze. 'Mine was a giant slushie followed by the Tango Train.'

That sets her off again, and this time, Cameron joins her. The laughter feels like unspooling tension and by the time Jules has laughed herself out, his limbs feel jelly-like in the best way.

'Oh gosh. Well.' Jules takes a deep breath in through her

nose, flapping her hands at her eyes. 'A Luna Park trip is off the cards.'

'What if we just went on the Ferris Wheel over and over?' he asks, half teasing, half serious. 'Nice views.'

'Tempting. But I'm sure there are other nice views that don't involve me getting close to the location of childhood trauma.'

'Plenty.'

'I'm not sure that really counts as the adult side of Sydney, anyway,' Jules says, starting on her half of the banana bread.

'Ah. That's right. In that case,' Cameron leans across the table and wiggles his eyebrows. 'I know a good sex store in Newtown that we could check out.'

She rolls her eyes but he doesn't care about the dismissal. He was after the blush, and he got it. Pink spreads over her cheeks and down her neck. It makes him want to get up from the table and have his way with her.

He's obviously broadcasting his thoughts, because the flare of heat in her eyes is unmissable. She glances across at the bed and his gaze drops down her chest to see her nipples hard again through her shirt, begging to be played with.

The moment is ruined by his phone buzzing on the table. Several times.

He checks the messages. All from his sisters, like they planned a simultaneous interrogation.

> *Carrie: Update needed. What's going on with Jules? Did you kiss last night, Y/N?*
> *Chloe: Good morning! How's the conference? How's Jules?*
> *Chloe: I'm so glad we could meet her the other day. Carrie told me about the hand holding! Yay.*
> *Chloe: Can we see her again before you leave? I can come pick the dress up today, maybe? Say hello?*
> *Chloe: Actually, got uni stuff all day then musical stuff in the evening. Tomorrow? Friday? Let me know.*

Carrie: Did you think about what I said last night? I was serious.

Cameron's frowning by the time he's read them all. He's been getting texts like this every day since they had lunch together. Scratch that, since his phone call with them on Saturday, even though they promised to table it over the weekend. Ignoring the texts has not dissuaded his sisters in the slightest.

'Everything good?'

Cameron lifts his gaze to Jules. She's staring at him with a furrowed brow.

'Yeah. It's good. My sisters are—' His phone starts buzzing in his hand. 'Calling me. Apparently.'

'Do they make a habit of calling you at breakfast?' Jules asks, as Cameron stares at Carrie's face on his phone. He has no plans to answer.

'Uh, no. I think it's because I've been avoiding their texts.'

'Why?'

Because they're hounding me about asking you out and wondering if we've started dating.

The call times out and he switches his phone to airplane mode. He'll take it off when he leaves Jules's room.

He returns his attention to Jules. 'Because they're meddling.'

Jules laughs, expression clearing. 'I know that feeling. Can't give them the satisfaction of an immediate reply. My brother used to be so bad at it.'

'Used to. How'd you get him to stop?'

'I didn't do anything. He had a kid and our conversation topics changed.'

'You're an aunt?'

Jules's smile could give the sun a run for its money. 'Yep. Got a little nephew down in Tasmania. Another on the way, actually.' She pulls out her phone while she speaks and taps at the screen, before placing it on the table and spinning it to face him. 'That's me and my brother and his wife, Cecelia. And little Toby.'

She gestures to the people on the screen as she names them. Cameron leans over the table to have a closer look, brushing a section of Jules's hair behind her ear so it's not tickling his cheek. She blinks at him and bites her lower lip. No fair. He wanted to do that.

Not even risking a kiss in case he gets carried away, he looks back at the phone. Jules's brother — Finn, if he's remembered correctly — looks like a male version of Jules. Same hair and eyes, but taller and hairier. Cecelia's beautiful, with curves and wavy blonde hair and a smile made for the cameras. Her wheelchair is bright blue and matches her glasses. In her lap is a brown-haired boy with a cheeky smile and plump cheeks. Jules has her arm around Cecelia's shoulders and she's tickling Toby.

'Beautiful,' Cameron breathes, eyes stuck on Jules's disarming smile, the pure joy on her face.

'Pardon?'

He clears his throat, looking up at the real deal. The beauty is magnified in person. It sends a rush of heat along his spine and his words get caught in his throat a moment as he stares into Jules's blue eyes. His mind conjures a fantasy picture like the one on Jules's phone, of him and her and a little girl sitting on his shoulders.

Shit. Where'd that come from?

He swallows roughly, blinking to clear the image. 'It's— They're, uh, a beautiful family.'

'Thanks.'

Jules smiles down at the picture. There's a wistfulness in her eyes that has him asking, 'Do you miss not having them around? Your family?'

'Yeah,' she sighs, swiping along to another similar photo, this one with two older people who must be her parents. 'I really do. We were very close. I mean, we still are, obviously, but phone calls and video chats aren't really the same.'

She swipes back to the original photo and chews her lower lip. He wants to reach across and smooth his thumb over it so she'll stop.

'And sometimes I worry,' she says, so quietly he almost misses it.

'About what?'

She hovers her fingers over the phone, breathing shallowly. 'That I'm left out. Forgotten.'

'No way.'

Jules's gaze lifts to his, eyebrows raised. He didn't mean to speak so forcefully, but the words flung themselves from his chest, squeezed out by a band of tightness. How could Jules think that?

Her blue eyes are watery and his gut yanks hard again. Softening his tone, he places his hand gently over hers. 'No one would ever forget you. *Especially* not your family.'

She nods slowly, her hand twitching beneath his. 'I know that, logically, but… You know, Mum and Dad have each other, and Finn and Cecilia and Toby are a little unit and I'm just… me. Here by myself.' Her attention drops to the phone again for a moment before she switches it off and flips it over on the table. 'A little like you, I guess.'

Her gaze travels over his face, bottom lip abused by her teeth again. 'Do you ever…?'

She trails off without finishing the question, withdrawing her hand from beneath his so she can reach for more croissant. She chews, glumly, while fiddling with her silver bracelet. He can practically feel the melancholy drifting off her. She shouldn't be feeling that way. He wants to soak it up somehow, so she can go back to the laughing and the teasing. Kissing it out of her is appealing, but he knows that's the wrong approach, as much as he's been craving her lips all morning.

He'll have to go for a different technique. He clears his throat, then says, 'It can feel like you're missing out.'

She lifts her head, brow furrowed.

'Being away from family,' he clarifies.

'Yes,' she says softly, nodding. 'You're right. Even though I have wonderful, amazing friends, and an awesome place, and a stable job, so it feels silly to even worry about that.' Another twist of her bracelet around her wrist. 'But I do worry.'

'We can't control how we feel about stuff all the time.' Like how he still wants to kiss her, despite, or maybe because of, the sadness in her eyes.

Her gaze roves over his face, inquisitive. 'No. I guess we can't.'

Otherwise, he'd choose not to feel like Canberra is home, but not homey. And he doesn't think that can be fixed by buying some houseplants and finding the best Thai place in his area.

And now he's the one swimming in melancholy.

He pulls back to his side of the table and grabs his half-eaten croissant. 'So, uh. I forget what we were talking about before this deviation.'

'You were telling me about places in Sydney.'

'That's right. What kind of places are you interested in?' He'd guess museums, shows and bakeries. Some typical Sydney tourist places as well since she was in awe of the Opera House and Harbour Bridge last night.

'Where would *you* go?' she asks. 'Any nice restaurants? Bars?'

'Heaps. Maybe I should send through a list.'

'Will you colour-code it based on type?'

'Type?'

'Yeah, like.' She picks up her coffee and cradles it in her palm. 'This is good for families. Um, nice brunch place. Cheap.' Her eyes dart over his face and away. 'Nice date location.'

His stomach tightens. Date locations? Why does she need to know about those?

'I can do that.' And if no date places make the list, so be it.

'Thanks.' She smiles, finishing the last of her coffee. 'What would you do if you were here for a week? Not for work, just on holiday.'

'Well, aside from visiting the family, I'd probably... head

to a few beaches. Do some walks around the coast. Go out for drinks with—' He stops. He used to go out regularly with people from Cable. That wouldn't happen now. 'Go out and see some live music.'

'Is that what you did when you lived here?'

'Pretty much.'

She drops her chin onto her hand and stares at him.

He wipes at his chin. 'Have I got food on my face?'

She gives a throaty laugh and shakes her head. 'No. I like hearing you talk about Sydney.'

'Really?'

'Yeah. You get this look on your face. This little smile like people do when they get a nice text or remember something funny. You obviously love it here.'

His body doesn't know what to do with all the warmth spilling from his chest. It's like it's flowing out of his body, trying to wrap Jules in this same feeling.

He nods slowly. 'True. I didn't realise until I came back here, how much. I've actually been wondering—'

He cuts the words off. Why is he doing this again? Jules doesn't want to hear about this shit. You don't offload your worries onto a woman you're having a fling with. Even if it feels normal to do just that, like this whole morning with her has felt normal. Natural.

'Wondering what?' Jules's blue eyes show clear interest in the conversation.

It's on the tip of his tongue to tell her, 'I've been wondering if I made a mistake leaving Sydney'. To tell her that he didn't realise how much he missed Sydney. Didn't realise how lonely he'd been until he came here and spent time with her, and his sisters and Matteo. That he may have made a mistake and that, maybe – shit, the thought sinks like a needle right into his muscles – maybe the solution is to move back. Away from Canberra. Away from Jules.

His mouth twists, a stickiness coating his insides.

Her hand lands over his on the table, warm and soft, and it

almost pulls the words from his chest anyway. But the contact also shoots that familiar electricity down his spine and the desire reminds him of what this is. What Jules asked for and clearly defined, their first night together.

A fling.

It's not right to burden her with his worries when this thing between them is only temporary.

He sends her a smile and pulls his hand out from beneath hers.

'Never mind.' He wipes his hand on a napkin and takes a long swig of coffee. 'Should we get started on your presentation now?'

CHAPTER 17

Jules is in the middle of dressing for her presentation after lunch when her phone starts vibrating with an incoming video call from her friends. She accepts quickly and Cat and Tori's faces appear on screen.

They're squished together in the corner booth of the tiny cafe in between the Infinity office and where Tori now works, where they sometimes meet up during the day if there's big news to spill or someone is craving a chocolate oatmeal biscuit. That cafe makes the best ones. Big as your hand and fifty per cent chocolate.

'We need a Cameron update,' Tori says immediately.

'Hi, Jules. How are you?' Cat asks with clear sarcasm.

Jules shakes her head at them. 'Hi. I'm good. Got my talk soon.'

'Feeling ready?' Cat asks.

'Yeah. I am.' Which is the truth. There are some nerves, for sure, but she doesn't mind those when it comes to public speaking. They help keep her energy up. 'I can't believe you're at Big Drip without me,' she accuses, propping her phone up against the tissue box on her bedside table so she can continue getting ready.

'We missed you. We needed comfort food.' Tori lifts her giant cookie up to the screen. 'Not sure that's the outfit I'd wear for your presentation, by the way. You look hot though.'

Jules does a twirl in the matching blue bra and pantie set she's currently in. 'Thank you. And no, I'm going to go with the outfit you picked for me, Tor.'

Jules pulls open the wardrobe door and takes down the pencil skirt and blouse combo.

'How *is* the conference going though?' Cat asks again.

'Really good. I didn't realise how down I was in the office until I wasn't there anymore.'

'Down like, stressed?' Cat asks.

'I don't know. A little. But more like uninspired? I just feel lighter out here.'

'Could it be – and this is just a wild guess,' Tori says, 'all the sex you're having?'

Jules taps her chin and pretends to think it over seriously. 'Maybe.'

She drops the act and laughs, stepping into the skirt and pulling it up over her hips, zipping it at the back and checking her reflection in the mirror.

'I'm actually... not to be brash but I think that is actually a part of it. The freedom and the spontaneity and being in the moment. I know it's sappy, but...' Jules shrugs. 'I don't know. It got me thinking about being more confident. Making changes.'

Jules pulls the blouse on and tucks it into her skirt, trying to figure out how to phrase the nebulous thoughts that have been floating in her head these past few days.

'You know I've been toying with the idea of resigning?' She picks up her phone and sits on the edge of the bed.

'Yeah.' Her friends nod.

'Well... I actually finished a draft resignation letter,' she confesses.

Her friends erupt in a flurry of well-wishes, Tori knocking over Cat's water. Jules laughs at the unfettered enthusiasm and support.

'We need to celebrate when you get back!' Tori announces, mopping up the spill with a stack of napkins while Cat pats at the splash on her slacks. 'A toast to you finally taking charge of your professional life. I'll make any dessert you like.'

'Bombe alaska?'

'I'll make any *other* dessert you'd like.'

Jules laughs. 'Thanks, Tor. I'll think on it.'

She carries her phone into the bathroom to start on her hair and make-up.

'So you *were* lying when you said Cameron doesn't have a magical penis,' Tori says, which Jules is sure would be getting her some strange looks in the cafe.

'No, it's not like that,' Jules says, grabbing her hairbrush. 'I haven't been sexed into a revelation. I mean, that probably laid a bit of the groundwork, because, like I said, it's been freeing not really having any plans and not thinking ahead so much, just taking opportunities as they come.' Like in the Opera House green room. 'Which is not my usual way.'

'Yes,' Tori says. 'You normally wave at the opportunities as they go by.'

'Okay, there's a little more that usually happens.'

Like Jules talking herself into and out of reaching beyond her comfort zone for so long that all she can do is wave, having missed the window of opportunity. It's just so nice and safe and stable in there. But she said yes to Cameron's offer this week and it's worked out wonderfully. She asked James for his presentation slides and he said yes. Speaking of.

'But actually, I saw a talk on Monday by this guy called James McCarthy about research methodology.'

Tori does a large fake yawn and Cat elbows her in the ribs.

'Ow!' Tori rubs her side.

'Don't disrespect Jules's emotional moment.'

'Thank you, Cat.' Jules smooths foundation over her face. 'Anyway. My point is, I was sitting there and it was like lightbulbs going off over my head. Everything he said was so interesting. I had a look at his website, and he has a whole business teaching courses and workshops and contracting out to businesses. It sounds really awesome. I mean, you two know how much I loved all the research we did before we revamped the e-commerce site.'

'Yes,' Tori nods. 'You nerd-ed out about it every night for weeks and made us be a practise focus group.'

Jules laughs as she refits the lid on her foundation bottle before returning it to her make-up bag. 'They don't have any job openings at the moment, but even just looking for them made me realise I want that feeling again that I had listening to him talk. I haven't been excited like that since my first promotion at Infinity.'

Cat nods fervently. 'That is so great, Jules.'

'Yeah. I know it's a little outside of my previous experience but... I don't know.' Jules shrugs and starts working on her eyes. 'I spoke to James a bit after his talk and he gave me a business card without me asking for one and I was just thinking... this is one of those opportunities right?'

'Lady, it's like a sign from on high,' Tori says.

'Definitely worth pursuing,' Cat agrees.

'That's what I thought. And Cameron said my presentation was really engaging. And I know James is going to be in the audience today, so it'll be like a little self-promo.'

'Cameron's heard your presentation?' Cat asks.

'Yeah. He was here at breakfast. He helped me work out a cleaner ending, which was nice.'

'Oh my god,' Tori exclaims. 'Am I looking at a Jules who has had morning sex?'

Jules rolls her eyes, trading mascara for highlighter and a brush. 'You are not. Well. Unless you count, like, one am as morning and not late at night?'

Tori wolf-whistles. 'You are going *all in* on the fling.'

'You told me to!'

'Yeah, because I thought if I said that you'd at least go half-way. You're kind of shit at letting go of your comfort zone. But now you're getting your rocks off at all hours of the day and talking about quitting your job.'

'So you *will* make me a bombe alaska?'

Tori laughs. 'In your dreams, lady.'

Cat taps her fingers on her collarbone. 'So no sex this morning, but he helped you out with your presentation. Is it just me, or is that very couple-y?'

'I thought that too!' Jules abandons the make-up for a moment to focus on her friends. 'But I didn't want to point that out to him and freak him out. I'm enjoying the fling side of things, but I'm still trying to have some deeper conversations where I can.'

She's discovered so much about him already. He's dorky and charming and loves his family. Apparently has terrible luck with technology and is a massive sweet tooth, like her. He laughs easily, even during sex, and he looks at her like she's important. The ache in her chest is getting soft at the edges but Jules knows there's more to discover. Like what happened at Cable and the full story about his ex. But even without all that...

She takes a deep breath and her voice is soft when she tells her friends, 'I really like Cameron, more every day. I wanted to see if we clicked enough that dating was a potential and... I think we do. The way I feel around him is like... like I can do anything. Say and ask and be what I want.'

Tori sighs. 'That's special, Jules. I'm not even going to turn what you said into a sexual thing, except to say, maybe you're the one with the magical vagina.'

Jules laughs. 'You know what? I'm going to take that as a compliment. Thank you. My years of abstinence was obviously just my vagina transforming from standard model to magical.'

'Maybe I should take a sexual vacation, then,' Tori muses. 'I want a magical vagina.'

'But if Jules is our case-study,' Cat points out, 'you might accidentally end up in a relationship when you start having sex again.'

'Fingers crossed I end up there,' Jules says while Tori shudders.

'Urgh. Good point.' Tori addresses Cat. 'I'm glad it's working for you Jules, but continued promiscuity for me it is.'

Jules shakes her head. 'I miss you guys.'

Tori clutches a hand over her chest. 'It took you *three days* to start missing us?'

Jules pokes her tongue out at them. 'I'll buy you both souvenirs to apologise. Now, what do you think works better? Hair up or down?'

CHAPTER 18

Jules listens to her pump-up mix while waiting for the MC to introduce her talk. Filled with 80s pop anthems, it has her bouncing on her feet on the side of the room, excitement running through her veins. Nerves too, but they're to be expected, especially since she only finished writing her presentation yesterday. She knows the content, and her run through this morning went smoothly, and with Cameron sitting in the audience like a good luck charm, Jules knows she's going to do well.

The MC introduces her and she walks over to the lectern to a smattering of applause. One clap rings louder than the others, and she easily picks out Cameron in the small crowd. She's surprised to see Matteo sitting beside him, since Cameron mentioned he also worked in marketing. Cameron shoots her a dimpled grin and Matteo sends her a double thumbs-up.

Rolling her shoulders back and down, she stands in front of the podium with a smile. 'Good afternoon everyone. Thanks for coming to this talk on e-commerce technology and the way readers navigate and use e-commerce systems.'

The Auslan interpreter over on the left side of the stage starts signing as she speaks. Her gaze travels over the crowd as she continues with an introduction, finally catching on the wire-rimmed glasses and checked shirt of James McCarthy. Her heart beats a quick jive in her chest, recognising the weight of this moment.

She takes a deep breath and reminds herself this is an opportunity she doesn't want to let pass her by. That she's intelligent and studious and put in the effort and knows what she's talking about backwards, forwards and upside-down. Then she finds Cameron in the crowd. She takes a moment to absorb the belief radiating from his smile, and she's off again.

* * *

Jules walks off stage feeling like she's got neon lights buzzing inside her instead of blood and veins. She spoke eloquently, and people laughed at the jokes, and she couldn't get to everyone at question time because so many people had their hands up. James McCarthy had even asked her a question. Her confidence is at an all-time high.

Cameron's waiting for her outside the hall, leaning against the wall opposite the exit door. He smiles at her and Jules's heart does a little flip inside her chest. She doesn't even think before crossing the corridor and leaning against him, kissing him with all that dizzy energy inside her body.

She pulls back after a few moments, breath heavy and skin buzzing.

'Sorry. I had the urge.' She drops her hand off his shoulder, realising this is the most overtly couple-y they've been in public at the conference. And that they're not a couple, despite her recent clarity that she thinks they could be. That she wants them to be.

'Hey, don't apologise for that.' Cameron grabs the hand she dropped. 'I like it. Kiss me any time.'

'In that case.' Jules leans up again and kisses him without restraint. Who knew public speaking could be such an aphrodisiac? Or maybe it's the fact that Cameron came to watch her even though it's outside his field, that he waited for her after the talk, after he already helped her this morning on it and they hadn't done anything sexual. Pure boyfriend stuff, as Cat pointed out. Another big tick in the 'do we have couple potential' column.

Though with all the energy running through her right now, the only thing she can think about is taking things to the bedroom for some more of the 'is this only a fling' column.

'I think you're glowing,' Cameron says when they part for air. 'Pleased with how your presentation went?'

'I am.' Her skin is hot but every moment of contact with Cameron makes that less about the presentation and more about him.

'You smashed it. And you didn't even need to include any baby pics.'

Jules laughs, remembering back to their car ride over and his joking suggestion to include pictures of Samantha's baby in her talk. She can't stop touching him, rubbing her hands up and down his arms, feeling the muscles beneath his shirt.

'Also.' Cameron grips her hips lightly and leans in to speak low against her ear. 'You were very sexy up there.'

Jules shivers, anticipation unravelling like a fern inside her. 'Oh, was I?'

'Mm-hm. If you weren't so engaging, I probably would have spent the entire time picturing you in your underwear.'

Jules laughs breathily, angling her head so she can stare into his caramel eyes. 'That's the opposite of how that trick's meant to work.'

'I know. And like I said, I got too caught up in the presentation for it anyway. Besides.' He drags his hands slowly up her arms. 'I quite like you in a pencil skirt.'

'You know what a pencil skirt is?'

'Chloe's my sister. I also know that this is a Peter Pan collar,' he touches the hem of her shirt, 'that the colour is teal, and that this whole outfit would look fantastic on the floor of my hotel room.'

Jules's mouth pops open. 'I can't believe you just used that line.'

Cameron laughs and she feels the vibrations against her body where they're pressed together. Her nipples stand at attention.

'I feel like it's working though. Want to prove me right?'

Jules narrows her eyes at him. She'd love to say no, just

to tease him, but it's like that first night all over again. She's too horny to even try.

* * *

Jules starfishes out on Cameron's bed, head down at the bottom end, feeling the sweat on her body slowly cooling.

'Does that count as an afternoon delight?' she asks.

Cameron starts singing at her and Jules flops her left arm over his face. It's not the sexiest move, but she's exhausted from some very athletic sex.

'Nothing against your singing voice, but I do *not* want that song stuck in my head.'

Cameron starts humming it instead, so Jules rolls onto her front and tickles Cameron's side.

'Woah, hey.' He twitches away from her, grabbing her hands and pinning them between his body and the bed. 'No tickling.'

'No humming or singing that song.'

'How about whistling?'

'No.'

Cameron laughs and releases her hands. 'Fine.'

He crosses his arms beneath his head and stares at the ceiling. Jules travels her gaze down his lithe body. The defined chest, the trail of hair leading down from his belly button, those thick thighs she was bracing her hands on not so long ago.

She exhales. This is like a dream. A beautiful, erotic fantasy.

'And yes, by the way.' Cameron rolls his head her way with a dopey smile on his face, dimples pressing into his cheek.

'Yes what?'

'I'd say that qualifies as an afternoon delight.'

'Cool.'

'But I've also got some meringues for you that I grabbed this morning, if you want that kind of afternoon delight. They're over on the desk.'

Jules's stomach trembles happily. He remembered from their car ride that she loves meringues. 'Maybe later. I'm too blissed out right now.'

She shuffles closer to Cameron, snuggling into his side and throwing her right arm over his torso.

He manoeuvres his arm from beneath his head and starts running it lightly up and down her bare back. She smiles and leans in to kiss him softly, all the fizzling, frantic sexual fervour of earlier dissipated. Satisfied thoroughly. Like she's gotten through the hot, smoky outside of a well-toasted marshmallow, and now she's in that soft gooey centre.

She hums against Cameron's lips, enjoying kissing him for the sake of kissing him.

'I've never had afternoon sex before,' she ends up confessing into the blissful quiet, lulled into exposing her own squishy bits by her post-orgasm bliss haze and being surrounded by his arms.

Cameron's fingers still on her back and Jules's heart starts beating fast and unsteady. Shit. Why'd she have to say that? Way to make herself alluring.

'Really?' Cameron sounds surprised, which helps rehabilitate her ego somewhat. His fingers resume tracing over her back, which helps too.

'Yeah.'

'I'm honoured to have been your first.'

Jules pushes onto her elbow, grabbing at the opening for a joke. 'Don't get cave-manish on me.'

Cameron beats his chest and thrusts his chin out.

Jules drops her head to her chest and laughs. 'Holy shit. Even that, *even that* I find appealing.'

Cameron looks bemused, eyebrows drawing together, but says, 'If you want me to dress up in a loincloth, I'll do it.'

It's not a bad mental picture at all. 'I think we'll table that for now.'

'Probably for the best. I don't know where I'd source a loincloth in the next few days.'

The reminder of their impending deadline drops an ice cube into Jules's chest. Two more nights here, and then it's back to Canberra and the office and the way things were.

Jules lays back down, pillowing her head on Cameron's arm and committing to memory the feeling of his fingers on her back. As her heartrate calms, the ache at her centre pulses for attention. It's flipped between satisfied and needy over the past few days, these quiet moments with Cameron taking the edge off momentarily before the ache starts again. She doesn't have the new turn-a-fling-into-a-relationship list yet, but relishing in the fling isn't enough anymore.

She told her friends from the start she's not a fling person. She needs the emotional side, too, and she's grown restless waiting.

That's always been her move. Waiting. Maintaining the status quo and watching things around her move, hoping the ripples aren't enough to dislodge her from her place, holding on tightly to the things closest to her so they form a buffer against the shifting world. But with Cameron, waiting won't work.

When they get back to Canberra, they won't have nearly as much time together. They were literally never in the same room before, though some of that can be attributed to her being content to keep his identity an enigma. But she wants this, so she has to take every moment.

Sex and pillow talk. That was meant to be the plan. Spilling her own slightly-embarrassing intimate secrets probably wasn't the pillow talk Tori and Cat were encouraging, but maybe exposing more of her vulnerable parts will encourage Cameron to do the same.

She opens her mouth to talk but a pressure appears at the base of her skull. Her shoulders twitch and the ants start marching over her skin. Last time she stepped outside her comfort zone, she endured a rejection so severe that when she leaped back into it she found it had shrunk in size.

But outside her comfort zone is now the place where she

finally spoke face to face with Cameron. Where she stepped up to fill in for Samantha with no notice and walked offstage glowing. Where she and Cameron have kissed and laughed and she's learned the many perfect ways their bodies fit together.

'I think when I was younger and inexperienced,' she starts, haltingly peeling back a layer of herself, 'I thought sex should happen in the morning or at night.'

Cameron continues his light *up down up down* stroking on her back. His eyes stay steady on her with interest, absent of any judgement.

'I wasn't naturally adventurous, and the thought of initiating anything made me nervous. What if I got shut down?'

Cameron's fingers ground her while she forms her next words. They're barely a whisper, but she's speaking them. 'With you, I feel different. The way we are together, and how we interact, it makes me feel confident. And sexy.'

'You were both those things already,' he says immediately.

Jules's skin flushes. 'I wasn't. Not the former, at least. But being with you makes me see myself differently. And besides, I never met someone who makes me want sex so constantly.'

Cameron wiggles his eyebrows but his reply is serious enough. 'The feeling's mutual.'

Jules kisses his chest and spreads her palm over his heart, feeling the steady beat of it. 'I've read about this feeling, you know.'

'Which feeling?'

'Unignorable horny-ness.'

Cameron huffs and his lips quirk upwards. 'Your erotica?'

'Yes, my erotica.' Jules rolls her eyes. 'But other novels, too. Part of me thought that was creative license, exaggerating for the sake of a story. There's always been attraction in my relationships, but I guess there was never that desperate, "I have to get this man naked and inside me" like there is with you.'

She drops her gaze to his torso, concentrates on his steady

heartbeat beneath her palm. 'Even with my last ex, I can count on one hand the number of times I initiated anything sexually adventurous.'

Cameron's hand flattens in the dip of her back. 'Well. I'm glad you feel like you can be open with me about sex. Ask for things you want.' He picks her hand off his chest and presses kisses to her knuckles. Jules's body goes boneless at the touch and the softness in his caramel eyes.

'It's like I said on the first night,' Cameron reminds her. 'Less thinking. If you want something, ask. What's the worst that could happen?'

'You judge me.'

'Wrong, because I'd never do that.' He says it firmly, like it's an unmovable truth. 'The worst that could happen is I say no.'

Jules winces. That *is* the worst thing. They're talking about sex right now, but eventually she'll need to tell Cameron what she actually wants – to date him properly. What if she opens up and he says no? It'll be like Todd all over again.

'You don't like to be told no?' Cameron has clearly picked up her discomfort.

'Does anyone?' She pushes off his chest and rolls onto her back beside him. 'It's not that I want everyone – you – to agree with me all the time. But when it comes to relationships. I guess...'

Cameron rolls onto his side and props his head on his hand, looking down at her. She fumbles for the sheet and pulls it over her torso, curling her hands into the fabric.

'That ex I mentioned. He, uh... well. He said no to me.'

'And you're still alive. See? Not so bad.'

Jules shakes her head. 'I asked...' She swallows, throat dry, her words pulling a vanishing act.

Cameron continues to look down at her, his hand a light pressure at her hip over the sheet.

When the words do appear, they come out as a whisper. 'I asked him to marry me.'

There's a pause.

'You asked him to marry you?' His hand slips off her hip.

'Yeah.' Her whole torso is covered in prickling now, down the backs of her thighs too.

Regret comes over her like stepping through a waterfall. What has she done? Telling him about Todd? She's trying to get him to open up, but scooping out her insides is a step too far.

She looks down at her feet, skin growing tacky with sweat. She can barely breathe.

Cameron makes a noise in the back of his throat and her gaze snaps to his.

Their stare is charged, but not with anything Jules can name.

A lump travels up her throat, and then she's opening her mouth and words are pouring out to end the silence. 'He said no, obviously. Then he broke up with me. Then I didn't date or even approach anyone for three years. Until you.'

She curls her tongue up inside her mouth to stop any more nervous rambling. She's gotten perilously close to revealing her feelings for him. The dots are all there to connect.

Cameron's gaze is steady on her, but his expression remains unreadable. She can't look away from him though, because what if he disappears the moment she does?

'And earlier you were telling me you weren't confident,' Cameron finally speaks.

Breath fills her lungs. 'It wasn't about confidence. It was—to be honest, I wasn't asking for the right reasons.' The words keep spilling out. 'Finn had been living in Tasmania for a few months, and then Mum and Dad announced they were moving back to Ireland. They were all leaving and I... I wanted something stable.' And now her hands are getting involved, flapping around above her chest. 'A person who was going to stay. Proposing to Todd made sense, but a proposal shouldn't make sense, should it? I mean, it should *feel* right. Necessary, even. Not logical.'

'Jules.'

Cameron's hand fits at her waist. Jules exhales noisily and lets her hands fall to her chest. It's the first he's touched her since she confessed about Todd. The heat of his palm spreads calm through her body.

'Thank you for telling me. I'm sorry he broke up with you.'

'Thanks.'

Swallowing past the lump still in her throat, Jules waits for Cameron to take his turn, open up about Braden and whatever went on between them. Needs his honesty to make the fact she's lying here with her insides all scooped out to have been worth it. Needs it like a balm on sunburnt skin.

Nothing.

Maybe if she asks? But as she opens her mouth, her throat closes up and static starts filling her head. What if she asks and he dismisses her?

Her body sinks into the mattress like someone's dropped an encyclopedia on her chest, weighing her down.

At least he's still touching her.

She blinks as her eyes start to itch. He's not opening up.

Jules sighs, squirming on the mattress. 'That conversation really took a turn. Can we, uh, get back to talking about sex now?' She rolls onto her side and slides her palm up his chest. 'Or having sex, again? Something that doesn't require me speaking.'

Cameron smiles loosely at her, warmth returning to his expression, though it's a mere simmer compared to how he was looking at her before this awkward conversational corner. 'I like you speaking, though.'

'And you know I like *you* speaking.'

He grins, then presses his lips against her ear. 'I do know that.'

Jules's body doesn't disappoint her, shivers sliding along her skin and nipples hardening, even as the ache in her chest expands, empty still and seeking.

She pushes against his chest until he's on his back and

she's half on top of him once more. 'So can we move on from the conversation? I made myself sound so vanilla compared to you.'

'Vanilla?' Cameron's fingers slip beneath her chin and he moves her head back so they're staring at each other. 'You're talking about someone else, right? Do you remember what happened last night at the Opera House?'

She presses her thighs together. 'Vividly.'

'Good.' His palm spreads out over her lower back. 'And hey, even if you were 'vanilla', there isn't anything wrong with that. Sex is about pleasure, right? And that means different things for different people.'

Jules's stomach goops around like a lava lamp, spreading a soporific warmth that halts the expanding ache. 'I love how assured you are about sex.'

'I've been told my body is one of my top features.'

'It is a good body,' Jules agrees, 'but you know that's not what I meant.'

'Do I?' The hand at the dip of her back grows heavy and a tightness creeps onto his face at the corners of his eyes.

'I like your confidence, of course, but I—' Jules's heart starts racing, body understanding she's struck a nerve before her brain catches up. 'I like your personality more.'

Cameron stills beneath her and the air in the room presses heavy against her skin.

'You're goofy, and you're a music nerd with a sweet tooth, and you love your sisters endlessly,' she lists, wanting the furrow in his brow to disappear. 'You're kind.'

Cameron looks away, the palm on her back curling into a fist. His caramel eyes go wary and he stops breathing beneath her.

She slowly separates their bodies and Cameron immediately swings his legs off the side of the bed, hiding his face. It's like a kick to her stomach.

'Cameron?' Her hand hovers over his back where the muscles are tensed.

'I'm fine.' He pushes off the bed and starts redressing, keeping his back to her as he pulls on his slacks.

'Are you?'

He pulls in a harsh breath, stilling, and Jules holds her breath too, waiting for him to let her in.

'Do you—do you want to tell me about it?' she tries. She can feel his hesitation like a breeze on her skin. He's about to let her in. This is the moment she's waited for.

But then he snaps back into motion and Jules's stomach drops.

'I've got to get to my next session. We both do. I'll... I'll see you later.'

Rejection stings like bluebottles around her chest as Cameron hastily pulls on his clothes. She dresses clumsily, fingers shaking, unable to get a proper breath in as space builds between them, harsh and dark like the feeling in her torso. Cameron hides his face from her but when she steps past him at his door, she catches a glimpse. His expression is shuttered.

Her stomach twists. So much for opening up to Cameron to encourage him to do the same. Their impending separation made her greedy to fill her ache with all things Cameron and she's pushed too far.

CHAPTER 19

Cameron strides along the walkway around from Sydney Harbour to The Rocks, hands shoved into his pockets and shoes slapping hard on the path. It's sunny, but instead of warming his skin, it dries him out. His eyes itch. He should've grabbed his sunglasses but he rushed out of the hotel after the last talk of the day without thinking.

Jules opened up to him today and he screwed things up. She told him about fears and insecurities and her ex and how comfortable she felt around him, and what did he do? Brush her off. Literally gave her his back and forced her out the room without any reciprocation of openness. Not even a goodbye kiss or another compliment on her presentation. She deserves those.

The kicker is, he wanted to reciprocate. Tell her about Braden, about his worries about his looks and his relationships and trusting new people.

Then she touched a nerve and he got spooked and ran, exactly like he did when he ran away from Cable.

I like your personality more.

Why the hell did that rattle him so much? He should feel relieved she's not like Braden, that she sees him as a whole person and not a body to have fun with, even though they're having a fling. He doesn't, and it's pissing him off because it's proving his sisters right. He's not over what happened. Now it's poisoning what he has with Jules. They've only got two more days at the conference and she may not even look at him again after his departure this afternoon.

Fight, flight, freeze. No prize money for picking which one he is. Flight every time.

Fuck that. He doesn't want to be that guy. He knows he hurt Jules, and that hurts him. Deep in his chest there's an ache like something heavy is pressing down on him. He's got to go back to her. Make things right with them. Apologise. He'll stop by that cafe on the way back and grab some more meringues. And an entire packet of marshmallows from the convenience store next door.

The sound of a distinctive laugh has his attention shifting from his feet to the crowd ahead of him, pace slowing until his gaze lands on a curvy woman with dark blonde hair and tanned skin. He freezes.

Braden.

His legs tense with anticipation of launching himself along the pavement away from her. He doesn't want to make a scene though, and she's walking with a handful of people from his old work. He's already caused enough bad blood with them all, barring Matteo. He wanted to use this week to repair his image with them, not run like a kid scared any time he sees them. Which he's failed at so far.

His legs are still tense when Braden spots him. The double-take would be hilarious if she didn't immediately start walking over to him. At least no-one follows her. He's not in the headspace to deal with a full reunion. He's not in the headspace to deal with his ex, either, but she's standing right in front of him.

'Cameron Parker. I thought I saw you.'

Braden smiles with enough wattage to power a small vehicle, but Cameron doesn't feel it. A vacuum like a black hole opens inside him, sucking in all his heat and breath.

'Hi, Braden.'

'I thought you lived in Canberra now?'

'I'm here for the Australasian Publishers Conference.'

'Oh, that's right. I heard Matteo mention that.' She tilts her head in an oh-so-familiar way. 'Are you watching? Presenting?'

She waves her hand around as she speaks and her phone

screen catches the sun. Cameron's eyes glue to it like it's a venomous spider. 'Presenting tomorrow.'

'I'll have to swing by. What time?'

The conversation is so normal, but Cameron's body is rioting. Talking with Braden used to be so easy, and now it feels like any avenue of conversation is fraught, layered with hidden meaning.

'Cam. Time?'

His hands twitch by his sides. 'Uh, eleven am.'

'Perfect.' She enters it into her phone. 'Picture for old-times sake? My photo roll misses you.'

Cameron isn't so panicked that he misses the subtext there. She's telling him she misses him too.

He swallows but his throat is dry and all it accomplishes is making him cough enough that Braden reaches out a hand to pat his back.

'No thank you.' Cameron declines, shrugging her hand off.

'Are you camera shy now? You used to love posing for photos.'

That was before she took those photos, fun things that he thought were for personal enjoyment, goofy dress-ups and sweaty post-run pics, and she plastered them all over social media in the name of marketing, no permission requested. It might not have stung so much if he didn't hear her talking to her friends about it, how Cameron 'wasn't much of a brain, but his abs made up for it'. That the best marketing strategy he brought to the company was her posting photos of him reading their novels shirtless at the beach.

That 'he wasn't someone you get serious with, he was the fun one before you settle down'.

Cameron had broken up with her the next day. He was never opposed to relationships being about fun over long-term commitment, but not when that wasn't made clear to both parties. Like what he and Jules have.

The weight in his chest morphs into a giant fist grinding into his spleen.

'Not right now.' Cameron rejects the offer.

'No worries. I should catch the others up anyway, but I'll be at your talk and hope to see you around. Maybe we can fit in a coffee at some point?'

He can't tell if she means it euphemistically.

Goosebumps break out over his skin despite the sunshine. Cameron smiles and nods, not wanting to make a scene by asking her not to come to his presentation and requesting she never speak to him again. Would that get him the closure he needs? Distance hasn't brought it, obviously, and if Braden is harbouring some hope that they'll get back together, their relationship is clearly unresolved. At least on her end.

Fuck. Fucking fuck.

* * *

Cameron's head is still spinning with thoughts of Braden when he gets back to the hotel. Honestly, he'd actually managed to forget she was at the conference for a peaceful 24 hours. Jules has been taking up his time and his thoughts, their fling a blessing on a level he didn't realise until face to face with Braden today. Another reason he needs to make up for bailing on Jules this afternoon.

A noise from down the corridor pulls his attention.

Jules is crouched in front of her door, picking up her phone and key card from where they've dropped onto the floor.

Seeing her, his body loses all tension for a second before catching up with what sent him running from the hotel in the first place.

'Jules! Wait.'

She pauses with her door open, then turns slowly and watches him walk over.

Every step towards her wraps a band of tightness around his chest. She's not smiling at him. Hasn't even said a word.

Fuck. His gut lurches. He did that. He made things awkward between them. Two days of sex they've survived fine, but one moment of emotional vulnerability and he flees, screwing it up. By his own rules – their own rules – he's got two days left of the fling and then things have to go back to normal. He wants those final two days.

She shifts on her feet and glances inside her room.

Shit. Now he's got to say something. He doesn't even have the marshmallows as an apology token, since seeing Braden threw him for a loop and he forgot he'd planned to buy them.

'Hi.' It's a clunky opener.

'Hey.' Jules tucks her hair behind her ears and looks into her room again.

She wants him to leave.

Well he doesn't want to leave. Not like this, with awkwardness in the air and not having seen her smile since his bed earlier.

'Do you want to grab dinner together?'

Jules's eyes widen at the tactless question, surprise clear before her emotions hide away. It's like a light dimming.

His gut sinks. He should want her to say no. He's got his presentation tomorrow and this was meant to be his night off to rehearse, but the weight around his chest won't go away until he gets them back to where they were before he ran.

He waits, feeling like he's standing in front of a storm about to eat him whole. 'Please? I want to apologise for earlier.'

'You don't need to.'

'Explain, then,' he offers recklessly. He doesn't *want* to explain. He doesn't want Jules to know how screwed up his thinking was. He only wants to get rid of the weird tension between them, clear the air.

Unfortunately, that gets her attention. She stills and her head tilts to one side.

'Okay,' she says after a beat. 'Dinner would be great.'

* * *

Cameron takes them to a Thai restaurant below street level a few blocks away from their hotel. The hostess greets them and leads them to a small, round table along a side wall, with a softly glowing light cube in the centre of the table.

Jules takes her seat and looks out over the restaurant. The warm glow of the light emphasises the length of her neck and swoop of her cheekbones, and turns her brown hair golden.

His throat goes dry while his palms get clammy. It feels like a date.

He waits for the slamming door of denial but it doesn't come. He's got bigger things to worry about, like how to explain to Jules why he acted how he did without telling her the full story.

They had a stilted conversation on the way over and now there's silence between them. He doesn't know what the absence of her nervous babble means but it can't be good. At least he can read her expression again, thank god, though he hates the wariness in her tight eyes and the way she's avoiding looking at him. Her spine's stiff, too, and her hands are folded tightly together on the table.

'Jules?'

She turns to him, blue eyes cloudy in the dark room.

'I'm sorry for walking out earlier. I didn't mean to hurt you.'

'You didn't.'

Her gaze skitters off his face and he frowns. 'I thought we agreed to be honest with each other.'

'Yes. About... *sex stuff*,' she lowers her voice and leans into him.

'Jules.'

'It's fine, Cameron. I get it.' She pulls back, dragging a menu with her and proceeding to focus on it as she talks. 'Maybe I was a little hurt, but I meant it when I said you don't owe me an apology. We're having a fling. By definition it's about sex, and I was getting emotional and you made it clear you didn't want that, as is your right.'

Ice stabs at his spine. 'Not true.'

'It's fine. I accept your apology.'

The band around his chest doesn't loosen. In fact, it gets tighter, making his heart compress and start beating faster. Why is he pushing this so much? He should be taking the out, grateful she's keeping this to their agreed terms. No emotions. Just the physical.

Yet his chest squeezes tighter and not seeing her smile at him is like a song without a resolution. He *needs* her smile. He needs her warmth filling him up to make this discomfort go away.

'I'm terrified of spiders,' he blurts.

Her eyes lift to his. 'Pardon?'

'Fucking terrified. I once didn't sleep in my room for four nights because I saw a huntsman in there. This was recently, too.'

Her eyes narrow and she tilts her head. At least she's not ignoring him.

'Uh... once, when I was a kid, I stole money from Dad's wallet to buy myself a terrible pair of Nikes I never wore. I don't understand people who don't listen to music. I failed my driver's license test twice. I do paint-by-numbers for fun. Which I already told you. Crap.' His heart races despite having done nothing but blurt out facts about himself.

'You failed your driver's license test twice?'

'Yes. My sisters like to remind me of that often.'

Jules's lips quirk. It's not a full smile but the band around his chest loosens a fraction.

She drops the menu on the table and focuses fully on him. 'None of this explains what happened this afternoon.'

'I have a habit of running from my problems.'

Jules's mouth pops open and she blinks at him.

A bit too real, but still true. Poorly worded though. 'Not that you're a problem,' he adds.

'Good to know.' She bites her lip and cocks her head. 'So what was the problem?'

'Uh...' The problem was Cameron got spooked by their emotional intimacy and reverted to his original tactic for handling potential feelings for Jules. Avoidance. No way is he telling her that though. It'll make him sound pathetic.

'If I say it's not you, it's me, would that be enough of an explanation?' He crosses his fingers beneath the table, and guilt tinges his next breath for hoping for an easy out.

'Partially.' She chews on her lower lip some more. 'Is that what happened at Cable, too? You... ran away from a problem?'

His jaw locks tight. She's too perceptive by far. He should've remembered that about her. But he can't berate her for not being honest with him and then lie to her face.

It takes a mammoth effort for his jaw to unlock enough for him to say, 'Yes. I was running.'

'Why?'

'It's — I don't talk about it.'

'Would you prefer to explain why you practically kicked me out of your room instead?'

He swallows painfully, throat dry. He feels renewed guilt for evading even as he replies, 'Not really.'

'*Cameron.*' Jules purses her lips and her disappointment claws his skin like talons. 'You said you were going to explain what happened. I opened up to you about Todd and you can't give me anything in return? You think I talk about him regularly?'

Cameron shifts in his seat. 'No. So I appreciate what it means that you did. But emotional vulnerability isn't a tit for tat thing.'

She jerks back in her seat and folds her arms over her chest, her gaze flitting off over his shoulder.

Fuck. He's upset her. This dinner was meant to be about *un*-upsetting her. How's he managing to make it worse? 'Jules. I'm sorry.'

'I already accepted your apology. I want the explanation.'

Her gaze is flinty and it makes his chest heavy. 'It's not easy for me to talk about. I barely told the story to Matteo, let alone my family.'

'And you think it was easy for me to talk about Todd?'

'No.' Fuck. He drags a hand down his face. 'That's not what I was implying.'

'Can you at least give me *something*? Please?'

'I—' He swallows roughly, multiple times. His throat is so parched it doesn't achieve anything.

Give her something. Okay. How about the fact he's physically in pain because she hasn't smiled at him all evening? Or that he saw his ex this afternoon and he's not sure his brain has returned to full function? That he wishes they were having this conversation over the phone so he wouldn't have to feel the weight of her stare on him as he fails to give Jules what she wants.

Or what about the other, harsher, more personal realisations he's been having this week? That leaving Sydney may have been a mistake. That he's lonely in Canberra. That in moments of weakness he pictures more than a single week with Jules and it scares him shitless.

'Did it work out at least?' Jules asks with a dollop of sarcasm. 'Running away from Cable?'

'I met you.'

The look she shoots him shrivels his insides. 'You're avoiding again.'

He feels like he's playing that game, what's it called, *Operation*, where you have to pull things out of the board without touching the sides. Only the things he's pulling out aren't plastic bones, they're emotions he's shoved down so far they're embedded in *his* bones. And instead of the loud buzz when he fails, he gets a frown from Jules and his own gut twisting.

He clears his throat and yanks the words out as best he can. 'It worked. I left because my... there was someone who...' God, why is this so hard? Why can't he just say the damn words? Spit them out, then move on.

Jules stares at him like she never has before. With narrowed eyes and a shade of doubt. It makes his stomach bunch and he hates it.

'It wasn't a comfortable working environment,' he forces

out. 'I was getting anxious and the quality of my work was affected. Leaving Cable was the right choice for me.' Leaving Sydney, well, that's still up for debate.

Jules's hard stare doesn't shift from his eyes. He fights the urge to look away from the eye contact.

After several seconds during which Cameron's heart attempts to break his ribcage from the inside, her arms loosen and drop into her lap.

'Running from something doesn't make it go away, you know.' It's half resigned, half accusatory.

He begs to differ. *Out of sight, out of mind* is a foundational pillar of his personality. Look how he tried to handle Jules before this conference.

'No, it doesn't,' he says despite his beliefs, because he doesn't want to push Jules away when she's starting to thaw. He needs this distance between them gone so he can appreciate and savour Jules for the final two days of the conference. The Jules from this afternoon, not the one glaring at him across the table. Though even this steely Jules has appeal, and Cameron fears there's nothing sexual or fling-like about the way her 'take no shit' expression affects him.

'It's quick, though,' Cameron adds. 'Clean.'

She lifts a shoulder, gaze dropping to the tablecloth which she runs her fingers over. 'Maybe for you, but not the pers— the *people* you're running from.'

'Jules.' He'd reach for her hand if he thought she wouldn't pull away from him. 'This afternoon I made an impulsive, wrong decision. It's not the same as what happened at Cable.'

The regret was far more immediate this time.

'Can we...' He reaches for her hand anyway, aborts at the last moment and curls his fist on the table. 'Are we good? We've only got another two days of the conference.'

Jules stares at him, her blue eyes still holding an edge of anger. As he waits, that icy shard pierces his spine again and twists. What if she says they're not good? What if he has to give her up? Because of something he did. Fuck.

Yet as the seconds drag on and Jules doesn't give him her assurance, a deep feeling, bursting forth with painful force from somewhere buried inside, has him speaking again. 'Okay. You want something? I hate that my actions have hurt you, Jules, because I... I care about you.'

There's still no response, but the wariness in Jules's gaze eases fractionally. 'You haven't smiled at me since this afternoon, you know,' he says.

'I know.'

'But did you know I miss seeing it?'

She narrows her eyes at him but it's the honest truth. She must see it on his face, because the last of the hardness in her expression fades, and she sighs.

'Alright. We're good.'

The band around Cameron's chest loosens and he sucks in a big lungful of air. 'Thank fuck.'

Jules's lips quirk, then she drops her gaze to the table. 'And I'm sorry.'

'Sorry? Why're you sorry?'

'I shouldn't have forced you to talk about the Cable stuff.' She shrugs and twists her hands together. 'It made you uncomfortable.'

An understatement. 'Yeah, but hey.' He leans over the table and she lifts her gaze to him. 'If it gets me back in your good graces, I'd do it again. I've always liked talking to you. And—' He swallows, stopping the words by rote. Then realises, heart racing, he doesn't want to.

'I don't want to be the guy that keeps running away from shit,' he says. 'I want to be able to talk about my emotions and my fears. Of spiders and more serious stuff. I want to talk to you. I want to talk *with* you.'

The words feel true as they leave his mouth, even though five minutes ago he would've sworn the exact opposite.

The twinkling look in her eyes and the first genuine smile she's given him all night may have something to do with the change of heart.

CHAPTER 20

They order food and drinks and when Jules smiles at him after the server leaves, all is right with the world. Mostly. He feels like he's experienced an earthquake and his insides are still jostled out of place, but he can breathe normally, so he's claiming a win.

Jules's fingers tap on the table to the beat of the background music in the restaurant. She's relaxing in her chair, looking at him without any hardness in her eyes, and there's a surge of sunny emotions racing through his body as he watches her. The little smile on her lips, the way her hair falls over her shoulder, drawing his eyes to the hint of cleavage. Those fingers *tap tap tapping* and her silver bracelet catching the light.

'Sorry.' She flattens her palm against the table when she notices where his gaze is.

'No need to apologise. It's cute.'

Her brow furrows. 'I thought you didn't like the descriptor 'cute'?'

'Applied to me, yeah. But I think it suits you.'

She blushes a *cute* pink. 'You don't think I'd prefer—what word did you use the other night? 'Desirable'?'

He laughs. 'Don't worry. You're that too.'

She gives him a sultry look from beneath her lashes and his blood diverts southwards. He's not even mad he's getting half-hard in a restaurant after one flirty look. These are the kind of bodily reactions he wants. Not that constricting tightness in his chest because she wasn't smiling at him.

'What's your go-to album when you need a pick-me-up?'

he asks, feeling music is a safe topic for them, and it's either initiate a conversation or lean across the table and devour her. The way he wants to drag his teeth up her neck isn't suited to a public place.

'Album or song?' Jules folds her arms on the table and leans over them. Her gaze drops to his lips.

'Both.'

'Okay. Song is probably 'Don't Leave Me This Way', The Communards version. Album is... ooh, that's trickier.' She laces her fingers together and scrunches her nose up. 'It's actually probably this compilation album I have of 80s pop songs, otherwise... maybe *She's So Unusual*, Cyndi Lauper's first album.'

'Have you ever dressed as her for a costume party?'

Jules narrows her eyes at him. 'Maybe.'

Cameron laughs. 'That's a yes. Do you have photos?'

'If I did, you wouldn't be seeing them without some begging.'

Cameron leans over the table. Jules doesn't lean back and they're close enough he can feel it on his face when she exhales. He's torturing himself with her proximity. 'I can beg. I'll happily go to my knees for you.'

He makes sure his voice is nice and deep for the line, and Jules shivering is the payoff.

Her skin flushes pink and her eyes drop to his lips. 'Naughty.'

'I play to my strengths.'

He would've begged her for forgiveness earlier if that's what it would take. And hell if that isn't telling of how much he likes being with Jules.

Braden's voice swims in his head, a hazy memory of a lascivious compliment she once gave, but he distracts himself from both previous thoughts by slotting his knee between Jules's legs beneath the table and pushing them apart slightly.

Jules bites her lip and Cameron's blood pumps thick through his veins. She's not opposed to some semi-public sex, but slipping his hand up her thigh to brush against her underwear may be too forward.

The server drops off their food, cutting through the sexual tension and his ill-thought-out desire. Jules takes a long drink of water while Cameron divvies up food evenly onto their plates.

'Okay. Your turn,' she says. 'Song and album.'

'Song, 'Good Vibrations'.'

Jules laughs, pulling her plate toward her. 'The Beach Boys?'

He shrugs. 'What can I say? It gives me good vibrations.'

Jules rolls her eyes. 'Okay. It's kinda catchy. And album?'

'*The B-52s.*'

'You had that answer ready to go.' She shovels a mouthful of curry and rice onto her fork. 'Hey. Are you into trivia?'

'Very. My family used to do a monthly trivia competition. We're all incredibly competitive. *Incredibly.*'

Jules's eyes light up and her knees lock around his beneath the table, sending heat straight to his dick. 'Do you know The Blue Alcott?'

'Uh, you mean the pub back in Canberra?'

'Yeah. They do a trivia night on Thursdays. I go with some people from work.' She reaches a hand across the table and squeezes his wrist. More blood rushes south. If the table were shallow enough for him to slide his leg between hers until he could press his knee to her heat, he would.

'You should come along,' Jules continues, oblivious to his salacious thoughts. 'I'm the only muso in the group, but I don't know everything. It'd be good having you there. I know Zoe from marketing is there most weeks.'

The five-foot nothing Jewish woman has invited Cameron every week since he's been at Infinity. Maybe he'll say yes next time. Jules will be there and he does love trivia. Should help with the loneliness too. If he decides to stay in Canberra.

Ignoring the thought, he twists his hand so their fingers link and gently squeezes her hand. 'I'll think about it.'

Jules returns the squeeze then slips her hand from his to resume eating dinner.

'Can I come back to something?' she asks.

'Not if you're going to mock the Beach Boys again.'

She scoffs. 'Have you heard their Christmas album? There's a lot to mock.'

'You don't include Christmas albums as part of a band's true discography. Everyone knows that.'

'Oh, do they?'

'All the cool people.'

'Hey!' Jules kicks her foot into his shin beneath the table. It's a solid hit and he winces, hissing. 'Shit. Sorry. Forgot I was wearing the pointy heels. Are you okay?'

She ducks her head below the table and pushes his pant leg up to his knee to check. He hopes she doesn't notice he's half-hard from the hand holding, and getting harder by the moment with Jules under the table for him, fingers pressing at his calf. Or maybe he does hope she sees.

A waiter comes around to check on them, clocks Jules under the table, and scampers away with an, 'I'll come back later'.

Jules reappears. 'Oops.' She pushes her hair behind her ears.

'Prognosis?' Cameron inquires, eying the flush down her cheeks and neck.

'Fine. Only a little red mark.' Jules gaze darts over his shoulder to where the server must be. 'But we're probably about to get kicked out of the restaurant. They probably thought I was *doing something* to you.'

'You don't need to be under a table to *do something* to me. You sitting there works just as well.'

'Really? That's...' Jules blinks owlishly, the flush over her cheeks and neck growing darker. 'Really?'

Cameron drops his voice. 'Really.'

Jules swallows and licks her lips. 'You too, you know.' She leans across the table, gaze dropping to his lips, the V of his shirt, sending heat spiralling down his torso.

Then she stops.

'I'm getting the evil eye.' She looks past his shoulder, frowning.

Cameron looks over at the waiter. 'That's not the evil eye.'

'I think it is,' she whispers. 'Tori does it all the time and it looks just like that.'

'The light's too low to tell. We're fine.' Jules is still fixated on the waiter, her fingers tapping on the table again.

'What were you going to say earlier?' Cameron prompts to distract her. 'About coming back to something.'

'Oh. Yeah.' Jules picks up her drink and puts it down again without taking a sip. 'Um, I wanted to ask – and I know you tried to move the conversation on with the music question, and we can go back to that after, promise – but you said you run away from problems.'

Cameron's next bite of food goes down like a stone. 'I did,' he says slowly.

'And I know you said I wasn't the problem.' She reaches for her drink, but spins it around on the tablecloth instead of drinking. 'But did you mean that generally? I mean, maybe it wasn't me, but was it something I did or said? I want to make sure I don't do it again.'

Cameron frowns. She's concerned about him when he's the one who behaved like a dick?

But also, she wants him to talk about the whole running thing more? His body flushes cold, then hot. He did say he wanted to talk about his fears with her, but turns out unearthing those buried emotions is easier said than done.

Maybe this is what his parents are going on about when they talk about relationships being about communication and talking through issues. God knows he and Braden didn't do that. He kept all his hesitations inside and then after one big problem he pulled the plug. Not that it's comparable with now. He and Jules don't have a relationship, they have a hookup with an end date, an arrangement that he's worked hard tonight to revive.

His silence must have gone too long, because Jules starts talking like she had in the car ride over, quicker than normal and using her hands for emphasis.

'I asked because I wanted to make sure things weren't weird between us. I know this arrangement is... is temporary. But I don't want to lose what we had before then when we go back to the office. Chatting on the phone with you. Guessing your soundtrack for the day. Because I, um, I care about you too, you know.'

Heat like sunshine flares in his chest at her soft words.

'You won't lose it,' Cameron promises, meaning it all the way through. After tonight, he doesn't think he'd be able to say no to anything Jules asked of him. A shocking thought, when it seems all he'd done today is throw up a big no to all her questions.

She nods, loosing a breath. 'So you'll tell me what I did?'

'You didn't do anything wrong,' he assures her. 'I overreacted to something.'

Jules's lips purse. 'To what?'

Cameron tries to cross his ankle over his knee but there's not enough room under the table. He settles for gripping his knees tightly.

Jules holds his gaze with steady blue eyes. He could lie or obfuscate, but she just spent the afternoon telling him he made her confident to be honest with him. He did promise her the same, though at the time he'd been thinking only of sex. Yet sitting in this restaurant with her now, he doesn't want to lie to her. She doesn't deserve that. And she obviously cares about not hurting his feelings.

Tightness snaps around his chest. He's out of practice with this whole emotional vulnerability stuff. He and Jules are good again though, so why burden her with more of his messy past. They'll be back to normal in a few days anyway.

Jules waits patiently and like the jealousy geyser when Matteo held her hand, the truth is born out on a rush of something needy that burns away the tightness in his chest.

'You said you liked my personality more than my body.'

Exhaling slowly, he focuses on her face while his intestine tries to tie itself into even more of a knot.

'Oh.' Stillness, then a slight frown. 'Do you... not want me to compliment you?'

'No. No, please. It made me feel...' Alive. Happy. Valued. Worthy.

The words are on the tip of his tongue, but voicing one feels like a big move. Like a relationship move. So he goes for the joke. 'My ego likes it.'

It's a pitiful answer, and he can tell from the slight tilt of Jules's head she's joining dots again. Does he want her to connect these ones?

He goes for his drink, tips back a large mouthful. It doesn't taste like anything. Neither does the next mouthful.

'Alright.' Jules's forehead smooths, dot-joining completed or abandoned for now. She smiles at him and bumps her knee against his under the table. 'I'll try complimenting your personality more in future.'

'Thank you. And if you could call me 'cute' some more, that'd be great.'

Jules rolls her eyes, thankfully missing how his hand trembles faintly as he returns his drink to the table, trembles because he's starting to join his own dots in the back of his mind, and the picture it's turning into, one of him and Jules, doesn't resemble the one he saw at the start of this week. No, it looks an awful lot like the one that's been coming in flashes when he least expects it. Flash-*forwards*.

CHAPTER 21

Cameron suggests taking the scenic route back to the hotel and Jules agrees. Anything to keep this portion of the night going. Cameron is finally opening up. Granted, she was hoping for more about the Cable stuff, and less about his fear of spiders. But he did confess about his running away thing, which she could tell was a big deal. It's not the most hopeful trait he could have confessed to possessing, and since he did there's been a persistent prickle on the back of her neck, because running is exactly what Todd did.

But nevertheless, she's learning more. Though she practically had to force it from him, since her own opening up didn't inspire immediate reciprocation. Which in hindsight, of course it didn't, because Cameron was right. Emotional vulnerability isn't 'tit for tat'.

But the ache in her chest is filling in more tonight and she loves him.

No. *It*. She loves *it*.

Shit.

Where did that word slip come from? She's only just realised she wants to try for something long-term and serious with him, but you don't go from liking to love, just like you don't go from flirting to sex. Which, bad analogy. She did that this week. But it's still skipping a bunch of points in the plan.

And she had that scare today when he shut himself off, so really, she should be taking a half-step back, if anything, not racing a hundred steps forward. What if he runs again? Like Todd had? He confessed tonight that's something he does.

'Let's get gelato,' she says. A brain freeze should shock the

L-word out of her system. It's way too early for those kinds of feelings when they're not even actually dating, just going on very date-like outings. It's probably because they haven't had sex since... actually, it's only been a few hours. But maybe if she reminds herself this is a fling?

Jules taps Cameron on the shoulder, then plants her lips on his when he turns to her. He makes a little *oomph* noise but kisses her back eagerly, hands locking around her lower back. A familiar heat spreads through her limbs. She licks at his lower lip then slides her tongue inside his mouth, tasting curry, kissing him until all thoughts of *that word* are out of her head. Until all she's thinking about is racing back to the hotel and getting naked.

There.

She pulls back, satisfied in one way, thoroughly unsatisfied in another.

Cameron looks stunned. Wide eyes with blown-out pupils, hair mussed and lips slightly parted. Now she definitely needs that gelato since she's on fire.

She pulls him over to the gelato stand and orders a butterscotch in a waffle cone.

'What flavour?' she asks him.

'Uh...' Cameron's still looking at her lips and he doesn't look away when he says, 'caramel.'

She's not sure why he's so fixated, they've kissed plenty of times before, but she doesn't hate it, even though her skin is now probably as pink as the raspberry gelato.

She pays, despite Cameron's protests, and then they meander along Circular Quay as they eat. Jules watches Cameron's tongue swipe up the side of his gelato with jealousy. By the wink he gives her after darting his tongue out to scoop the top into his waiting mouth, he's aware of the effect his ministrations are having.

Two can play that game.

It's the oddest, silliest foreplay Jules has ever engaged in. Tastes good, too, when she steals a taste of Cameron's gelato and he braces her against the railing by the wharf and kisses her with an ice-cold tongue. There's way more people around than there were at the Opera House but she doesn't care. A little possessive part of her is elated, soaring in her chest that he's being openly affectionate with her. Out in public. Kissing. Like they're a couple.

And there she goes again with the dating thoughts.

Cameron presses a cold kiss to her cheek, then her temple, then rests his lips against her ear.

'You know what I've been thinking about all night?' Cameron asks.

From the hot hardness pressing against her hip – a hardness she spotted when she ducked below the table at the restaurant earlier – Jules is pretty confident it's something along the lines of smearing gelato all over her body and licking it off slowly. At least, that's what she's thinking about doing to him.

'Your presentation?' She goes for the joke, but the instant way he stiffens up – his entire body, not the part Jules was thinking about sliding gelato over – has her realising the misstep. Damn, she should have gone for a sexy answer.

'Fuck.' He pulls off her and she shivers. 'No. I haven't been.'

He runs a hand over his face. When it drops away, it's like he's painted worry lines and tension onto his skin.

Batting away her hormones takes some concentration, but his presentation is something that matters to Cameron. If she can help him with it, that's as good as an orgasm on his tongue. Kind of.

Fighting through the lust, she checks the giant clock on the facade of the art gallery behind him. 'It's only just after eight. Let's head back and we can run through it.'

Cameron exhales roughly and throws his half-eaten gelato into a nearby bin. 'Sorry to end this so abruptly,' he says. He sets a blistering pace to the hotel.

Jules tries to match his stride which involves a shuffle-hop and then some fast footwork. 'No apology needed.' It's the honest truth. 'I know how important this presentation is to you.'

'Did I tell you that?'

'You didn't have to. You're the most studious person I know, and I've seen your desk. You have so many printouts of your presentation and reminders of when and where to be.'

'I want it to go well.' He says it like he's calling on the universe to help. 'Everyone from Cable will — '

He doesn't finish the sentence.

Jules reaches for his hand and holds on tightly. He squeezes back with enough force she worries about bruising.

Cameron continues his hurried pace. For a man totally confident and at ease in the bedroom, there's an alarming tension to his body. His over-preparedness for the conference was charming to her, but is it more than a personality quirk?

'It will go well,' she repeats.

'And what if it doesn't?' he says tightly.

Jules wants to yank him to a stop on the sidewalk and wrap her arms so tightly around him she's like a security blanket. 'Then... we'll eat an entire block of chocolate together then move on.'

He scoffs. 'I'm not sure a sugar high will help me recover from making an ass of myself twice.'

'Making an ass of yourself?'

'Yeah. You know I ran from Cable for personal reasons. It was shit timing. I'd spearheaded a massive blitz campaign for a new Australian YA series. I left right before it launched. My manager's expression when I told her I was resigning was — ' He jerks his head side to side. 'So disappointed. I let her down. And the rest of the team.'

'What does that have to do with your presentation?'

'The second book in the series is due to release early next year and so the whole Gen Z focus should be useful to them. It won't be if I fumble my talk. Or if my bad luck with tech means the slide show doesn't work. What if the microphone fritzes?'

Jules's heart pangs like a string plucked. He's so concerned about making amends in his own subtle way.

'Cameron, you're... it *will* go well.' She's breathless from the pace and she can't make eye contact with him this way. That won't do.

She digs her feet into the ground and yanks on Cameron's hands.

'Why're you stopping?'

'Listen.' Jules grabs his other hand so she's grasping them both. He's not running from what she wants to say to him. His eyes are bright and wide and his hair is a mess. Jules falls a little more for him in this second.

'You're so prepared. And intelligent, with years of experience. Patricia sings your praises at work, you know that?' His mouth opens and shuts, and he swallows. 'The first thing she said when she told me you were attending the conference with me, was that you've been making major improvements with the digital side of the company. Patricia doesn't sugar-coat. She thinks you're the best thing since lab diamonds.'

His gaze is unblinking. He's staring at her like he's searching for something. She hopes he finds it.

She squeezes his hands tight. 'I think so, too. But you need to not hyperventilate right now.'

Cameron's eyes flutter shut and he drops his head to his chest.

'Here's what we're going to do,' she says. 'We're going to get back to the hotel and go to your room, you're going to run through your presentation, and I will sit there and listen, and give feedback if you want, as many times as you need.'

Cameron's head lifts. His fingers squeeze around her palm. They're sweaty, and she's not sure if it's from the speed walking or nerves.

Her heart seems to exist in her chest and throat at once.

'What if it's six times?' he whispers.

'Then we better grab some coffee and chocolate on the way back.'

There's no warning as he grips her face tightly between his hands and presses a hard kiss to her lips. It lacks finesse, but the sheer fervour in it makes Jules's toes curl and steals her breath.

He pulls back and presses their foreheads together. 'Jules. You—thank you.' Another fast kiss. *'Thank you.'*

CHAPTER 22

Back in Cameron's hotel room, Jules sits on one of the desk chairs, watching Cameron give his presentation on targeted marketing for Gen Z. He's marginally calmer now he's running through his presentation, though he's speaking a tad fast.

It's still Cameron's voice though, and it rolls over Jules's skin like an erotic aural massage, so she can't be blamed that it takes ten minutes for her upper brain to kick into gear.

'Stop. You're too tense.'

Cameron grips his palm cards tight. Jules suspects they're only a security blanket. He hasn't looked at them once. 'Excuse me?'

'You're tense. Your shoulders are all bunched up and your neck is jutting out,' Jules waves her hand toward him. 'It's affecting your breathing and that's causing all kinds of problems.'

Jules gets out of the chair and walks over to Cameron, pressing down and back on his shoulders. Tingles rush up her arm but she ignores the physical thrill. She honestly does want to help him. Besides, it'll be good for that ache in her chest.

'You seem very knowledgeable on this stuff,' Cameron says.

'I did a public speaking course a few years ago.'

'Right.' He rubs a closed fist in a circle over his chest. 'So what's the fix?'

'Picture the audience in their underwear.'

'Jules.' Cameron's eyes lock onto hers and Jules's fingers tighten on his shoulders. 'If I picture you in your underwear, I'm not going to be able to get through this speech.'

Heat burns in his eyes. His voice has dropped in pitch and she's not sure if it's intentional or not, but it makes her thighs squeeze together.

Her gaze drops to his mouth but she reins in the impulse to kiss him. 'That was meant to be a joke to get you to loosen up. Don't actually do that. Here.'

Jules removes her hands from Cameron, then takes a deep breath in and rolls her shoulders back and down, like she did before her own talk. Cameron copies her movement.

'Once more,' she directs. 'Perfect.'

'Thanks.' He runs a hand through his already dishevelled hair. 'So, no picturing people in their underwear. What's the actual fix then?'

'Dancing.'

Cameron laughs right up until Jules steals his palm cards from him. 'That was the serious suggestion.'

All mirth drops off his face. The panic is adorable.

'Dancing is—you want me to dance?' He sounds like she's asked him to walk backwards over hot coals.

Jules nods, bouncing a little on the balls of her feet. 'Yes. It'll loosen you right up.'

'But I can't get up in front of everyone and dance.' His voice is strained.

'Why not?'

'Because I'm here in a professional capacity, and aside from that—'

Jules bumps her shoulder against his chest. 'Another joke, sorry. Couldn't resist.'

Cameron groans and runs his hands through his hair. 'So I don't need to dance?'

'Oh no, we're still going to dance.'

She shimmies over to the desk to put his palm cards away, then dances her way back over to him. The look of terror is still on his face, and he stands stiff as a flagpole. 'Then tomorrow you can listen to whatever song we use now and your body will remember how it felt. Which should be relaxed,' Jules adds, grabbing Cameron's hands and putting them onto her hips which she sways from side to side. 'It's a pretty cool technique actually. Haven't got quite the timeframe to repeat it as much as you should, but I think it'll help.'

'Jules. I'm not sure...'

'Do you trust me?' Jules lays her hands lightly on Cameron's forearms, encouraging him into a gentle twist. She keeps moving her hips while Cameron thinks, a furrow on his brow.

The silence stretches a little long for her comfort, but with her hands on him and his on her, she's not complaining. It's not exactly how she imagined dancing with Cameron – not that it's been one of her most prominent fantasies – but it's still nice being so close to him, getting to see the little vulnerabilities beneath his cool, calm and collected exterior.

'I trust you,' he eventually says, stepping in closer until their hips are an inch apart.

'Perfect. Do you dance?' Jules moves her hands up behind Cameron's neck, her fingers playing with the ends of his hair.

'I had to learn a waltz for Carrie's wedding.'

Cameron shifts without warning, taking her right hand off his neck and extending it out to the side, while his other hand shifts up to her waist.

Jules loses her footing but Cameron snaps her body up against his, causing a rush of air to puff out between her parted lips, and a pleasant *zing* to shoot down from her nipples to her toes.

Cameron smiles at her and Jules gets waylaid thinking about dancing him over to the bed. Her toes curl but she bats away the thought. He helped her this morning, now she's helping him. With his speech, not with an orgasm.

'Not this kind of dancing,' she says. 'I meant the kind of dancing you do after half a bottle of wine to an 80s playlist.'

'I haven't done that in years.'

'What?!' Jules pulls herself away from Cameron and goes for her phone, bringing up her pump-up playlist. 'Well, we're changing that right now.'

'I don't have a bottle of wine on me.'

'You'll have to work harder to let go of your inhibitions then.'

She hits play and drops the phone to the table. Synth chords sound out in the room and Jules starts banging her head along with the beat, raising her arm in the air waiting for the beat to drop.

Cameron watches her, back to being stiff as a flagpole. Jules skips over to him, picking up his hands and spinning him in a circle with her as the first verse kicks in.

Jules drags him all the way through the first verse, but his body stays tense. 'Let go, Cameron.'

He pulls her hands from her grip, discomfort clear in the twist of his mouth. It's not the letting go she meant. 'You look—'

'Ridiculous? Free? Childish? Like I'm having a hell of a good time?'

'All those things.'

'And don't it feel good. Here.' She grabs his hand and places it over her racing heart. 'My adrenaline is up, my body is loose and I feel like I can take over the world! That's exactly the energy you want for your presentation.'

'I'm not sure.'

'Come on. There's no one else here. I don't care what you look like.'

Cameron's facial expression does an odd twitch and jump. 'You don't?'

'*No*. So come on. No excuses. It's just you and me, here.'

Jules isn't sure what it is about her encouragement, but one second, Cameron's motionless, and the next he's jumping up and down like he's in the mosh pit at a festival.

Jules laughs, clapping her hands furiously. Whatever energy is pumping in Cameron's veins, she wants some of it. The smile on his face, growing bigger every second, pressing those swoon-worthy dimples into his cheeks, makes her whole body come alive, tingling all over.

'Yes. Yes! That's fantastic.'

She jumps up and down with him, fist-pumping and clapping along with the chorus, spinning on the spot and even throwing in a terrible attempt at a high-kick which has Cameron doubling over to laugh.

They get through the entire song, laughing like they're high. Cameron's hair loses any semblance of order and Jules may be getting sweat patches under her arms, but it's infectious. This moment – she's going to take it all the way to her grave.

The song eventually segues into another, and Jules winds down her dancing. Cameron wraps her in a massive hug and lifts her clear off her feet, swinging her around until she's laughing and dizzy.

'Now, lay it on me!' Jules says.

Cameron drops her to his feet and seals his lips to hers, kissing her with the same fervour he's just been dancing with. There's a lot of tongue, and some playful nibbling of her lips. Jules's knees wobble, making her glad for Cameron's arms still locked tight around her back, squishing their flushed bodies together.

Jules's focus shatters into dozens of pieces and it takes, oh, four entire minutes of kissing before she remembers the point of the dance break was not to get them in the mood, but to help Cameron loosen up for the presentation.

Reluctantly, after one more suck of his lower lip, she pushes against his shoulders.

He pulls back only enough to press their foreheads together. His hair is a mess and his skin has a sheen of sweat that Jules wants to lick off.

'That's...' Jules presses her fingers to her tingling lips, laughing. 'That's not what I meant.'

'You said lay one on me.'

'I said lay *it* on me.'

'Oh. In that case.' Cameron scoops her up easily and carries her across to the bed, dropping her onto it before crawling on top of her and letting his body press hers into the mattress.

Jules gyrates her hips against his body. It's a natural, subconscious reaction to Cameron but she stops after two, okay, five thrusts.

'Also not what I meant.'

'I know.' Cameron grins like a kid on Christmas morning.

Jules stopping her own movements means nothing because Cameron's got his own rub-and-circle manoeuvre going on. She's only just repaired her focus. She wants to provide support for him like he did for her, but with every shift of his hips against her pulsing clit, it's harder to remember that.

Jules grabs his biceps to push him back but her arms pull him closer instead. 'We're meant to be working on your public speaking.'

'By relaxing my body. You know what's really good for that?' Cameron plays dirty, leaning close to her ear and dropping his voice low. 'Sex.'

Jules shivers. Her nipples, already hard, get somehow tighter, pebbling beneath the cups of her bra. 'Cameron. We're meant to be working on your confidence.'

'Then this is perfect. I'm most confident in bed. I'm confident I'll make you come, that we'll both be satisfied. Then I'll get up and do the speech.'

Jules's traitorous hips grind up against him a few times. Can't be helped when he's still saying all this right in her ear with warm breath and that rough, sex-deep voice. Her underwear is a wet mess right now, and she wants to yank the hem of her top down, then the cups of her bra so she can rub her eager nipples against him.

But she's starting to get the sense she's witnessing Cameron running away from something in real time. It's startling, and a truer insight into his depths than she's seen so far. And what did he mean by 'most confident in bed'? Why would he think that?

Regardless, she doesn't want to aid and abet his coping mechanism. She wants to help him face it and work through it. Like a partner would.

'Yes, but what about outside the bedroom?' She prompts. 'What are you going to do tomorrow, huh? Have a quickie before you go on stage?'

'Sounds perfect to me.'

His breath tickles her ear, sending shivers right through her. As Cameron continues his rub-and-circle hip manoeuvre, Jules sees the Rubicon approaching.

'Cameron. Come on.'

Her clit yells at her as she shuffles out from under Cameron's body, but this is the choice she needs to make. This is a perfect chance for her to show Cameron she can offer more than sex, that they can have a relationship that's more than sex.

'Take this seriously. I know you want this to go well. Are you scared or something?'

Jules expects another witty comeback, but instead, Cameron's expression darkens.

'Oh.' Her throat dries up. 'You actually are, aren't you?'

Cameron sighs and drops onto his back on the mattress, rubbing his hands roughly over his face, then holding them there while he breathes.

Jules can see he's hard still, but now that she's aware of his fear, the desire to rid him of his pants and wrap her hand around him has vanished.

'Cameron?' she prompts softly, padding away from the bed to stop the cheerful pop music playing from her phone.

'Scared? No.' Cameron crosses his arms over his chest and stares at the ceiling. 'Anxious. Yeah. A lot.'

Jules presses a palm to her chest, right where that ache to know Cameron lives. 'I had no idea.'

Cameron shrugs, gaze still fixed on the ceiling, the dark expression on his face miles from the carefree laughter while they were dancing.

Jules bites her lip, desperate to get the look off Cameron's face. She wants to bring the dimples back. She wants to be the person who can help Cameron out of wherever he's gone, but her earlier attempt at emotional openness backfired. He bolted away from the room and her.

But then he came back. He asked her out to dinner and they talked. So even with those familiar ants crawling over her shoulders, she takes a deep breath and lays down beside Cameron.

She tilts her head to the side to stare at him, debating asking the question she's been wanting to since their night at the symphony. 'I know you're worried about presenting to the Cable people but, this seems... is this about Braden?'

Cameron stops breathing. 'How do you know about Braden?'

'Chloe told me.'

Cameron swears on an exhale. He turns his head to look at her, wariness in the set of his eyebrows. 'How much did she tell you?'

'Not much. That you used to work together, and you had a bad break up and it affected you.'

'All true.' Cameron sighs, shifting to stare at the ceiling again.

Jules chews her lip. 'Is she why you left?'

Cameron makes a non-committal noise, then sighs. 'Yeah.'

'Oh.' Jules's stomach does an unsteady slosh inside her. What the hell happened? Something bad enough he left Cable despite the terrible timing.

She slides her leg across the mattress to rest her foot lightly against his leg. A little contact to ground him, show him she's here with him.

'We were together for almost a year and things were good,' he says slowly, uncrossing his arms only to shove his hands into his pockets. 'Then I found out we wanted different things. That she didn't see me or our relationship the way I thought she did.'

'Different things?' It doesn't sound so terrible, but then again, she and Todd wanted different things and that shook her for years.

'We weren't on the same page about how serious it was.' Cameron looks over at her again and his lips quirk in a facsimile of his usual smile. 'It's actually one of the things I like about us. We've made it clear what this is.'

A little section of Jules's heart breaks off. Shit. He's here praising their relationship for being well-defined, and meanwhile, she's working for something way beyond the boundaries they set.

'I'm glad,' she says, concentrating on pushing away her own hurt to focus on Cameron's.

'My sisters think I need closure. They think our break-up is holding me back.'

'Do you think that?'

She bites her tongue and waits, staring at Cameron's profile. The straight jaw and the slope of his nose.

'Braden's going to be there tomorrow,' he says after a minute, ignoring her question. 'In the audience. And all the other Cable people.'

'That's making you anxious?' She rolls onto her side to face him better, wishing she knew how to truly comfort him, but she hasn't learnt yet. Will she ever get the chance to?

'You know I didn't leave on the best of terms. The phrase 'burning bridges' comes to mind.' His mouth twists into a frown.

'Matteo doesn't seem to think so.'

'Yeah. That's Matteo for you. The others? Probably not going to be looking at me kindly.'

'So you're worried they won't like the presentation you created for them?'

Cameron rolls onto his side and their knees knock, sending a fissure of warmth down Jules's calves.

'Yes. Or that they won't be able to see past my actions to actually listen to it. The way I left was completely unprofessional. Minimal notice, projects unfinished.' His bitterness coats Jules's insides with tangy sadness for Cameron. He cares so much.

'But you did that for your mental wellbeing. They can't fault you for that.'

'They can't know about it either.'

'Does Matteo?'

'Yeah. He's the only one, though.'

'That sounds... isolating.'

Cameron hums. He reaches out and trails his hand over the slope of Jules's shoulder. 'I'm beginning to see that.'

His fingers glide down to her elbow, then back up to her shoulder to repeat the movement. There's nothing sexual about the warmth that spreads through her body. It isn't a bonfire, or fireworks. This is heated floors in winter, or a patch of sunlight to read a book in. Her body soaks it up greedily.

She reaches out to touch his elbow but Cameron rolls onto his back again, leaving Jules's arm to flop onto the mattress.

'Sorry. Sorry,' Cameron says. 'You wanted a conference fling and I'm here talking about my emotional crap.'

'Hey. Just because we're having a—a fling,' Jules forces the word out, 'doesn't mean I don't care about your emotions or what's going on in your head.' She would've hoped that was clear from all the times she's tried to squeeze her way in there this week. 'I like that you can share these parts of yourself with me. Besides. We were friends before this anyway. Weren't we?'

Cameron's gaze finds hers and his expression softens slowly as she watches. 'Yeah.'

'And we will be after.' It comes out as a question.

'Hope so.'

And friends don't lie to each other.

Jules needs to come clean about her feelings. She knows it like she knows every word to 'Ordinary World' and the track listing for every B-52's album.

After his presentation.

She can't rock his confidence before then, so she'll continue to act as if the fling is all she wants. There's truth there, at least. She does want Cameron, wants him like she hasn't wanted anyone before, with a loud heart and her entire body.

For now, they stare at each other across the sheets. A heat builds between them, but it's different to normal. More a slow fog gathering round them, as opposed to a flash of lightning.

Cameron takes her face between his palms. His caramel eyes stare into hers, right down to the soft squishy parts inside her. She stares back, finally seeing some of his soft squishy parts too.

'You're an incredible woman, you know that?'

Jules's heart soars, though her stomach twinges with lingering guilt over masking her real intentions for their relationship.

When he kisses her, it's with that same, thick foggy lust that makes her bones limp. It's so slow, so delicate how he shapes his lips to hers, that it's like moving through a dreamscape, half awake and half asleep.

Cameron presses her back down onto the sheets and crawls on top of her, pressing kisses over her body, shoulders, neck, nose, ear. Lifts her palms up and kisses those too.

She breathes deeply and lets it out slowly as Cameron takes his time divesting her of her clothes, then strips down to his skin. When he lays his weight over her, thighs between her parted legs, it feels perfect. The way their bodies align, and the hypnotic heat they share with each other.

Tomorrow she'll tell him the truth about how she feels about him, and what she wants from him. Today, she'll enjoy this like it's the last time she gets to have him like this. She knows there's a possibility he'll turn her down when she asks for more from him, especially with Cameron's self-confessed propensity for running. But earlier today, her subconscious said 'love' and while it's not right for how she feels today, it could be. In the future.

She can see herself falling in love with Cameron, a man who understands the depths of her musical passion, who indulges her sweet tooth, who makes her confident enough to reach for things beyond her comfort zone.

She lets the thoughts flee as Cameron kisses her, taking his time, running his fingers over her skin until she's trembling and aching for him to be inside her.

'Cameron,' she whispers.

'I've got you,' he says, his beautiful face hovering above hers as he kisses her deep.

He puts a condom on then stares into her eyes the whole time as he pushes in and this, finally, this is the connection Jules was searching for. The sex *and* the emotion. She can read it in his eyes. There's an openness there, a vulnerability that steals her breath and makes her cross her legs behind his waist and squeeze, hold him deep inside her so he knows she's right here with him.

Together, they glide toward pure pleasure. Taking their time. Kissing slowly. Fingers and hands and tongues exploring, all the while, the slow thrust in and out, Cameron moving inside her, and his caramel eyes catching hers and holding her, lifting her up whenever they connect.

She slides her palms across his broad shoulders, to meet at the back of his neck and draw his face to hers.

'This feels so good. You make me feel so good,' she confesses.

Cameron's smile is filled with something Jules can't place, close as she is to ultimate pleasure. Fondness?

Her body jolts as Cameron changes his angle slightly, and she drops her head back and sighs.

His lips find that place on her neck that turns her to goo, and his fingers trail down down down, over her breasts and down her torso, right to where she's pulsing and needy.

'Incredible,' Cameron tells her, his fingers working her slow. She rides the wave for endless moments, pleasure filling her up, magma through her very bones.

'Jules. Julianne.' Cameron whispers her name and she's gone, shaking and clenching and spiralling down through layers of feeling until Cameron's fingers on her clit are too much and she has to pull his hand away.

She can feel her wetness on his hand when she links their fingers together.

'You're incredible too.' She stares into Cameron's eyes and hopes he knows how deeply she means the words. How much she hopes she'll get the chance to say them again and again into the future. 'An incredible, wonderful man.'

There's more she'd like to say, but Cameron speeds up, pulling out further and driving in with increasing need, and Jules is transfixed watching his face, seeing the way his own gaze flicks around Jules's face and body.

He grabs her other hand and lifts both their linked hands beside her head. Jules lifts her hips to meet his thrusts, wanting to give this man everything and anything if he'll keep looking at her like he is now. With need and devotion.

His lips crash into hers seconds before he comes and he kisses her through it with messy fervour.

Cameron's head drops to the crook of her neck. He presses soft kisses to her skin that send happiness racing through her like champagne.

They stay linked, coming down together, Cameron pressing soft kisses to her heated skin until reality starts licking at the edges of the dreamscape.

'Are you going to get up and do your speech now?' Jules asks.

'I don't think I can move. That was... intense.'

Jules's heart flutters. 'I thought so too.'

He does move enough to deal with the condom, but he falls straight back into bed and up against Jules's cooling body, facing her.

'You don't need one last run-through?' Jules checks. He'd been so worried earlier.

'I'll find you in the audience and you'll give me confidence.'

'Okay.' Trusting Cameron is being honest, Jules's body melts into the mattress, indulging while she can. 'I should go. Leave you to sleep.'

Cameron's arm tightens around her waist. 'It's after midnight. Stay.'

A fist grips her heart and squeezes. 'Are you sure?'

He presses a light kiss to her shoulder and smooths hair off her face. 'Very.'

Jules relaxes into the bed, rolling onto her side and letting Cameron pull her close until her back is pressed against his front. He slips a foot in between hers and tangles their legs together.

Cameron kisses her shoulder again and splays his hand out over her stomach. 'Thank you for listening tonight.'

'Any time,' she replies, meaning it from the top of her head to the tips of her toes.

Jules lays her hand over his and lets his warmth loosen her limbs. That aching part inside her doesn't strain so much anymore. Tonight Cameron opened up to her about his past and his emotions, and the sex... it was different from how it's been before. Less driven by need and more by want. Less libido and more tenderness. The way he'd looked at her while they moved together, that wasn't the expression of a man who doesn't have feelings for her.

She falls asleep with a smile on her face and hope inside her heart that tomorrow, when she tells him she's got feelings for him, that she wants to date him properly, he'll say the same back to her.

CHAPTER 23

Cameron's alarm goes off at 6 am. A female groan sounds from the sleep-soft body curled against his front. He smiles and buries his face in Jules's hair, inhaling the fruity scent of her shampoo. It's been ages since he's had the pleasure of waking up with a woman, and this isn't any woman. It's Jules.

He spreads his hand out over her belly, revelling in the warmth that moves through his limbs. It's dangerous to indulge but he hasn't got the energy or the want to squash the feelings down, that sunny whirlwind pulsing through his body like it had at dinner last night. The conference ends tomorrow. He's only got one more day to be with Jules like this. Why not indulge, when the simple act of waking up with a woman he likes is enough to buoy him toward the sky. He'll take any luck he can get today for his presentation.

The moment is broken by his alarm getting louder. Jules groans and rolls her head to squint blearily at him. Her voice is rough with sleep when she says, 'What the hell time is this?'

'Six in the morning.'

Jules groans again and Cameron laughs quietly, pressing a kiss to her bare shoulder. 'I'm going to the gym. Go back to sleep.'

'With pleasure, you monster.'

Cameron sweeps the hair off her face to kiss her cheek before climbing out of bed and changing into his gym clothes. He catches Jules staring at him from one opened eye.

'I thought you were going back to sleep.'

'Couldn't resist catching a look.'

'You've seen me naked several times this week.'

'And I love it every time.'

The white sheet drapes tantalisingly over Jules's curves. Her bare knee and lower leg poking out from beneath the covers calls to him, but he finishes dressing instead, promising himself he'll kiss his way up the limb, and a little higher, after his presentation.

He brushes a kiss to her forehead before heading for the door, closing it softly on his way out.

Down in the gym, where he's planned to work out with Matteo this morning, he steps onto the treadmill in the corner. Without Jules by his side, the familiar nerves start jangling up his arms. He speeds through a warm up then sets the pace high, hoping to burn away some of that distracting energy.

He runs through his presentation as he jogs, muttering the words to himself beneath his breath. It's less fun than Jules's technique. Dancing around with abandon in his room.

He bumps the pace up again, smiling. Jules's careless freedom had been infectious. He hadn't let loose like that in ages – unless you count in bed with Jules this week – and letting go of worries about what he looked like was like taking off a ten-kilogram jacket he wasn't aware he'd been wearing.

In fact, this whole week, any time he's with Jules, it's been... he doesn't even have the words. It's been so long since this feeling – the lightness in his limbs and the easy smiles that come any time he thinks of or sees Jules – has happened to him. Not even that homecoming feeling of returning to Sydney compares. He kissed her forehead this morning, for crying out loud. He doesn't think he even pulled that totally boyfriendly move out when he was with Braden. But he can't resist Jules.

He shakes his head and wipes sweat from his forehead with the bottom of his shirt. His thoughts are getting away from him. Presentation. He needs to run through it again.

A few minutes later, Matteo joins Cameron on the machine next to his.

'Ciao.'

'Hey.'

Matteo drops a water bottle into the holder and hits the start button. 'Big pressie today. You ready?'

'Hope so. Just ran it through now. Practised with Jules last night, too.'

'Is that what we're calling it these days?'

'Very funny,' Cameron replies dryly, while Matteo laughs. 'Might see if I can fit another run-through after my shower.'

'I never understood why you rehearsed these things so much.' Matteo increases the speed of his machine and starts a light jog. 'You used to make me sit through dozens of practices before you pitched marketing strategies to the CEO. You're naturally charismatic. You could waltz into a meeting wearing board shorts and thongs and get a CEO to sign over their company.'

'Maybe that's because I practice the delivery so much.'

He doesn't feel charismatic these days. He can count on one hand the number of friends he has at Infinity, hell, in Canberra. He's made it so no one's eager to spend time in his presence. Except Jules. And even that's about to end.

They run in companionable silence, Cameron feeling the pull of muscles in his thighs and calves. He should look into starting a running club at Infinity, make some better connections with people. Or work harder on picking up the slack of the connections he left behind in Sydney.

He wonders if Jules would be into a running club? Clearly not at six in the morning. He already knew she wasn't a morning person from their early start on Monday, but hearing the groaning complaint was cute.

'Dude,' Matteo drawls out, pulling Cameron from the memory.

'What?'

'I know that look. You've got *feelings*.'

'No I don't.' The warm whirlwind in his chest begs to differ.

'I dropped it the other day because you asked, but I don't think I can ignore it any longer.'

'My debilitating crush on you? Yes. Caught me.'

Matteo laughs. 'Thanks. Nice dodge. But obviously, I'm talking about Jules. You've fallen for her.'

'No I haven't.' The reply is automatic and sets off a lurch in his gut. Because it's a lie.

Fuck.

He should've realised yesterday at dinner when he decided to let the warm weather phenomena in his chest rage on, assuming it would blow itself out. Yeah. That didn't happen. He asked her to spend the night. He didn't even get a complete run-through of his presentation in. He *made love* to her.

Shit. Does that mean he loves her?

No. Ridiculous. But you don't make love without some depth of emotional connection. Which means he's got feelings for Jules beyond friendship. Beyond a fling.

Cameron jumps off the treadmill while it's still going. Anything to get away from Matteo's line of questioning and his own revelation. Thank fuck no-one else is in the gym with them.

He's behaving like a kid with his hands over his ears chanting 'la-la-la-la' but he's got his presentation today. It's a lot of pressure and he needs to be in the right headspace.

'Cameron?' Matteo stops his own treadmill before stepping off it.

Cameron paces across the floor of the gym, shaking out his arms like he can flick away the thoughts Matteo is planting in his head. Well, if he's being honest, less like planting and more like giving them permission to bloom. It's not like he hasn't been sporadically slammed with visions this week of him and Jules still together far in the future.

'Not gonna lie, I'm a little worried by this reaction.' Matteo gestures at Cameron. 'This doesn't seem like a man who's got his shit together.'

Cameron laughs. 'I do. I'm fine. Why does no-one believe that?'

'Uh, because you do things like jump off moving treadmills to avoid talking about your feelings.'

'There are no feelings to talk about.' The lie twists worse now he's aware of it, like a giant fist grinding his organs.

Matteo rolls his entire head along with his eyes. 'I've been friends with you for years. I know the signs. You like Jules. What's the issue? Why aren't you trying to make anything more of what you have with her? You guys seem to work well together. I mean, if I didn't know about your fling thing, I'd guess you were already a couple.'

'Well, we're not. So.' Cameron pivots and retraces his path across the floor. His limbs feel jittery.

'Look, man.' Matteo steps into his path and he draws to a halt. 'I went easy on you the other day because you were clearly fixated on this thing with Jules being a fling, but you've been emotionally invested the entire time. There's nothing wrong with that. Bottling up emotions again, however...'

Cameron frowns. 'If you've been talking to my sisters this time—'

'I haven't been but I probably agree with everything they've said. Look.' Matteo drops his hands onto Cameron's shoulders. 'You're a great guy, you deserve a great woman who makes you feel a million bucks. Is Jules not that woman? Because from what I can see in your face when you're thinking about her, or talking about her, she is.'

Cameron ducks under Matteo's arms and resumes his pacing. 'Jules is great. She's fantastic. So is what we have, just like this. We know what we are to each other. We have clearly defined boundaries and expectations. The sex is awesome. I know exactly what she wants from me and it's a body, not a boyfriend.'

Matteo clears his throat. 'Are we still talking about Jules?'

'Yes.' Cameron fists his hands into his hair, spinning to face his friend.

Matteo's disbelief is clearly communicated by the shape of his eyebrows.

Cameron deflates. 'No.'

'Okay. Now we're getting somewhere. Let's backtrack a little.' Matteo sits on one of the padded weight benches and pats the one parallel to it.

Cameron eyes the bench like it's got fangs. This feels like it's about to be a deep and meaningful conversation, like the kind he had yesterday with Jules. Two in as many days is a lot, but Matteo stares him down until he relents and takes a seat. This grinding feeling inside him is crap. He has to get rid of it before his presentation.

'You agreed to the fling,' Matteo says, 'so you must like her in some way.'

'Of course. She's... Jules. I like *being* with her.'

'Why?'

'She's nice.'

'A little more, man. Come on.'

Cameron exhales and rubs his knuckles under his jaw. It's not hard to list her attributes when he lets himself think of them. 'She's incredibly smart. Funny. Kind of has a dry humour. So beautiful. She loves music as much as I do. She makes me... I don't know, happy. Comfortable.'

Matteo hums, nodding sagely like he's a therapist and Cameron's laid out on his couch. 'Funny how none of that was sexual.'

'Shit.' Cameron's eyes widen. Busted.

Matteo nods slowly. 'See what I'm saying now?'

'Shit,' Cameron repeats. Why couldn't he have answered Matteo's questions with his lower brain. Then he'd be able to avoid what surely comes next.

'You do like her. You're just holding back because you're afraid.'

Yep. There it is.

'Afraid she'll hurt you like Braden.'

'Stop. Look, I—' He takes a deep breath and pushes up

from the bench. If he's going to come clean, he doesn't want to see the I-told-you-so look in Matteo's eyes as he does.

'I see it now,' he tells Matteo. 'Braden fucked me up for relationships. I do get scared.'

Claiming the truth isn't empowering. It makes his bones shrink until he feels all of three feet tall.

Matteo hums. 'She hasn't fucked you up, there's just some added internal complications now. Acknowledging it is a good first step.'

Cameron rubs a fist over his chest as he starts pacing again. 'Running into her yesterday... it's clear I've got some unresolved shit in my head about it.'

'Not feelings for her?' Matteo asks with horrified wide eyes.

Cameron's gut spasms at the mere idea. 'No way.'

Matteo tips his head up to the ceiling. 'Thank fuck.'

'Though she was clearly still interested in hooking up.'

'Oh, damn.' Matteo's eyes widen again.

'Yeah.' His skin tightens remembering the clear interest in her face. 'Thing is, it's not great timing to figure my shit out. I've got my presentation today and I have to make up for the mess I left at Cable when I resigned. You know how important word of mouth and professional reputation is in this field. What if I can never get a job in Sydney again?'

'You're thinking about moving back?' Matteo doesn't hide the surprise from his tone.

'That's—' He didn't mean to say 'Sydney' instead of 'Canberra', but it's true. 'Yeah. Maybe.' Cameron shrugs. 'But that's a whole other thing I don't want to think about right now.'

'Well, I'd love to have you here again, man, but only if it's the right thing for you.'

'Thanks,' Cameron nods. 'But yeah. I can't be stressing about Braden hinting she wants to get back together. Or have sex again or whatever. I've already been stressing that leaving Sydney was a bad move. I'm trying to placate my sisters, who keep bugging me with texts about Jules. And *Jules*. I'm spending so much time with her it's getting impossible to stop feeling things and thinking about her. So I really need—'

'Hold up.' Matteo throws his palms up. 'There's so much to unpack there. But first. Feeling things? What happened to your 'you've got it wrong, we're having a fling, it's one hundred per cent sexual' argument from, like, two minutes ago?'

Cameron's heart *thump-thumps* hard in his chest, gearing up to say the words he won't be able to take back. 'I was lying. It stopped being one hundred per cent sexual.'

'What? When?' Matteo asks with a massive gasp.

Cameron shakes his head. 'You're as bad as my sisters. They've been pushing me to ask her out from day one.'

'No dodging the question.' He grabs Cameron's arm and yanks him onto the bench beside him. 'When did it happen?'

'Yesterday.' Cameron focuses on peeling Matteo's fingers off his arm as he speaks. 'She opened up to me, told me stuff about her past and her fears. It was... nice knowing she trusted me enough to share those things.'

'Nice' isn't a strong enough word, but he doesn't want to go too sappy and say 'validating'.

'Did you do the same?'

Cameron barks out a self-deprecating laugh. 'Should have. But no. I did something bad.'

Matteo groans. 'Please don't tell me you said, 'that's nice', and then shoved your dick inside her.'

'Urgh.' Cameron shudders and pushes hard at Matteo's shoulder, regretting it when Matteo doesn't budge and his hand ends up covered in sweat. 'You seriously think I'd do that?'

'I don't know, man.' Matteo hefts his massive shoulders. 'You were the one saying 'it's a fling, it's a fling'.'

'Thanks for the vote of confidence.' He wipes his palm on his shorts several times.

'So what did happen?'

'She, uh, gave me a compliment and I freaked out and ran.'

'You ran away from a compliment?'

He drops his hands between his legs and looks out at the treadmills, the belt on his abandoned one still cycling around. 'She said she liked my personality more than my body.'

Matteo lets out a low whistle. 'So kinda made you question your whole attitude towards the fling, then.'

'And it made me want to tell her about Braden. I don't tell people that. I hate how it makes me look. And yes, I am aware now that's unhealthy.' Cameron pushes his hands through his hair. 'Point is, I ran and I felt awful. Everything was weird inside me because I thought I'd screwed things up with Jules. I knew the only way to make it right was to apologise and explain. So I did.'

Matteo whistles slowly through his teeth. 'You told her the Braden stuff.'

'Uh, a little.'

Matteo raises his eyebrows at that and the fist grinds Cameron's insides some more. 'But other stuff. Personal stuff. She kind of had to force it out of me, though, to be honest. I've been, uh, keeping a lot of shit inside recently. But then after, she smiled at me and my insides all slotted back into place. So, it was worth it. I'd do it again for that smile.'

Matteo grins, elbowing Cameron. 'You're a romantic. That was poetry.'

'Shut up.'

'So you're actually admitting your feelings are there?' Matteo inches closer to him on the bench.

'The possibility has always been there.' He wouldn't have gone to such lengths to avoid seeing her at work if there wasn't.

'And now?'

Cameron's got a summer storm inside his chest, pushing warmth every which way. Jules is upstairs in his bed waiting for him, and damn if it doesn't put a smile on his face. 'It's not a possibility, is it? It's reality.'

Matteo slides right up to him and wraps his long arms round Cameron.

'Urgh. Matteo. Dude. You're covered in sweat.'

'So are you, mate. I don't care. You confessed to feelings and I gotta support that.'

'Wish the support stank less.' But he braces his arms around Matteo's torso anyway.

'So you two are gonna start dating now?' Matteo cuts straight to it when he finally releases Cameron from the sweaty purgatory of his hug.

'Don't get ahead of yourself. Jules wanted a fling. I have no idea if she'd be keen on a relationship with me.'

Shit. He hadn't thought that far ahead until now.

His gut lurches. He was so comforted this whole time knowing they were on the same page. Now he's flipped to the next chapter without knowing if she wants to follow.

Anxiety becomes a dryness in his throat, tempered marginally by a warm hopeful breeze in his chest.

'I can't think about it right now, anyway. About any of it.' He stands and grabs his stuff abandoned at the treadmill, shutting the machine off. 'I've got my presentation. I don't need more unrelated stuff crowding my head.'

'As long as you're not going to run from your emotions. Or from making a decision,' Matteo says, hopping back onto his treadmill and starting it up.

Cameron's not running. He's delaying, making the 100-metre sprint into a marathon, or a hurdle race. The first hurdle being his presentation. Then figuring out if Jules wants more, then dealing with Braden, then whatever else pops up, like that niggling question in the back of his mind around whether he made a mistake leaving Sydney and what that would mean for him and Jules.

CHAPTER 24

Jules wakes to the sound of a shower running. She jerks up in bed, heart rabbiting away in her chest, before it sinks in. She's in Cameron's room, in Cameron's bed.

Her body tingles all over and she flops back onto the bed and rolls over to smash her face into the pillows. They smell like Cameron. Like the man she spent the night with. The one she likes enough that she's going to tell him the truth today about how she feels.

The ants appear on her skin, digging sharp feet into her muscles, making her shudder as a vision plays in her mind of Cameron turning his back on her after she confesses her feelings to him.

No. She's not going to let them dissuade her. No risk, no reward, as Tori would say. She's normally talking about the spontaneous alterations she makes to her Nonna's recipes, but it can be applied here, too.

The shower is still going and Jules follows the tug in her abdomen into the bathroom. Cameron's left the door ajar so she doesn't even have to knock.

Cameron wet is a sight to behold. A sight that sends heat flooding into her core as she watches sheets of water slide over the muscles on his back and over the curve of his ass.

'Room for one more?' she asks.

Cameron turns to face her, brushing his hair off his forehead. His arm muscles bunch and Jules's insides clench.

A smile spreads over Cameron's face, at once sensual and innocently happy. 'Not sure. Shall we test it?'

Jules steps inside the shower and goes straight for a kiss,

sliding her hands over wet muscles and hot skin. Cameron kisses her slow and soft, with obvious tenderness that makes her knees weak and the sensation of butterflies appear in her stomach. She thought that was a turn of phrase, but she swears there are wings fluttering inside her.

'Hair wet or dry?' Cameron checks with her, feathering kisses over her forehead. 'I think there's a shower cap in that vanity kit out there.'

'Because shower caps are the epitome of sexy.'

'*You're* the epitome of sexy,' Cameron parries, rubbing his knuckles on the underside of her breast.

She grabs the shower cap and a condom.

Shower sex is something she's done before, but though it's sex, she's never found it sexy. The awkwardness of limbs in an enclosed space, arguments about water temperature and getting soap in your eyes. The precariousness of balance and grip.

Not with Cameron. Everything is slow and measured and steamy, in all senses of the phrase. Cameron goes to his knees for her, teasing out pleasure with his tongue and fingers until her moans are bouncing off the tiled walls.

After, she braces her forearms on the tiles and cants her hips back for Cameron to slide in. Water sluices between their bodies. He's got one hand on her hip, the other kneading a breast, and he tries a few angles until he finds the one that makes the little 'oh' noises fall from her lips with every thrust.

There's little speaking between them, but Jules has had the pleasure of Cameron enough times this week to read his body, and he hers. It steals her breath and makes her heart beat loud in her ears. They *know* each other. They come seconds apart, then lean against the tiles, kissing languidly until Jules's skin starts pebbling from cold and Cameron gently pushes her beneath the warm spray and steps out of the shower to dry off while he watches her, a soft smile on his face the entire time that creates more butterflies in her stomach.

* * *

Jules moves through the rest of her morning routine – going back to her room to dress and heading down to the breakfast buffet – with half her thoughts back in Cameron's room, and half her heart tangled in his sheets. She almost told him this morning, when she stepped out of the shower and he wrapped her up in a towel. Almost said, 'I've got feelings for you. I want to date you.'

She'd taken a breath to prepare and everything, but then her throat closed up. What if he didn't have feelings for her? What if he laughed? What if he ended things, even their phone calls in the office? She'd gone light-headed, unable to take a proper breath until he'd pressed a gentle kiss to her forehead and made some of the tension slip away.

Then she remembered she was waiting until after his presentation anyway.

Now she has time to push through her fear, to focus on the vision *she* wants, of her and him together after she sews her heart onto her sleeve for him and asks him out. It's not what she expected she'd be doing today, based on yesterday afternoon when she'd tried to open up to him so he'd return the favour and he'd run away from her instead. Just like Todd.

You can't force emotional vulnerability from someone. Cameron was right. It had been foolish to try, and it left her roaming around the hotel that afternoon feeling like someone had thrown a bunch of daggers between her shoulder blades. Exactly how it had felt when Todd left her after she proposed. This leap was smaller in comparison but the result was the same. Knives in her back and a lump in her throat.

It goes to show how deep her feelings for Cameron have grown in a handful of days, to garner the same level of reaction as from her rejected proposal of her ex-boyfriend of four years. Using the L-word in her head yesterday may have been an accident at first, but this morning, waking up with Cameron, seeing him sleepy and unguarded, she's more certain than ever she wants the whole package. Dates and hand holding and learning more about him and kisses that don't lead to anything. The chance to fall in love.

It feels natural, right, to think about loving Cameron. Like sitting across from him at that fancy restaurant had felt right – after he'd apologised and explained in a stilted way why he'd run from her. It had also felt like she was crossing off item number three from her list. Go on a date.

Which means she's now crossed off everything on the list. Talked face-to-face, flirted and gauged his interest, gone on a date, hanky-panky. *Lots* of hanky-panky. Like it was step one and four and all the way through to 20.

But they're still not dating.

Her friends were going to help her make a second list when she's back in Canberra, how to turn a fling into a real relationship, but she doesn't need a step-by-step. All she needs is honesty.

If things go to plan, they'll be official by the end of the day. All she's got to do is tell him how she feels and ask him out.

That brings the ants marching across her shoulders. She rolls them a couple of times but the feeling stays. If the sensation was in her stomach, she'd call it nerves, not fear. At least there's no back-stabby feeling. It's day four of the conference and she woke up this morning in Cameron's bed, with his arm weighing her down into the mattress and his warm breath fanning across the back of her neck.

She smiles as she moves through the breakfast buffet without Cameron by her side since he's gone to investigate the room he'll be giving his presentation in. She passes the muesli stand and her stomach swoops. That's what Cameron eats for breakfast.

It's official. She's a goner.

She sits at a table and brings up the group chat with Tori and Cat, but barely gets through the missed messages from last night before someone stops by her table.

'Julianne. I was hoping to see you.'

She looks up to see James McCarthy, patched jacket and glasses on, carrying a plate of eggs and sausages.

'Good morning, Mr McCarthy.' She places her phone on the table. 'You were?'

'James, please. I wanted to offer my congratulations on your presentation. I found it very engaging.'

'Thank you, James,' Jules says. 'I was worried I might have rushed a little through the research development justification section.'

'Not at all, at least not in my opinion. I'm sure Ms Liu will be very proud of you.'

'Thank you. And thank you for sending those files through. I looked over them again. Really fascinating stuff.'

'I'm glad you think so. I know it's not a particularly attractive area for a lot of people.'

As he talks, an idea takes shape, looking like another opportunity for Jules to grab. Maybe she can practise the whole confidence thing and being honest about what she wants before doing it with Cameron this afternoon. She doesn't want to choke in front of him again.

Cameron was confident enough to leave Cable when he knew it wasn't right for him. She thought she didn't have it in her to do the same with Infinity, but if being with him this week has shown her anything, it's that she's more confident than she thought. She can step outside her comfort zone if she tries hard enough. The rewards are out there waiting.

'Would you like to join me?' she asks James, gesturing to the empty seat.

'You're not waiting on anyone?'

She shakes her head and James places his plate and mug of tea on the table and folds himself into the seat.

Jules is hit with a sudden attack of the ants, so she takes a breath around the lump in her throat and eases into the conversation with a question about something from her presentation. James is as enthused and engaging one-on-one as he was in front of a crowd, and quickly, the ants are forgotten in the flurry of excitement in her brain. Lightbulbs flicking on one after the other as she parries intellectually with James. They talk for twenty minutes, she's surprised to see after glancing at the clock on the back wall.

'Can I ask?' she says, riding a wave of enthusiasm, 'I was looking at your website yesterday, and there weren't any job listings. Is there a way I can get an alert when something comes up?'

'Ah.' James removes his glasses to clear the lenses on his sweater. 'You're interested in working for the company, are you?'

'Yes. Potentially.' Saying the word is exhilarating. 'I think your ethos is fantastic. I'd love to be part of that.'

'Hmm. Well.' He slides his glasses back on and folds his hands atop the table. 'You're located in Canberra, if I'm not mistaken?'

'I'm in Canberra.'

'Unfortunately, we don't have offices there, or plans to open a branch any time soon.'

'Oh.' Jules swallows. 'Of course. It was wishful thinking to ask.'

'Not necessarily. There will be something opening up soon, though... would you consider moving to Sydney?'

'I...' Pinpricks dig into her skin. Move? Leave Canberra? Her friends? Cameron?

She's getting ahead of herself with that last one, but all the rest are valid. Yes she's ready to leave Infinity, but moving to Sydney is a big change. There's stepping outside her comfort zone, and then there's crawling inside a canon and shooting herself so far away she doesn't see the zone anymore.

'I know that's a big question to drop on you with no warning,' James says, understanding in his eyes.

'It is, yes, and honestly, it's not something I've considered.'

She takes a beat to do it now. The thought of returning to the office after this week is uninspiring. And it's not only the Cameron stuff, it's the work stuff too. These talks have reignited her passion and having experienced that electric thrill again, she doesn't want to give it up. Infinity saps her energy, she can see that now. Working somewhere like James's company could boost it.

No risk, no reward.

'I'd consider it,' she tells him. 'Though I suppose it depends on the job.'

'Of course.'

'Is there scope to work remotely?' she asks as the thought occurs. 'All or some of the time?'

'A fair question.' He reclines his head. 'Not at this stage, but potentially further down the line, yes. But we're looking to grow our Sydney office in the new year.'

'You are?'

'Yes. It's not been publicly announced yet, but we're hoping to set up a new team to create targeted courses for sustainable business practices.' He takes a sip of his black tea, staring at her over the rim of his cup. 'It would involve a lot of work, since we'll be researching and designing the program from the ground up, and we find that process works best if people are in the office together. Better for brainstorming and team cohesion.'

'Right. Makes sense.'

'I predict the clients would be a broad scope of businesses, perhaps even not-for-profits and government agencies, as opposed to mostly publishing and media companies like it is now. Would you still be interested?'

She's never looked beyond the publishing industry, but it doesn't require much thinking to see how stepping outside of it will help counter the feeling of having stagnated professionally. 'I've worked in mass media for... ever since I graduated uni, actually,' she says. 'A change sounds good.'

'Wonderful.' James smiles like he means it. 'The hiring process starts next month. I'll be on the interview panel, so you'll know at least one face.'

'And I should just keep checking the website?'

'That'd be best. And you do have my email, so if you have any queries when the listing goes up, don't hesitate to get in touch before submitting your application.'

'Fantastic. Thank you. I will.'

'No need to thank me. From what I saw yesterday, you'd be a wonderful asset to the company.' James checks his watch. 'I should head off, but if you want to catch up tomorrow to talk about the company, I'll have a stand set up in the trade hall. Come find me and we can get a coffee.'

'That would be brilliant. Thank you.'

James farewells her and heads off.

Jules grins, digging back into her breakfast with renewed appetite. She's practically got a job interview lined up a day after drafting her resignation letter. That has to be a good sign. Hopefully it bodes well for her discussion with Cameron later today, as well.

She looks around the room to see if she can spot him, but he must still be preparing for his presentation. Her insides go all goopy. He's so nerdy and dedicated.

Her phone starts ringing. She glances at the screen. It's Samantha. Does she sense that Jules has been talking about leaving Infinity?

Stomach bubbling, she accepts the call. 'Hi, Samantha.'

'Jules! Hello! How did the presentation go yesterday?'

Jules relaxes slightly into the chair. No sixth sense, just a well-intended follow up. 'It went well, I think. People seemed pretty engaged and I got some good questions at the end.'

'That's fantastic. I knew you'd do well up there. I didn't pick you to cover my maternity leave without reason.'

'Thanks. How are you going with everything?' Jules asks, reaching for her orange juice.

'I'm wearing a dress over jeans and the longest uninterrupted sleep I've had lately is three hours.'

'Sounds... hectic.'

'Oh yes, for sure. Hope you're having a more relaxed time up there. Presentation over! That's always the scary bit. Then it's just soaking up knowledge and networking and seeing if any stalls are handing out freebies on trade-stall day.'

Jules laughs at the leading tone. 'Are you angling for something in particular?'

'Since you ask, a few years back there was an educational publisher from Perth, I think it was, that was handing out little bottle openers with book quotes engraved on them. I lost my old one.'

'I'll keep an eye out.'

'Oh. And if James McCarthy has anything set up, like any info packs or conference deals for client meetings, let me know. I got those slides you sent through and they were very useful. Or I assume they will be. My work brain has gone a little soft recently.'

'I'm actually, probably, going to be meeting up with James for a coffee tomorrow, so I'll ask him then.'

'Really?' Her tone is pure shock. 'How did you finagle that?'

'There was no finagle-ing involved. I talked to him after his presentation, he talked to me after mine.'

'Does he still wear jackets with the patches on the elbows? He always reminded me of that nerdy linguist guy from the animated film. You know the one?'

'Yes to both.'

Samantha laughs. 'I guess academia never goes out of style. Hope he's not trying to poach you from us!'

'Uh... no? No.' Is it poaching if she's the one pursuing a position with his company?

Samantha hums. 'That's not a comforting response.'

'Sorry. He's not trying to poach me. But, um...' Jules clenches and unclenches her hand. Should she go for broke? Make this a Jules-takes-big-risks day? She's had a one hundred per cent success rate so far.

'Jules?' Samantha prompts.

'I am thinking of looking for another job,' she rushes out. 'Leaving Infinity.'

The silence on the other end of the line quickly cuts through the momentum of her announcement, and fill-in-the-silence Jules emerges.

'I mean, obviously I'm not handing in my notice right now. But I was thinking, when you get back full-time, once you find your feet again, I'll let Patricia know. It's not because—I've loved working at Infinity, really, but I've been there for almost seven years now, you know, there's not—'

'Jules, hey. *Jules*. Stop.'

She sucks a breath in past the lump in her throat and holds it.

'You sound worried,' Samantha says. 'Honestly, I've been waiting for you to tell me this for a while.'

'You have?' Jules folds her arm around her torso and squeezes.

'Yes. I can tell you've been restless.'

Jules lets the breath go finally. 'Why didn't you say anything?'

'I didn't want you to feel like I was forcing you out. Besides, you're a great employee and a real asset to the team. Losing you will be tough. But I don't want you sticking around if you don't want to. There's no faster way to kill passion or enthusiasm.'

Jules exhales and slumps back into her seat. Samantha's words are a year too late. She already feels that way, and now she's wondering if she should've had this conversation ages ago and saved herself the tension and energy depletion. And resorting to reading erotica at work.

'Thank you, Samantha.'

'No worries. Thank you for giving me the heads up. And to save you from asking, I will very happily provide a letter of recommendation for you.'

'You're amazing.'

'I know,' she laughs. 'Enjoy the rest of the conference. I know I've still got another while of maternity leave but when you get back to Canberra, let's grab a coffee and chat. It'll be my baby break for the day.'

Jules hangs up and stares at her phone. She told her boss she was thinking of resigning and the sky didn't shatter around her. She got her blessing, and the promise of a recommendation letter. Holy shit. That's two-for-two now.

She hopes her success rate holds steady after her confession to Cameron.

CHAPTER 25

Cameron checks his outfit in the bathroom mirror one more time. Buttons all done up. Tie straight. Collar flat. His hair is sitting neatly and his jaw is clean-shaven. He takes a long breath in through his nose, then pushes the air out slowly through his lips.

He's got this. He knows his presentation back to front. He's run through it another two times this morning after breakfast, and he's triple-checked his slides work on the projector in the conference room.

And Jules will be there in the audience to buoy him.

He hasn't seen her since their shower this morning and the little tug in his gut can only mean he misses her. Fair enough, since he's jumped off the platform and is now summersaulting his way into an Olympic-sized pool of feelings for her. An ocean of them, potentially. He hasn't hit the water yet.

Which steals the breath from his lungs, because what if she doesn't want him? She did say she was only after a conference fling. She's said to his face she wanted them to go back to being friends after this. She told him she's constantly horny for him. It'd be an ego boost if it wasn't tinged with the bitterness of Braden, plus it's not exactly the stuff long-lasting relationships are built on.

Shit. Cameron jerks his head side to side. The tie he's been fiddling with has gone crooked and too tight. He loosens it and smooths it back down, returning to his measured breathing.

He can't lose his focus now.

Even if there doesn't seem to be many signs pointing toward a relationship for him and Jules.

Braden and his ex-Cable colleagues are also going to be in the audience. He's extending an olive branch and reclaiming his professional reputation. He can't fuck it up because he's worrying if Jules will want anything to do with him once they're back in Canberra.

The tightness pulls on his shoulder blades, but he takes a steadying breath and rolls his shoulders back and down like Jules taught him. God, he wishes she were still here in his room, smiling at him from the bed or laughing at his hardcopy colour-coded schedules and scribbling her name into all the blank spaces like she had the other night. He could do with the boost of comfort she always injects in him. Listening to the song they danced to isn't the same as having her with him, hearing her laugh and seeing her smile and smelling her shampoo.

Fuck. He really does want to be with her properly.

He shakes his head before he can start that line of worrying again, stopping the music playing from his phone and sliding it into his pocket. After his presentation, and after he's kissed her breathless, he'll try to figure out if she's interested in more than a fling.

He pulls his room door shut behind him, feeling ready if not nerve-free. He doesn't expect to see Braden waiting in the corridor.

She shoots him her mega-watt smile and his stomach starts shrivelling up.

'Hey, Cam.'

'What are you doing here? How'd you get my room number?'

'I wanted to wish you luck before your presentation.' She slides up to him and he shuffles backwards, flight response thwarted as his back hits the wall. 'I know how nervous you get about these things.'

'Ambushing me on my way to give my talk was meant to help?'

'You'll be great. You always are.' She dismisses the

question. Her gaze roves over his face. He feels on display in a bad way, like an animal at the zoo. His fingers itch to push her away.

'I've missed you.'

Cameron's stomach bunches. She's really doing this now? After saying she remembered how nervous he gets? He doesn't doubt part of her means that, but his body floods with anxiety like spinning tops, making his hands shake. He crosses his arms, shoving them beneath his armpits.

'We broke up, remember.' He keeps it brief. He's got a presentation to get to and he wouldn't want to shoot the breeze with her even if he didn't.

'I remember. And I don't get it. We were having fun together, weren't we?'

'Maybe I didn't want just fun.' The words don't feel like a lie, but they make a hypocrite of him, considering what he's been doing with Jules.

Hang on. Back up.

Fuck.

A clear comparison forms from his anxious brain, one that sends his pulse into overdrive.

Is he in that same place again? Wanting something more out of a relationship with a woman he works with? A woman who doesn't see him as someone worthy of a serious relationship?

Tackiness creeps over his skin, but the thoughts crumble when Braden slides a hand up his bicep to his shoulders. Her fingers land on bare skin at his neck.

Braden tilts her head. 'Are you sure?'

He shudders. She's really offering *that*? Was she even serious about the coffee, or was this her end goal the whole time? Get Cameron between the sheets again. His breath tastes stale.

Braden continues to smile at him, ignoring every signal his body is giving out, while he works to unlock his clenched jaw and tell her to stop touching him.

His phone starts buzzing in his pocket, giving him an

excuse to move. 'I need to go. I have to get to the conference room.'

'Of course.' She shrugs, removing her hand and her gaze dips down his body quickly. 'I'll catch you later.'

It's not a question. It's probably not meant to be a threat either, but with the way his insides itch and rub against each other, it feels like it.

He flees down the corridor with the superimposed image of Braden and Jules stuck in his head like the afterimage of a nightmare.

* * *

Cameron's thoughts are all over the place as he waits at the side of the stage for his presentation to start. Jules in his bed that morning, in his shower. Matteo and his sisters telling him how he's feeling. Him finally realising they're right. His run-in with Braden, and the horrible tacky déjà vu sensation that history is repeating. He wanted more from that relationship too, just like he wants more from Jules now.

He tries to bat the thoughts away, the birds and anvils circling his head like a cartoon character, bashing into each other and ignoring all his attempts to centre himself and focus on his speech. No amount of blasting 80s pop through his headphones and rolling his shoulders makes it go away. Must be backlash from all the times over the last year he's kept them bottled up. Feelings for Jules, and how things ended with Braden, and how lonely he was in Canberra. That bottle has completely shattered since he confessed he likes Jules to Matteo this morning. There's nowhere for his feelings to settle now so they swirl around his body.

He smooths his shirt down and tugs at his tie. It feels like it's choking him, but he can't take it off or he'll look too casual.

From the side of the stage, he spots Jules in the audience. She winks at him and gestures to his phone.

He pulls it out and sees a text.

Jules: Sorry I can't provide a quickie in the wings, but just imagine what hearing that sexy voice of yours speak for an hour straight is going to do to me.
Jules: ;) ;) ;)

Cameron's blood pumps thick through his veins, rushing south, his body responding by rote to Jules's come-on even as a black hole starts seeding in his chest. Sex. She's talking about sex right before he's about to go onstage and give the presentation she knows is important to him.

There's no 'good luck', 'break a leg', 'you'll do great', 'roll your shoulders'. His phone trembles in his hand. No emotional support. Maybe he's an asshole for wanting it after the attitude he started this week with, but he craves it anyway.

Unable to blink or look away from the screen, he sees the Instagram notification pop up, covering whatever new messages Jules has sent.

BookyBraden has tagged you in a post.

His finger hovers over the notification. He shouldn't, he knows it can't be anything he'll want to see, but his finger is already pressing the message.

Cameron winces as the picture loads, black hole sucking more of him inside.

In the picture, he's lying on a beach towel, one hand braced behind his head and the other holding a book above his head to read. Braden has captioned it with an inoffensive description about the talk he's about to give, but he remembers it being worse when she first posted. Something about strong arms and reading books. It weirded him out at the time, but after hearing her dismiss him and their relationship, he'd gone back through her profile and the Cable account and the words had hit differently. He remembers the sick, roiling feeling in his gut he got when he went through her profile.

He's feeling it again now.

Because he's done it again. Given a co-worker power over his heart and his confidence.

He's been kidding himself with Jules, hasn't he? All those mushy feelings and impulsive desires to kiss her forehead in the morning and sleep curled around her and buy her fucking marshmallows. Jules has been clear from the start. All they have is a fling.

CHAPTER 26

His presentation was shit. He knew it ten minutes in by the fidgeting of people in their chairs and the lacklustre laughter at his jokes. He used to revel in public speaking, the ability to connect to a hundred people at a time and bring them all along on a journey with him. But he couldn't find that connection, no matter how hard he tried. As if the wall Chloe said he had against connection was operating at full force, invisible at the edge of the stage but tangible inside him. Maybe it wasn't at the edge of the stage at all, maybe it was wrapped around him like a cloak, travelling everywhere with him.

He had seen Braden and his ex-Cable colleagues in the audience and his throat dried up and he stumbled over a sentence. Then he'd caught Jules's gaze and his skin pulled tight and his focus slipped, thinking back to her texts and Braden's Instagram post, and his stomach had twisted into even more knots, the black hole Cameron-sized and inescapable.

Now, as he heads up to his room, it feels like he's swallowed an entire length of scratchy rope and it's rubbing his insides raw.

Jules is leaning against the wall by his door, her long legs stretching out in front of her. She smiles at him. It's pure seduction and it makes his stride falter. Where's the awkward woman from the car ride over? Yeah, Jules confessed to being comfortable around him, but this look on her face is like... like Braden.

'Good job up there.'

And now she's lying to him. His skin heats. 'Don't sugar-coat. It was crap.'

'It wasn't—' He shoots her a look and she drops the platitudes. 'Okay. The delivery wasn't your best, but the actual content was really good. If those Cable people didn't take copious notes, then they missed out.'

He pushes open his door with a heavy hand and she follows him inside.

'Content is only half the presentation,' he drops his stuff on the table, not caring as it spreads out messily. 'I was meant to make up for my dented professionalism with the Cable people, and instead I proved how deserving I was of demoting myself to Infinity. They're probably glad I don't work there anymore.'

He tugs the suffocating tie off and throws it away, then drops into one of the desk chairs, running his hands through his hair and messing it up. Like he did with his presentation.

'Their loss,' Jules says, walking over to him. 'Infinity is lucky to have you. Patricia thinks you're a marketing genius.'

She massages the tight muscles of his shoulders and it feels good, it does. Physically. But.

'I'm not in the mood, Jules.'

'That's okay. We can just do this.'

She continues working the muscles in his shoulders but he doesn't get any less tense. 'I don't want to do this.'

'No worries.' Her hands fall away. 'I have no idea how to give a proper massage anyway. What about a walk down to Circular Quay? Another ice-cream on me? Or one of those sugary coffees you like.'

'No. Not this.' He sucks in a breath, digs his own fist into his stomach. Spits out the words with his back turned so he can't see her expression. 'The fling.'

'What?' The word carries mixed emotions, enough he can't pick any single one out.

He spins the chair to face her. Her lips are parted and her brow is furrowed. She stares at him, her blue eyes the shade of a summer sky.

He fumbles the top two buttons of his shirt open. 'It was a

bad idea from the start. Mixing work and relationships never works. I know that. I'd forgotten temporarily because you...'

'Because I what?'

'Distracted me.' He curls his fists on his thighs. 'You saw my presentation. That's what happens when I let myself get distracted.'

'Hang on.' She shifts her weight on her feet and frowns. 'Are you blaming me for how your presentation went?'

'I've been spending all my free time with you.' There's an annotated schedule on the table behind him that will attest to that. 'I only ran through my presentation once last night because of your ridiculous dance suggestion. And you spent the night here.'

'Because you asked me to stay.' Her voice gains a harsh edge and his insides jolt and jar.

'Well I shouldn't have.'

'You were—you were the one who offered to be in this fling with me that first night.'

'And now I'm taking it back.' The words fall like granite boulders into the heavy air of the room. Hurt as much lurching out of his throat, too. 'This fling is over.'

Jules takes a few steps away from him, crossing her arms over her body and pursing her lips together.

He can't look at her, at the defensive state he pushed her into. On purpose. Because he has to if he wants to protect himself from destruction. So he's pushing her away, pushing her so far back they'll probably never even get back to what they had before this.

He stands and starts sorting his desk, gathering all the wasted paper of his presentation speech and programs into a pile. They're going straight in the bin. Or maybe he'll take them home and set them on fire. Seems fitting.

Because he's annoyed and watching something burning down to ash could be poetic. Annoyed at Jules, sure, a little, but mostly at himself for getting played again. He's the one who offered to be her fling on that first night, who can't resist his urges around her, who let his feelings grow beyond his control and ended up getting himself into the same fucking mess that tanked his relationship with Braden and his career at Cable in a matter of days.

Even now, as he glances over at her, he finds her alluring as fuck with her flushed cheeks and fiery eyes, but he can't go there. Infinity is going to hear about how much he bombed his presentation and it's going to be another smear on his professional name. He can't fall back any further after the step down he took to leave Cable. He's got some kind of wall around him? Great. He's going to shore it up so he doesn't put his job at risk by letting his focus be pulled.

So he has to stop being with Jules. Fling, friendship and all. Now he's aware of his feelings, he can't be anything less than all or nothing with her. And she obviously doesn't want all of him.

'There's still another day of the conference.' Jules moves to stand on the other side of the desk from him, braces her hands on the surface.

'You haven't had enough sex already? Worked me out of your system?' He yanks papers from beneath her splayed hands. They rip but it doesn't matter anymore.

'Worked you out…' She jerks her head side to side. 'When have I ever given you the impression that I only wanted you for sex?'

He laughs harshly. 'The fling was a bit of a giveaway. How about all the sexting? When you stared at my ass when I got out of bed this morning? The text before my talk about having a quickie.' The list is easy to assemble, everything right there for him. What a fool he's been to think they could have had more.

'I was trying to distract you! Get you to relax.'
'And instead I bombed my presentation.'
'That wasn't—that's unfair to pin that on me.'
'I'm not pinning it on you. I'm at fault, too.' And Braden.

The papers buckle in his hands. 'Which is why I'm taking steps to make sure it doesn't happen again.'

'No.' She straightens up and stares him down. 'You're running. From this. From us.'

He never should have told her about the running thing. Her throwing it in his face now, like she knows him, hurts. The grinding in his chest kind of hurt.

'There is no us.' Listing all those anecdotes, it's clear he never had an opening with Jules, no matter what Matteo and his sisters thought they saw. They were outside observers. He got the real inside look. 'This was a one-week fling and it's over now.'

The table between them may as well be a continent.

He watches Jules's expression morph from anger and determination, through something like disappointment, skirting around hurt, before her eyes start glistening.

'Cameron, please. Don't. This isn't...' Her voice is choked and barely above a whisper. She looks around the room, searching for what, he has no idea, but the more she lingers, fighting for them, the worse he feels. Shouldn't she be saying 'this sucks, but fine' and walking out? All she's losing is another day of sex. He's losing a potential relationship and a friend.

He grabs the edge of the desk tight so he doesn't walk around to fold her body against his. Whisper reassurances into her silky hair and smooth his palm down the curve of her back.

Moments pass, Cameron's stomach grinding itself down, until she focuses back on him.

She faces him front on, takes a breath so big he sees her chest push out. Can't she just go? So he can get on with moving on? From her and his disastrous talk and his poor decisions. He can see it in her stance though, the way her fists are curled by her side, the way her eyes don't glisten anymore. She's going to fight for them.

A flurry inside his chest attempts to dispel the grinding,

even before she speaks, slow and steady like she wants every word to be chiselled into his brain.

'It isn't just sex, Cameron.'

'Yes it is.' The reply is automatic. And a lie. He wouldn't have fallen for her if it was true.

In her eyes, determination fights with vulnerability. The slight tremble in her hands makes her next words all the more precious. And all the more painful. 'Not to me.'

Something inside his body pangs, the part that wants to believe. But how can he when all evidence points towards him being her fling and nothing more.

He can't have hope. He's already fallen so far. He can't let the temptation of Jules exist. He has to end things permanently.

'It was to me.' The words are charcoal on his tongue. 'It was just sex.'

He sees the words hit her and her eyes become watery again. She jerks like he's gone over there and punched her in the gut.

Part of Cameron wrenches off inside him, the hopeful part, and plummets painfully into his gut like a sheet of ice into the sea. He knows exactly how she feels in this moment because he's been in her shoes before, with Braden.

He's an asshole for turning it on her but he knows it works, and sure enough, Jules gathers herself with her arms folded around her middle and walks away from him.

CHAPTER 27

Her hands wrapped around her middle are the only thing holding Jules together as she enters her hotel room. If she uncrosses them, she'll fall apart. Her skin feels thin and insubstantial, and her insides swollen and tender.

She makes her way out onto the tiny balcony and slides down to the floor, tilting her head back to chase the warmth of the sun. It reaches her as if through layers of glass. Muted and dull. The fresh air doesn't help either, because she can barely get a proper breath in. Her stomach shifts, nausea creeping up her throat.

So much for her perfect track record. Goodbye one hundred per cent success rate.

Cameron doesn't want her. Never really wanted her in the way she did him, and now even their fling has been ripped from her. It's like Todd all over again, right down to the stabbing pain between her shoulder blades.

Her breath rattles into her body unsteadily. Sex and pillow talk. What a ridiculous idea. She should have been honest from the start and told him she liked him, because now, even when she did tell him it was more than sex for her – fought through those stomping ants crawling all over her skin, in her lungs and down her throat to tell him – he didn't believe her.

And why would he? She *has* been focusing mostly on sex this week. Initiating it in his shower, at the Opera House, letting her body drive her instead of making him rehearse his presentation last night.

A sob breaks through and she squeezes her arms tighter around herself.

She should message Cat and Tori. They'll make her feel better. But her phone is in her room and she can't find the energy to move. She may throw up if she does.

Thinking about Cat and Tori at least brings some clarity to her stuffy head. There may have been those sexual interactions, but there was other stuff between her and Cameron too. Their dinner date and their breakfast chats and their discussion last night. He even said himself he was opening up to her, getting emotional. Has he forgotten those moments or—

Another sob and the tears start sliding down her face. He can't have forgotten something that happened less than 24 hours ago. It mustn't have meant anything to him, except maybe regret. It doesn't matter what he said in bed last night now, because he's made his feelings clear. It was only about sex for him.

She keeps her arms wrapped around her torso and lets the tears drip off her chin.

* * *

The next morning is tough. After a restless night, she wants to stay in bed and avoid Cameron and her feelings, but she's made commitments. To have coffee with James and to get that replacement bottle opener for Samantha.

She tries to focus on the positives from yesterday, remind herself how invigorating talking with James was, but it all comes back to Cameron. Being with him made her confident in voicing her wants. Without him providing inspiration with his own story, she wouldn't have been so open with James, or told Samantha she was thinking of looking for a new job.

But she didn't have the confidence when it really counted. To be honest with him sooner.

She slips quietly into the breakfast area after scanning the tables for Cameron and not seeing him. She avoids the muesli station and sits at a table facing away from the entrance, or else she'll be looking for him every second. She doesn't want to know how he's coping. She doesn't want to see his expression when he sees her. Dismissal, anger, friendliness without heat.

She plays with her food more than eating it, until a voice interrupts her brooding.

'Jules?'

She moves her head slowly, looking up at the man beside her table.

'Matteo. Hi.' She sounds like she's got feathers shoved down her throat.

'Hey. Mind if I join you?'

She has no energy to feel either way on the request, so she gestures to the free seat.

Matteo drops into it. 'So. Cameron told me you guys ended your fling.'

The words are unexpected. Her knife scrapes against the bottom of her plate. She waits to feel strange that Matteo knows about what she's been doing with his friend, but she doesn't feel much of anything except resignation.

'You've seen him already?' Maybe she does want to know how he's dealing with the end of them.

'Gym this morning.'

'Oh.' So Cameron felt normal enough, unaffected enough to get up as usual and head to the gym, while she snoozed her alarm five times and had to talk herself into a shower. Great. If she was hoping he was as distraught by their break-up as she was, it doesn't seem like it.

'So you know what happened?' she asks.

'I got an incredibly truncated version from Cameron and I've filled in the blanks with my own observations.'

'Which are?'

'That he made a mistake and he still wants you. Wants to date you.'

Jules laughs harshly, dropping the cutlery and giving up on eating. 'Doubt it. He told me it was only about sex.'

Matteo swears and runs a palm over his shaved head. 'He didn't tell me that part. What a self-sabotaging bastard.' He drops his hand onto the table. 'Look. I know Cameron, so I'm certain that was a lie.'

'He sounded pretty sure to me.'

'He's good at talking himself into believing something, even if it isn't true. Besides.' He leans in and whispers, 'He told me yesterday morning he wanted to be with you properly.'

Jules's stomach flips over. He did?

Then warmth turns to fiery heat as anger bubbles in her gut. If that's true, why did he break things off so brutally a few hours later? What changed? His feelings mustn't be as strong as hers, if she believes Matteo that they're there at all.

'Why're you telling me this?' She clenches her hands around her orange juice.

'Before I answer that, can I ask you something personal?'

'Okay,' she says slowly.

'Was it just about sex for you?'

Jules blinks. She knows Matteo is Cameron's close friend, but she doesn't know the guy. How can she tell him when it took her so long to work up the courage to tell Cameron?

But Matteo is clearly working up to something and if nothing else, she's curious to hear more about Cameron. That ache in her chest has had no time to fade and it wants to learn. Wants to understand how they got to where they are when it thought they were doing so well.

'It wasn't.'

'And would you want to date him if you could?'

A lump forms in her throat as images flourish in her mind; their dinner together, gelatos by the wharf, even as far back as sitting with him and his sisters on their first day here. Further back. Their phone calls at work, how he's been the bright centre of her days for months.

She nods.

'Thought so. In that case…' Matteo leans further in, lowering his voice. 'There are some things I think you should know about Cameron. Then you can tell me if you still believe he meant what he said.'

* * *

Matteo wanted the conversation to be private, so they end up outside the hotel, walking down to the harbour, nursing take-away coffees that Matteo paid for. Jules's stomach roils like a ship in a storm so she wraps her hands around the cup without trying to drink any.

'So. You know about Braden?' Matteo begins his explanation.

Bringing up Cameron's ex can't be a good sign.

'A little,' she says. 'Cameron said she was his ex. That they worked together at Cable.'

'Yep. Both true. Did he say anything about their breakup?'

'All he said was they didn't want the same thing. That they weren't on the same page about how serious it was.'

'Of course he did,' Matteo sighs. He takes a slow drag of coffee as they pass beneath Circular Quay train station and head in the direction of the art gallery and the railing that Cameron kissed her against two nights ago. When she'd been flying high to be acting like a couple in public with him.

Though her coffee is hot in her hands, her fingers feel cold.

'Alright,' Matteo says. 'I'm going to tell you the full story of what happened, because I love that man, and I think he deserves another chance with you. And you with him. Obviously, no pressure to do anything after you hear it, but you need to know where he's coming from to get why he reacted so strongly. And why I think he lied to you about it being just sex.'

Should she say no? It's Cameron's story to tell. But the ache inside her quivers and she wants, *needs* to understand. 'Okay.'

Matteo leads them to a wooden bench in the sun with a view of the Opera House, and a portal to memories with Cameron.

'So him and Braden,' he starts after they sit. Jules focuses on him like it'll blur out the memories all around her. 'Both worked in marketing. Hit it off straight away and started dating pretty quickly. All normal stuff. He was smitten, but then Braden started posting pictures of Cameron to the company's social media accounts. It's not uncommon, a lot of publishers try to go for that personal angle these days, all that behind the scenes, meet the team stuff. But the thing is, they weren't always staged photos.'

'Staged?' Jules risks a sip of coffee.

'Like Cameron in the office holding a stack of the new releases. She was sharing private pictures.'

Jules's eyes widen. The coffee curdles in her stomach. 'Private pictures?'

'Not that kind of private.' Matteo holds a hand up. 'But pictures of him at the beach reading a Cable book, or like, after a run with an audiobook. She never asked his permission and the traffic on them was too good for them to be taken down.'

'That's terrible.' Jules cringes, putting her coffee beside her. Her stomach is too unsettled to contemplate it.

'No shit. Cameron wasn't comfortable with that, but he liked her, so he let it slide. Too damn giving for his own good, sometimes. One of those moments where he talked himself into being fine with something he wasn't actually fine with.'

Jules nods slowly, foreboding creeping like spiders up her spine.

'Then a couple of months later, me and Cameron were in a meeting room hashing out – doesn't matter.' He shakes his head and rests one leg over the other, gripping his calf. 'Point is, Braden was in the room next door on the phone with someone and those walls aren't exactly soundproof. Meant Cameron heard every word of her explaining to her friend how he wasn't the guy you settled down with. That he was the hot guy you had fun with before looking for that other guy.'

Jules's skin goes icy, as cold as Matteo's voice has become. 'I had no idea.'

'Neither did he. So hearing the woman he was dating tell her friend they weren't serious, that he was just a bit of fun...' Matteo's eyes are hard. 'Plus she also said he was dead weight in the marketing team and his best contribution was his abs. He couldn't talk himself into being okay with that.'

Jules's mouth hangs open.

There aren't words. The insensitivity. The immorality. The—

She balls her hands and presses them to her stomach. 'I don't know what to say.'

'Neither does he. He doesn't talk about it,' Matteo says needlessly. 'I'm ninety-five per cent sure if I hadn't been with him at the time, he wouldn't have told me the full story of what happened.'

'And that's why he left Cable? He said working there wasn't good for him. But—that's—'

'Yeah.' Matteo doesn't seem to have the words either. 'And that's why I think he ended the fling. He's mixing you and Braden up. He's trying to protect himself from getting hurt again.'

Jules stares out at the water, trying to connect what Matteo's told her with what she's heard from Cameron himself. It's worse than he let on. His sisters' concern makes so much more sense now, how they talked about him being his old self around her, and how much they worried about what being around Braden would mean for him.

Then the realisation hits.

'Oh god. Oh god.' She turns to Matteo, the chill moving up her fingers to her heart. 'He's mixing us up? But that means… he agreed to a fling with me! He's practically been reliving that whole situation, but with full awareness he was, and I've been letting him. Why would he do that? Put himself in a position that's just like what he went through with Braden?'

Matteo raises his eyebrows. 'You need me to spell it out? He likes you, Jules, even if he was pretending he didn't. I could see it at the welcome drinks. That's probably why he said yes in the first place.'

'But *I* never would have said yes if I'd known.'

Matteo nods, eyes losing the last of their hardness. 'Which

is why I'm trusting you with this story. Cameron goes to great lengths to make sure no one knows it. He doesn't like people thinking poorly of him.'

Jules's hands itch. She reaches for her cold coffee, drinking it for something to do. It doesn't sit right in her stomach.

'So what now?' she asks.

He shrugs. 'Like I said, no pressure to act, but I thought you deserved to know where he was coming from, in case that changes your perspective on things. Do you still think he meant it when he said it was just sex to him? That he'd agree to be a bit of fun to someone again if there wasn't something more behind it?'

'I… I don't want to believe he meant it.' But the hard look in his eyes when he said it to her didn't show anything but determination. The only way to test if Matteo is right is for her to be completely honest and hope the truth of how she feels will cut through the untruths he's convinced himself about their relationship.

Matteo nods, standing up and throwing his coffee cup into a nearby bin. 'If you'd met Cameron before he'd been with Braden… I think things would have worked out a lot differently between you two. And if you can get Cameron to pull his head out of the sand, I think he'd see that.'

Matteo departs with a nod, leaving her sitting on the bench with a million new thoughts and feelings to process. She stares at the harbour without really seeing it. People walk past her, birds flock, a busker plays guitar further along the path, but it's all background noise to Cameron's voice inside her head saying, 'there is no us', 'it was just sex', 'mixing work and relationships never works.'

At least she's got better context for that last one now.

She drains the last of her cold coffee. The fact that she's had a part in piling on Cameron's insecurities makes her stomach clench uncomfortably tight until she's worried the coffee is going to come back up.

It's obvious what she needs to do now. She needs to tell

the truth, like she'd been planning to. Tell him she wants a proper relationship, not a conference fling. She wants the entire man, flaws and vulnerabilities and all. He's given her the confidence this week to be honest about what she wants. With him, with James, with Samantha. With herself. She can't hold back from him any longer, not if she wants the chance to be with him, and that means laying her emotions bare and hoping Matteo was right that Cameron does want to date her, despite what he told her last night.

But even if she doesn't believe Matteo, even if Cameron did mean what he said, that she was just sex to him – Jules's stomach lurches and she presses a fist to her lips – she has to make it up to him. Make him understand that for her at least, he'd been more than sex the entire time. That he offers so much more to someone beyond what happens in the bedroom.

She shudders as a legion of ants appear over her entire body. He's already broken things off with her and this could make it all that much worse, completely kill her chance at a relationship with him. But she has to do it. Even if he doesn't take back what he said, even if they don't end up dating, he needs to know he's more than a bit of fun to her. He's more than that. Period.

CHAPTER 28

Jules keeps her trade stall visit short, consulting the vendor map to avoid seeing Cameron at Infinity's stand as she locates Samantha's bottle opener and finds James's stall to load up on pamphlets. She asks him for a raincheck on the coffee, since she's not in the right head space to talk about job prospects when she's busy figuring out what exactly she's going to say to Cameron.

She still hasn't messaged Cat and Tori about what's happened, despite them checking in with her. Hopefully, after what she's about to do, she'll have something more definite to say. Either 'we're dating' or 'he never wants to see me again'. There won't be a middle ground for them after her confession.

She still has to do it.

Her ant friends take up residence across her back and shoulders as she stands in front of Cameron's room, taking breath after breath, waiting to feel ready, for the ants to disappear or her pulse to not be quite so fast. There's no feeling ready for this though. Proposing to Todd barely prepared her. The stakes seem so much higher now, though they've only had four days of being together.

She still wants more, and she hopes she gets it, but equally as important is making sure Cameron sees his value and worth. Understands she wasn't treating him like Braden did. For her sake, yes, but more so for his.

She knocks on his door and holds her breath.

It only takes a few seconds and then he's there, framed in the doorway wearing grey slacks and a navy polo. His hair is a mess and there's stubble on his jaw again. He looks gorgeous. He looks weary.

'Jules.' The door closes a fraction and his eyes narrow.

'Hi.' Her pulse ticks up again.

This is where she should start talking, or blurt out 'I'm falling for you', but the urge to fill in awkward silences has fled from her. Maybe the ants crawling over her skin have carried it away, along with all the phrases she'd planned while walking back to the hotel.

Cameron's gaze hovers at her ear. 'What're you doing here?'

She swallows. Her fingers start tapping the side of her thighs. 'I want to talk. I don't think you meant it when you said it was just sex to you.'

'Don't worry, it was good sex.' His caramel eyes focus on hers. They're so hard, none of the melting warmth they normally possess. 'But it didn't mean anything.'

Her blood heats, chasing away the cold she's carried since her conversation with Matteo. She feels better equipped to deal with the conversation, can see behind the smoke and mirrors. Cameron's pushing her to get a reaction he wants, some kind of justification for his running away.

She doesn't buy it, and she won't let him take away what it meant to her. 'What about last night? We shared something special. It was deeper than sex.'

He averts his gaze and swallows roughly. Has she struck a nerve?

She tries pushing against it again. 'Matteo told me about Braden. The full story.'

There's a pause, long enough for hope to start growing in her chest that Cameron's going to listen to her, but when his head angles back to her, anger is on his face.

'That wasn't his story to tell.' His jaw clenches and his eyes glint like steel.

He goes to shut the door but Jules slams her hand against it and locks her elbow.

'I know it wasn't. I would have preferred it coming from you, but you've been hurt and you're hiding and Matteo was only trying to help me see where you were coming from. He doesn't think you meant it either.'

'Because he's a romantic.'

'No, because he's your friend and he had a backstory that I didn't.' Jules wedges the door further open. 'But now I do and I see you clearer than before, and I get – I *hope* I get – why you're running from me.'

His eyebrows lift. 'You still think I'm running?'

Her heart jumps into her throat at the incredulous tone. But she has to believe he is.

'You told me yourself that's what you do. I think our arrangement reminded you of your relationship with Braden. Sex focused. And because that didn't end well, and because you worked together, you're running away from us so it doesn't have the chance to go bad too.'

Her hands are sweaty and her back itches. Remembering to breathe is less a priority than getting the words out. 'So sue me, or call me naive or a hopeless romantic, but knowing that, it makes me… I don't think you meant what you said the other night.' Her shoulders bunch up. 'At least I… really hope you didn't.'

Cameron's gaze drops to the rise and fall of her chest. His fingers tighten around the door but he doesn't try to shut it. It's a small encouragement, but Jules will take what she can.

'You've had your fling,' he says, voice hollow. 'Why should it matter?'

'Because the fling isn't what I really wanted. It's never been what I wanted.'

'You literally told me you wanted a conference fling.'

'No, I said *my friends* said I should have one.'

Cameron's hand drops from the door and he shifts his weight on his feet. His hands go to his hips for a moment, then slip inside his pockets instead. She watches them curl.

'What are you saying.' His voice is scratchy, gaze darting over her face. 'You didn't want that? I coerced you?'

'No, Cameron. *No.*' She reaches out to touch him then

snatches her hand back when he shies away. The empty ache inside her pulses. 'Of course not. I went willingly and very, very eagerly.'

'After you saw me with my shirt off.'

'I—what?' Jules blinks. He says it like a fact but she doesn't get where his assumption is coming from.

And how are they getting so far away from what she wants to say? She can't stand here and watch him talk himself into believing the worst of her. Of him. Of their relationship.

The ants crawl but she puts as much force into her rebuttal as she can. 'That's not true.'

'In case you've forgotten, you denied pretty heavily in the car that you would say yes if I was the person offering to have a fling with you. Then less than 24 hours later, *after seeing me shirtless,* suddenly you're interested.'

'That is... that's completely...' She doesn't know what it is, but after hearing Matteo talk about Cameron's history with Braden, she's horrified, literally sick to her stomach, that Cameron thought she was using him the same way.

'That's bullshit,' she says firmly. She'd already been interested, for one thing, and if anything pushed her over the edge, it was seeing him around his sisters at lunch, and the way he comforted her when they bumped into each other outside the bathrooms.

'Not from where I'm standing.' His arms fold across his chest.

Jules doesn't know what she can say. Everything she says or does, now and for the past week, he's twisting up to fit his belief. Talking himself into things, just like Matteo said.

'Don't twist my actions up to justify your choice.' She tries to make him see what he's doing.

'You got your fling. Why're you trying to turn this into something else?'

'I already said it. This was never just a fling for me, Cameron!'

His entire body goes tight. She sees the strain in his arms, at his neck and in the pursing of his mouth. It's like he's closing himself off to her. Like he's building a wall.

She takes a fortifying breath then confesses to her feelings, hoping she can break through with pure, unfiltered emotion. 'I have never wanted you just for your body and for sex. I want... I want *you*. All of you. The music nerd and the marketing geek and the fitness junkie and the paint-by-numbers guy, the one who jumps around the room to 80s pop with me.'

Jules takes a deep breath. It shakes unsteadily into her lungs but she powers through.

'I've liked you for months, Cameron. We spoke so many times on the phone and you're so patient and kind and, honestly, the one person whose phone calls I actually *wanted* to answer. You were like this little calm in the storm of my day.'

His jaw clenches. 'But you hadn't seen me.'

Knowing why he's fixated on the point digs blades into her stomach. She can't walk away from this conversation without him believing he's more than his appearance, even if that's all she walks away from it with.

'That didn't matter. I may not have seen you but I *saw* you, the person you are. This was never only about sex for me. It was about you, being with you. I was working up the courage to ask you out after this week. I want to date you. And have sex with you, sure, but I thought that would come later. And I'm so sorry, Cameron, so sorry for putting you in a position that made you feel how Braden made you feel. Please believe that it meant more to me than that. You're not just some *body* to me.'

His arms drop heavy to his sides. 'How can I believe that, Jules? You started our whole thing off by asking us to define what a fling was. I've seen the way you look at my body.'

It sounds dismissive on the surface, but she's had months of listening to Cameron speak, so she can pick out the hint of want there too. Like he wants to believe her.

'How I look at *you*.' She shakes her head and dares take a

half-step closer to him. 'You offer more than your appearance, so much more. I should've been clear with you from the start about my feelings, then you'd get what I'm saying.'

He swallows roughly. 'Feelings?'

'Yes. I... I'm... I want to be with you, Cameron. Long-term. I want the chance to fall in love with you.'

Her stomach drops as she says the words, because she knows this is her final lifeline back to their relationship.

Jules waits for words or actions, but his face goes slack, lips parting on a punched exhale. Gradually, his eyes pinch at the corners, and his mouth compresses into a flat line. And then he stays cast in stone, barely moving except for the rise and fall of his chest.

Her stomach plummets then lifts, sickeningly quick. This moment? It's worse than Todd ending things. Worse than her parents announcing they were moving overseas, or her brother leaving her behind for Tasmania. Because Cameron's right here still, but he's moved beyond her reach.

The nervous rambling returns, making up for lost time.

'If you say yes, we can take it slow, as slow as you need. We don't have to have sex again until you're ready. You can blindfold me. We can do it in the dark. But that's not—that's not what I want to focus on.' She reaches for him then. Grabs for his hand and holds it tight between hers. His gaze flicks to her and she sees it, vulnerability and hope. The same emotions she's feeling right now. 'I want to be with you in every way two people can: emotionally, romantically, physically. I'm asking you to be my boyfriend. I'm asking you to not run from us.'

His fingers twitch in her grip. She hears him swallow, and a tiny sound, almost a whine, emerges from his throat before he speaks. 'I can't.'

Ice slides down her spine as he pulls his hand from her grip. She can't move her limbs quick enough to halt the door this time. The snick of the lock is as loud as a snare drum.

'Wait, wait. Cameron?' She presses her palms to the door.

Silence from inside. Only the sound of her blood rushing in her ears. She has to try anyway.

'Please. If we can't—' Her throat closes up, clogging with clambering ants. 'I can't bear walking away from this conference and have you assuming something untrue about yourself. Please tell me you at least believe you're more than your appearance. To me and the world.'

More silence.

'Cameron?'

She holds her breath, doesn't move, presses her ear against the door and strains. But there's nothing. No breathing, no footsteps, no acknowledgement of her words.

And now there's no them either.

CHAPTER 29

The end of the fling with Jules should be a clean break. It doesn't feel like it.

Cameron paces his room, antsy, like he wants to run, and it's not away this time. No. It's back to Jules.

But he can't.

Seeing her nearly crying, watching her fight for them, tell him that she wants the chance to fall in love with him... Only the toughest, most closed-off person could watch that emotional confession and not feel something. His gut was tugging him to her, but there was still that itchy doubt inside him. That history was repeating itself.

At the end of the day, words – no matter how pretty, or romantic, or gut-wrenchingly honest they seem – are only words. It's actions that truly reveal a person's wants and Jules's actions were pretty clearly about the one thing this week.

So she's not exactly like Braden, she came back and fought for them. Fine. But he still feels like a wreck in the aftermath of a relationship, same as with Braden.

He has to ride this out until it doesn't feel so raw. Expunge the feelings from inside until he can't remember the taste of her or the noises she makes when she comes or the warmth in his chest when she smiles at him, so when they're back in the office on Monday, his job performance won't be hurt. At least this time, he won't be forced to see his ex face-to-face every day.

His gut twists. He can't even properly claim Jules as an ex, since they were never officially anything. He can't loiter in the hotel room any longer, either. The place is stacked full of memories of Jules and he's chasing that clean break.

Cameron does a final check that everything has been packed and nothing is lost beneath the bed or in the wardrobe. Nothing. The only thing he's leaving behind besides memories is the pile of papers shoved into the bin by the desk.

Satchel slung over a shoulder and suitcase in hand, Cameron walks out.

Someone's waiting in the corridor for him. His heart lifts, foolishly, hopefully – and isn't that telling – but it clatters back into place fast. It's not Jules. It's Braden. Fuck.

He pulls the door shut with force, frowning already. 'What?'

'Hey, Cam.' The mega-watt smile appears. 'Let's grab that coffee before you head back to Canberra.'

She doesn't even phrase it like a question.

He wheels his suitcase in front of his body like a barrier. 'Stop. Just stop.'

Braden does. Arguing with Jules, having to force himself to follow through on his decision, has worn away all care for social niceties. He already tanked his presentation. Pleasantries here are barely going to make a dent. He may as well end this whatever-the-fuck-it-is with Braden today, too. Then he's leaving it all in Sydney, so things can go back to normal in Canberra. A new normal, maybe a lonely normal – his heart misses Jules's smile already – but a safe one behind his invisible wall.

He wraps both hands tightly around the handle of his suitcase. 'I don't want to get coffee with you. I don't want to chat with you. I have zero interest in getting back with you in any way.' Every word rips from him like pulling off a Band-Aid, revealing new shiny skin beneath. Is this what Jules felt when she confessed to him?

'You hurt me, Braden. You abused my trust and you made me doubt myself and every single relationship since.'

Like his one with Jules. It's over now because of that doubt.

'What?' Braden's eyebrows draw together. 'Where is this coming from? You never said anything about this while we were dating.'

'I shouldn't have had to.'

Braden rolls her eyes. 'I'm not a mind-reader, Cameron. We could have talked about this. We still can. Let's get that coffee.'

His grip tightens on the suitcase. 'Like you could have asked my permission before you posted photos of me to the company Instagram?'

'Oh.' Her eyes widen as she nods slowly. 'That's what this is about. I'm sorry for that. Of course I should have asked, gotten your consent, but I assumed—'

'That's not what this is about. This is about—it's about—' The words lodge in his throat.

She tilts her head in *that* way and they fly out of his mouth.

'It's about you telling your friend my brain was useless at work, but thank god my abs were marketable.' Acid drips from the words and his body heats like he's about to turn into a supernova. 'That I was the guy you had fun with before you found someone to settle down with.'

Braden rocks back on her heels. Pinpricks of colour dot her cheeks and when she speaks, it's not to apologise. 'When did you hear that?'

'At Cable. I was in the meeting room next door when you were having that conversation.'

She crosses her arms over her chest, voice small when she says, 'You broke up with me the next day. I remember wondering if it was karma.'

Karma? That's one way of looking at it. 'We wanted different things, things you never made clear to me, and after I found out I couldn't look at you without feeling like my chest was being crushed.'

She flinches, but steps in so her knees rest against his suitcase.

'I didn't realise.' There's true shame in her expression, but it's too little too late. 'I honestly thought we were on the same page about what we wanted. I'm sorry.'

The words hit his chest and bounce off. There's no place for any of her words to penetrate beyond the wall he had to throw back up to be able to end things with Jules. 'Bit late for that.'

Face pinched, she stares up at him with eyes he used to find alluring. 'I didn't mean to hurt you, Cam. You never should have heard that.'

'No. I shouldn't have *overheard* that. You should have told me to my face how you were feeling.'

Like Jules did. His hands go clammy, and a pressure settles on his shoulders.

'You could have, too.'

Braden's trying to protect herself, shift some blame to him for eavesdropping. The total opposite of what Jules did earlier. Confess immediately to what Matteo had told her, then fucking rip her chest open and show her heart to him.

Fuck. He accused her of being like Braden but she did the one thing he'd been angry that Braden hadn't.

He shouldn't be comparing Braden and Jules. It's crass. They're two entirely different people, and—

Shit.

Shit.

Shit.

It's what Carrie and Chloe and Matteo have been saying all along.

He turns away from Braden. He needs to be away from this. He's said what he needed to and he needs time to process the realisation.

'Wait, Cam.'

His fists curl but he turns around. Braden looks smaller than she ever has, a dejected curve to her shoulders.

'I hope you know... you are the kind of person someone would be lucky to settle down with. I hope you find her.'

He inhales slowly and counts to four. It's scarily close to

what Jules said, but hearing it from Braden is... he shakes his head. Incomprehensible. He doesn't pay attention to the quiet whisper from the part of him he thought had wrenched off earlier, the part that's been slowly reattaching itself throughout his conversation with Braden: that he's already found her.

When he pushes the breath out, he tries to expel all the negativity holding onto his breakup with Braden lined his body with. He can't carry that and his breakup with Jules. His body isn't made for it. 'I hope you find your person, too.'

He doesn't wait to see her react beyond a shallow nod before he turns and heads for the lifts, glancing once at Jules's closed room door, gut twisting as he forces himself to walk past without stopping.

CHAPTER 30

Getting closure feels crap. Like he's a sponge that's been wrung out by a giant pair of hands. His chest is tight and there's a pounding in his head. Yet as he loads his luggage into the hire car, those feelings turn into the kind of ache he gets post-workout. One that lets you know you've done something worthwhile for yourself.

His mind clears too, all the racing thoughts condensing down to the biggest, most important few.

He's got his closure with Braden.

He and Jules are done.

It's better this way.

Who's he kidding? The thing stuck on his mind is that Jules and Braden are different people.

Carrie said it to his face. Matteo said it to his face. They're different people.

Their actions may have been similar, but that doesn't mean their motivations were. He knows that, because Jules told him what was driving her choices, and god knows it was the exact opposite of what Braden's were.

He was given all the information he needed to make him and Jules work like he'd wanted them to yesterday morning, and he still screwed himself over. And Jules.

The clean break he was after? Yeah. Not so clean now. For him, at least.

He has to do something to fix this.

Thankfully, they've got an entire three hour car ride to sort things out. He'll apologise. He'll explain. He'll come clean, finally, about the Braden stuff while he can't physically run away. He'll tell Jules how he felt yesterday morning and the night she slept in his bed, that warm whirlwind inside him. He should've trusted that feeling instead of listening to his frightened brain banging on about Braden.

He leans against the open boot, waiting for Jules, planning it out. He'll tell her how he feels right now in this moment, how his chest hurts, a band of tightness snapped around his ribs because he knows she's hurt. Then he'll start from the beginning, with their first phone call and how it was sunshine on an otherwise grey day. He'll confess to avoiding her because he didn't trust himself not to catch feelings. He'll talk about every time he leaned into her, because it felt impossible not to.

She's going to be pissed at him and he deserves it, but if he can just make her listen, then maybe he has a shot at erasing the past 24 hours and all the shit he said.

His phone buzzes in his pocket. He pulls it out and his gut drops.

Jules: Don't wait for me to drive back. I'll make my own way.

His hand clenches around the phone, shoulders bunching. Fuck.

Now what?

He can't say everything he needs to in a text. Would she even read it?

His gut sinks like an anvil in his torso. What if it's too late? He didn't chase her and he didn't pull any punches when he broke them up. He fucking told her to her face it was only about the physical, and that seeds doubts that undermine an entire relationship. If he's any indication, you need an entire year to get over those, and you don't want to get back with the person who made you feel that way once you do. An apology text won't cut it. And wasn't he the one saying he wanted to talk *with* her, not *to* her? Yet he chose to end things in a way that made conversation impossible. He took that option from her.

Not wanting to leave her without a reply, he sends a simple 'okay'. He wants to add more, but no written words seem enough to convey his feelings. 'I'm sorry' or 'I didn't mean it', which the anguished yearning in his belly is screaming at him, loud and clear.

Of course he didn't fucking mean it. Only being interested in Jules for the sex? He rubs his fist in a circle over his aching chest. That's not what it was. How could it be, when from their first phone call he'd been avoiding her because he knew he'd fall for her if he didn't.

Being proved right isn't satisfactory. It's the opposite. Like he's been slapped around the head and his ears are ringing. A bitter laugh passes his lips. He was so desperate to stop history repeating, yet here he is, feeling like he had after things with Braden ended. Actually, scratch that. He feels even worse. Dried up and achy. Karma getting him this time and he deserves every sharp twinge inside him.

He slowly closes the car boot, then slides into the car, pulling the door shut behind him before clicking his seatbelt in and turning the engine on. The radio blares and his hand snaps out to shut it off.

Silence rings.

The car is quiet without Jules beside him.

She may not be there in person, but she lives in his head and in his chest. His hands wrap around the steering wheel, quickly turning white-knuckled. The reasons for keeping his distance, ones that made sense five days ago, hell, five hours ago, now feel like frail excuses he needed to convince himself of.

Taking a long inhale, he releases the steering wheel and pulls out his phone. His text message with Jules is still open, and he stares at the words she sent a few minutes ago, confirming she wanted to be away from him so desperately she's likely gone and paid for her own train ticket to Canberra.

His body figures it out a fraction of a second before his brain does, arm reaching to shut off the ignition before the thought fully clarifies.

She sent this a few minutes ago. Jules is still here, in the hotel. He can say all of this to her face.

He bursts out of the car, fumbling the door closed before racing to the lifts and pressing the up button. The taunting red numbers descend in slow-motion. Fucking hell, why won't they go faster? Each second is precious. Jules could be leaving her room at any moment.

Finally, the doors open and he throws himself inside the lift, only for the ascent to drag too. The tightness in his chest constricts with every breath, every stride in the confined space, back and forth, floor by floor. He needs to catch her so he can explain, finish digging the emotions out of his bones for her so she knows it did mean something to him. It'll hurt like a gut-punch doing it and will she even want him still? But fuck, he needs to try. He can't leave this be, like when he ran from her after she complimented his personality. Did he learn nothing from that?

Memories of the past week play like a highlights reel in his head, now with a filter of this-woman-is-falling-for-you overlayed onto them. It doesn't take long to understand with his entire cowardly, unworthy heart, that although he denied it at the time, she was telling the truth. She wanted him for more than a body. She wants more now, like she apparently did when they started the fling anyway. She wants him as a boyfriend. She fell for him.

And he's fallen for her too. Plummeted. And he's yet to land.

He's hoping Jules will catch him.

The lift arrives on the right floor and he squeezes himself sideways through the still-opening doors. No-one is around to witness his desperate run, but he'd still do it even if there was.

Without hesitation, he knocks twice on Jules's door, then steps back to wait, heart hammering inside his chest.

A few seconds pass. Then another few.

Her door remains shut.

'Jules? I need to talk to you.' He knocks again, then presses his ear to the door, but there's no sound coming from inside.

A chill moves over his skin. It steals the air from his lungs and halts his heart.

She's gone. She's left.

He twists his head, pressing his forehead against the door and letting his eyes shut.

Well, he's finally landed and there's no Jules to catch him. A shiver wracks his body as he drops not into calm ocean waters, but into iciness. Choppy seas, a roiling vastness of feelings that have been waiting for him for days. Weeks. Months. He's caught in the white-water of his past and he's flailing.

Time hovers as he stays pressed to the door, body shivering sporadically, processing emotions he's been keeping at bay and barely started letting in this week with encouragement from Carrie and Chloe, Matteo, Jules. Letting these feelings in hurts like getting dumped by a wave, but he submits himself to the force of his emotions until he resurfaces, shaky and breathless. Alone.

He isn't sure how long passes before his phone buzzes in his pocket.

Exhaling, Cameron levers himself from the door, feeling his bones ache. He's got new texts from Matteo and Chloe. And a direct Instagram message from BookyBraden.

In self-flagellation at its finest – because why not make himself feel that much worse – Cameron opens Braden's message. He reads it without taking the words in until his third time through.

> *BookyBraden: If it makes any difference coming from me, you're a great marketing manager. Intelligent and perceptive. If your presentation at the conference was meant for Cable's benefit, then thanks. It'll help us launch book 2.*

BookyBraden: Plus. So you know I meant my apology. My friend at Lin & Luther says their senior marketing manager is thinking about taking long service leave. They'll be looking for someone to temp the role. I know you always wanted to work for them.

Cameron closes the app without replying. The news of a potential job in his dream company in Sydney should make him want to run around the block, but all he feels is a hollowness in his chest.

Because it's clear now, standing in the corridor where everything intersects – outside Jules's room, where Braden confronted him twice – that since Braden and Jules are different women with different motivations, then he's the common denominator.

He's the one imploding his relationships.

Braden. Jules. Even non-romantic ones, like Matteo and his sisters.

He let his sisters' messages go unanswered. He stopped reaching out to Matteo. He didn't talk things out with Braden while they were dating, though she's got culpability too. And Jules. He didn't see how she wanted him even when she said it to his face. He spewed lies to Jules, and Jules gave him nothing but truth.

He digs the corner of his phone into his chest, emotions coagulating inside him until he feels heavy, until his breaths struggle to get to his lungs past the lump in his throat.

He ran from Jules when emotional intimacy started creeping in. He could barely tell her the truth even when she asked for it. He didn't appreciate her enough when they were together, every beautiful facet of herself she chose to share with him. Why would she want to settle down with him?

It's his fault things are over between him and Jules, but at least there's one slim, silver lining. Jules deserves someone better than him anyway.

CHAPTER 31

Jules feels suspended in time as she rides the train to Canberra. Scenery blurs past the window, but she's not seeing it. She's stuck back in Cameron's hotel room with him, watching his face as she tells him how she feels.

His reaction plays in slow motion in her head. How rigid he'd been holding himself as she led up to it, then the instant way he went slack after she confessed. The surprise conveyed by his parted lips, the way his caramel eyes softened with hope when she grabbed his hand, hope that only lasted a split second before he turned to stone again.

She clings to that moment of hope. It wouldn't be there if he hadn't wanted to hear she had feelings for him. And the more she replays their exchange, the more she believes Matteo was right about Cameron's coping techniques. The running she knew about direct from the source, and him talking himself into things fits with what he was saying, how he was pulling all these tiny moments from over the week to back up the decision he'd already made. Her texts and checking him out. The fact they defined it as a fling in the first place.

Jules's chest warms to an uncomfortable heat, like standing too close to a fire, and she yanks her jumper over her head, balling it atop the tray table.

What about all the other moments they shared, huh? Joking about ringtones and baby pics in the car ride over. Exchanging coffee and marshmallows. Sharing gelatos at Circular Quay. Dancing around his room together. Spending the night wrapped in each other's arms. Cameron calling her an incredible woman. And that's not even counting all their phone calls at work, and the guess-the-song game they've been playing for months.

She fists her hands into her jumper. She wants to send him a list of all of those moments. Would it change anything if she did? Does she want it to?

Her heart swells, pressing against her lungs, demanding attention.

Yes. She does.

Jules drops her head onto her jumper and shuts her eyes. It doesn't seem to matter anymore though what she wants. She's already said all she can. Conference is over, the fling is done, and come Monday, they'll be back to how things were, except Jules's fear will have come true. They won't be going back to what they had. He did reject her after she told him how she felt.

But that look of hope.

She sees it again now. Her heart can't ignore it, and with Matteo's insight into how Cameron works, the ember of hope it sparks survives the entire trip home to Canberra.

* * *

Jules steps off the train and Tori and Cat are waiting for her, holding an oversized brown paper bag with the Big Drip logo on it.

She bursts into tears.

Immediately, she's wrapped in the warm arms of her friends while she shakes with sobs, getting tears all over Tori's dress before Cat pulls a handkerchief from her pocket and passes it over.

'I'm sorry.' Jules dabs under her eyes and blows her nose once the tears have passed. 'I don't get why I'm crying so much about this. We weren't even properly together.'

'No need to be sorry,' Tori says. 'It's totally natural to cry over that douche.'

'Don't... don't berate Cameron,' Jules tells Tori.

'Can I rag on him a little, though?' Tori runs her fingers through Jules's hair. 'He made my friend miserable.'

'We brought you choc-oat cookies.' Cat offers the bag to Jules and she opens it. The smell of chocolate and butter and sugar is like a warm hug but her stomach feels too leaden to eat yet.

'So, what happened?' Tori starts shepherding them to her car, grabbing hold of Jules's suitcase while Cat picks up her handbag. 'Your text was skimpy on the details.'

Jules presses the still-warm cookies to her chest. 'There was too much to put in a text.'

'Uh-oh.' Cat says. 'Should we stop for more cookies on the way home?'

'No. No, I want to go home and shower and put on comfy pyjamas.'

'And then tell us everything that happened?' Tori tacks on, unlocking her car and sliding Jules's suitcase in.

'Of course. I think I need to talk it all out to make sense of it. I really... didn't...' Jules's throat thickens. She swears and takes a sharp breath. She will not cry over this again. 'I really didn't think it'd end how it did.'

Cat leans her body against Jules and she leans back.

'While you know I can't wait to hear all about it,' Tori slams the boot shut then turns to Jules, gripping her wrist lightly. 'More importantly, before any of that... are you okay?'

Jules's throat feels thick. Again. Damn it. 'Not really. Not yet.'

She's wrapped in another hug and it eases some of the ache in her bones.

***

Back at home, Jules takes a long, scorching hot shower then gets changed into her softest pyjamas. The cookies are warmed up to melty-chocolate perfection, and Tori makes Italian-style hot chocolate, so rich and thick she brings three teaspoons across to the coffee table.

Her friends pile her onto the couch, Cat on her left and

Tori on her right, like they had after Todd ended things with her. It feels different now. She feels different. Back then, her thoughts had been about what she was losing, and how Todd's rejection reflected on her. Now, her thoughts are full of Cameron. Is he back in Canberra yet? Is he thinking about their last conversation? Does he feel regret? Relief? Loss? Do his bones ache like hers do?

Does he believe her that she fell for him in his entirety?

Jules nibbles at a cookie while Cat and Tori fill her in on a week's worth of gossip, then start comparing notes on a romance novel they both read recently, waiting for Jules to be ready.

'Okay.' Jules pulls her legs beneath her, crossing them.

'Feeling more yourself?' Cat asks, running her fingers through the damp strands of Jules's hair.

'Much.'

'So what happened?' Tori asks gently. 'We thought things were going well.'

Jules pulls the plate of cookies on her lap so she can pick one up and break it in half. 'They were. He was really opening up to me. I even slept the night in his bed on Wednesday. But something happened yesterday and he ended things.'

'Did he say why?' Cat asks, fingers still running through Jules's hair.

'He thought I was using him for sex.'

Tori cocks her head. 'He does know you were having a fling, right? '

'Yes. Like I said, we made that very clear from the start.' Jules starts breaking the cookie into smaller pieces, letting them fall onto the plate. 'Which is why it was so weird hearing him say that, and why – at least after I spoke to Matteo – I didn't believe him.'

'Matteo?' Tori asks.

'A friend from Cable he reconnected with while we were there.' Jules lifts another cookie and begins the process of breaking it apart.

'What did Matteo say to you that made you change your mind?' Cat brings the conversation back.

Jules hands are covered in melty chocolate, so she reaches for a napkin to wipe her fingers. 'I think Cameron had been telling Matteo about what we were doing because the morning after things ended, Matteo found me and told me... well, some private stuff about Cameron and his ex. And, I don't know, it was like having my eyes opened. I knew where he was coming from, why he interpreted the situation how he did.'

Fingers clean and no more cookies to demolish, Jules settles for tapping her fingers on her crossed knees instead. 'And also, it made me feel rotten. I don't... it's his story to tell, but I wish I could go back. I would've been honest from the start. I should have taken the risk and told him what I wanted. Instead, I went along with the fling thing and unknowingly put him in a position where he was reliving his awful relationship with an ex.'

Tori lets out a low whistle beside her. 'Jules. That sounds shit. But you didn't know about his ex, so you can't be at fault.'

Jules nods, but her stomach squirms anyway. She lays her palms flat over her abdomen. 'I know. And I know there's no point worrying when I can't change what we did. So this morning I did what I should have done from the start.'

Even after the fact, echoes of pinpricks settle on her shoulders. She takes a deep breath and looks between her friends.

'I told him everything. I was completely honest about having liked him for months, and that it was never just sex for me. That I was—that I wanted to have the chance to fall in love with him.'

Tori makes a soft noise then wraps her arms around Jules.

'And he didn't change his mind. He—' Jules laughs thickly, an itch appearing at the back of her eyes. She grabs onto Tori's arm. 'He told me *he* was using *me* for sex. That it was only ever about sex for him. That really hurt to hear.'

'Of course it did.' Cat removes the plate of cookies before they slide off Jules's lap.

'But then later I realised—how hypocritical is that?' Jules's chest flushes hot.

'Are you sure I can't bad-mouth him?' Tori props her chin on Jules's shoulder. 'What a load of inconsistent bullshit.'

'Well, that's the thing. Realising that contradiction makes me believe even more that he didn't mean it. I knew he was only trying to justify all that stuff to himself, like Matteo warned me he does. And I *can't* believe it was only sex for him. I won't let him change what being with him meant to me.'

'And he won't.' Cat drops a hand on Jules's knee. 'Your memories and your feelings are your own.'

Jules focuses on taking measured breaths, willing the clogged throat and itchy eyes to disappear.

Tori and Cat slowly eat the broken cookie pieces while Jules grabs her hot chocolate and sips it, letting the warmth combat the coldness inside her.

'Can I ask,' Cat says after a few minutes of quiet. 'Do you regret the fling?'

Jules knows her answer, because the spark of hope is still fighting the cold inside her. 'No.'

'Do you still want to be with him?'

'Yes.' She puts her hot chocolate down. 'I've still got feelings, strong ones, and he didn't do anything wrong, except let his insecurities get the better of him so he thought he had to push me away. And yes, it feels shit that he thought he had to – especially the second time after I told him how I felt – and he needs to apologise for that. But after our week together, I know him and I honestly believe he didn't mean it.'

'Okay,' Cat says simply.

'Yeah.' Tori slings an arm around Jules's shoulders again, leaning her forehead against Jules's temple. 'If you believe it then we do too.'

'Let's make another plan, like we said.' Cat reaches for her pens but Jules grabs her arm to stop her.

'I don't want a plan.'

'You sure?' Tori checks, pulling back slightly. 'You're not retreating back into your comfort zone, are you?'

Jules shakes her head. 'I laid it all out for him. My feelings for him and what I want. I have no more cards to play.' She travels her finger over the patterns on her pyjama pants. 'It's up to him now. He'll either pick me or he won't. And if he doesn't…'

'If he doesn't?'

Jules takes a deep breath and reaches for her friends' hands, squeezing them. 'I don't want to hide from opportunities for another three years. I've got coffees with James McCarthy and Samantha lined up, and a resignation letter ready to submit.'

CHAPTER 32

The weekend sucks. Cameron can't stop thinking about Jules, about the tight look on her face when he had the nerve to lie to her about their fling just being about sex. Like he hadn't got intimate with her in more ways than that. He dreams in rose-tinted highlight reels and wakes up with momentary warmth before it gets sucked out and he's left with that dry, grinding feeling again.

He reads through their text chain, finally seeing the message he'd missed before his presentation.

> *Jules: You're going to be fantastic. You're intelligent and eloquent and you care about your topic. You've got this. I believe in you.*

Re-reading it is akin to holding his palm over a flame, but he still looks at it multiple times a day.

At work on Monday, he doesn't listen to music at his desk. He gets Rawiri to call IT on his behalf. He takes the stairs so he doesn't end up in the lift with her, because he won't get to push her against the wall and kiss her until she moans this time. And he'd be thinking about it like a creep because the sex *did* mean something, and he can't shake it from his head. Or his heart.

In their team meeting, Zoe tells him he looks, 'Like death warmed up', which is better than he feels.

Not seeing Jules in the office used to be about self-preservation. It's more like self-flagellation now, and he deserves every stepping-on-Lego sensation he feels for kicking her heart. For lying to her. For running away like she begged him not to.

God, he's a fucking dick.

She deserves better.

* * *

Tuesday is much the same. As is Wednesday. Toss and turn then dream of Jules, wake up and remember betraying Jules, go to work and avoid Jules and things that remind him of her. Wash rinse repeat. Step on another Lego. Feel another organ grind itself to rubble.

Thursday offers a break in routine when someone bangs loudly on his door in the evening. He's happy for anything that helps drag him from the depth of the trench he's dug himself into.

He opens the door and freezes.

His sisters are at his doorstep. 'What the hell are you doing here?'

'We're here to talk some sense into you.' Carrie marches past him.

'Shouldn't you be performing?' he calls after her as she makes herself at home.

'I'm between programs.'

Chloe gets in a quick hug as she walks past at least, before following Carrie down the hall.

'This is going to be painful,' Cameron mutters as he shuts the door and drags himself into his living room where his sisters are already seated at the dining table.

He drops into a chair and crosses his arms. The silent treatment will have no effect on his sisters, but their intervention will go faster if he doesn't interrupt with his own thoughts. He wanted a break from Jules-shaped thoughts. He suspects from the flat line of Carrie's lips, and the disappointed twist to Chloe's mouth, that this conversation won't be it.

'You screwed up with Jules.' Carrie says.

Yep. There it is. His insides shrivel up as Carrie stares him down. 'How—'

'Matteo told us.' Chloe drags his half-eaten dinner toward her and steals a dumpling from his plate.

'Hey.' He steals the plate back from her.

'Sorry,' Chloe says with her mouth full. 'It's a long drive and we didn't stop. I'm starving.'

Cameron sighs and pushes up from the table, heading to his kitchen. He pulls out crackers from his cupboard and grabs a tub of hummus from his fridge.

'So what's the deal?'

'Fuck!' Cameron fumbles the crackers. His sisters have followed him into the kitchen. It's only a small rectangular space to begin with, now it feels claustrophobic. He's penned in at the far end by the sink with his sisters between him and the door.

Chloe takes the crackers from his hands and rips them open, shoving one into her mouth without bothering to get any hummus on it.

'Matteo was light on the details,' Carrie says, popping open the hummus and dipping a cracker into it, before passing it to Chloe. 'He said you had some sort of falling out.'

'Is he spilling all my secrets now?' He presses a fist to his chest over his racing heart. He needs to have a talk with Matteo about his honesty pledge, and how it doesn't mean he has to spill everything about other people.

Carrie leans a hip against the countertop to his right. 'He's concerned about your wellbeing. As are we.'

'Thanks. But you don't need to worry. I'm fine.'

Chloe scoffs, digging a cracker into the hummus and coming away with about a quarter of the tub piled onto it. 'You're eating takeaway dumplings on a Thursday and there's two completed paint-by-numbers drying on your coffee table. Plus, your living room is more spotless than normal. Like you've been cleaning as an avoidance tactic.'

She's got him there.

'I'm fine,' he repeats as she lifts herself to sit on the counter next to the fridge, opposite Carrie.

'If you don't want to talk about Jules, what about Braden then?' Carrie says.

Cameron crosses his arms over his chest and widens his stance, trying to convey authority. 'I don't want to talk about her either.'

Carrie lifts an eyebrow. 'Because?'

Clearly, posturing doesn't work on an older sibling. 'Because it's in the past. I got my closure, or whatever.'

'Hey.' Chloe beams at him and swings a foot out to tap his leg. 'That's great.'

'Whatever.' He shrugs off her sincerity but warmth blooms inside his chest. It was a big deal for him and he feels better for it, but it's been smothered by what's going on with Jules. Or *not* going on.

'So guess it's back to Jules then,' Carrie says. 'Did you end up asking her out? Were you dating? Your texts have been evasive.'

Cameron shuffles his bare feet against the tiles. 'No.'

Chloe gasps. 'But you were so into each other! Carrie said you were holding hands at the symphony.'

'Holding hands doesn't mean I like her.'

'You liking her isn't what we're discussing here,' Carrie says, reaching across to Chloe for a cracker and dip. 'We all know you do. Including you, so I'm not sure why you're trying to convince us you don't.'

'Yeah,' Chloe agrees. 'How're we meant to encourage and support you if we don't know what's going on and if you lie to us about your feelings?'

'You want to know what's going on?' He swings his head back and forth between his sisters. 'Fine. Yes, I like her. But we weren't dating. I didn't ask her out. We had a fling. We were having sex. And now that's over.'

The shock factor doesn't shock as much as he was hoping. His sisters are as immovable as boulders in a creek.

'So you were two consenting adults having sex,' Chloe surmises without hesitation.

Carrie grimaces and casts her gaze to the ceiling. 'So much information I didn't need to know about my younger brother.'

'I've had flings before.'

Carrie winces. 'Yet more information.'

'Hey. You're the ones who started this conversation.'

'We weren't expecting it to end up here,' Chloe says through a mouthful of food.

Carrie drops her gaze to him. There's something in her expression that resonates with Cameron, a knowing that makes the hairs on the back of his arms stand up. 'You haven't had a fling before with someone you actually like as much as you do Jules,' she says. 'It's different when you already care for them.'

He doesn't know with who, or when, but he'd swear she's talking from experience.

Seeing the empathy in Carrie's eyes erases his desire to say as little as possible during this intervention. His sisters have come all this way and, he realises, watching them pass the crackers back and forth, he's missed their company. His heart feels lighter, even as they take him to task. Which is saying something with how heavy it's felt these past few days.

And maybe – *maybe* – there's a small part of him that's not yet been ground down into nothing. That's survived his self-flagellation and now yearns, hopeful his sisters come bearing answers for him and Jules.

Cameron deflates, leaning back against the sink. 'Yeah. It is different.'

'We thought you'd asked her out in a more romantic sense,' Chloe frowns. 'You don't think making it a fling was a little... self-sabotaging? Maybe?'

He doesn't tell them the fling was Jules's idea. She wouldn't want his sisters to have that knowledge, and he has culpability too. She mentioned it in passing. He's the one who actually made it happen because he *wanted* her so damn bad, and wanted to appease her even more. 'What're you saying?'

Chloe shrugs a shoulder. 'I'm wondering if you were giving yourself an out if things didn't go well. Because then you could do exactly what you've done and compare her to Braden and justify letting her go for the sake of your job.'

Cameron frowns, his skin tightening. It sounds cheap hearing it. Ending a relationship because of a job? No, worse, not even trying for one because of a job. 'I didn't say that's why I ended things. I didn't even say I was the one who ended things.'

'Matteo,' Chloe offers in explanation. 'And no, he didn't tell us those details. But you've been vocal about not dating someone you work with, so it's pretty easy to join the dots.' Chloe puts down the crackers and focuses her attention on Cameron. 'Am I right?'

Cameron scrubs his hands over his face then drops his gaze to the floor.

His pulse beats thick at his wrists and he leans on the solid support of the kitchen counter. His sisters are forcing him to face the actions he made and take a hard look at the motivations behind them. It's uncomfortable, but he needs to have this conversation, because Canberra this week has sucked for more reasons than the Jules thing.

It's cold here. Lacking. He doesn't have connections or people to hang out with, someone to invite over so his house doesn't feel so empty. He tried Steven and Fredrich, but they're on holiday up north. He's missed Matteo. He's missed his sisters like he missed Sydney. He's missed their teasing and stealing his food and elbowing into his life. How they can cut through his bullshit excuses to the fears he'd rather hide away.

'You're partly right.' He keeps his head dropped. It's easier to talk when he's not seeing their expressions. Still feels like he's pulling parts of his insides out. 'It was only meant to be at the conference anyway, but I ended it early because I freaked out. Shit had happened and I saw too many parallels with my relationship with Braden. I saw my career tanking because I'd fallen for the wrong woman, so I ended things. Brutally.'

'Cameron.' Carrie's harsh tone has his head snapping up to look at her. 'What did I tell you right from the start. She's not Braden.'

Carrie's anger is alive in the air between them and he holds her stare, facing her judgement because he knows in his gut, his heart, it's warranted.

'God, we thought you'd gotten over this.' Carrie fists her hands onto her waist. 'This seeing Braden in everyone you interact with. You just told us you got closure.'

Cameron swallows roughly. 'I have. I do. But that was after all the Jules stuff. The damage was done. I'd lied to Jules and diminished her and what we had because I was trying to push her away to protect myself. I hurt her.'

His hands go clammy recalling their fight. Fuck, it feels like he's taken a baseball bat to his chest for every shit thing he spat at Jules the other day. His disgust with himself runs deep as the Mariana trench. The clamminess spreading to his neck, chest, the dip of his back.

'Have you explained any of this to her?' Carrie asks.

'No.'

'Apologised?'

'No.'

'Why not?'

'Because I'm fucking scared!' His voice cracks but Carrie doesn't back off.

'Of what?'

'Take your pick.' Cameron throws his arms out. 'Rejection. Falling back into being distrustful of her intentions. Hurting her again. Feeling like this.'

'Like what?'

He groans, the sound torn from his soul. 'Like my insides are grinding together, constantly. Like my lungs are filled with sand. This sucks.' He slaps his palm onto his chest and his heart batters against his ribcage below it. '*This sucks* and we were together for less than five days. What's going to happen to me if it doesn't work out?'

The words hang in the kitchen, no one speaking while they float there like a storm cloud. He hears the words ring in his head and they sound like more excuses.

Excuses to run.

Cameron's chest rises and falls sharply beneath his palm. Carrie's still staring at him with an inscrutable gaze while his heart attempts to fracture his ribcage it's beating so hard and fast.

Chloe slides off the counter, the sound of her feet hitting the floor loud in the stillness. She focuses her attention on Cameron and tilts her head. 'What happens if it *does* work out? Do you want long-term with Jules? Forget about all the other factors and answer that.'

'I do.' It's what he's been dreaming about all week.

Chloe smiles, nodding slowly. 'It's not too late to fix this, then. You've just got to let your walls down. All the way, not a little bit. *All the way.*'

'What does that mean?' Cameron lets his hand fall to his side. He doesn't mean to sound so desperate, but that yearning part of him swells, injected with new hope.

'It means you've got to be honest with her, not just about what happened at the conference, but everything before that too. Your no-dating a colleague thing, and the Braden stuff, and why you agreed to the fling in the first place,' Chloe lists, Carrie nodding along. 'At the very least, you gotta make her understand she shouldn't feel guilty about the fling.'

'She knows about the Braden stuff already.'

'All of it?' Carrie asks.

He shrugs. 'Most of it.'

'Then tell her the rest. Start there.'

'Matteo already did. It's why—' Cameron snaps his jaw shut.

'Why what?'

Cameron averts his gaze but there's not many safe places to look in the small kitchen.

'The silence is implying it won't look good for you,' Carrie says. 'Spit it out.'

He stares at his bare feet. His sisters already think he's been a dick. Spitting it out will only make things worse.

Or they could help him figure a way out of this funk. Chloe said it wasn't too late for him to fix things, but if he wants their help – which they're clearly here to give whether he asks for it or not – they need to know the full story.

He sighs. 'It's why she told me she wasn't interested in only a fling.'

'Cameron.'

'I know. I know.' He scrubs his hands over his face then folds his arms over his chest, trapping his trembling hands beneath his biceps.

'And?' Carrie says. 'I can see you're holding something back.'

'How do you—' Cameron sighs again, every confession still raw like he's pulling his insides out into the open. 'She told me she'd liked me for months and wanted all of me. Not just my body. She said—' His throat constricts and he has to swallow four times before he can speak again. 'She wanted the chance to fall in love with me.'

'Ah.' Chloe lifts a finger into the air. 'There it is.'

'There's what?'

'The real reason you ended things. We know,' Chloe gestures between her and Carrie, 'your job doesn't come into it. That's an excuse. It's really about protecting your heart.'

Cameron's stomach swoops. 'Protecting my heart?'

'Yeah, you know. Your thing with the wall.' Chloe prompts.

'And your trust issues,' Carrie adds.

Cameron looks back and forth between them. 'You're saying I broke up with Jules to protect my heart?'

They both nod.

'You did basically say as much when you were yelling a minute ago,' Chloe reminds him.

'Well I did a shit job of it because I'm pretty certain my heart is crumbling in my chest.'

Chloe makes a wounded noise and lunges to wrap him in a hug. He holds stiff for a few seconds before sighing and wrapping his arms around her. It doesn't make the raw pain go away, but it helps.

'I'm sorry you're hurting, Cameron.' Carrie walks over and lays a hand on his back. 'You obviously care a lot about Jules. I know we've been pushy about this and I'm sorry if that complicated things.'

'Thanks,' he grumbles. 'But pretty sure I made it complicated all on my own.'

Carrie laughs softly and bumps her knuckles on his shoulder. 'I've got one more pushy thing to say.'

He sighs, pulling out of the hug. 'Of course you do.' He takes a deep breath and rolls his shoulders back and down before facing Carrie. 'Let's hear it.'

'If our parents have taught us one thing, it's—'

'No phones at the dinner table,' Cameron and Chloe say in unison.

Carrie rolls her eyes but her lips quirk. 'It's that clear communication is important in relationships. You think me and Jesse are still together because we didn't talk through the hurdles along the way? 'Course not. It sucks sometimes, but you've got to be that vulnerable with your partner if you want the long-term. Hard conversations are worth it for what's on the other side. Your heart may take a bruising here and there, but it'll recover stronger for it.'

There's nothing but sincerity in her words. Cameron wants to scoff, and maybe a week ago he would have, but not tonight. He wants to be on that other side with Jules. He wants to be *with* Jules.

'That was truly sappy,' he can't help but say.

'It was true.' Carrie lifts a shoulder. 'You should talk to Jules. Apologise and explain and give her space to process. Then ask her out.'

'Romantically,' Chloe clarifies.

'It's not too late.'

'Isn't it? I fucked up. The things I said to her...' Cameron shakes his head, wishing he'd done things differently that day. 'I don't deserve her.'

Carrie raises an eyebrow. 'Shouldn't she get to make the choice about who she deserves?'

'And won't you regret it if you don't tell her how you feel?' Chloe adds.

He already regrets it. They promised each other honesty and he trampled over their vow, acting a fucking hypocrite because he was scared. He sees Jules's face in his mind, the way it crumpled and her eyes filled with tears before she walked out of his hotel room. He groans and drags his hands through his hair, realising his sisters are right, yet again. He's already taken the choice away from her once. Twice, if he counts the time he ran to her room to explain himself and she'd already left. And he should count that. He does.

'You're right. Of course she deserves that. She deserves anything she wants.' He'll count himself blessed if she decides that includes him after he tells her the full story. 'I need to tell her. Everything. All of it. I can't let her go without giving us a chance. I don't want to live the rest of my life wondering 'what if'.'

'Of course we're right,' Chloe says. 'You love her, right? Or at least, you want that same chance to?'

There's a hollowness in his chest that feels Jules-shaped. It's been part of him since before the conference. Time to see if he can fill it in. 'I want the chance to love her.'

'Come on then.' Chloe starts shoving the food back into the fridge. 'Do you know where she lives? Let's go.'

'What? No. Why?' Cameron's heart falls over itself, pulse skittering, then racing. 'I only just decided this.'

'You've got to go tell her everything. *Now*.' Chloe slams the fridge door shut. 'We aren't going to let you chicken out of this like you apparently did at the conference when you went for the temporary fling instead of asking her to date you.'

'Well that was before I realised my feelings.' His heart is in his throat. 'So you don't need to hold my hand now.'

'Oh no, this isn't hand holding.' Carrie grins with a wicked glint in her eye. 'This is pushing you down the gangplank.'

'Geez. Alright.'

'So?' Chloe prompts. 'Jules's address?'

'I don't know. But it's Thursday, so she's probably at trivia at the Blue Alcott, anyway. I'll do it tomorrow.'

'Did you say trivia?' Chloe perks up like a puppy hearing the word 'treat'.

'Yes.'

'Perfect. No time like the present. Come on.' Chloe grabs his hand and drags him out of the kitchen, through the living room, and down his front hall. She's stronger than he remembers. Or maybe he's not putting up much of a fight.

'But I haven't practiced what I'm going to say to her.'

'This isn't one of your marketing presentations,' Chloe says. 'Speak from the heart. You don't need practice for that.'

'I'm not wearing shoes.'

'I've got them,' Carrie calls from behind him.

'I left the iron on.'

Chloe yanks his arm, and he stumbles over the threshold. 'No you didn't.'

'The oven?'

'Nice try.' Carrie throws his jacket at his head and pulls the door shut with a definite bang behind them.

Cameron pats his pockets down. 'My house keys are actually sitting on the side table though.'

'Cameron. Look at me.' Carrie steps in front of him, facial expression reminiscent of their mother's when she's dishing out advice. 'You're half in love with her already. You want to be with her. *Stop running.*'

She shoves the shoes at his chest and he wraps his arms around them.

Stop running. Can he? There's been times already with Jules where he didn't want to, when the only running he wanted to do was straight into her arms. But will they still be open for him after he's fucked things up so badly?

His chest tightens and his hands heat, prickling like he's pressed them to a hot plate. Goddamn. He's got to try. Try for something real with Jules, or he'll be living with that hole in his chest for eternity.

Carrie nudges him and he stumbles a few steps. He's a mess. Trembling legs and sweaty palms. He stops metres from the car, watching Carrie get into the driver's seat, swallowing compulsively. Jules is a car ride away and he's barefoot and scruffy and his tongue weighs 20 kilograms in his mouth.

'Hey.' Chloe steps in front of Cameron with a solemn look on her face. 'Do you really think you don't deserve Jules?' she asks softly. 'Or is that another excuse for you to not try?'

'I...' He stares into the steady hazel of his little sister's eyes, wondering when she got to be so wise. Is this something else he missed while he's been isolating himself in Canberra?

He's mostly confident when he answers, 'The second thing.'

Chloe nods. 'Good. I'm glad. But I'm going to text you the contact info for my therapist, okay? Just to have.'

He opens his mouth but he has no air to speak. He nods instead.

Carrie honks the horn and Cameron takes a deep breath, straightening his spine.

Dammit, he's doing this. At the very least, Jules deserves to hear an apology and his explanation. But he's beyond doing the bare minimum. He's going to lay his heart bare for Jules because holy hell does she deserve it.

CHAPTER 33

The Blue Alcott is packed. They're doing a 2000s trivia night and Jules is convinced every single university student has shown up to play. Nothing like the lure of a free meal to the winning team for those on a student budget.

The excitement of the game and the atmosphere in the pub can't quite erase the ache inside her, the place that's needy still for all things Cameron. She hasn't heard from him or seen him in the office all week and it turns out that 'out of sight out of mind' is total bullshit. He's in her thoughts more than ever. Every time the phone rings, or she hears someone talk about marketing, or synth-pop plays on the radio. And when he's in her thoughts, that ache in her chest pulses, not ready to give up.

But how long can she wait for him to make his move? She doesn't want to miss out on opportunities again or become stuck in her comfort zone. If he doesn't reach out to her, or he does but it's to confirm his original choice, then she'll have to move on.

The bartender drops the drinks in front of her and she heads back to the table where several Infinity staff sit with Cat and Tori, who she retakes her seat between before divvying up their drinks.

'Thanks, lady.' Tori sips her drink, making eyes with a woman a few tables along like she's been doing all night.

'Think she'll come over before the next round starts?' Cat whispers in Jules's ear.

Jules looks between Tori and the woman. 'I think Tori will go to her.'

'Hmm. I think you're right.'

She doesn't need to live vicariously through Tori's exploits anymore since she more than made up for her years of inaction at the conference, but watching Tori undressing someone with her eyes makes her stomach tense. Cameron used to look at her like that.

Which isn't even the look she's missing most. She wants that other one, the soft one, when he framed her face with his hands and called her incredible.

The MC announces the next round and Jules focuses in. That is, until a familiar voice sounds from behind her with an answer to the question.

'It's Universal Studios.'

Goosebumps break out across her skin. That voice. Oh, she's missed it. Missed the man who it belongs to as well. Her heart flips over then races.

Cat presses a supporting hand to her knee as Jules turns slowly in her seat.

'Cameron. Hi.'

His caramel eyes are fixed solely on her, reflecting the bar lights. He looks beautiful. Magnetic. Uneasy.

There's a loosening in her chest despite that last one. 'Are you... here for trivia?'

'No. I—' He pulls his hands from the pockets of his tan slacks. 'Can we talk? Please?'

Tori leans in close to Jules, but keeps her voice loud enough for Cameron to hear when she says, 'You don't have to go with him.'

'We're in the middle of a round,' Cat tells Cameron, a rare note of steel in her voice.

'I can help,' he offers immediately. 'Jules said you could do with another muso.'

He's replying to Cat, but he's looking right at Jules with a plea in his eyes. She bites her lip, chest warming.

Tori kicks a chair towards him with her foot, and he grabs for it, sitting at the edge of their group with his gaze still fixed on Jules.

His focus barely leaves her as the MC asks the next question, even as he debates with his co-worker Zoe about the answer. His steady attention has those mythical butterflies once again proving they're not a myth by appearing in her chest.

Tori was right to say she doesn't have to talk to him, but she wants to. Already, that ache is softening at the edges. And they left things so abruptly at the conference. She doesn't want that to be their last interaction, even if they can't go back to what they had. Did he believe she saw him as more than a body? She never found out.

'Let's go,' she tells him before the MC asks the next question.

'Thank you.'

Tori points a warning finger at him as he stands, but neither she nor Cat try to interfere.

Cameron lets her lead them through the packed floor. His hand lands on her lower back and tingles spread out, fierce, hitting her heart and making it pump even faster.

'Are those your sisters at the bar?' Jules asks, spotting a head of pink and purple–streaked blonde hair as they walk past.

'Yeah. They drove down from Sydney this afternoon.'

Both notice her and wave. She returns the gesture. 'Why?'

'To be meddling sisters.'

The words are prickly but the tone is pure love.

Outside, they walk down the street away from the pub until they reach a nature strip. The cool air pebbles Jules's skin and she wraps her arms around herself.

She stops and turns to Cameron. His hair is glossy and his jaw, which is clenched tight, is stubbled. Her thighs tingle with remembered sensation. She presses her legs together and notices he's not wearing socks. 'Are you okay, Cameron? You look a little... dishevelled.'

'Am I okay? You're asking if I'm—' Cameron slides a hand through his hair. 'Jules. Are *you* okay?'

She tucks her hair behind her ear and shrugs. 'I'm fine' is on the tip of her tongue, but they promised each other honesty. She's not sure if it still means anything to him, but she wants to stay true to it.

'I've been better,' she says.

'If any of that is because—' Cameron cuts off with a scoff, jerking his head side to side. 'Of course some of it's because of me. I'm sorry, Jules.'

She rubs her palm up and down her bare arms. 'Yeah. The, uh… the conference didn't end the way I wanted.'

Tension brackets Cameron's mouth. His head drops to his chest and he exhales roughly. 'I fucked things up.'

Jules blinks. It's not what she was expecting. She isn't sure what she was expecting. Something less definitive and without the raw emotion, probably. Whatever he thinks he's 'fucked up' sounds like it's killing him.

'What did you fuck up?' she asks.

'Us.'

He lifts his head and the emotion in his eyes wallops her in the stomach. Regret. Shame. Desperation.

Because of how things ended? But. She swallows. 'I thought there wasn't an us?'

He shakes his head. 'Of course there's an us.'

'You didn't make it sound that way in Sydney.'

'Because I…' He looks over her shoulder, shuffling on his feet. 'My sisters drove here to tell me you deserve my honesty and an apology, and that you deserve to make your own decision about whether you want to be with me still. They're right. I knew that before they came but I've been…'

He trails off, swallowing harshly. His gaze flits over her face, moving from her eyes, her lips, nose, chin, ear, along the length of her hair draped over a shoulder. It'd make her heart race if it wasn't already speeding because of his words. Be with him still?

'You've been what,' she prompts, her own breath quickening.

His eyes meet hers and Jules's breath catches. 'Scared. I've been running scared.'

The bare emotion in his wide eyes sends her heartbeat into adrenaline-fueled overdrive.

'But I don't want to do that anymore,' he says. 'You need to have all the facts, the honest truth about what I've been thinking. You were honest with me, and we promised we'd be with each other, right?'

Jules nods.

He takes a deep breath. Tension lines radiate from his eyes. She doesn't want him to feel forced to open up to her because she did. At one point, she played that emotional vulnerability card like it was a trick. It's not. It's something you have to earn, something you give only when you're comfortable and you trust the other person.

'Cameron. You don't have to bare your soul to me.'

'I want to.'

The ache inside her quivers hopefully.

'Here goes.' He takes another deep breath in, gaze focused on her. 'I haven't practised this at all so I apologise in advance if I speak in circles.'

'Should we dance for a bit first?'

Cameron stills for a second before laughing. 'Maybe.'

Jules's stomach goops around. His laugh. She wants to wrap herself in it like a hug. She settles for wrapping her arms tighter around herself.

'Okay. Um. Where to—right. First thing. I know you weren't using me for my body.'

Again, it's not the words Jules thought she'd hear straight off the bat. When he continues, it makes a little more sense. 'I know I meant more to you than that, and you trying so hard to make sure I knew that meant a lot. Thank you. So don't feel guilty about the fling thing. I have no regrets. Even if it... didn't end how it should have.'

Jules swallows the 'how should it have ended?' question.

He takes a deep breath then lets it out slowly. 'I was a

fucking hypocrite. I know Matteo told you the full Braden story. I should've done that, but I don't like how it makes me look. Or feel.'

'He did tell me, so if you don't want—'

'I do. I should have earlier, because it's why I did what I did.' Cameron takes a step in closer to Jules. His hand reaches to touch her but he pulls it away at the last second.

Jules's skin tingles where he would have touched.

'When I was with Braden,' Cameron begins, a hesitancy to his words. 'I thought we had something serious, or something that was heading that way. When I found out she only saw me as this 'hot guy' to have fun with before she went looking for someone to get serious with, it hurt me. She didn't think I was worth settling down with and since that I've—I sometimes—' He pushes out a breath and shakes his head. 'It's made me doubt myself and what I bring to a relationship. So I retreated from others. Including you. First in the office, and then at the conference.'

Hearing the story from Cameron is immeasurably worse than hearing it from Matteo. She can see the shame in his eyes and see the tremor in his hand when he moves it through his hair.

She touches his arm lightly when it drops back down, holds his gaze while she links her fingers through his.

He exhales roughly, looking at their joined hands. 'I'm so sorry I was an ass who tried to make you believe I was doing the same to you. I thought... I thought I was.' His hand tightens on hers. 'I had made myself believe a conference fling was all you wanted from me, because after the Braden stuff it made sense to me.'

His gaze lifts to hers. 'I was lying to myself. And to you because of it. I was trying so hard all week to only make it about sex, because I was worried I would fall for you if I didn't. So all those times you opened up to me, instead of me treating it like the fucking gift it was, I shoved my walls back up and I... I made it about sex and the physical.'

His palm is sweaty, but he doesn't pull away. Jules's own hands feel sweaty too. This is... a lot. He's not just opening up to her, offering an explanation or an apology. He's digging deep into his heart and letting her see everything, the good and the bad.

'The thing is... I failed.' Cameron lifts their joined hands and kisses her knuckles. 'Because we did connect emotionally. We already had a connection before this conference, with all those phone calls at work. Then so many times last week I forgot about trying to keep my distance, and god Jules, you made it so easy for me to open up to you. You said you felt comfortable around me? Well, I felt the same with you. There was no artifice. Except the huge lie I was telling myself the whole time.'

He steps in and Jules has to tilt her head back. His caramel eyes swim with emotion, making her light-headed from the way he's looking at her. Like she's the most important thing in the world.

'Cameron,' she breathes.

He presses her hand to his heart. It's racing as much as hers is.

'And it wasn't even just forgetting to be closed off, it was actively wanting to open up to you. You know the real reason I ran out of the room when you told me you liked my personality more than my body? Because I wanted so badly to tell you all of this then. About Braden and how screwed up that made me, and about how much I valued you and the safe space you created when we were together. I was running from the strength of my feelings. But I couldn't even do it right because I came back and begged you to go to dinner with me. It was impossible to ignore how I felt after that.'

Jules's inhalation is shaky. 'Thank you. For explaining how you were feeling. But you still...' The ache in her chest pulses, needy. 'Why did you end things if you felt like that?'

His mouth opens and closes a few times with false starts. 'I ran into Braden before my presentation.' His hand flexes on

Jules's, still over his racing heart, and he clears his throat. 'I felt blindsided. She... implied she wanted to hook up again.' Jules's chest pangs at that, though it's clear by Cameron's shudder he wasn't interested. 'It's an excuse, I know, but I let her get to my head and I freaked out. I accused you of being like her when you're not.'

He kisses her knuckles again, then shifts back a fraction so he can grab her other hand and cradle them both in his. 'Jules, I've... after your text telling me you'd make your own way back from the conference, I raced to your room to try and stop you so I could tell you all of this then.'

Sparks of warmth ignite in her chest. He did?

'But you weren't there and I got lost in my anxiety. I've spent the past few days telling myself you deserve someone better than me, but I was only giving myself an excuse to keep running. Because I'm scared of being rejected again.' His hands tremble, but his gaze is steady when he says, 'Of being the only person to fall in love in a relationship.'

Jules freezes. 'In love?'

'Yeah. Yes.' He drops his forehead to rest against hers. 'I want the chance to love you, Jules. I've been fighting the feeling for a while but I don't want to anymore. I can't. Because I feel too much for you.'

Jules can barely breathe, let alone form words. Every breath is shallow and her hands feel limp in Cameron's. Is she having an out of body experience? No. She's entirely present. Can feel the warmth from his hands, the thud of her pulse in her neck and fingertips, the breath filling her lungs on shallow inhalations, the puff of his breath over her lips, the way his hair tickles her forehead. The way her heart is growing bigger inside her, filling with love.

'So that's... what's been going on.' Cameron pulls away, nose gliding over her cheek as he does. 'And now that you know everything, the decision about us is up to you.'

'What decision?'

'I want to date you, Jules. Properly. Romantically. I want

to romance you and I want the chance to prove I'll never run away again.' He runs a hand gently over her hair. 'But only if you still want me.'

He goes to drop her hand but she holds on tight. 'Shouldn't it be up to *us*? If there is an us. Do you want there to be an us?'

'I said I want the chance to fall in love with you.'

'Is that a yes?'

He smiles, wide enough his dimples come out. 'Yes. Always.'

'I want an us too.' Jules closes the distance between them and slides her hands up his arms until they're resting at his neck. She stares into his eyes, which are swimming with hope. She smiles. 'Because I want the chance to fall in love with you.'

Cameron makes a sound of relief in the back of his throat and with barely a second's warning, Jules is wrapped in his arms. He pulls her tight to his chest and her arms wrap around his torso. He smells like Cameron. Like spearmint and coffee.

'I'm so sorry,' he says against her temple, voice thick. 'I did exactly what your ex did. What I always do. I ran.'

'Not exactly like my ex.' Jules squeezes him tighter, trying to imprint his body and his warmth and his presence. 'You came back.'

He pulls back and brushes her hair behind her ear, smiling softly. 'I'll always come back to you. Even if I get scared and try to run again, I'll come back.'

The butterflies take flight at that, travelling through her chest and abdomen. His eyes hold nothing but earnest promise.

'Maybe you can try skipping the running part?' Jules says. 'This past week hasn't been fun.'

'For me either. And I'm so fucking sorry.' He cradles her face, like he had in bed the other night, before things got derailed. 'So sorry. I don't—' He swallows and presses a quick kiss to her nose. 'Okay, then. No running.'

'Next time, we can try talking first.'

'Sounds good. But I'm talked out tonight.'

Jules hums and plays her fingers over his skin. Yes, they had a big emotional moment, but it has been an entire week since they've touched. She's not a saint. 'What do you want to do instead?'

His voice drops low and gravelly. 'So many things. You have no idea.'

'I have some idea. We never did get around to that loincloth thing.'

Cameron laughs and shivers race up Jules's back. 'That's still tabled. There's something else I want to do more now, anyway.'

'What's that?'

'Can I kiss you? *Please*?'

Jules's stomach swoops. 'Yes.'

His lips descend on hers. Fire. Like the first time they kissed. Heat spreads from Cameron's hands and his lips until Jules is alight. She tastes spearmint and Cameron and she smiles against his lips while he pulls them closer together, bowing her body against his, feeling the shape of him like walking through her front door.

EPILOGUE

Jules paces the length of the room, her footsteps on the wooden floorboards echoing in the empty space.

'What're you thinking?' Cameron leans against the doorframe, watching her with that soft smile that teases at his dimples which means he's feeling content.

'I'm thinking... this feels right.' She runs her hand over the off-white walls and does another slow loop.

'What about you?' she asks when she makes it back to him. 'Not feeling like running?' After ten months of dating, it's almost an in-joke now, and a gentle way for her to check in with Cameron.

'Bit late now, isn't it? The moving van will be here in half an hour.'

Jules digs her fingers into his side and tickles. Cameron gasps and bats her hands away, before bundling her in his arms and kissing her breathless.

'I'm joking.' He runs a hand over her plait, tugging it around to lay over her shoulder. 'Not a chance I'm running from this.'

'Good. Because there have been times when—'

'One time. There was *one* time, and I lasted all of ten minutes before I was running back to you, calling you on the phone to apologise and tell you I loved you too.'

Jules grins and slides her hands up his arms. 'I remember.'

It had been oddly romantic, with the stormy weather and the desperate way Cameron announced his love on the doorstep of her share house, even with Cat and Tori snooping from down the corridor.

'And now I have no issue with it. Watch this.' He takes her hands in his and faces her head on, a confident smile on his face, love shining in his eyes. 'Jules. Julianne. I love you.'

Butterflies in her stomach. They still appear every time. She leans in to kiss him, getting carried away tracing his lips with her tongue. 'I love you too.'

He presses a kiss to her temple, then throws an arm around her shoulders and turns to look at the empty room. Large enough to work as a combined living and dining area, with the kitchen through one of the doors at the far wall, the other leading to a tiny, paved courtyard.

'You're right, though.' Cameron rubs his palm up and down her arm, sending pleasant warmth through her body. 'This does feel right. We were practically living together in Canberra, anyway. It was time to move in together officially.'

Jules sighs and leans her face into his chest, breathing him in, trying to imprint this moment in her soul. The solidness of his arm around her, the steady beat of his heart beneath her cheek.

The moment she moves in with the man she loves.

'But we're not accepting your dad's offer to build us a custom storage unit for our record collection when he's next in Australia,' Cameron says.

She looks up at him. 'Why not?'

'Because I've heard the stories your mum tells and I prefer not to live with the risk of the shelving falling off the wall onto my head when I'm sitting on the couch.'

Jules winces at the image. 'Agree. But we're letting your mum give us some artwork, right?'

'She's got the canvases stretched, ready to go. I was thinking of asking her for a nice Luna Park face.'

Jules fake vomits and Cameron laughs, dropping a kiss on her nose. 'Let's bring some stuff in from the car before everyone else arrives.'

They walk out hand in hand, down the few front steps onto the path that curves through a small but meticulous front lawn.

Cameron has promised to be responsible for all lawn mowing and other gardening-related activities, because god knows it wouldn't stay meticulous if Jules were in charge.

The street is quiet, with lots of one-storey houses, a mix of old and newly renovated. Trees line the pathways and there's a bike path from here all the way into Sydney CBD. Not that Jules will be using that form of transport. She'll leave that option for Cameron. She'll take the bus into the city for her new job at McCarthy Media.

Smiling, she grabs several bags and hauls them from the car up the path into the house, heading for the kitchen to start unpacking a few essentials before the moving vans get here, and Cameron's family and Matteo turn up to help.

'Remember, crockery in the second draw by the dishwasher,' Cameron says, dropping a large cardboard box onto the kitchen island.

'I remember.'

'Good. But just in case.' Cameron pulls a folded piece of paper from the back pocket of his jeans, smooths it out, grabs some Blu-tack and sticks it on the window above the sink. It's a diagram of the kitchen with all the cupboards and drawers labelled.

Jules shakes her head and tugs Cameron over to her by his Spandau Ballet t-shirt. 'Is this why you wanted the Blu-tack in the essentials boxes?'

'Hell yeah.' He grins, dimples pressing into his cheeks.

Jules's stomach goops around.

'Come here.' She cocks her finger and Cameron leans to press his forehead to Jules's. 'You're adorable.'

'I think the word you're looking for is 'cute'.'

Jules presses up and kisses him. Her body tingles all over with excitement. They're doing this. They're moving in together. Moving to Sydney. Together.

'I'm unbelievably happy, did you know?' she tells him, sliding her hands below his shirt to press against his torso. His abdomen twitches below her hands and a zing shoots down her spine. 'Moving in with you. *Being* with you. My new job at McCarthy Media. Your new job.'

'Mine's only a temp position.'

'At Lin & Luther. That's incredible.'

She runs a finger down from his belly button to the top of his jeans. Cameron's hands fit to her hips and she slides her mouth by his ear to whisper, 'Should we go christen our bedroom?'

Cameron hums. 'Tempting. But maybe we should wait until we have a bed in there?'

Jules pouts, withdrawing her hands from below his shirt. 'You're no fun.'

'I'm plenty fun, but my whole family will be here soon. You know how they are with arriving early everywhere.'

It's been a minor argument between Jules and Cameron through their relationship so far. Jules a firm believer that on time is anywhere from the designated arrival time to 30 minutes after, Cameron believing early equals on time. It's obviously an inherited trait since whenever they've caught up with his parents or sisters when they were driving up to Sydney on weekends to look at places, they were always the last to arrive.

'But I packed something else in here for the occasion. It probably won't be as good as sex with me—'

Jules elbows him in the side.

'—but I think you'll like it.'

Cameron rummages through the cardboard moving box, pulling out a Bluetooth speaker, a kettle, and a box of tissues before he unearths an unmarked white cake box which he places on the kitchen bench between them.

'Ooh. Fancy.' Jules sidles up and presses into his side.

He slowly opens the lid, humming a suspenseful melody which crescendos into a loud, 'Ta-da!' as the lid is flipped back.

Jules gasps. 'Giant marshmallows! Yes! And—hang on.' She peers into the box. 'Did you get these custom made?'

Cameron pulls one out and holds it up. 'Sure did.'

On the big white square is an artistic rendering of the Luna Park face with a speech bubble emerging from its mouth containing the words, 'Welcome to Sydney, Jules and Cameron'.

Jules groans and laughs at the same time. 'It's terrible.'

'Hey! I spent hours designing this.'

'Sorry. I should've said, 'it's terrible and I love it'.'

Cameron smiles, holding the marshmallow up to her lips. She takes a big bite, feeling bubbly and warm all through her body as the pillowy sugar melts on her tongue.

'And I love you,' he says, taking his own smaller bite of the marshmallow, proving his commitment and love for her like he does every day.

They share the treat between them until the sound of a van pulling up out the front of the house interrupts the quiet.

'Must be the movers.' Cameron offers her the final bite of marshmallow, and she eats it from his fingers, swirling her tongue around the digits as she does. His caramel eyes flash at her and her heart thumps hard in her chest. 'Ready?'

His sticky fingers wrap around hers and he squeezes her hand.

'Ready.'

ACKNOWLEDGEMENTS

Where to begin? Apparently, the answer is crying while I start to type. Writing is something I've always loved. I've been proud of things I've written since I penned my own version of Goldilocks in kindergarten for a homework task. But it wasn't until fairly recently that I started getting serious about actually becoming an author. And that kind of decision doesn't happen if you don't have a support network around you that inspires and encourages you to chase after dreams that spent years as a whisper in the back of your head.

To my family. Mum – who encouraged me to start writing my own (fan)fiction back in the day – and Dad. You've backed me from day one and I love you so much for that and everything else you do. My sisters, who share my excitement and help amplify it. To Nanna, who reads everything I write (even the steamy bits that Dad skims over) and compliments my stories, but also once reminded me she 'wasn't getting any younger' so I needed to hurry up with getting a book published.

To my partner, who is my sounding board and trouble shooter, and my biggest, proudest, yell-it-from-the-rooftops supporter.

To all my friends, who are incredibly supportive even though many of you aren't romance readers. Special shout out to the Darlings, who got the behind-the-scenes look at my writing process, and my sometimes unfiltered rants about whatever I was working on.

To Dani McLean and Sharyn Swanepoel, who beta-read an early version of the story. Your feedback made this so much better. Thank you, thank you, thank you! And to Antonella Licciardi for helping with the Italian.

Suzanne, Laurie, Vicky and everyone at Escape. You work so hard to get books out into the world and though I know there's always about seven million things on your plate, you were patient and kind with me and made the process exciting as opposed to terrifying.

To the Romance Writers of Australia. I'm so glad I joined your organisation! The amount of knowledge I've gained from your courses and attending the annual conferences cannot be measured. And more importantly, through RWAus I've met so many wonderful, generous, funny, kind romance writers. You've read my work and been cheerleaders. Not many others will happily talk about plot structure and tropes and cover design for hours. You are my people.

To the Bookstagram community. I can't think of a lovelier group of people. All the comments, all the likes, all the DMs, all the catch-ups – it's such a joy to have them in my life. You've embraced me with open arms; my booksta side and my author side. (And also, as devourers of books, you keep the publishing world spinning and I'm grateful for that.)

And finally, to the readers. To *you*. The magic in a book isn't unlocked until someone reads it. So basically, you're magical. May you always love reading. Thank you for choosing *Four Night Stand* from your (probably overwhelmingly large) to-be-read pile.

~ Georgia Moore

Thank you for reading *Four Night Stand*. I know there are millions of books out there to choose from, and you decided to pick up mine – that means a lot. I hope you enjoyed it.

Want to leave a review? Reviews can help readers find books! I am grateful for every single honest review. Thank you so much for taking the time to let others know what you thought of *Four Night Stand*.

~ Georgia Moore